First published in Great Britain 1990
by Methuen, Michelin House,
81 Fulham Road, London SW3 6RB

Copyright © 1990 David Nobbs

ISBN 0 413 63300 4

A CIP catalogue record for this book
is available from the British Library

Printed in Great Britain by
Richard Clay Ltd, Bungay, Suffolk

Contents

First Do

January:
The Church Wedding

A scruffy pigeon, a hopeless straggler in a race from Leek to Gateshead, shuffled across the hard blue sky as if embarrassed to come between the Social Liberal Democratic candidate for Hindhead and his Maker. Gerry Lansdown didn't see the pigeon. His eyes were closed. He was praying.

'Oh God,' he prayed silently, gripping his top hat with tight, tense fingers, 'thank you for what I am about to receive. Thank you for Rita Simcock.'

He opened his eyes and gazed up towards the God whose existence he had never doubted, although he had never thought of Him as a being so overwhelmingly superior to himself that it was necessary to worship Him, except during election campaigns.

The sun was astonishingly powerful for January, as if there were a hole in the ozone layer directly above Gerry's head. The pigeon had gone. There was no sign of God either.

The ravishing Liz Badger bore down upon Gerry, arm-in-arm with her second husband, the immaculate Neville Badger, of Badger, Badger, Fox and Badger.

'Hello, Gerry. You look wonderful,' she said.

'Thank you.' Gerry tried to look as if the compliment was undeserved. He smiled cautiously at the woman who had once run off with his fiancée's first husband. He kissed her, carefully, so as not to disturb her make-up.

'Doesn't he, Neville?' said Liz.

But Neville Badger, immaculate in his morning dress, was months and years away, attending other services at this massive Norman abbey: his marriage to Jane, Jane's funeral, and the marriage of Liz's daughter Jenny to Paul, younger son of today's bride.

'Neville!' Liz sounded as if she were summoning a recalcitrant Pekinese.

Her husband of four months sailed gently through time and made a soft landing beside her.

'What?' he improvised.

'I was saying, Gerry looks wonderful.'

Neville gave Gerry a brief, unseeing glance.

'Oh yes,' he said. 'Absolutely. Wonderful. Absolutely wonderful.'

'Isn't Rita lucky?'

'Oh yes. Absolutely. Lucky old Rita.'

'I mean . . . isn't he a simply gorgeous man?'

'Yes, he . . . er . . . I mean, gorgeous isn't a word I . . . you're looking very handsome, Gerry.'

The rising star in the Social Liberal Democratic firmament simpered. 'Well . . . ' he said. 'So are both of you. I mean, you're handsome and Liz is gorgeous.'

'Thank you . . . ' said Neville.

'Very much,' said Liz.

The Badgers walked slowly towards the West Door. The path ran between old, neglected graves. Beyond the graveyard, blackened stone and brick and rusting concrete buildings jostled in narrow, untidy streets.

At the porch Neville stopped. 'Liz?' he said. 'I don't query the basic truth of what was said, but wasn't that rather too much of a mutual admiration society?'

'Oh, Neville,' she said. 'I was trying to make you jealous.'

'What?'

'By praising Gerry.'

'Why should I be jealous?' Neville was struggling to understand, knowing from experience that his puzzlement would irritate her.

'I wanted you to think I find him attractive.'

'Maybe you do. He is attractive . . . I imagine . . . to a woman . . . which you are.'

The wedding guests were strolling slowly into the church. Two glorious hats bobbed past, wide-brimmed navy to the left of the stationary Badgers, bowl-shaped orange to their right.

'I'm trying to get you to show me how fiercely possessive you can be when aroused,' explained Liz.

'Oh, I see,' said the doyen of the town's lawyers. 'Sorry.'

'Oh, Neville, you're hopeless.'

'Sorry.'

'No. It's why I love you, I suppose.'

'Because I'm hopeless?' Neville was aroused now that Liz no longer wanted him to be. 'I see!'

'No, you don't. You see nothing.'

'I see Jenny.'

Liz's daughter Jenny was smiling broadly but nervously. Her hair was cropped shorter than her mother would have liked. She was almost eight months pregnant. She would soon become the first person ever to enter this most English of churches wearing a dress which illustrated the life cycle of the llama.

'Hello, Mum,' she said, knowing that Liz preferred to be called 'Mother'. 'Hello . . . ' she hesitated, as if making a serious attempt to call Neville 'Dad' for the first time. 'Neville.' She kissed her mother and almost kissed Neville.

'Where's Paul?' said Liz.

'He wouldn't come. He says he'd find it impossible to dredge up a smile.' Neither of Rita's boys had welcomed their mother's engagement to a man more than ten years younger than herself.

'Oh dear,' said Liz. 'Honesty can be so socially inconvenient.' She made the remark sound as though it might just possibly be witty.

Neville had dredged up a faint smile which appeared to be set in concrete as he listened to the conversation between his second wife and her daughter.

'I think Paul's trying to be ultra-honest in order to try to make me forget the time he was dishonest over Carol Fordingbridge,' said Jenny.

'How sophisticated his feelings are,' said Liz. 'No wonder he's doing so well with his road sweeping.'

'Oh Mum.' Jenny began to cry, big drops out of clear eyes like a summer shower. 'Oh Lord. Now look what you've made me do.'

She hurried off, blowing her nose angrily.

Liz clutched Neville's arm. 'Oh Lord,' she said. 'I didn't . . . why do I always . . . ? Darling, say something very nice, very quickly.'

As people drifted almost reluctantly into the great church, Neville Badger stood at his wife's side, his baggy face creased with mental effort.

'Those scrambled eggs we had this morning were really delicious,' he said at last.

'Oh, Neville, you're hopeless.'

Liz swirled into the church, the sun glinting on her large silver three-leafed clover earrings. Neville scurried immaculately in her wake.

As soon as Gerry Lansdown saw Jenny blowing her nose, he extricated himself without reluctance from a discussion on the ethics of High Street credit with a loss adjustor from Camberley, and hurried over to favour her with one of his most winning smiles and eliminate this blip of sorrow from the great joy of his wedding day.

'Jenny!' he said. 'Are you all right?'

'Yes. Fine. Great.' She gave him a brave but watery smile. 'Terrific.'

'Good. Good.' He kissed her. He liked her. He felt that she might make a good Liberal one day, when she had learnt to accept the compromises necessary for the conduct of civilised life. 'Is Paul all right?'

'No, he's got a touch of . . . er . . . ' To her fury, Jenny felt herself blushing. 'A touch of . . . er . . . a slight . . . I can't lie. Paul and I promised. No more lies. He's refused to come.'

'I see.' Gerry frowned. He didn't really care whether Paul came or not, but Rita would be very upset, and that would upset him. Blast the ghastly youth. 'I see. But you did.'

'Oh yes. I think one has to accept what happens in life, and try to make the best of it.'

'Terrific.'

'Oh Lord,' said Jenny. A stylised llama on her chest heaved with embarrassment, looking as if it might be about to give stylised birth. 'I shouldn't have said that. Not today.' A distant siren put her agony into context. Somebody might be dying out there. She rallied. 'Amazing day,' she said.

It was indeed. Later, the Meteorological Office would announce that this had been the hottest January day since 1783. That day, in fact, Pontefract was hotter than Algiers.

14

Paul's elder brother, the cynical Elvis Simcock, strolled semi-insolently towards them, running a hand through his hair to make sure that it was ruffled. At his side was his fiancée, the long-haired Carol Fordingbridge, whose one night stand with Paul was ignored but not forgotten. At Jenny's wedding to Paul, when all the men had worn suits, Elvis had worn a sports jacket. Now, when the men were in morning dress, he was wearing a suit, a grey chalk-stripe, single-breasted suit, which matched his insolence, but not his ruffled hair.

'Well Elvis has come anyway,' said Gerry. 'In a suit, not morning dress. How carefully calculated his little acts of rebellion are.'

'You see, Gerry. You laugh at us,' said Jenny.

Gerry ignored this remark, as he ignored all suggestions that he was less than perfect.

'Couldn't bring myself to wear morning dress, I'm afraid,' said Elvis.

'Why should you?' said Gerry, smiling warmly, as if grateful to Elvis for giving him the opportunity to show his broad-mindedness. 'What do appearances matter? Good for you, say I.'

Two low-flying jets from the American base at Frissingfold hurled themselves against the elegance of the scene, banked steeply over the sturdy Norman tower and were gone, leaving behind them a crying baby, several barking dogs, two shattered greenhouses and a group of Social Liberal Democrats staring at the ruthless blue of the winter sky with a range of emotions, from fury to reassurance, which reflected the unbridgeable gulfs between their various views on defence.

Carol Fordingbridge was the first to drag her eyes down from the ruptured sky. She was therefore the first to see Ted. Ted Simcock, first husband of Gerry's bride-to-be, former owner of the Jupiter Foundry, was approaching in a hired grey morning suit that almost fitted.

'Ted!' said Carol.

'Dad!' said Elvis.

'Hello.' Ted smiled, well pleased with the effect that he had created. Gerry couldn't have looked sicker if he'd come fourth behind the Green Party. 'I . . . er . . . I just happened to be passing and I thought, "Good Lord! There's Gerry in morning

dress. It must be Rita's wedding today. I'll just pop in and . . ."
Hello, Jenny.' He broke off to kiss his daughter-in-law, frowning
only briefly at the llamas. 'Hello, Carol.' There was a kiss for
Carol too. 'Hello, Elvis. ". . . just pop in and see the woman I
was married to for twenty-five years launched on her new idyll
of bliss." As it were.'

'You just happened to be passing, in full morning dress,' said
Gerry drily, his poise swiftly recovered.

'Ah. Yes. I'm . . . er . . . ' Ted couldn't help glancing down
towards the pale stain on his hired, striped trousers, which he'd
only noticed as he was putting them on. 'I'm on my way to
another wedding, funnily enough. Quite a coincidence. The
wedding of . . . ' Ted's attempt foundered ignominiously on
the rocks of their disbelief. 'Am I hell as like? I wanted to
bury the hatchet. Give my blessing to Rita, who still means
a lot to me, on what is after all the second happiest day of
her life. It's unconventional behaviour, I know, but then Ted
Simcock has never given a fig for convention. I mean, I'm not
coming to the reception, obviously.'

'Obviously.'

'Quite. I mean, that's invitation only.'

'Quite.'

'Obviously. But churches are public. I have the right, if I read
our unwritten constitution correctly. So, I thought, I'll come to
the church. In morning dress.' Ted glowered at his elder son.
'As befits.'

'I thought you didn't give a fig for convention,' said Elvis,
smiling with a self-satisfaction that he couldn't quite conceal,
even though he knew that his hero, Jean-Paul Sartre, would
not have regarded such a tiny conversational triumph as worthy
of self-satisfaction. But then Jean Paul Sartre hadn't got a bad
third at Keele University.

'You have to know which figs you give for which conventions,'
said Ted. 'That's known as maturity of judgment in my book.'

Jenny's brother Simon Rodenhurst approached, splendid in
his wedding attire. He saw Elvis and Ted, tried not to look like
an estate agent, and failed.

'Hello!' he said. 'Ted! You here? Good Lord.'

They gave him looks which said, 'Shut up, Simon. We've
just been through all that.'

'Hello, little sister,' he said. 'Where's Paul?'

They gave him looks which said, 'That's another can of worms best not opened.'

'What have I said?' he said.

They gave him looks which said that it would have been better if he hadn't said 'What have I said?'

'Come on, Simon,' said Jenny. 'Let's get inside.'

'We all better had,' said Carol. 'It's nearly five to.'

Jenny approached the porch with Simon. Carol followed with Elvis.

Elvis called out, 'You're looking very spacious today, Simon.'

'Oh belt up.' Simon Rodenhurst, of Trellis, Trellis, Openshaw and Finch, tossed his reply over his shoulder. A gust of wind caught his 'Oh belt up' and sent this example of his repartee swirling over the jumbled roofs of the town, over the turgid brown waters of the River Gadd, over the central Yorkshire plain, up and up through the weakening ozone layer into the blue beyond, to become a whisper around the planets long after this earth has been destroyed.

Rita's fiancé and her ex-husband stood alone together, as the last of the guests made their way into the church, along with the funny little man with the big ears who went to all the weddings.

'I hope my presence isn't unwelcome, Gerry,' said Ted.

'Do you really want Rita to be happy?' said Gerry.

'Course I do, Gerry.' Ted met Gerry's piercing gaze firmly. 'Course I do. I mean, what do you take me for?'

'In that case you're very welcome indeed, Ted.'

They shook hands.

'Is there . . . er . . . ?'

'Somebody in my life? Yes, I'm glad to say my recent amour still flourishes.' Ted had taken to using the occasional French word now that he was in catering.

A tall, attractive woman who had taken great pains to be of indeterminate age walked elegantly past them. Ted caught a whiff of expensive scent. She was wearing a bright yellow fitted top, yellow skirt, yellow pill-box hat, with a yellow bag and yellow shoes. The general effect was . . . yellow. On a summer's evening it might have proved irresistible to moths and midges. On an early winter's afternoon it proved irresistible to

Ted. She turned and gave him a look which was unmistakeably meaningful although he felt that he must be mistaken over the meaning. Then she entered the church.

'I'm . . . er . . . ' Ted tried to sound as if he hadn't even noticed her. 'I'm a very lucky man.'

He hurried into the church. Gerry Lansdown looked at his watch, and followed at a much more leisurely pace.

Ted Simcock, once the town's premier maker of fire irons, now living in a furnished flat off the wrong end of Commercial Street with a waitress called Sandra, whom he had met at the DHSS when she was an unemployed bakery assistant, hesitated briefly on entering the church. He was about to sit on Rita's side . . . after all, he hardly knew Gerry but had been married to Rita for a quarter of a century . . . but then he realised that this might not be entirely tactful, so he settled himself down near the back, on Gerry's side, behind the thinning hair of moderate politicians, the carefully tasteful hats of their moderate wives, and the more arrogant hats of the wives of the microchip men.

Facing the massed ranks of Gerry's friends and relations were the somewhat less massed ranks of Rita's friends and relations, spiky aunts, uncouth uncles, spotty cousins, several of them not in morning dress. Less than two years ago, when she had been Liz Rodenhurst, Liz Badger had sat opposite them, and had tried to ignore them. She felt strange now, sitting among them, though still trying to ignore them.

Three rows behind her sat Rodney and Betty Sillitoe.

'She's late,' whispered Betty, who was over-dressed as usual.

'She's exercising her prerogative,' whispered Rodney.

'You make it sound like a breed of dog,' whispered Betty.

They shared a whispered laugh.

Ted Simcock, former provider of quality boot scrapers, now head waiter at Chez Albert in Bridge Street, looked round at exactly the same moment as Liz. They looked at each other with horror. At that other wedding eighteen months ago their exchanged glances had led to events which had broken up and reordered their world. Neville Badger, beside Liz, smiled blandly at Ted. Ted and Liz shied away hastily from the possibility that history might repeat itself. Ted craned his head to examine the great hammer roof. This was generally regarded as a magnificent

18

example of early church architecture and a triumph for modern woodworm techniques, but Ted had no eyes for the vast pale beams, the carved angels, the faded red and gilt of the medieval paintwork. His head swivelled on, down again, towards the back of the church, where he met the gaze of the gleaming yellow lady. He looked away, she looked away, then they both looked back to see if they really had been giving each other meaningful looks. She smiled. He tried a smile that would make him look like a cool international sophisticate. It was a failure. He looked like a randy cocker spaniel.

The church clock proclaimed the quarter. Several people on Gerry's side frowned. While a bride was expected to be late, a politician's wife was expected to be punctual enough to be only slightly late.

Leslie Horton, water-bailiff and organist, who hated to be called Les, thundered through his limited repertoire without subtlety.

The best man, a drainage engineer from Dundee, who had been Gerry's best friend at school, though more perhaps in retrospect than at the time, glanced at his watch and sighed.

Gerry smiled serenely at the new young vicar, who had not yet won the hearts of his congregation.

The long-haired Carol Fordingbridge was the first to mouth the possibility that had begun to form in a hundred barely credulous minds.

'Wouldn't it be awful if she didn't turn up?' she whispered.

'Carol! She wouldn't,' whispered her fiancé with less than his usual cynicism. 'She couldn't. That'd be . . . awful.'

'I know,' breathed the former Miss Cock-A-Doodle Chickens excitedly. 'Awful.'

They considered the awesome prospect in awful silence.

'It'd be rather wonderful, though, wouldn't it?' she whispered.

The moment Leslie Horton had dreaded arrived. He had exhausted his programme of suitable pieces. The buzz of speculation in the congregation was growing steadily louder. Hats bobbed in horrified excitement. The new young vicar looked at Leslie Horton and shrugged with his eyes. Leslie Horton sighed with his shoulders and returned to the beginning of his repertoire.

The huge ribbed radiators had to fight valiantly against the stony chill of the abbey, even on this unseasonal day. With no joyous emotion to warm them, the ladies began to shiver. One of Rita's uncles had a sneezing fit.

The vicar advanced upon Gerry, who tried to smile confidently. His smile curled at the edges like a slice of tongue approaching its 'sell-by' date. The eyes of the congregation were upon them.

'If she isn't here soon,' whispered the vicar, 'I'll have to truncate the ceremony.'

'Truncate the ceremony?' hissed Gerry Lansdown. 'I don't want a truncated ceremony. I haven't paid a truncated licence fee.'

'I don't approve of divorcees marrying in church, even though I understand your fiancée was not the guilty party,' whispered the vicar, who was still referred to by his congregation as 'the new vicar', as if he would have to prove himself before earning the dignity of a name. 'My predecessor was less strict. I've inherited you as a *fait accompli*. I do not intend you to be a *fait accompli* worse than death.' He laughed briefly, with more self-congratulation than humour. 'I have another wedding later, the groom is a councillor, and I do not intend to have to delay an important wedding in my very first week here.'

Gerry Lansdown's hackles rose. His back arched. He was an insulted cat, ready for battle. But the vicar had gone.

'She's not coming, Rodney,' whispered Betty Sillitoe, overexcited as usual. 'She's jilted him. How awful!'

'She may have had an accident,' whispered Rodney.

'No. I know it. I feel it.' She sighed. 'I don't know whether to feel glad or sad.'

'I never do these days,' whispered Rodney. Affection softened his florid face as he added hurriedly, 'Except about you.'

'Aaaah,' said Betty, so loudly that several heads craned to identify the source. They heard her, oblivious to them, saying, 'I'd kiss you if we weren't in church.'

In front of them, the ravishing Liz Badger whispered into the immaculate right ear of her husband, 'Maybe Gerry isn't getting married after all. Maybe you'll still have cause to feel jealous.'

'Liz!' Neville's protest was too heartfelt to be contained in a whisper. 'I respect you far too much to feel that I need ever feel jealous.'

'Oh, Neville,' whispered Liz. 'You're hopeless.'

The clock struck the half hour.

'Five more minutes,' whispered the vicar.

Gerry's lips twitched. 'Your precious councillor will have to wait, vicar,' he hissed. 'I think you should know that I just happen to be the prospective Social Liberal Democratic parliamentary candidate for Hindhead.'

The vicar smiled thinly. 'He's a serving councillor, not prospective. And he's chairman of the Tower Appeal Fund Committee. Five minutes.'

The hum of conversation grew louder still. Leslie Horton's playing grew slower. The sun lit up the garish battle scenes in the modern stained-glass window, dedicated to the King's Own Yorkshire Light Infantry.

Ted's eyes were drawn to Liz's again and he realised that he was smiling. Hurriedly he tried to look horrified.

The new young vicar made a signal to Gerry.

Gerry nodded resignedly. A crescent of blue, reflected from a stained-glass window, was falling across his face.

'Ladies and gentlemen,' said the vicar. 'It looks as if something has happened. I'm afraid we have no alternative, for the moment, as we have further nuptials pending on a tight schedule at this ever-popular venue, but to respectfully suspend the wedding for the moment. Mr Horton, would you please play us out?'

Leslie Horton, water-bailiff and organist, who hated to be called Les, would wonder to the end of his days why he played 'The Wedding March ' at that moment.

The vicar raised his eyes to heaven, but received no immediate help.

In the town the traffic moved slowly. A police horse, en route to football duty, crapped hugely outside the Abbey National Building Society. Four overweight railway enthusiasts, sitting on the top deck of a bright yellow corporation bus, with engine numbers in their notebooks and no rings on their fingers, peered at the hats and morning dresses without envy, so far removed from any of their remaining hopes was the glittering scene. A six-year-old girl with an empty water pistol said, 'There's no bride. Mam, there's no bride.'

'Don't be silly,' said her mam, giving her a whack for her accuracy.

The wedding guests stood uneasily in the tactless sunshine. The women had to hold onto their hats as another gust announced the fragility of the fine weather. The men found no opportunity to wear their top hats and wondered why they had hired them. The funny little man with big ears who turned up unbidden at all the weddings walked slowly away, shaking his head.

All those who were saddened by the turn of events wore long faces, to prove that they were saddened.

All those who weren't saddened wore even longer faces, to hide the fact that they weren't saddened.

Nobody looked sadder than Ted Simcock, except perhaps the photographer, the pasty-faced Wayne Oldroyd, from Marwoods of Moor Street. He cast a last baleful glance at Gerry, before shuffling off with his unused tripod.

Out of the inhospitable gravel on the south side of the church there grew a lone tree, a sickly, unshapely ash. Around this tree a munificent council had placed a round slatted seat. Onto this seat jumped Gerry Lansdown. His face was pale. His eyes were hot. His complacency was a distant memory.

'Ladies and gentlemen,' he cried, and silence fell instantly. Everyone wanted to hear what he would say. What could he say? 'Ladies and gentlemen. It seems that something has delayed Rita . . . or something. Until we find out what . . . and bearing in mind that many of you have travelled a long way, many from Hindhead and some from even further afield . . . and as the reception . . . er . . . and it seems criminal to waste all that lovely food.' Gerry's voice gained assurance as he touched on political matters. 'We in the Social Liberal Democratic party believe that all waste of food is totally unjustified in a world where so many haven't enough to eat . . . so, whatever has happened, if indeed it has, I think the best course will be to proceed with the reception as if nothing had happened . . . I mean, as if nothing hadn't happened. Thank you.'

Gerry jumped down off the seat, and marched firmly through

the throng, which parted before him like the Red Sea before the Israelites.

Ted's spine tingled as he realised that Gerry was about to confront him. Illogically, he flinched. But Gerry's voice was mild, almost pleading.

'You know Rita better than any man on earth, Ted. Why has she done this to me?'

'Look on the bright side,' said Ted encouragingly. 'She could have had an accident.'

'What?'

'I mean, not that I . . . just a minor accident. I heard a siren.'

'I've checked. There's been no accident. That was an officer going home for his lunch.' The public figure in Gerry rose to the surface even at this moment of private grief. 'I shall write a strong letter of protest.' Then the private anguish returned. 'She's jilted me, Ted.'

The guests, drifting past towards their cars, tried to ignore them.

'What can I say, Gerry, except . . . ' Ted fought to keep the tell-tale gleam out of his eyes ' . . . I'm very, very sorry. I mean, I am. I'm shattered. Devastated. Goodbye, Gerry.'

He held out his hand.

'There's no need to go now,' said Gerry, spurning the proffered extremity. 'You may as well come to the reception.'

'You what?'

'We're colleagues now. Members of the same exclusive club.'

In the distant, ordinary town, another siren blared urgently.

'He's had his lunch,' said Ted, and immediately wished he hadn't. 'Exclusive club? What exclusive club?'

'The club of men who've been made miserable by Rita Simcock.'

'Ah. Well. Yes. I suppose we . . . but, I mean, even so, is it appropriate that I, her ex-husband, should be present at . . . '

The elegant yellow lady turned to smile at Ted as she passed.

'Thank you very much, Gerry,' said Ted.

So Ted found himself back in the Garden Room of the Clissold Lodge Hotel, where, at another wedding, he . . . he didn't even want to think about it.

The Clissold Lodge was situated in large, gently rolling grounds that had once belonged to Amos Clissold, the glue tycoon, whose slogan, 'Ee! Buy gum! Buy Clissold's', still occupied a prime site on the station forecourt. Now it was a country hotel on the edge of town. 'The hotel where country meets town,' as its brochure claimed. Its red-brick exterior was austere and forbidding. The interior was more gracious, but slightly faded. In the appropriately chintzy, over-furnished lounge, four slightly faded chintzy ladies were keeping amnesia at bay with an afternoon game of bridge.

The Garden Room was a spacious function room of pleasing Georgian proportions. Outside its French windows, the low January sun shone on a charming walled garden. Bouquets of hot-house red tulips and imported freesias studded the room. The guests were chatting animatedly. Two smiling waitresses in smart black and white outfits were dispensing non-vintage Moet. There was a splendid three-tiered cake. On the long buffet table there sat a superb Bradenham ham, a magnificent sea trout in wine jelly, a large walnut and spinach terrine spiked with green peppercorns, fleshy langoustines from Brittany, cold roasts of Scotch beef and Welsh lamb, bowls of green salad, Waldorf salad, salade niçoise, bean salad, avocado and mangetout salad, and not a tuna-fish vol-au-vent in sight. It was a perfect reception, save only, a purist might complain, for the absence of the bride.

Gerry Lansdown was doing the rounds, welcoming, smiling, urging people to eat, not that they needed urging.

'It seems wrong to enjoy anything on such an awful occasion,' said Liz Badger, 'but I have to admit, this sea trout in wine jelly is absolutely delicious.' She was wearing a black and white tunic with sweetheart neck, black skirt, and an elegant black cocktail hat.

But Neville Badger, now the only Badger in Badger, Badger, Fox and Badger, wasn't listening.

'I must go and say something to Gerry,' he said.

'Why?'

'I'm not an unimaginative man, Liz. I can imagine how he must be feeling.' Neville searched for the *mot juste*. 'Upset. I mean, I was thinking how I'd have felt if Jane hadn't turned up at our wedding.'

'But not me?' Liz's voice was icy. The sea trout was forgotten.

'What?'

'You married me as well. Or had you forgotten?'

'Of course not. How absurd!'

'It's just that it was Jane not turning up that you instinctively thought of, because she meant so much more to you than I do. Thank you, Neville.'

'No, Liz! Of course not. I love you. I'm the father of your child.' Ted sauntered past, trying not to look down at the stain on his hired trousers. 'Hello, Ted.' He turned back to Liz and lowered his voice. 'Well, no, not actually the father, but . . . no, I mentioned my marriage to Jane, I suppose, because I was married to her for so much longer than to you.' Liz glowered. 'So far,' he added hopefully. 'Anyway, Gerry needs support and it's up to me to give it.'

'Why you?'

Neville stared at Liz in astonishment, as if the answer were self-evident.

'Because I'm a man of the world. An experienced professional man. A man whose working life brings him into daily contact with sorrow and distress. A man who knows what to say.'

'What are you going to say?'

'I don't know. Oh Lord.'

Neville wandered off, to prepare himself for his errand of mercy. Left alone, Liz flashed a dazzling smile at the world, reducing the dazzle level sharply when she realised that she was smiling at Ted.

Ted approached his ex-lover cautiously.

'Marvellous spread,' he said.

'Paid for by him, I should imagine. And rather more generously than the one poor Laurence laid on for Jenny's wedding. Not a tuna fish vol-au-vent in sight.'

'Odd, isn't it?'

'I think it's very sensible. I hated those tuna fish vol-au-vents.'

'I meant . . . ' Ted lowered his voice and looked quickly round the room, hoping most people weren't looking at them, hoping the woman in yellow *was* looking at them. 'I meant you and me, here, in this very room, where, less than two years ago, in this very room, we . . . went upstairs to the very room above this very room and . . . made love.'

'I *had* remembered.'

Liz looked up at the ceiling, then at Ted, and shook her head ever so slightly at the memory of what she had done.

'How is my baby?' whispered Ted.

'Flourishing. I wish you wouldn't talk about him, Ted.'

'I care about him. Does he . . . er . . . still takes after me, does he?'

'No. He's losing the resemblance rapidly. Which, I would say, shows a remarkable degree of tact for an eight-month-old baby.'

Liz walked away. Ted went to the buffet table, seeking a displacement activity. He grabbed the first bit of food that didn't need cutlery – it was a slice of leek and stilton quiche, as it chanced – rammed a great piece into his mouth, and chewed slowly while he tried to regain his composure. He looked up to find the attractive yellow lady at his side smiling radiantly. He chewed desperately, tried to swallow, chewed again, tried to smile, chewed, and mumbled, 'Hello. I'm Ted Simcock,' through a porridge of half-chewed quiche.

'Of course you are,' said the symphony in yellow.

'You what?'

'I've had my card marked.'

At last the quiche was gone, and he could speak freely. He failed to take full advantage. 'What?' he said.

'You're opening a new restaurant in Arbitration Road.'

'What?' Really he might as well take another mouthful, if he couldn't do better than this.

'I've made it my business to find out about you.'

Her voice was cool, but not cold. It was classy without being shrill. He liked it. He liked her. He tried to think of something interesting to say. He said, 'Good heavens.'

'You interest me.'

'Good Lord.'

There was a loud crash of plates.

'Good God.'

It couldn't be.'

He turned slowly, towards the kitchen door.

It was.

It was Sandra. Sandra, whom he'd met at the DHSS. Sandra, whom he had found a job at Chez Albert. Sandra, with whom he lived.

'Oh no,' he said. 'Oh heck.'

As she bent down to pick up the broken plates, the cake-loving Sandra Pickersgill flashed Ted a look of defiance. The left leg of her tights had snagged.

Gerry Lansdown, hoping that the dreadfulness of his predicament would disappear if he ignored it, was holding a determinedly casual conversation with his best man and his best man's wife. They had exhausted the charms of Dundee and its environs, the state of the jam industry, the rope industry, and the royal burghs of Fife, and had turned to his native Surrey, far from this hard North Country into which he had strayed with such disastrous results.

'I love that whole area,' he was saying. 'Farnham. Guildford. The Hog's Back.'

Neville approached, concern creasing his bland face.

'I'm not interrupting, am I?' he said.

'No. No.' Gerry excused himself reluctantly from the enjoyable geographical chit-chat.

'Only, I . . . er . . . I felt I had to come and talk to you. You see, Gerry . . . ' Neville became portentous, 'I've been there.'

Gerry was puzzled. 'Been there? Been where? Guildford?'

'Guildford?' It was Neville's turn to be puzzled.

'We were just talking about Guildford,' said Gerry.

'Oh! Oh, no. No, no, no, no.' Neville felt that these repeated negatives might be construed as an unworthy slur on a fine town. 'I mean, I have been to Guildford, but no, I . . . nice town, specially the old part. No, I meant, I too have . . . Jane and I went to the theatre, with friends . . . no, I . . . er . . . and a little Chinese restaurant, nice crunchy duck, funny how these things stick in the . . . no, I meant, I too have been through great sorrow. I too have visited the pit of despair. I know how you're feeling.'

'Ah.'

'Dreadful.'

'What?'

'You're feeling dreadful.'

Gerry's lips twitched. 'Fancy you sensing that,' he said. 'How shrewd.'

Neville was oblivious of Gerry's anger. 'I want to promise you,' he persisted, earnest concern etched on his rather tired face, 'not as a cliché, because it can be a cliché. You'll get over this, Gerry. Time is a great healer.'

Gerry smiled faintly, and spoke very quietly, so that it was a while before Neville realised that he had actually said, 'Why don't you stuff a sea trout in your gob and drown yourself in wine jelly?'

Sandra came in from the kitchens bearing, somewhat precariously, a magnificent sea trout on a large Royal Doulton plate. Her expression matched that of the fish. She looked not to left nor to right. Guests made way for her. She plonked the fish on the buffet table, behind the wrecked carcass of its fellow.

Ted had been standing by the locked French windows, looking out on the paths and patios of the walled garden. The shadow of a cloud cast a brief winter gloom over the bare, pruned roses, the empty urns, the ornamental pond where silver carp lived out their monotonous lives. What a lot had happened, what monumental changes there had been, since he had sat in that garden, at Jenny and Paul's wedding, trying to give Rita the courage to face the throng. And now . . . had her courage failed her, or had she shown a great degree of courage? He didn't know. He didn't know anything. He didn't know what to do about Sandra and the yellow lady. He sensed Sandra's entry with the sea trout.

He adjusted his trousers, remembered the dirty mark, shrugged, tried to look taller than he was, and sidled through the guests to the buffet, where he stood irresolutely beside his inamorata, trying hard to look as if he was interested not in her, but in the buffet; because, as far as he knew, nobody in the town knew of his affair with Sandra, except the staff at Chez Albert and, inevitably, the postman. In fact Ted had even promised Monsieur Albert, the eponymous owner of Chez Albert, that he had ended the association, since Monsieur Albert – who hailed from Gateshead – was installing Ted as manager in a sister restaurant, and thought Sandra insufficiently classy to be the bedfellow of one of his managers.

'Sandra! What are you doing here?' hissed Ted.

Sandra turned her hurt, pert face on him. 'They phoned just after you left. They'd been let down. I held out for double overtime. I thought you'd be chuffed.'

'Well, yes, very nice, Sandra, more than useful, we can put it towards those curtains, I'm dead chuffed. But.'

'I know,' said Sandra, 'but I never dreamt you'd be here.'

'No, well . . . ' The Sillitoes drifted past. They smiled at Ted. He changed his tune rapidly. 'Could I have a sliver of salmon, please, waitress?' The Sillitoes had passed out of earshot. 'I didn't know either, Sandra.'

'You're ashamed of me,' said Sandra flatly. 'You don't want anyone to see you talking to me. And it's sea trout, anyroad.'

They began to move along the buffet table. Sandra put dollops of the various salads on Ted's plate as they talked.

'Rubbish,' said Ted. 'It's rubbish, is that, Sandra. I don't want anyone to see *you* talking to *me*.'

'You what?'

'In case you get sacked and lose your double overtime.' Liz was approaching. 'I'll have a bit of the salad niçoise, as we in the catering industry call it.'

Sandra put a sizeable dollop of salad on Ted's plate. A piece of anchovy slid onto the carpet unnoticed.

'So!' she said, when Liz had gone. 'A sensational development.'

'Sensational!' said Ted with relish, forgetting that he was supposed not to be pleased.

'And you're pleased.'

'I am pleased. I admit it. But only because he's not right for her, not because I . . . Rita and I are over, Sandra.'

'I know.'

'Honestly, love! We are! Over. Finito. You what?'

'I know. I've seen how you talk to that tarty piece.'

'Sandra! She is not a tarty piece.' Ted realised his mistake. 'And I've no idea who you're talking about.'

'So!' A scoop of potato salad. 'You're smitten!' A scoop of Waldorf Salad. A couple passed close by. 'Bean salad, sir?' said Sandra, playing Ted's game scornfully.

'Thank you, Sandra.'

The couple threw hostile glances at Ted. He recognised Rita's

29

sneezing uncle and his wife. Her hat matched his nose. They moved on without speaking. It was a deliberate snub, for what Ted had done to Rita.

'I am not, Sandra,' he said. 'I am not smitten. But I like to get my facts right. And the lady to whom I assume you refer, with whom I had a brief sophisticated exchange of views on Beaujolais Nouveau, happens not to be a tarty piece. All right?'

'"Beaujolais Nouveau"! The only Nouveau you've ever drunk is Theakston's Nouveau. She's a tarty piece and you're besotted.'

Ted began to raise his voice, forgetting that he was supposed to be having a casual conversation with a waitress who happened to be a colleague.

'She's a classy, elegant, attractive woman and I am not besotted.'

For a moment they glared at each other, eyeball to eyeball. Ted, expecting a deadly insult, was surprised to hear Sandra say, 'Mayonnaise, sir?' He was even more surprised to see the huge scoopful of mayonnaise that she plonked onto his absurdly heaped plate. It dropped off the edges. There would be a yellow stain just beneath the pale stain on his trousers. He turned away, trying not to show his anger.

The Sillitoes sailed unsuspectingly towards him and met the full force of the gale.

'Hungry?' said Rodney, seeing Ted's piled plate.

'Get stuffed,' said Ted, as he stomped off.

'What did I say?' said Rodney.

Betty indicated Sandra with her head.

'Ah!' Rodney nodded, as if he understood, then realised that he didn't understand. 'What?'

He found himself staring into Sandra's disconcertingly knowing young eyes and turned away. Now the Sillitoes were on collision course with Neville and Liz.

'Ah!' said Neville. 'The Sillitoes! Calmer waters!'

'What?' said Rodney. 'Well, who'd have thought Rita'd ever do a thing like that?'

'Will we ever understand the minds of . . . ?' Neville hesitated, ' . . . people?'

'You were going to say the minds of women, and then thought I'd accuse you of being sexist,' said Liz.

'What an awful thing for Rita to do, though,' said Betty Sillitoe, over-explicit as usual.

'Yes,' said Liz. 'How to upstage everybody by not being present.'

'That wasn't what I meant,' said Betty.

'So, what are you two planning now that your chickens will never come home to roost again?' enquired Neville.

Rodney Sillitoe, who still looked as though he had spent the night in a chicken coop in his suit, even though he was no longer the big wheel behind Cock-A-Doodle Chickens, having let all his battery chickens go free in a fit of remorse, explained their new plans briefly, but with evident enthusiasm. 'We're opening a health food complex.'

'With wholefood vegetarian restaurant,' added Betty proudly.

Liz laughed. Her laugh trilled through the tense gathering like the cry of a curlew on a misty morning.

'Liz!' said Neville.

'Sorry.' Liz seemed contrite. 'But Mr and Mrs Frozen Drumstick selling nut cutlets!'

'Why does everybody think vegetarian food is just funny laughable old nut cutlets?' protested Betty.

Liz's dainty hand fluttered to her neck, to be impaled there, a dying butterfly. 'My God! You're serious converts,' she said, and laughed again, a less elegant laugh, a magpie's malicious cackle.

'Liz!' said Neville.

'Oh Lord,' said Liz. 'I shouldn't laugh at anything today, should I? Sorry, Neville. Social lapse over.'

There was an uneasy pause. Neville, usually the first to fill uneasy pauses, leapt in. 'Can I get you two a drink?' he asked, before remembering that it wasn't wise to offer the Sillitoes drinks.

'Oh thank you,' said Betty. 'Grape juice, please.'

'Apple juice, please,' said Rodney.

This time Liz's laugh was an owl's hoot.

'Liz!' said Neville.

It would have been impossible for all the guests to have remained hushed all afternoon. It would have been unnatural if they had all continued to behave unnaturally all afternoon. So, as the sun

31

dipped, as clouds bubbled up in the increasingly unstable air, as champagne flowed and sea trout slithered down throats, and an Egyptian cherry tomato with no respect for class squirted down the waistcoat of a merchant banker from Abinger Hammer, it was only natural that stories should be told, that laughter should be heard, that cautiously desirous looks should be exchanged between the head waiter at Chez Albert and the mysterious yellow lady whose blonde hair might have been natural.

By the time Simon Rodenhurst, of Trellis, Trellis, Openshaw and Finch, approached the cynical Elvis Simcock and his long-haired fiancée, Carol Fordingbridge, a casual observer could have been forgiven for thinking that it was a happy occasion.

'Hello,' said Simon. 'What an extraordinary . . . er . . . what can I say? What can one say? I'm . . . er . . . I'm . . . '

'This is an unprecedented moment in our island's history, Carol,' said Elvis. 'An estate agent lost for words.'

'Here we go again,' sighed Simon. 'It's bash an estate agent time. It's mock an easy target time.'

'You could say the situation leaves considerable scope for improvement,' said Elvis. 'Which is estate agent-ese for a ginormous cock-up.'

'Except it isn't,' said Carol, who looked charming in an apricot crêpe, short-sleeved, belted dress.

'What?' said Elvis.

'You never wanted your mum to marry him.'

'No, but . . . I didn't want her to do that to him.'

'I believe you're starting to like him now he isn't going to be your new father.'

'Well . . . he's quite a nice bloke.'

Carol was appalled. 'He's a faceless, ambitious, self-satisfied, crummy, crappy, yuppie smoothie prig,' she said.

'He's quite a nice faceless, ambitious, self-satisfied, crummy, crappy, yuppie smoothie prig.'

'Hey!' said Simon. 'When are you two love-birds going to name the day?'

'Poor Simon. Thank God I'm not cursed with good manners,' said Elvis.

'What?' said Simon.

'Trying to change the subject so tactfully.'

'Except it wasn't tactful, was it?' Both men were shocked by Carol's vehemence. Vehemence wasn't her stock-in-trade.

'What?' said the philosophy graduate feebly.

'He won't name the date, Simon, till I've passed my philosophy finals.'

'What?' said the bemused young estate agent.

'Oh, bloody hell, stop saying "what" alternately, will yer?' said this new vehement Carol. 'I've yet to satisfy Elvis, Simon, that I'm a mentally worthy partner for his philosophic journey through life.'

'What?' said Elvis.

Carol stormed off, leaving one rather surprised young man and one very surprised young man.

'Women!' said the very surprised young man.

'I know,' said the rather surprised young man. 'They have an uncomfortable habit of hitting on the truth, don't they?'

'Simon! That was almost clever.'

'I know. I have the occasional flash.'

'How *is* your sex life?'

'Non-existent.' Simon dropped his voice. 'I've given it up. That married woman I showed round one of our properties was the last woman I will ever have in my life.'

'That's funny,' said Elvis. 'I had the distinct impression she was the first woman you'd ever had in your life.'

Simon's concern for his image wrestled with his need to confess. The need to confess won.

'She was the first woman and the last woman I'll ever have in my life. I hate sex. It terrifies me,' he said. 'There! I've admitted it. I'm a happy man, Elvis.'

Simon's sister Jenny was staring at the fading day, trying to fight back tears as she thought about her own wedding day, only seventeen months ago.

The sky was dotted with clouds now. Jenny watched their shadows. At her wedding, she had been real. Now she felt that she was a shadow.

These dark shapes that floated across the neat rectangles of that over-careful garden, what could they be to a young woman so sensitive to the prospect of cosmic disaster but the shadows of strange flying creatures, birds and mammals rendered enormous and grotesque by nuclear radiation on a vast scale, huge deformed multi-breasted limbless freaks with pitted scaly skins? She shuddered and turned away from the horror of it, towards the horror of the pretended normality of the Garden Room. She walked instinctively towards Elvis, her husband's brother, and he seemed to walk equally instinctively towards her, so that what he said became curiously important to her.

On the whole, she wished that he hadn't said, 'Hello, Jenny. What on earth are you wearing?'

'Thank you,' she said bitterly. 'It's made out of llama wool by very poor Peruvian Indians who need our support.'

'Several llamas died to make it possible,' said Elvis. 'And you a vegetarian.'

'Nobody's ever suggested that having a social conscience is easy, Elvis.'

At last Elvis noticed that Jenny was close to tears. 'I'm sorry, Jenny,' he said, and he looked momentarily surprised at his own sincerity. 'You look lovely.' He kissed her, warmly, on her cold cheek. 'Paul's a lucky man.'

'So are you.'

'You what?' Elvis was puzzled.

'Carol's lovely too.'

'Oh. Yes. Right. Right. You don't resent her for what she did with Paul, then?'

'Not any more. That's all over. Sorted out. Helped us to move on to a deeper and ever more satisfying plateau of shared feelings and emotions.'

'So you're happy?'

'Happy!' snorted Jenny. 'I thought you were a philosopher. Happiness is unattainable.'

Jenny left behind her a rather lost young philosopher, who, for all his cynicism, found it easier to cope with plateaux of shared feelings and emotions than with the possibility that happiness was unattainable.

Rodney and Betty Sillitoe steamed up, two frigates in rigid formation.

'Elvis,' said Betty. 'We've a proposition to put to you.'

'How would you like to work for me again?' said Rodney.

'For us,' corrected Betty.

'Oh yes. Absolutely. Us. Quite. What I meant.'

'Work for you? What as?' said Elvis.

'In our health food complex,' said Betty.

'With wholefood vegetarian restaurant,' said Rodney.

Elvis laughed. The Sillitoes looked hurt. He wiped the laugh from his face.

'Sorry,' he said. 'I was just . . . surprised. No, it sounds great. Sadly, though, it clashes with my career structure.'

'Career structure?' echoed Rodney faintly.

'I've got a job,' said Elvis. 'With Radio Gadd. I'm . . . ' He couldn't resist a self-satisfied smile, although later he would regret that he hadn't been more modishly cool. 'I'm moving into the media.'

Elvis hurried off, as if hot-foot on his first scoop.

Rodney and Betty exchanged looks of amazement, saw Gerry collapse wearily into a chair, and exchanged looks of social responsibility. They were lifeboats now, speeding to the scene of disaster.

'It's a lovely buffet, Gerry,' said Betty.

'Thank you,' said Gerry politely, but from a long way away. He stood up, wearily.

'It's usually sit-down these days, isn't it,' said Betty. 'But I like a buffet myself, on an occasion such as . . . this would have been.'

'Betty!' said Rodney. 'It's a very nice do altogether, Gerry. A great . . . er . . . well, not success exactly.'

'Because of the . . . er . . . the non . . . er . . . '

'Betty!'

'It's quite all right,' said Gerry coldly. 'I do still remember that my fiancée hasn't turned up.'

They watched him stride away.

'She's well out of that,' said Betty. 'There's a nasty streak there.'

'Are you surprised?' said Rodney. 'He's not exactly having a nice day.'

But Betty was no longer listening. Now that she didn't touch alcohol, curiosity had become her tipple. And her sharp, sexual antennae had spotted Ted, far across the room, beyond the bewildered Liberal Democrats, beyond Rita's guzzling, puzzling uncles.

35

'Ooooh! Rodney! Look!' she exclaimed. 'Who's that woman Ted's talking to?'

Rodney Sillitoe, the big wheel behind a planned health food complex with wholefood vegetarian restaurant, tried not to swivel round and look.

'Betty!' he said. 'Don't be so inquisitive. It's not the right social attitude now you're joint managing director of –' Yet swivel round he eventually did. 'Oooh!'

The objects of Rodney and Betty's interest were oblivious to these 'oooh's'. They were oblivious to anything except each other.

'You're a fascinating man, Ted,' the striking lady in yellow was saying. 'You have a wonderful earthy appeal.'

'Good Lord!' said the man who had once made the best toasting forks in Yorkshire, bar none.

'Are you surprised that I find you interesting?'

'Oh no, not about that. Well, yes, a bit. I mean, I wouldn't want you to think I was big-headed or anything.' Ted gazed into the yellow lady's blue eyes. 'No, I was surprised because . . . I mean . . . they say lightning never strikes twice in the same place twice.'

'What?' She was puzzled. 'What lightning?'

'Nothing. Er . . . Ted returned hastily to more mundane matters. 'I . . . er . . . I don't even know your name.'

'Corinna Price-Rodgerson.'

Even mundane matters didn't seem mundane. Ted Simcock was found interesting by a woman with a double-barrelled name. He caressed both barrels. 'Corinna Price-Rodgerson! Corinna, would you . . . ?' The forgotten Sandra stalked past, a pile of plates wobbling dangerously. 'Oh, you sauté your mushrooms first! How clever!'

'I beg your pardon?' said the astonished Corinna.

'I . . . er . . . I didn't want the waitress to overhear our . . . er . . . '

'You know her?'

'No.' There was a crash of plates. Ted closed his eyes. It was the best attempt he could make to blot out the incident, since it is impossible to close one's ears. 'No! No, but . . . not in front of the servants, eh?'

'My God!' There was double-barrelled astonishment in Corinna's voice. 'That's an old-fashioned attitude even for my family.'

'Tell me about your family.'

'They're all in East Africa. Daddy's a bishop. He's also a dish.'

'You what?'

'A lovely man.'

'Ah. And . . . er . . . do you have . . . or I mean have you had . . . er . . . ever had . . . a husband, as it were?'

Corinna smiled. 'No. I've never married.'

'Good Lord!'

'Thank you. Some women are choosy, Ted. They wait for Mr Right to come along.'

'Yes, well . . . I'm divorced, as you probably . . . I was in business. I had a foundry specialising in . . . domestic artifacts.'

'Domestic artifacts?'

'Toasting forks. Boot scrapers. Door knockers. Fire irons. I needed a sea change. I moved laterally into catering. Oh, Corinna, you're lovely.'

'This room is so public,' said Corinna. 'Ted, I have an idea.'

'Good God!' said Ted. He couldn't resist a quick glance at the ceiling. 'Good God!'

'What?'

'Lightning *does* strike twice in the same place twice!'

'What?'

'You've got a room upstairs.'

Corinna Price-Rodgerson may have been a bishop's daughter, may have regarded herself as pretty nimble socially, but Ted's remark left her frankly at a loss. 'What?' she said. 'Room upstairs? What room upstairs?'

'Ah! No, I . . . er . . . when you said . . . I mean, there's room upstairs. I mean, there are rooms upstairs. I mean, I imagine, I've never . . . funny hotel if there weren't . . . and I thought, I'd like to book one. A double room.' Sandra passed them again, giving Ted another glare. 'Double cream! And a touch of kirsch! So that's the secret!'

'No,' said Corinna Price-Rodgerson, with gentle rebuke in her voice. 'You do know that waitress. That's the secret.'

37

She handed Ted a card. 'I think you and I should get together.'

'"Financial consultant"!' he read.

' 'Fraid so. I leave God to Daddy, and I look after Mammon. I might be able to help you, Ted. Why don't you take me to dinner next Tuesday?'

Sandra bore down on them with a plate of canapés.

'Sir? Madam?' she said with controlled fury. 'Some canapés?'

'Oh, thank you, waitress,' said Ted. 'I'll . . . er . . . I'll try one of these Tuesdays.'

Ted reeled away, chewing his untasted canapé. Rodney and Betty Sillitoe loomed through the smoky afternoon fog and fetched up neatly on either side of him.

'Ted!' said Rodney. 'The very man! We have an emerging new business, and you have a great big hole.'

'What?'

'In life,' said Betty. 'Where your foundry used to be.'

'Oh!' said Ted. 'No. No.'

'Can we let bygones be bygones?' said Rodney. 'Will you work for me . . . us?'

'But I don't have a great big hole,' said Ted. 'Monsieur Albert's installing me as manager of his sister restaurant to Chez Albert. It's called . . . ' He had the grace to hesitate. 'Chez Edouard.'

'Oh Ted!' said Betty.

'So, what's this business of yours?' said Ted.

There was a fractional pause, as though neither Sillitoe wanted to be the first to speak.

'We're opening a health food complex,' said Rodney.

'With wholefood vegetarian restaurant,' said Betty.

Ted laughed, an honest snort of a laugh.

'Yes, well,' said Betty, 'isn't it lucky you have Chez Edouard and don't need to join our rib-tickling, side-splitting venture?'

Betty and Rodney swept onwards, on a tide of injured pride, through the increasingly animated gathering.

'Here's somebody who won't find it funny, anyroad,' said Rodney. 'Hello, Jenny love.'

Jenny accepted Rodney's semi-avuncular kiss without enthusiasm. 'It's great,' she said. 'I can kiss you without feeling hypocritical, now you've given up battery chicken farming.'

'The perfect cue!' exclaimed Betty.

'Betty and I are opening a health food complex,' said Rodney proudly.

'With wholefood vegetarian restaurant,' enthused Betty.

And Jenny laughed. She shook with laughter. The baby in her womb shook with her. Several llamas shook with her. Then she saw the Sillitoes' hurt faces, and a guilty hand flew to her mouth.

'Sorry,' she said. 'Oh, that's wonderful. That's terrific. Oh, well done!'

'So, why the mirth?' said Rodney.

'Well, not because of the business,' said Jenny. 'Because . . . it's you! Sorry.'

She laughed again. Rodney and Betty joined in, but not with much conviction.

Gerry Lansdown, standing with the Badgers, said grimly, 'What a lot of laughter this gathering is causing.'

'It's nerves, Gerry,' said Liz. 'People are finding this difficult.'

'Me too, funnily enough,' said Gerry.

'Marriage isn't all it's cracked up to be, Gerry,' said Neville. His remark cut through the discussion like a rifle shot.

'What?' said Liz.

'I was married for many years, Gerry. My wife died. Did I move quietly into the peaceful backwaters of bachelordom? No! Dived head first into the chill, choppy waters.'

'Neville!' Liz stormed off.

'Oh Lord!' said Neville. 'Sorry, Gerry.'

Neville hurried off in pursuit of Liz, who had ceased storming a few yards away, in order to wait for him.

'Liz!' he said. 'Don't be a fool. I was only cheering him up.'

'But how could you say such things?'

'Because I didn't mean them. I was just trying to get him to look on the bright side.'

'You're in danger of cheering up the whole world except me, Neville,' said his bride of four months.

Outside in the ornamental pond, as the afternoon sagged, the carp swam round and round, unseen.

Inside, in the Garden Room of the Clissold Lodge Hotel, it

39

seemed that social tension sharpened the appetite. A plague of locusts could not have made a more thorough job of the buffet. Just one lone langoustine languished on a vast plate. No one would have the cheek to eat it now.

Amid the debris, the cake remained conspicuously uncut. It would never wing its way, in tiny slabs, to expatriate nephews and trail-blazing uncles, who were assumed to be still alive, since no news of their death had been received. It would be sent, complete in its magnificence, to Sutton House, a home for mentally handicapped children, where a beautiful girl of seventeen with a mental age of six would burst into tears because she would believe that it was her wedding cake.

And in the foyer of the Clissold Lodge Hotel, on that darkening brideless afternoon, a budding radio reporter who had suddenly remembered that he was a budding radio reporter put his duty to his chosen profession above his duty to a family that he had been given no opportunity to choose, and rang the newsroom of Radio Gadd.

'Elvis Simcock here,' he announced urgently, while the receptionist fed guests' mini-bar purchases into the computer, and pretended not to listen. 'The old abbey church has seen some sensational scenes, but it's seen few scenes more sensational than the sensational scenes it's seen today. The glittering wedding of popular local personality, Rita Simcock, ex-wife of prominent local ex-foundry owner, Ted Simcock, to Godalming micro-chip magnate Gerald Lansdown, a rising star in the Social Liberal Democratic firmament, was called off today when the bride failed to turn up, but the reception in the Garden Room of the famous old Clissold Lodge –'

He broke off as Rita entered through the swing doors. She stopped by the door to the Garden Room and turned towards Elvis. She raised a finger to her mouth, pleading for silence. Then she drew a deep breath and entered her reception.

'Cancel all that,' barked Radio Gadd's ace reporter. 'Cancel all that, urgent. The bride has just swept in, in a sensational scene. Await further news. This is Clissold Lodge . . . this is Elvis Simcock, the Garden Room, the Clissold Lodge Hotel.'

He banged the telephone into its cradle and hurried after his mother.

Heads turned to look at Rita. Other heads turned to see what it was that the heads were staring at. Silence draped the room like a hollow fog. Cousins and uncles and aunts shivered. Leaders of moderate opinion in Hindhead felt cold tingles down their spines. A description of a memorable meal in Esher was cut off in mid-timbale.

Rita stood in the double doorways of the function room and smiled, a brittle smile. She was wearing an inappropriately virginal white satin embroidered three piece suit, with a small flowered headband. She was clutching a small posy of freesias, which she hadn't had the heart to dump in a rubbish bin.

'Hello,' she said brightly.

She walked towards Gerry. The guests parted before her as if she were a line of police horses.

Gerry Lansdown, white-faced, grim-lipped, tried on several expressions without success. Anger. Self-pity. Stoic resignation. Manly dignity. All failed him. He ended up smiling stiffly, sardonically, with eyes that hid everything.

'Oh, Gerry,' said Rita. 'I think this is the worst moment of my life.'

'I'm not enjoying myself as much as I'd expected, either.' Gerry whipped her with sarcasm. 'I can't quite work out why. Can't seem to put my finger on it.'

'Oh, Gerry.'

'Am I to get some more eloquent explanation of your incredible behaviour?' asked her jilted fiancé coldly. 'Or am I to have to make do with "Oh, Gerry"?'

'Oh, Gerry.'

Janet Hicks, the red-headed waitress, remembered that Rita had smiled at her at the wedding of Jenny and Paul. She hurried up now, to reward that smile with a glass of champagne. Rita nodded her thanks. Janet, a martyr to verrucas, hobbled off.

'How can I explain?' said Rita.

'Try.'

'Suddenly I just couldn't.' Ted had edged his way to the front of the listening throng, and was hanging on his ex-wife's words. 'Suddenly I realised that it was a case of "out of the frying pan into the fire".'

'I'm a frying pan now. Terrific,' said Ted.

'Shut up, Ted,' said Rita.

'Yes, shut up, Ted,' echoed Gerry.

'Ted!' Rita was belatedly astounded. 'What are you doing here?'

'I wanted to see you happily launched on your new life.'

'Oh, Ted.' Rita turned back from her ex-husband to her ex-fiancé. 'Oh, Gerry'. What words could begin to explain? 'For the best part of my adult life I've felt like a doormat.'

'Terrific. Thank you, Rita,' said Ted.

'Shut up, Ted,' said Rita.

'Yes, shut up, Ted,' echoed Gerry.

'I'm a frying pan,' grumbled Ted. 'She's a doormat. What are the boys? Garden gnomes?'

'Shut up, Ted,' said Rita.

'Yes, shut up, Ted,' echoed Gerry.

For the first time, through the mists of her emotions, Rita saw the rapt, staring faces of the guests. She was appalled.

'Is everybody listening to us?' she said. 'For God's sake! Please! I'm trying to have a private conversation with my fian . . . with my ex . . . ' She shook the freesias in frustration, ' . . . with Gerry.'

There was a brief, stunned pause. Neville turned hurriedly to Rodney and said, 'How were your roses last year, Rodney?'

'Covered in greenfly,' said Rodney.

'Really? Ours weren't. Isn't that extraordinary, Liz? Rodney's roses were covered in greenfly and ours weren't.'

'Good old Neville,' said Liz. 'First to the social rescue yet again.'

All over the room, trivial conversations were cranked into fragile life, and Rita turned back to face her jilted fiancé, in total privacy, in the middle of the crowd.

'I'm dreadfully sorry, Gerry,' she said. 'And after you've paid for all this.'

'That's hardly the aspect that upsets me most, Rita.'

'Oh, Gerry. I had no idea I wasn't going to be able to go through with it, or I'd have broken it off earlier. I'd have done anything to spare you this humiliation.'

'I think anybody considering how you and I have behaved today might think it's your humiliation, not mine.'

'Thank you, Gerry.'

'What for?'

'For making it easier for me by being nasty.' Rita was shocked by Gerry's hot, hostile eyes, and tried an altogether less combative approach. 'I'm sorry. Look, I set out today to marry you. Probably I still love you.'

'Unfortunately it doesn't say that in the wedding service.' There was a remorselessly thorough quality to Gerry's sarcasm. '"Do you take this man probably to love, perhaps to cherish even, in minor illness and in health, maybe almost till death or a long holiday do you part?"'

'Precisely. So I couldn't marry you. Look, all this is entirely because of me and because of my life history and how I see my role as a woman.'

'Ah! Aha!'

'Well all right. "Ah! Aha!" away. Gerry, I'm afraid I realised that I just don't want to be a politician's wife. Your brother said . . . er . . .'

'What did my brother say? Why did I let him give you away? Where is he?'

Rita had found it difficult to decide who should give her away. Her father was dead, she had no brothers, her sons were out of the question. If she chose any other relative, she would offend her remaining relatives. So she had chosen Gerry's brother and offended them all.

People were trying not to seem interested in how things were going between Rita and Gerry. But they wished, even the most unselfish and thoughtful and well-mannered of them wished, even Neville wished, that they could hear every word.

'I wanted to face you on your own,' the lovely bride that wasn't to be was saying. 'We were driving along, we were more than half way there, I said, "I can't go through with it, Nigel." He took me for a drink.'

'He didn't even try to persuade you? The bastard!'

'He did try to persuade me. It was no use. I had four large gins in the Three Tuns, where my appearance caused quite a sensation. Pool players stopped in mid-clunk. "Nigel," I said, "I don't want to be the little woman who fondles his constituents' babies. I've played second fiddle too long. I don't want to be an appendage. I don't want to be a smile on his manifesto."'

'And what did he say, my wonderful brother?'

'I can't tell you.'

43

'Rita! You must.'

Yes. She must. In not turning up at the church she had exhausted her capacity for acting against Gerry's wishes.

'Oh Lord! He said . . . he said, "But, Rita, he'll never be elected. It'll just be one humiliating campaign and then 'Goodnight, Hindhead.'"'

'The bastard!'

'I said I didn't believe that.' Rita's head was swimming. She was finding it difficult to control her speech. 'You're intelligent, good-looking, energetic. Apart from an unfortunate tendency towards niceness and honesty you have all the qualities a politicians needs.' She frowned, aware that she had used too many plurals. She must concentrate. She must get things right. 'But you see, Gerry, when the crunch came, I found I didn't love you enough to give up my career.'

'What career?' Gerry didn't attempt to hide his scorn.

'Precisely! I must do something soon. I don't love you enough to fill my garden with Bulgarian wine, Lymeswold cheese, and hordes of frantically argumentative moderates. I don't love you enough to host elegant dinner parties for smiling Japanese businessmen with microchips on their shoulders. It came to me that I must release you before I trapped you. I'm so very, very sorry. And really, dear dear Gerry, there's nothing more to be said and oh God I must explain to them before I cry.'

Rita scurried to the end of the room, clutching her posy fiercely. 'Ladies and gentlemen,' she called out. Silence fell with suspect haste. She stood facing all her guests; all Gerry's guests; her ex-husband, whose face was a vault of secrets; his ex-lover, whose face was an open book; Neville, his face creased in concentration and sadness; Jenny and her llamas on the verge of tears; Rodney and Betty frowning in unison, synchronised swimmers in a pool of sorrow; Elvis, unaware of Carol Fordingbridge's drowning arm clinging hopefully to him; Simon, as concerned for another person's predicament as it's possible for a young man to be while remaining an estate agent; a pale shaft of late afternoon sunshine catching Corinna's yellow dress; Sandra, her corn-coloured hair dishevelled, her apron crooked, her hands clutching a disturbingly large pile of dirty pudding plates, her fierce young eyes uncertain whether to look

44

at Rita or Corinna; and, between Rita and all these people, the wrecked buffet, over which the uncut cake towered, a snow-covered cathedral that had miraculously survived the bombing of the surrounding city.

Rita looked at all this through wet eyes and saw none of it. Saw a blur. Lowered her eyes as if she might find on the floor the words that she sought.

'Ladies and gentlemen,' she said. 'I owe you all an apology for ruining this dreadful day. I mean this wonderful day that it would have been if I hadn't ruined it. Ladies and gentlemen . . . and everybody else . . . what I've done today is because of being a woman, and the unhappiness of my first marriage.'

'Terrific!' said Ted. 'I'm having a wonderful day.'

'Shut up, Ted,' said Rita.

'Yes, shut up, Ted,' echoed Gerry.

'Shut up, Gerry,' said Rita. 'Leave this to me. Ladies and gentlemen, Gerry's been very good to me. The best and most generous lover I've ever had.'

'Tremendous!' exclaimed Ted.

'Shut up, Ted,' said Rita.

'Yes, shut up, Ted,' echoed Corinna Price-Rodgerson.

'Starved of true love as I had been for most of my life – shut up, Ted!'

Ted, who hadn't spoken, looked outraged, as if he would never in his life dream of interrupting a woman.

'I mistook my gratitude, my freedom, for love,' continued Rita. 'I thought I wanted to marry Gerry, but I can't, because I'd only be a manifesto, and I don't want to end up as a smile on his appendage.'

'She's drunk,' said Betty quietly, but not quite quietly enough.

'Yes!' said Rita. 'And it takes one to know one. I am a bit drunk, because I had three tuns at the Four Gins . . . and tonic.' She raised her glass to her lips, then seemed to notice it for the first time. 'Oh no!' she said. 'No!' She put her hand over the top of the glass. 'Coffee, please. Black. For a black day. Ladies and gentlemen, Gerry will meet a fine woman who will love him as I can't, and you . . . you will all forget this day. Please! And . . . I'm so sorry.'

Rita hurried off, past people torn between compassion, horror

45

and the knowledge of what a good story it would make. She was shuddering and gasping.

Elvis rushed over to her and took her in his arms.

'Mum!' he said. Despite his years of study, despite the vast riches of the English language, he could think of no words to add, so he repeated the one word that seemed appropriate. 'Mum!' And Jenny hurried over, tears streaming, llamas heaving, and said 'Rita!' and kissed her, and Rita said 'Jenny!' and Elvis hugged them both, and they looked round for a chair, and a rather florid man – he was an architect who designed futuristic tubular shopping fortresses and lived in a Georgian house near Hazlemere, did they but know it – saw the gesture, and his good manners overcame his feelings of solidarity with Gerry, and he brought over a chair, saying unnecessarily, 'A chair,' and Jenny said, 'Thanks,' and Rita subsided into the chair, and Elvis said, 'Mum!' and the riches of the English language remained unexplored.

Rita gave a tiny, tired grin. 'I'm all right now,' she said. 'Suddenly I'm all right. I feel very small and very cold but very sober.'

'How lovely she would have looked!' Betty Sillitoe, over-sentimental as usual, gave a vast sigh. 'How magnificent her dress would have been.'

'It still is,' protested the former big wheel behind Cock-A-Doodle Chickens.

'You know what I mean.' Betty sighed again. 'It was sad to see her drunk, though.'

'It's always sad when somebody you like and admire lets themselves down in public. More grape juice?'

'Please.'

Carol Fordingbridge smiled at Rita, but could think of nothing to say, so, sensibly under the circumstances, she said nothing. She tried to link arms with Elvis, but he shrugged her arm off. Behind them, cold streaks of orange and red were fading slowly to mauves and purples as the short day died.

Sometimes Rita dreaded asking the most simple questions, but this one couldn't be avoided. 'Where's Paul?'

46

'He refused to come,' said Jenny, half embarrassed, half defiant.

'Good for him,' said Rita.

'Oh terrific,' said Elvis. 'I face up to the total embarrassment of the occasion, because I love you, and Paul gets praised for copping out.'

'Elvis! Your mother's got enough problems without you getting in a temper,' said Carol.

'Temper?' Elvis showed just a touch of temper at the suggestion. 'I'm not getting in a temper.'

'No. I know. I've seen your tempers,' said his fiancée. 'Like when I put tomato purée in the coq au vin.'

'Carol!'

'I don't suppose Jean-Paul Sartre ever lost his temper because Simone De Beauvoir put tomato purée in the coq au vin.'

'That's the whole point.' Elvis sounded wearily long-suffering beyond his years. 'Simone De Beauvoir would never have put tomato purée in the coq au vin.'

'Elvis!' said Jenny. 'Three quarters of the world are starving.'

'I know. And I deplore it,' said Elvis. 'But I fail to see any logical link between that and putting tomato purée in coq au vin.'

'This is ridiculous,' said Jenny. 'We've got more urgent things to think about.'

'No. Please,' begged Rita. 'I can't take any more talk about the urgent things. Let's talk about tomato purée.' Nobody spoke. 'Nobody has anything to say about tomato purée, it seems.'

'Hello!' Simon tossed his absurdly cheery greeting into their resonant silence.

'Hello, Simon,' said Rita. He was a man made for morning dress. In sweaters he was a fish out of water, in jeans a laughing stock. He was made for great occasions and Rita had ruined his great occasion, she had ruined everybody's great occasion. Oh God! 'Sorry to ruin your day.'

'Not at all,' protested Simon, with that bottomless willingness to please that would surely take him far up the ladder with Trellis, Trellis, Openshaw and Finch. 'Not at all. It's been a terrific . . . well, not a terrific . . . not at all terrific, of course, but . . . apart from not being terrific, it's been . . . well . . . '

Elvis finished it for him. ' . . . terrific.'

'Well, yes. Well, it has.'

Carol turned the torch of her beauty full onto Elvis's face. It was a beauty to which only he, it seemed, was blind. And he was her fiancé. Strange are the ways of young love.

'I've spotted a flaw in your logic,' she said.

'You what?' Elvis was incredulous.

'You said you'd faced up to the total embarrassment of the occasion, but you didn't know it was going to be embarrassing when you faced it.'

'I was talking of the embarrassment of Mum marrying Gerry, not the embarrassment of her not marrying him.'

Elvis stomped off. Carol gave a little embarrassed laugh.

'I can't seem to do anything right these days,' she said.

'Settle for celibacy, Carol,' said Simon. 'I have, and it's terrific. I mean, look at all the chaos the sexual urges get people into.'

'Yes! Oh yes!' said Rita.

'Oh Lord.' He was appalled. 'Oh no, Rita. I wasn't meaning you.'

'Come on, Simon.' Jenny led her brother away as one would a small child who has become a nuisance.

Alone with Rita, Carol looked young and vulnerable. 'Well, I'd . . . ' she began.

'No, please, Carol, stay with me,' begged Rita. 'I have an awful feeling that the moment I'm on my own Ted will loom up, and I can't face that yet.'

'Oh. Right.' Carol fetched a chair just vacated by Rita's sneezing uncle, and sat beside Rita. Behind them, a large flock of rooks chattered homewards towards the long narrow wood that screened the hotel grounds from the Tadcaster Road. Their day was ending. Rita felt that hers would stretch ahead of her for ever.

There was an awkward but affectionate silence between the two women as each searched for a topic.

Carol found one first.

'Is it wrong to put tomato purée in coq au vin?' she asked.

'I wouldn't know,' said Rita. 'Ted never let me cook anything foreign.'

Times change. Ted Simcock, ex-foundry owner, ex-husband,

ex-refuser of foreign food, handed his ex-lover and her second husband a card and said, unnecessarily, 'Our card.' They studied the card's limited text without interest. He continued unabashed. 'Our cuisine will be basically a marriage of the bountifulness of Yorkshire hospitality . . . ' he stretched his arms, to etch in the size of the portions, ' . . . with the flair and *je ne sais quoi* of *cuisine nouvelle.*' He garnished the air with his fingers.

'Who's your chef.' It was just a social noise, not inquisitive enough to justify a question mark.

'Ah! That's the only slight snag at the moment. Genius doesn't grow on trees.' Ted handed his former lover's husband a bright orange voucher. 'Present that during our first week, you'll get a free half-carafe of house wine.'

'Thank you,' said Neville politely.

'Very generous,' said Liz, her voice drier than Ted's house wine was likely to be.

Ted moved on, to distribute his vinic largesse more widely.

'I must go to Rita,' announced Neville.

'Neville!' said Liz sharply.

'She looks rather trapped with Carol, who has no conversation, poor girl. She'll be feeling awful.'

'No. You mean she's found today an ordeal?'

Liz felt that she had delivered these little shafts of sarcasm rather well, dressing the depth of her feelings in an elegant lightness of tone, rather as a lark might sing if livid. Neville appeared not to notice. Liz raised her eyes larkwards as he ploughed on earnestly.

'In Rita's case I feel it's my particular duty to talk to her. I suspect that she once carried a bit of a torch for me.'

'Good God, Neville.' Liz realised that her raised voice was attracting the interest of one of Rita's aunts. She didn't care. 'I'd have thought that was a special reason for not talking to her.'

'I'm going to talk to her, Liz. By all means come too, if you feel like it.'

'Righty-ho, sir.' Liz gave a mock salute and wished she hadn't. If she kept longing for Neville to be masterful, it wasn't fair that she should wax sarcastic every time he approached that state.

Carol was giving the lie to Neville's assertion that she had no

49

conversation, although perhaps laying herself open to the charge that she did not have a wide range of topics.

'I use tomato purée in lasagne,' she was saying.

'I'm sure it's delicious.'

Behind them a single shaft of crimson defied the onset of night. In front of them, the talk was frenzied. Only Rita and Carol and a couple of footsore aunts were seated in all that throng. Only Carol had the task of keeping a conversation going with the architect of the day's sensational doings. She searched for something further to say, and, happily, inspiration struck.

'I use tomato purée in moussaka,' she said. 'Probably that's wrong too. Probably I'm dead ignorant.'

'I'm sure you're a very good little cook.' Rita winced, regretting the 'little'.

'No. Elvis says he'll have to do all the cooking when we give media dinner parties.'

'"Media dinner parties"! My son, philosopher, rebel and slob, plans "media dinner parties"! Oh, Carol!' She surprised Carol by leaning over and kissing her warmly.

Neville and Liz arrived, Neville smiling earnestly, Liz faintly.

'Hello!' said Neville too brightly. 'All ship-shape and Bristol fashion?'

'Absolutely.' Rita managed a smile. 'Carol and I have been having a fascinating chat about tomato purée.'

'Jolly . . . good.' Neville frowned as he considered the possibility of fascinating chats about tomato purée. 'Rita, I wanted to say that, whatever you may think, and whatever you may think anybody else thinks, and I think if you knew what they were thinking you might find that they aren't thinking what you think they're thinking, I think, in fact I know, that I have never admired you as much as today.'

Rita burst into tears, threw her posy of freesias at Neville, and rushed from the room.

'Neville!' said Liz, before rushing off to comfort her old enemy.

Ted's ex-wife and the woman who had taken him from her left the room arm-in-arm. Some heads turned to watch, others turned so as not to watch.

'What did I say?' said Neville Badger, puzzled doyen of the town's legal community.

Ted stood beside Sandra, his waitress, his mistress, and watched as his ex-wife and ex-mistress left the room. The dollop of trifle on his plate was forgotten.

'Well!' he said. 'Could this be the start of a beautiful friendship?'

He didn't want the trifle. He was full to bursting. But he'd felt obliged to take some notice of Sandra, and, since he was determined to keep their relationship secret, he could hardly say, 'Sandra! I want you. How about a bit tonight?' He had therefore said, 'Waitress, I wonder if you could rustle up a last dollop of trifle.' An excellent ruse, the only drawback being that, the dollop of trifle having been rustled up, he now had to eat it.

'She can't keep her eyes off you.' There was withering scorn in Sandra's voice, as if anybody who couldn't keep her eyes off Ted must be mentally deficient.

'What?' Ted was puzzled. 'Who? Liz? Rita?'

'The tarty piece!'

Ted willed his neck not to swivel. It was no use. He found himself gazing, across Rita's craggy relatives, past Gerry's poncy friends, far across the crowded function room towards his vision in yellow. Corinna was waiting for him to look. She smiled. His heart churned. He turned back to Sandra, who was also smiling, grimly.

'Sandra!' Ted spoke with a mouth full of trifle. 'The "tarty piece" only happens to be double-barrelled. Her father's only a bishop. And a dish.'

'You what?'

'A lovely man. And she's nothing to me, anyroad. So, I've nothing to hide. So, I'm going to talk to her. All right? Good.'

He was aware of Sandra's eyes boring into his back as he negotiated a path between the wedding guests, refusing to meet the eyes of uncles who had drunk all his whisky every Boxing Day and aunts who had given him so much aftershave and deodorant that he had begun to wonder about his personal freshness. What did Rita's relatives matter now, in this wonderful world in which Corinna Price-Rodgerson had eyes only for him?

'You've been avoiding me.' She seemed amused.

51

'No! Look, Corinna, meeting you today has been very, very exciting for me. I feel . . . '

'Aflame with desire?' She smiled, slightly awkward in her advances, as one might expect from a bishop's daughter.

'Lightning does strike twice in the same place twice!'

'What?' Corinna was again puzzled.

'Nothing. I want to be alone with you, Corinna. I can't wait for Tuesday . . . ' Sandra arrived with champagne. ' . . . s will be stewsdays, stewsdays every Tuesday, Sundays and most days will be roast days . . . Sandra!'

Sandra continued to pour champagne into Ted's glass long after it was full. The champagne cascaded onto the floor around his feet. Sandra smiled. Her smiles were formidable.

'Ladies and gentlemen.'

Ted turned eagerly to listen to Gerry. Anything was better than this confrontation between Sandra and Corinna.

Silence fell rapidly. Rita and Liz entered, having repaired Rita's shattered face and make-up. Rita looked as if she might faint. Liz clutched her arm and squeezed it encouragingly. Nobody saw them. All eyes were on Gerry. What would he say? What could he say? On this, the worst day of his life, he held an audience spellbound for the only time in his inglorious political career. The irony escaped him.

'Ladies and gentlemen.' He stood where Rita had delivered her emotional speech. Gerry's speech was carefully unemotional. His face was pale and pinched. He looked very young, and so very, very old. 'Ladies and gentlemen. I'm off now. I'd just like to apologise for the way the day has turned out, and to thank you all for coming, and for all the presents, which were just what we . . . would have wanted, and will be returned. I'm off to Capri. I had hoped that my bride would be with me, as I understand that this is customary on these occasions. But I'm going anyway; it's all paid for, and I deplore waste of every kind. It says so in my bloody manifesto, so it must be true.'

Gerry Lansdown looked neither to left nor right as he walked past his wedding guests. He didn't so much as glance at Rita. He strode out of her life forever, with his head held high.

Rita trembled.

'Feel up to facing everybody?' said Liz gently.

'Oh yes. I don't think I should run away now. And . . . thank you, Liz.'

Rita kissed Liz, and Neville, watching, beamed.

'Our Liz is turning into a real trooper,' said Rodney Sillitoe, watching from their position beside the apple juice.

'Well she doesn't see Rita as a threat, now she's made such a fool of herself,' said Betty.

'That's a bit ungenerous, isn't it?'

'No. It's realistic. I don't believe anybody ever does anything except for selfish reasons.'

'Betty! You do.' Rodney was astounded. 'You're a very sentimental person.'

'Sentimentality is selfish. When I pat a little boy on the head and go, "There, there! Who's a clever boy, then?", who loves it? Me. Who hates it? The little boy. Selfish.'

'But you're an incredibly wonderful wife to me.'

'Because you're such an incredibly wonderful husband to me that it's in my interest to be an incredibly wonderful wife to you.'

'Aaaah! Let's clink juices and drink to us.'

'To us.'

They clinked juices.

With Liz at her side, Rita felt able to face her ex-husband at last.

'Well!' said Rita.

'Yes,' said Ted.

'What a mess,' said Rita.

'Yes,' said Ted.

'Oh well,' said Liz.

There was a brief lull, as if their loquacity had exhausted them.

'So how did you feel, Ted?' asked Rita. 'Sad? Happy? Triumphant?'

'Rita! As if I . . . I mean! Really! I felt embarrassed. For you. For Gerry. For me.'

'For you?' said Liz.

'Rita made some rather nasty insinuations about my prowess as a lover.'

'Ted!' said Liz. 'Not now.'

'No, no. I know. Subject closed. Not the time or place.' He paused. 'But. Well, it was, wasn't it? A bit below the belt. As it were.'

'No, Ted, it wasn't below the belt,' said Rita. 'I was referring to your emotional commitment, not your physical prowess. You're all right in that department, and there are people in this room who could second that, I'm sure.'

Liz blushed. She was thoroughly disconcerted. Ted was astounded. He didn't realise that Rita's abrupt return to acidity had made her feel angry and confused about her dramatic new role as Rita's friend and saviour.

'I really must go and . . . er . . . ' Liz couldn't find any way of ending her sentence.

Ted, not known for his social rescues, leapt to her aid. 'See if Neville's all right?'

'Yes! Exactly! Thank you, Ted!' Ted wished that Liz didn't sound so surprised.

Ted and Rita looked into each other's eyes and saw only the past, their marriage, the painful separation and divorce. The duty manager, Mr O'Mara, trim, precise, prissy and finger-clicking, was fussily organising the drawing of the curtains. It was that moment, on late winter afternoons, that is the most magical of the day for those who are happy at home, as they enfold themselves in a womb chosen and furnished by them; but which, for the lonely, the bored, the inadequate, the defeated, the frightened, is the bleakest moment of all, as they face the long dark evening, and welcome into their homes a group of Australians because, empty-headed and indifferently acted though they may be, they are better than loneliness, or more fun than their nearest and dearest.

Ted, feeling the bleakness, shivered, and reached out to touch Rita.

'No,' she said. 'No. I have to say, Ted . . . we have to get this straight . . . my not marrying Gerry has nothing to do with any feelings for you. I'm not coming back to you, ever.'

'Oh no,' said Ted. 'No, no, I know. No. I've . . . er . . .'
Corinna walked past behind Rita and flashed Ted a quick
invitational smile. 'I've . . . er . . . I've reconciled myself
to that.'

'So I see.'

'What?'

'That rather striking woman who just passed.'

It wasn't the first time that Ted had wondered how Rita could
see behind her.

'Do you notice everything?' he said.

'I'm a woman.'

'Yes.'

'You're worried about your sexual prowess, and here you are
surrounded by your conquests.' Rita shook her head at the absurd
neuroses of men.

'Rita! Don't exaggerate.' But Ted couldn't help looking
slightly pleased.

'Me. Liz. The striking woman. The waitress.'

'Waitress? What waitress?'

'The one you're living with. The one you're so busy trying
to keep secret that everybody knows about her.'

Ted was appalled. 'Rita! You mean . . . ? Oh heck.'

'I even saw Doreen from the Frimley Building Society going
into the other bar. All we need now is the blonde Swedish
nymphomaniac and Big Bertha from Nuremberg and we'd have
the full set. Ted and his women.'

'Rita!' said Ted, desperately trying not to think, 'Well, yes,
I've had me moments,' even more desperately trying not to
think, 'What a pathetic list, compared to Don Juan and President
Kennedy and Simenon.' 'Why rake over cold ashes, Rita? Why
spoon up dead custard? The past is dead. Dead. How is Doreen?
How's she looking?'

Rita gave Ted a long, hard stare, and didn't tell him how
Doreen was looking.

The immaculate Neville Badger of Badger, Badger, Fox and
Badger approached. Liz followed, as if on this occasion *she* were
his lapdog.

'Well, here we are,' said Neville. 'Almost like . . . well, no,
not really very like old times.'

'No,' said Rita with feeling. 'Not really.'

It was as if Neville's approach had been the signal for the full social rescue of Rita Simcock to be put into operation. Elvis and Carol arrived next. Rita's mind whizzed. Would Carol talk about tomato purée? Did Elvis know that she had never been able to love him quite as much as she loved Paul?

'Hello,' said the great philosopher.

'Hello, Elvis,' said Liz, and a stranger would have sworn that she was pleased to see him. 'I heard your sports bulletin yesterday. Very pithy.'

Elvis swelled with pleasure. 'Thank you, Liz,' he said. 'I aimed for . . . pith.'

'Then you succeeded.'

Was she mocking him? Could he avoid blushing? Luckily Simon and Jenny scurried up, Simon breezily, Jenny more warily.

'Hello!' said Simon. 'Everybody gathered! Almost like . . . well, no, not really at all like old times.'

'No,' said Ted. With what depths of regret he invested the monosyllable.

'I'm very grateful to you all for rallying round,' said Rita, 'but I think I ought to face the massed ranks of Gerry's friends and relations now.'

'I don't think you should,' said Ted. 'They might lynch you.'

'Thank you, Ted.'

'No, but is there really any point?' said Jenny. 'Will anything you can say to them make anything any better? You've explained already. Can you add anything?'

'Perhaps not,' admitted Rita. 'Perhaps we should just go home. "Home"!'

And indeed a few people were beginning to drift off, now that the curtains had been drawn. It was dawning on them that it wasn't appropriate to linger to the end of such an occasion. Others were staying because they weren't quite sure how to leave. Should one just drift away? That seemed rude. But was it appropriate to give thanks? And to whom?

'When I tell Paul!' said Jenny. 'He's going to be so sick he missed it. Oh Lord. I shouldn't have said that. Not today. Oh Lord. I think I'm going to cry.'

'Don't cry! Please!' implored Rita. 'Nobody cry. Once I start –'

She changed the subject desperately, the words pouring out. 'You know, Jenny, what you said about explaining. There's something I didn't explain. I couldn't. Gerry wouldn't have understood. One of the reasons I couldn't marry him . . . it'll probably sound very silly . . . he never had any doubts. I doubt whether I could live with somebody who had no doubts.'

'I don't understand,' said Simon.

'I do,' said Carol Fordingbridge. Elvis couldn't prevent his eyebrows from rising caustically. 'I do, Elvis!'

'I didn't say anything,' said Elvis.

'I have doubts,' said Rita. 'Tremendous doubts. I'm constantly testing my beliefs against my doubts. I don't intend to hide that even from the selection committee.'

'Well, no, quite right,' said Ted. 'Why should . . . selection committee? What selection committee, Rita?'

'I'm trying to enter politics myself,' said Rita. 'In a modest way.' She smiled modestly, shyly. 'I'm putting myself up to be Labour candidate for the Brackley Ward council by-election.'

Jenny was the first to recover, but even she wasn't quite quick enough. Later, Rita would wish that her friends hadn't all been quite so stunned.

'Great,' said Jenny, hurrying forward to kiss her mother-in-law. 'Fantastic. No, that's really fantastic. Great.'

'You! In politics!' Ted didn't attempt to hide his incredulity.

'Thank you, Ted.'

'I'll have to preserve the full impartiality of my reports, Mum,' said Elvis grandly.

'Well of course you will,' said his mother. 'I'd have expected nothing less from you.'

Elvis sniffed her remark, suspecting mockery.

'*Labour?*' said Neville, as if the enormity of it had just filtered through.

'Do you know nothing of my beliefs?' said Rita.

'Sorry,' said Neville.

Liz let her head sink onto Neville's arm in an affectionate exasperation.

'If they'll have me after this,' said Rita. 'Oh God.' She doubled up, as if in physical pain. 'Oh, I'm sorry. I just . . . I feel awful.' Ted and Carol grabbed her. 'Oh,' she said. 'Oh.' She tried to smile up at their concerned faces. 'You know,' she said, 'when I came in and faced Gerry and everybody, funnily enough I didn't feel as bad as I expected. I suppose the drama of it keyed me up. But now, when it's over, and when I wake up in the nights to come, in the months to come, and realise, no, it isn't a nightmare, I, Rita Simcock, did this dreadful thing . . . will I ever feel able to smile again? Will I ever feel able to laugh again?'

Betty and Rodney Sillitoe sailed up. They were two galleons, laden to the gunwales with sympathy.

'Hello!' said Betty.

'Hello!' said Rodney.

'All gathered together,' said Betty encouragingly. 'Almost like . . . well, no, not really very much like . . . '

'No,' said Ted. 'Not very. Not really.'

A heavy little silence sat on them, as they reflected upon how unlike old times it was. Rita, whom they had come to support, was the first to make the effort.

'So, what are you two busy bees up to these days?' she asked the Sillitoes.

Rodney and Betty exchanged uneasy glances.

'We're opening a health food complex,' said Betty.

'With wholefood vegetarian restaurant,' said Rodney.

Rita laughed.

Second Do

February:
The Christening

Neville Badger looked down at young Josceleyn, snug in his up-market pram, and thought, 'Will you, one day, ensure that there will still be a Badger at Badger, Badger, Fox and Badger?'

A male mistle-thrush, head on one side as he listened between the gravestones for the faint underground stirrings that would indicate the approach of his unsuspecting lunch, saw the pram out of the corner of his bleak bright eye and refused to give ground.

Liz Badger, resplendent at the side of her immaculate husband, looked down at young Josceleyn and told herself for the umpteenth time, 'There's nothing of Ted in him.'

Rita Simcock joined them, bent to admire Josceleyn, and thought, 'Is he really beginning to resemble Neville? Can emotional influences really produce so rapid a change?' But all she said was, 'Bless him.'

Neville smiled and said, 'Well, it could have been worse. It could have been raining.'

The ravishing Liz Badger looked slightly less ravishing as she frowned at her husband's banality.

A moist south-westerly air-stream had produced a soft, heavy, soupy grey day in which it was possible to shiver and sweat at the same time. Later, the Meteorological Office would declare it to be the most humid February day since 1868. That day, in fact, Selby was more humid than Rangoon. Yorkshire had awakened that Sunday morning to find a layer of red Saharan dust over everything. Compulsive washers of cars had smiled over their watery bacon, in their softly sweating, newly fitted kitchens. It wasn't much fun, week after week, washing cars that were already clean. Here was a challenge.

'We knew we were taking a risk, having it in February,' said

Neville to Rita. 'But we realised that if we didn't have it soon he'd be walking. He's very forward.'

'Neville's terribly proud of him. Almost as if . . . ' Liz didn't finish her sentence. She didn't need to.

'Quite,' said Rita.

Neville carefully negotiated an uneven stretch of pavement, taking care to give Josceleyn a smooth ride. A man born to be a father, he had never had a child of his own. Rita made a mental note to refer to inadequate maintenance of pavements in her maiden speech, and Neville, as if he could read her mind – an ability of which he had never given the remotest sign – said, 'Incidentally, congratulations . . . Councillor.'

'Thank you very much.' Rita couldn't help being slightly coy.

'Who'd have thought – ?' Neville stopped so abruptly that it was clear he had been going to say something tactless.

'When I was a down-trodden, neurotic housewife, that within two years I'd sweep onto the council by five votes after four recounts?'

'Well, not exactly, no, but . . . '

'Who would have?'

'Precisely.'

The pram slipped smoothly towards the abbey over a more even stretch of path.

'A small majority,' continued Rita, 'but a vital moment in our town's history.'

'What?' Liz bit her tongue. She had meant to show no interest whatever in Rita's political career.

'It changes the balance of the council. This town is now Labour controlled. Exciting, isn't it?'

Rita glanced at their faces, looking for the excitement which she knew she wouldn't see. Neville tried not to look too appalled. Liz didn't try.

'I hope you don't intend to talk politics today, Rita,' she said as they rounded the heavily buttressed South West corner of the great building. 'I hardly think it's the time. Have you heard from Gerry? Did he enjoy his honeymoon on his own?'

'Liz!' Neville stopped the pram abruptly. Josceleyn whimpered.

'Oh, I don't think these things should be swept under

62

the carpet, Neville, or they'll hang over us forever,' said Liz airily.

'You put your carpets on the ceiling, do you?' said Rita.

'You know what I mean,' said Liz. 'I mention it purely in order to exorcise it, not to be nasty.'

'I choose to believe you. And you're right.' Rita gave Liz a smile that was superficially innocent of malice. 'No skeletons in cupboards. No carpets hanging over us. I understand that he had quite a good . . . God, Ted!'

Ted Simcock, former owner of the Jupiter Foundry, soon to be manager of Chez Edouard, smiled at them rather awkwardly. He was wearing a somewhat flash suit which he believed befitted his new status as a restaurateur.

'Hello,' he said, and he only just failed to sound at ease.

'Have you invited him?' said Rita under her breath.

Liz shook her head.

'Ted! Really!' said Rita.

'Well, I . . . er . . . incidentally, congratulations, Councillor.'

'Thank you very much.' Again, Rita couldn't help being slightly coy.

'Who'd have thought . . . ?'

'Quite. But really, Ted! Turning up today!'

Liz leant across the pram, ostensibly to pull Josceleyn's coverlet up over his neck, but actually to hiss, 'Pretty tactless, Ted, even for you.'

Ted leant forward, ostensibly to have a close look at his son, but actually to hiss back, 'You once said you liked me because I was tactless and uncouth.'

'I hardly think we need mention that,' hissed Liz.

Ted gave the three of them what he hoped was a proud, dignified look. 'I think I of all people have the right to be here,' he said. He realised that there were people within earshot, and added, out of the side of his mouth, 'The baby is mine.'

'No, no, Ted. No, no,' said Neville. 'You're his father. He isn't yours. He isn't anybody's. He's himself. Circumstances have meant that it's my duty . . . and my great privilege . . . to look after him till he's old enough to look after himself.'

They were stunned. In the town, four young men roared out of the car-park of the Coach and Mallet in a souped-up Escort with a faulty exhaust, and the landlord's caged-up Rottweilers, sensing their aggression, barked excitedly.

'Well said, Neville,' said Liz at last.

'Yes. Marvellous,' said Rita.

'I wish you didn't sound so surprised,' grumbled Neville.

'I care about the boy,' said Ted, resuming his self-justification as if Neville hadn't spoken. 'I'd like to witness the service at least. I'll give nobody any reason to suspect the truth. I mean, I won't. I'm capable of being civilised and discreet. I mean . . . I'm a leading restaurateur. And I mean . . . I'm hardly likely to make a scene in front of my fiancée, am I?'

Rita and Liz were astounded. Ted's startling information took rather longer to filter into Neville's keen legal brain.

'Well, all right,' he said, 'but if you do, Ted, if you do . . . your fiancée?'

'You're not marrying your waitress?' Liz sounded as if she couldn't believe that a man with whom she had slept could ever sink so low.

'No, Liz. Nothing as disturbing to your social nostrils as that. I'm marrying Corinna Price-Rodgerson.'

'Oh, Ted.' It was Rita's turn to sound shocked.

'Thank you, Rita.'

'Well, congratulations, Ted,' said Neville.

'Yes, congratulations,' said Liz.

'Yes, congratulations,' echoed Rita.

Into the inappropriately cool silence that followed these congratulations there stepped the lady in question. Where before she had been yellow, she was now orange. She greeted them vivaciously, as if she had already taken them to her heart.

'Congratulations, Corinna,' said Neville and Liz in unison.

'Yes, congratulations,' said Rita, after just too long a pause.

'Thank you,' said Corinna graciously. 'And congratulations to you too . . . Councillor.'

'You see!' said Ted. 'Congratulations all round. Worry not. It's going to be a wonderful day.'

It began to seem that it would indeed be a wonderful day. A narrow gash of hard cobalt appeared in the gloomy sky, and widened and softened as the banks of cloud rolled away. The sun shone warmly. The humidity seemed to stream up through the gap in the clouds, towards the amazing blue of that winter

64

sky. Foreheads eased. People took sumptuous breaths. It was as if the lid had been taken off this pressured, gaseous universe.

Liz and Neville's guests were gathering on the paths around the church. The sun shone on the earrings of elegantly dressed ladies and on the port-wine noses of men who had lived well. It shone on Matthew Wadebridge, a colleague of Neville's at Badger, Badger, Fox and Badger, and on Mrs Wadehurst, who was big in the Red Cross, and pretty big in the sunshine outside the abbey church. It shone on the bald head of the bluff, egg-shaped Graham Wintergreen, manager of the golf club, and on his golfophobe wife Angela. It shone on the queenly Charlotte Ratchett, of the furniture Ratchetts, greying but undefeated, no mean wielder of a number two iron in her hey-day. It shone on Morris Wigmore, Deputy Leader of the Conservative Group on the Council, whose son had come to a sticky end in Brisbane, despite which, or perhaps because of which, he never seemed to stop smiling. It shone on Rodney Sillitoe, the former big wheel behind Cock-A-Doodle Chickens, in a crumpled suit and with a crumpled face, Band-Aid on his chin and no Betty at his side. It shone on Liz's skeletal, ramrod uncle, Hubert Ellsworth-Smythe, who had made his money in Malaya and Burma, and lost it in York, Doncaster, Wetherby and Market Rasen. It shone on Simon Rodenhurst, up-and-coming estate agent, assiduous cleaner of teeth.

'Hello,' beamed Simon whitely. 'Congratulations, Councillor!'

'Thank you very much.' This time Rita almost managed not to sound coy.

Simon beamed at the whole group: Neville and Liz and Rita and Corinna and . . . Ted!

'Ted!' he said.

'I think you've met my fiancée, Corinna,' said Ted.

'Yes, we've . . . er . . . fiancée? Good God!' Simon gulped. 'I mean, "Good God is certainly giving us something to celebrate today!" Congratulations!'

Simon was less than overjoyed to see, approaching at a fast lick, and smiling broadly, Andrew Denton, Neville's nephew, who was in banking in Leeds and not doing as well as had been hoped. Simon was even less overjoyed to see, approaching at a slower lick, Andrew's wife Judy, whom he had once shown round a house, and then round his flat, and then round his bedroom, and then round his body. He was even less overjoyed to see Judy's stomach. From what Andrew had said at his mother's wedding to Neville, Simon was certain that what was in there was the result of the one and only indiscretion in his unintentionally celibate young life.

'Fiancée!' said Andrew cheerfully. 'I heard that! Congratulations! Hello, all. Mrs Simcock! I heard! Congratulations!'

'Thank you very much.'

Simon tried hard to look at something other than Judy's stomach.

'Quite a warm day,' said Andrew Denton. 'We won't need heating. That's lucky.'

There was a mystified pause.

'Because we don't want it to be a baptism of fire,' he explained. 'Joke,' he added.

'You remember my nephew do you, Simon?' said Neville.

Curls of grey cloud swirled in from the West. The sun fought feebly, and was gone. The lid came down again. The day pulsed with moist pressure. The greyness, to which they had earlier been reconciled, was terrible now.

'Yes,' said Simon. 'Yes, I . . . er . . . I . . . er . . . yes.'

'And you know my wife Judy?' said Andrew. 'Heavily pregnant, but still lovely.'

'Yes, I . . . er . . . yes, I . . . I showed her round a . . . er . . . a . . . er . . . ' Simon was a rabbit frozen before life's full beam.

'House,' said Judy. 'It was a house, Simon.'

'Yes. Absolutely. A house.'

'And here's the godmother, even more pregnant, but also still lovely,' said Liz.

Jenny was wheeling her son, Thomas, in an altogether more mundane pram. She did indeed look fairly enormous, being due any day now.

'Hello, everybody,' she said. 'Congratulations, Rita. Fantastic! Fantastic! Ted!'

'You know my fiancée, don't you?' said Ted.

'Fiancée? Fantastic.' Jenny tried to invest this 'fantastic' with the enthusiasm she had shown in her previous ones. It was a gallant failure. 'Well . . . congratulations. What a happy day.'

66

'Where's Paul?' said Rita nervously.

'We had a terrible row this morning, and he's refusing to speak to me, and he wouldn't come. Oh Lord. I was going to say he has this mystery virus, but I couldn't lie, but I should have lied, I shouldn't have spoilt things, not today.'

The suave Doctor Spreckley glared at the Christening party, as if they had no right to be there. There were only thirty-six people gathered round the fifteenth-century font, and he had fifty-eight Belgians in tow. Doctor Spreckley, precise and delicate wielder of instruments at the General and, more frequently, the Nuffield, had thrown himself enthusiastically into the town's twinning with Namur. He had visited that charming city twice and on each occasion had managed to wield his instrument precisely, if not delicately. Since his wife had left him, because of his unfaithfulness, he had thought of very little except sex and food, and nowhere did that combination seem more promising than in gallant little Belgium. These last few months had seen an incomprehensible falling-off of these appetites, and today he was in a thoroughly sour temper. He no longer felt attracted to his physiotherapist from Liège. His roast beef dinner at the Grand Universal Hotel had been vile – goodness knew what the Belgians must have thought. He was damned if he would deny them a tour of the church just because of some blasted service.

And so, the new young vicar took that small gathering through the service of baptism accompanied by a loud echoing whispered commentary, in vile French, on the charms of his church, and by the tip-toeing of fifty-eight Belgians, many of whom may have been gallant, but very few of whom were little.

The three godparents stood at the front of the gathering, with Jenny between Simon and Andrew. She was holding Thomas, and she was terrified that he would cry.

The congregation recited along with the vicar, temporarily drowning Doctor Spreckley.

'Heavenly Father, in your love you have called us to know you, led us to trust you . . . '

Simon did something he hadn't done since boarding school. He prayed, silently.

'Oh Lord,' he said, 'I expect you know this, well you know

everything, but in case you were looking the other way or something . . . I mean, you must sometimes, you're only human, well no, you're not . . . anyway, the thing is, the only time I've ever . . . you know . . . it was with the wife of the other godfather. She's . . . you know . . . and I think it's very probably mine. I'm very sorry and I'll never . . . you know . . . again with anybody ever, but what am I to do? I should never have agreed to take on the moral welfare of this child. Should I back out now? Help me.'

He finished just in time to hear the vicar say, 'Therefore I ask these questions which you must answer for yourselves and for this child. Do you turn to Christ?' And the parents and Godparents responded, 'I turn to Christ.'

What should he say? 'Sorry, vicar. No can do'?

'I turn to Christ,' he said.

'Do you repent of your sins?'

This time Simon joined the others. 'I repent of my sins,' he said, so intensely that Jenny turned to look at him.

'Do you renounce evil?'

'I renounce evil.' Andrew Denton was also surprised by Simon's intensity.

'We will now sing . . . ' The vicar paused to glare at the Belgians. ' . . . hymn number one hundred and sixteen, omitting verses four and five.'

The dimly-lit House of God thundered to the uninspired playing of Leslie Horton, water-bailiff and organist, who hated to be called Les.

'All things bright and beautiful,
All creatures great and small,' sang the congregation.

Rita glanced at Rodney. He looked rough. 'Rodney's on his own again,' she thought. 'I hope nothing's wrong.'

'Each little flower that opens
Each little bird that sings.'

The Belgians began to file out of the church. They had tickets for the rugby league match against Featherstone Rovers.

Jenny, oblivious of everyone, including the Belgians, told herself, 'Concentrate on these young lives. Forget your own troubles. Pretend you believe, and pray.'

'All creatures great and small
All things wise and wonderful . . . '

Ted craned his neck to catch a glimpse of Rodney. 'Oh dear,' he thought. 'Don't say *they're* splitting up.'

'The river running by,
The sunset and the morning . . . '

The long-haired Carol Fordingbridge looked charming in a grey and white floral patterned dress with white collar, and a natural straw hat with a black band. But Elvis in his thrusting young media person suit had no eyes for her charms.

'Oh Lord,' she prayed, 'make the whole world happy. Get rid of poverty and disease, and make Elvis love me.'

'All things wise and wonderful,' sang that small congregation, dwarfed by the cool, echoing church. 'The Lord God made them all.'

Even Liz, the high and mighty, the haughty and naughty, couldn't resist a curious glance at Rodney.

'Rodney looks awful,' she thought. 'Don't say *he's* got marital problems.'

'How great is God almighty,
Who has made all things well . . . '

'I wish He could make me well,' thought Rodney. 'But I deserve it. I have strayed, oh Lord.'

'All things wise and wonderful,
The Lord God made them all.'

The last notes of the organ reverberated around the empty nave, and died. There was total silence. The vicar couldn't have taken Liz's son from her with less confidence if the boy had been a great lump of soap.

Ted Simcock, former maker of door knockers, macho Yorkshireman, found himself smiling inanely as the vicar held his son awkwardly over the font, and as the infant splashed water over himself, baptising himself before the vicar could do it.

Ted's smile died as he heard the vicar's words.

'Josceleyn Neville Selwyn, I baptise you in the name of the Father, and of the Son, and of the Holy Spirit.'

'Josceleyn Neville Selwyn,' he thought. 'My son is going to be known to the world as Josceleyn Neville Selwyn Badger.'

A greater sense of loss than he had ever known swept over Ted. He felt as if he was the biggest of a set of Russian dolls. He felt that if he could be opened up other Ted Simcocks would be found there, less puffed-up, less pretentious, better, more honest, more loving, more caring Ted Simcocks. Happier Ted Simcocks.

Liz Badger, mother of his baby, didn't acknowledge at that moment that he existed.

Corinna Price-Rodgerson clutched Ted's arm, and his sense of loss was almost swept away.

Stepping out of the church was like colliding with a damp flannel. The afternoon was as grey as the face of a dying man.

Outside the West Door, where mythological stone beasts hid among exquisite carved leaves, the new young vicar spoke with Neville and Liz, playing the conversation game, at which he was already being compared unfavourably with the old vicar by some inappropriately uncharitable Christians in his flock.

'He looks so very like you, Mr Badger,' he said. 'I find that extraordinary.'

'Yes, I . . . I find it rather extraordinary myself,' said Neville.

'So many people take these things for granted,' said the vicar. 'But the seed, the tiny seed, growing into a person that resembles its parents, every time I see it I think "This is a miracle."'

'In this case it certainly is,' said Liz, half to herself. She moved off, taking Neville in her slip-stream, and the vicar made a mental note to be less religious in his small talk.

The guests stood around, chatting, waiting for their hosts to set off for the party.

Rita tackled Rodney. 'Betty didn't make it then?' she prompted.

'No. She was hoping so much . . . Oooh!' He gasped with pain. 'Excuse me, Rita.'

'Oh dear,' said Rita as she walked away. 'Oh dear, oh dear.'

Rodney was just lowering himself onto a wooden bench beside the church when he saw Ted and Corinna bearing down upon him. With a sigh he stood up almost straight again.

'Are you all right, Rodney?' asked Ted.

'Yes. Grand.' His voice was as contorted with pain as it had often been with drink. 'Just grand. Right good. Top form.'

'You know Corinna, my fiancée, don't you?'

Corinna beamed at Rodney.

'Your fiancée!' said Rodney. 'What happened to . . . ' Ted, behind Corinna, shook his head furiously. ' . . . to the famous British reserve, our native shyness . . . ' Ted nodded. ' . . . that you've got engaged so quickly?'

'Love brooks no frontiers, Rodney.'

'You what?'

'Love breaks down barriers. Betty away again?'

'Yes, she's . . . er . . . ' he groaned again, ' . . . excuse me. I have sinned, and I'm reaping the whirlwind.'

Rodney collapsed onto the bench.

Corinna continued to smile. She seemed happy to be silently benevolent until called upon to speak.

'Oh dear,' said Ted, as they walked away from the ailing former imprisoner of chickens. 'Oh Lord. Oh heck.'

Liz and Neville stood watching the clusters of guests, as if they were outsiders who had no right to be there, rather than the *raison d'etre* for the elegant little shindig. Neville was looking worried.

'He'll be all right with his godparents,' said Liz.

The pregnant, charmingly shapeless, slightly fey Judy Denton had carried little Josceleyn off, in practice for the days ahead.

'It's not that,' said Neville. 'I was thinking, it'll look odd if we don't invite Ted and Corinna back now they're here. It'll set tongues wagging.'

'Oh Lord,' said Liz. 'Do we really still care that much about wagging tongues?'

'And they *have* just announced their engagement. It'll look a bit graceless.'

'Oh Lord. Today of all days, Neville, I would like to be free of memories of Ted.'

'He'll be discreet. He's with his fiancée, whose father is a bishop.'

'Ah! So that means she's so socially acceptable that we must ask her.'

'No. Of course not. No, I think that, accepting as we must that your son . . . our son . . . is in reality the product of Ted's . . . er . . . '

'Spermatazoa.'

'Liz! Well, yes, in a . . . that it would be a Christian

gesture, on a Christian day, to invite Ted to . . . wet the baby's head.'

A two-carriage Sprinter train clanked slowly through the quiet Sunday afternoon. A few married couples were walking along the paths that criss-crossed the churchyard. Their dogs were fouling the paths. They gazed at their shitting dogs with adoration. Ted and his orange fiancée bore down on Neville and Liz.

'Well . . .,' said Ted, ' . . . we'll just slip quietly away, so . . . good luck, eh?'

'No, no,' said Neville. 'No, no. No need. I'd . . . er . . . we'd . . . er . . . I'd very much like it if you came to the . . . er . . . '

'I thought it was family only,' said Corinna.

'Ted is very much family, Corinna, in a way,' said Liz.

Ted leapt in much too quickly. 'Liz is referring to the fact that our two families are linked by wedlock, darling,' he said.

'Well, yes, that's what I assumed she meant,' said Corinna with apparent innocence. 'What else could she have meant?'

'What else?' agreed Ted. 'Exactly. Nothing else. Precisely. My point exactly.' He turned to the Badgers. 'We'd love to come,' he said. 'Where are the junketings? À la maison de les Badgers?'

'No, Ted,' said Neville. 'At the Clissold Lodge. But the Brontë Suite this time. It's smaller.'

'Then we'll see you in the Brontë Suite,' said Ted, and he winked to show them that they could rely on him, because he knew how to behave in public, but Liz and Neville, seeing him wink, thought, 'Oh Lord. Ted doesn't know how to behave in public. Can we rely on him?'

Simon was unused to holding babies. You didn't get much call for it, at Trellis, Trellis, Openshaw and Finch. He realised that Judy had found Josceleyn heavy, in her condition, but her handing over of him in public had seemed a tactless symbolic gesture under the circumstances. He was terrified that the boy would slip from his grasp, or choke to death, or merely scream his head off. He held him as if he were a carrier bag of doubtful strength full of bottles of Château Lafitte. He was terrified that Judy intended to begin a meaningful conversation. He would have welcomed the arrival of a third party, had it not been Andrew Denton, fellow godfather, life-long wag, husband of Judy, and official father of the child in Judy's womb.

'He does look a bit like his father, doesn't he?' said Judy, who was practising having maternal feelings by gazing at Josceleyn fondly.

'Let's hope our baby doesn't look like his father, eh?' said Andrew.

'What?' said Simon and Judy, aghast.

'Because I've got an ugly mug,' explained Andrew Denton. 'Joke.'

'Ah. Yes. Joke. Right,' said Simon and Judy. And they laughed. They were worried that their laughs hadn't sounded convincing, but Andrew hadn't noticed anything suspicious. He was only too used to receiving unconvincing laughs.

The Brontë Suite, the fifth smallest of the fifty-seven Brontë Suites in hotels in Yorkshire, was barely half the size of the Garden Room. It looked out over the front of the hotel, where the gravel drive curved away through the park-like grounds, dotted with oaks and chestnuts, to the narrow woods that screened the hotel from the Tadcaster Road. It made no nod to the existence of the Brontë sisters beyond taking their name. There were dark polished wood panels interspersed with dignified striped green wallpaper. The modern stainless steel lights didn't go with the crystal chandelier. The three paintings – of Bolton Abbey, Fountains Abbey and Rievaulx Abbey – had known more apposite days, when it had been the Abbey Suite. But what they lacked in relevance, they also lacked in quality.

On trestle tables at one end of the room, beneath Rievaulx Abbey, as it chanced, there was a fine array of sandwiches – smoked salmon, cucumber, rare roast beef – and fancy cakes and biscuits. There was also a christening cake, with baby and cradle atop it, and this was widely held to be consistent with the standards expected of the Vale of York Bakery in Slaughterhouse Lane.

Eric Siddall, barman supreme, polka-dotted bow tie slightly askew, as if to suggest that he had a vaguely rakish past, stood by a table on which there were several bottles of champagne, two of them in ice-buckets. There were fluted champagne glasses and tea cups. Eric looked uncomfortable when Graham Wintergreen,

73

manager of the golf club, entered. Graham Wintergreen looked uncomfortable when he saw Eric.

The guests were filing in from their cars. Many carried little presents, which they handed to Neville and Liz, who didn't unwrap them.

Rodney Sillitoe collapsed into one of several Restoration chairs dotted around the walls, but singly, as if to discourage social sitting. There was also the occasional occasional table.

The cynical Elvis Simcock made a bee-line for Rodney, leaving his fiancée in the social lurch. He fetched a second chair and sat beside Rodney.

'Auntie Betty's been away quite a lot lately, hasn't she?' he asked.

'Yes. She's having to look after an elderly aunt. She's at Tadcaster more often than she's at home these days.' Rodney gasped and grimaced.

'Are you all right?' asked Elvis.

'No. Last night I succumbed to temptation. I'm reaping the whirlwind.'

'Would you be prepared to tell me what temptation exactly you succumbed to?' persisted Elvis.

'Meat.'

'You what?'

'Rump steak. Rare. Bloody. Marvellous. Bloody marvellous. Now I've got the gripes.'

'Oh, I see.' Elvis sounded disappointed.

'Disappointed? Thought I was talking about "another woman"?'

'No! 'Course not. Has it ever crossed your mind that when she's at Tadcaster Auntie Betty might be seeing "another man"?'

'It has crossed my mind, yes.' Rodney raised Elvis's hopes only to dash them. 'Once. Just then, when you asked it. Of course it hasn't, Elvis. We have the perfect marriage.'

'Of course you do.' Elvis sounded disbelieving, as befitted one so cynical.

Rita approached her new hosts. She sported a knitted navy suit with three-quarter-length coat and cream knitted top. Her hat, shoes and bag were white. Liz had plumped for a purple, pink and yellow silk jacket and skirt, with a lilac silk top and large lilac bows in her hair. Neville wore a dark suit.

'Rita!' he said. 'There's tea or champagne, except there isn't any tea yet.'

'Champagne then?' said Liz. 'Or does that clash with your image as a Labour councillor?'

'I don't deal in images, Liz,' said Rita. 'I deal in truth and justice. Oh Lord, that sounds pompous. I hope in time I'll learn to be serious without being pompous. Champagne, please.'

Eric Siddall, barman supreme, sidled up as if on castors. 'There you go, madam,' he said, handing Rita a glass. 'Just the job. Tickety-boo.'

'Thank you, Eric,' said Rita. 'Eric! Are you working here now?'

'As of last Monday fortnight, madam,' said Eric. 'There was . . . let's say there was a clash of personalities at the golf club.' He flung a hostile glance towards the bluff, egg-shaped Graham Wintergreen.

'I'm sorry to hear that, Eric,' said Neville. 'I noticed you'd gone of course.'

'Thank you, sir.'

Eric excused himself, leaving them regretting that they hadn't asked him to elaborate.

'So . . . ' said Neville, ' . . . how are you faring, Rita?'

'In what way?'

'Well . . . in life. At home. The evenings. The nights. Without . . . '

'Neville!' said Liz.

'Without what?' asked Rita. 'Gerry? Any man? Sex?'

'No! Well, yes.'

'Neville!'

'I'm faring well. I'm not the sort of woman who feels incomplete without a man.'

'Is that a dig at me?' said Liz.

'No,' said Rita. 'Good heavens, no, Liz. We're friends now.'

'Ah.'

'Subject closed. Feminist speeches over.' Rita did try to leave it at that. 'I just hate the idea that without marriage men are fine but women aren't. Men seem to have managed to project the idea that bachelors are admirable and spinsters are pathetic.

75

As if marriage was an institution for the benefit of women, when it's clearly almost entirely for the benefit of men.'

'I see corduroy's staging a revival,' said Neville.

'What?' Rita and Liz were as united in their bemusement as they had ever been in their lives.

'I read somewhere that corduroy is making a comeback. I was steering us towards safer waters,' explained Neville. 'Sorry.'

'No. You're absolutely right,' said Rita. 'Let's try and avoid ructions of any kind, just this once.'

Sandra entered hurriedly and inelegantly with a large pot of tea and a large jug of hot water.

'Sorry about that,' she said to the Badgers, 'but he's a right dozy ha'p'orth, him.'

'Sandra!' Rita sounded appalled.

'Oh Lord.' So did Neville.

'What's wrong?' Sandra plonked the tea and water down and picked up the milk jug.

'You'll see,' said Liz.

Ted entered with Corinna.

Sandra dropped the milk jug onto the cups.

'She's seen,' said Liz.

Ted also looked thunderstruck. 'Oh heck. That's torn it,' he said. 'Come on, Corinna. Let's leave. It's best. I mean, it is. Isn't it?'

But his vision in orange was made of sterner stuff. 'I don't want to leave, Ted,' she said. 'I enjoy champagne. And I'm not frightened of a waitress. My father's a bishop.'

Corinna Price-Rodgerson marched forward resolutely. Ted had no option but to follow.

'Ted! Corinna!' Neville's enthusiasm for welcoming new arrivals was a bottomless well. 'Tea or champagne?'

'Champagne for me, please,' said Corinna.

'There you go, madam,' said Eric Siddall, barman supreme. 'No problem. Just the job. They can't touch you for it.'

'I think I'll start with tea,' said Ted. 'I've got a mouth like an elephant's . . . ' he glanced at Corinna, ' . . . mouth.'

Ted's choice of tea involved an encounter with Sandra, lover of cake and, until recently, lover of Ted. Well, so be it. It was unavoidable.

Sandra, who had made a creditable job of clearing up the

worst of the mess that she had made, gave Ted a cup of tea and enquired, with suspect solicitude, 'Do you take sugar, sir?'

Ted was uneasily aware that people were listening.

'You know I . . . yes. Two, please,' he said.

'Nice to see you again, sir. We haven't seen you around lately,' said Sandra.

'No, I . . . er . . . I . . . er . . . I've been . . . er . . . '

'Tied up? I know how these things happen, sir.'

Jenny came in, carrying an electronic baby link.

'They've put the babies in room 108,' she announced.

'They've what?' said Ted.

'That's hardly appropriate,' said Liz. 'That's the room he was . . . put in last time.'

'Well they say they use that room as a kind of spare because it's next to the boiler so it's noisy at ni . . . What last time?' said Jenny.

'I didn't realise it had ever really gone away,' said Rita.

They all gave her blank looks.

'Corduroy,' she explained.

'You're religious,' Ted told Corinna. 'Come and have a look at our great Yorkshire abbeys.'

He led Corinna off to admire the paintings.

Rita slipped off without explanation.

'What last time?' insisted Jenny.

Neville excused himself without explanation.

'Mum,' said Jenny, suddenly alone with Liz. 'He's never been to the hotel before. Were you going to say "That's the room he was conceived in"? Was he conceived during my wedding reception?'

'I'm afraid so,' admitted her mother. 'I was so overjoyed at your marrying your road sweeper that I got carried away.'

'Oh my God,' wailed Jenny. 'No wonder our marriage is going wrong. Oh Lord. I shouldn't have said that. Not today.'

She plugged in the baby-listening device.

Ted and his fiancée stood beneath Fountains Abbey. The artist had imposed his romanticism on the natural romance of the ruins. He had imposed his concept of beauty on their natural beauty. The result was uniquely, inspiredly ugly.

'Your waitress showed a bit of style there,' said Corinna.

'Surprised?' said her fiancé. 'That's stereotyped thinking, Corinna. That's a very glib social judgement, is that.'

'I do not make glib social judgements, Ted.' Corinna's rebuke was cool but affectionate. 'I was brought up not to. Don't forget, my father's a bishop.'

'Some chance,' muttered Ted.

'What's that supposed to mean?'

'Nothing. Well, you do rather drag it in. "Nice cup of tea, this. Incidentally, my father's a bishop."' He lowered his voice, in order to talk about sex. '"That was magnificent. You're the best lover I've ever had, Ted. Not that I've had that many. My father's a bishop."'

'I've never said you're the best lover I've ever had.'

'No. You haven't. Why not?'

'Maybe you're the only lover I've ever had.'

'What?' Ted's astonishment slipped out. He worked hard to alleviate his tactlessness. He wasn't *entirely* successful. 'I mean, not that I'm surprised. No, it's just that . . . statistically speaking, it's very unusual for women to reach your . . . oh heck . . . I mean . . . well . . . great!'

'Don't forget, my . . . ' began Corinna. Ted joined in. ' . . . father's a bishop.'

They laughed.

Sandra watched. Her face was a rigid mask.

'Sorry if I was a bit edgy, love,' said Ted. 'But, I mean . . . I am. It's with seeing her. Being reminded what a . . . well, not a bastard exactly. I mean, I didn't intend when I . . . I had no idea I'd be passionately loved by a beautiful, glamorous, sophisticated virginal goddess. I forget sometimes how attractive I am.'

Liz's skeletal, ramrod uncle, Hubert Ellsworth-Smythe, who had never refused liquid refreshment in his life, stood with a cup of tea in one hand and a glass of champagne in the other, regaling Angela Wintergreen with anecdotes about *faux-pas* at tiffin, and Angela Wintergreen was enchanted, because he hadn't mentioned golf once. Matthew Wadebridge, Neville's colleague, whose wife did charity work six evenings a week and snored in her chair on the seventh, looked out over the grounds, watched a heron flapping indolently through the murk in search of more promising waters, shivered, thought how long

78

the night must be for herons and what jolly times he had in the Bacchus Wine Bar in Newbaldgate each weekday lunchtime, decided that perhaps being human wasn't too dreadful after all, and turned back to the jollifications with renewed enthusiasm. Jenny Rodenhurst, charming despite her advanced pregnancy in a red and cream chiffon tent-style dress, with a natural straw hat and a shoulder bag hand-woven by the wives of Bolivian tin miners, approached her mother diffidently, wondering how to present Paul's absence in a not wholly unfavourable light.

'Mum?' she began.

'Paul's absence from social functions is becoming habitual, Jenny,' said Liz, driving a coach and pair through her daughter's diffidence.

'He hates do's. Any excuse. Look, Mum, we've had difficulties arising from lack of mutual faith arising from Paul's lapse with Carol, but our troubles pale into insignificance compared to floods in Cambodia and earthquakes in Armenia and poverty in the shanty towns of El Salvador. So, let's not talk about it.' She wanted to get away from the mother she had longed to talk to two minutes ago. She saw Eric at his drinks table. 'Champagne!' she said, and set off without further excuse. 'Better not,' she said, looking down at her swollen body. 'Have you any orange juice, Eric?'

'Certainly, madam,' said the dapper, ageless Eric Siddall. 'No problem. Here we go. Tickety-boo. And how's that husband of yours?'

'Fine,' lied Jenny. 'Great.'

'Sometimes, I – not having ever myself – sometimes I look at married couples and I . . . but with you two, I see you, so devoted, such loving parents, and I . . . I do, I come over all unnecessary . . .'

'Oh, belt up, Eric. You know nothing about it,' said Jenny.

Eric Siddall, barman supreme, stared at Jenny aghast.

'Oh Lord,' she said. 'Oh, Eric. Oh, I'm sorry, Eric.'

Eric bore his hurt with dignity.

'No problem, madam,' he said.

Betty Sillitoe had intended to make something of an entrance. Entering a room without Rodney at her side was, after all, something of a rarity. She had planned to stand in the doorway, smiling, looking really rather fetching, she felt, in her coral crêpe dress edged with apricot ribbon, and throwing her arms out in a gesture of affection; embracing them all in the warmth of her personality, as if she were the Pope and the Brontë Suite St Peter's Square.

This touching tableau was ruined before it started, by Jenny hurtling tearfully towards her, trembling with self-disgust, wailing, 'I shouldn't have. Not today,' and hurrying out into the lobby. Betty turned towards her in amazement, then turned back towards the room, and was embraced by Rodney before she had regained her composure.

'Betty! You came!' His delight removed all traces of regret for her lost entrance.

'I'm sorry I missed the service,' she said, 'but I couldn't leave her while she was hallucinating.'

'Hallucinating?'

'She thought she was Joan of Arc. She might have burnt herself.'

'Oh, Betty.'

Rodney embraced Betty again, even more warmly.

'Rodney!' she protested. 'A bit of decorum in public, if you please. As befits joint managing directors of a major new business. I'd have been earlier but I popped home to change because this dress creases if you travel. Rodney, there's a dreadful, soggy, wobbly, smelly mess on the kitchen table. What is it?'

'Carrot and cashew nut roulade. A treat for tonight, for your homecoming.'

'Oh, Rodney. I'm sorry.'

'No. I knew it had gone wrong. I meant to throw it out.'

Neville, Rita and Liz came forward to greet Betty.

'Hello, Neville,' she said. 'Hello . . . Councillor! Congratulations.' Now at last she embraced the whole room in her gaze. 'Ted! Corinna! *Sandra!*'

Sandra approached, smiling serenely, ignoring Betty's surprise. 'Tea, madam, or champagne?'

'Oh tea first, I think, please.' Betty called out to Eric. 'Eric? Later I'd like a drink. Do you have any fruit juices?'

'What?'

'I do not touch alcohol. It *is* a poison. Do you have any fruit juices?'

80

Even Eric Siddall, barman supreme, found it impossible to hide his astonishment entirely.

'Yes, madam,' he said, recovering. 'Can do. No problem.'

Betty turned back to Neville, Liz and Rita. 'Well, she said, 'I suppose my absence has set you all wondering if Rodney and I'll be splitting up next.'

'No, Betty. Good Lord, no,' said Rita.

'You splitting up? That's a good one,' said Neville.

'That's the best laugh I've had in weeks,' said Liz.

'Absolutely,' said Rita.

They laughed. It would be hard to decide which of the three laughs was the least unconvincing.

Underneath the hideously romanticised painting of Bolton Abbey, Elvis Simcock, elder son of Ted and Rita Simcock, was questioning Simon Rodenhurst, only son of Liz and the late Laurence Rodenhurst.

'So, Simon, are you still planning to give up what it would anyway be an exaggeration to call your sex life?'

'Too right. Today has confirmed that.'

'What's so special about today?'

'The other godfather's wife was the woman in question.'

'The pregnant one?'

'Precisely.'

'Oh my God.'

'Exactly.'

Elvis tried to hide his excitement at this revelation. He assumed a dignified, caring expression as he sought the words that he needed.

'What exactly went through your mind,' he enquired carefully, 'when you realised that the woman you'd made pregnant on your one and only foray into the world-renowned delights of sexual intercourse was the wife of your fellow godfather?'

'What do you think went through it, you steaming berk?' countered Simon angrily. 'I thought, "I am unfit to undertake the moral welfare of a mature garden slug with psychopathic tendencies, let alone an innocent infant boy. I must tell them I can't do it."'

'But you didn't tell them you couldn't do it, did you?'

'Because what could I say? "I can't go through with this. I'm the twit who got Andrew's wife preggers"?' He changed the subject. 'How's things with Carol?'

'Terrific. Great. Couldn't be better.'

'Hello,' said Carol, as if she'd been waiting for her cue. 'You're Elvis Simcock, aren't you?' She held out her hand politely. 'I'm Carol Fordingbridge, your fiancée. Remember me?'

'Carol!'

Elvis was all the more furious because he knew that he had no right to be.

'I've got to sit down,' said Rodney Sillitoe, and, as though to prove that he hadn't been lying, he sat down.

Betty looked round for another chair. Morris Wigmore leapt to his feet and handed her his chair, smiling. When Betty said that he shouldn't have, he pooh-poohed the idea that he had made any sort of sacrifice. He smiled confidently, frankly at Betty, little knowing that she was thinking, 'Why don't I trust this man? Why does he send goose-pimples up my spine? If only his son hadn't come to a sticky end in Brisbane, so that I could loathe him without feeing a heel.'

'Last night I strayed,' confessed Rodney in a near-whisper, when Betty had settled herself in her Restoration chair.

'Strayed? How do you mean, "strayed"?'

'What do you think I mean?'

'Well, not a woman. You wouldn't.'

'Aaaah!'

'So it must have been either alcohol or meat. The way you look, I'd say . . . ' Betty examined his rough, red, battered face lovingly, ' . . . meat.'

'Steak. Rump. Rare.'

'Oh, Rodney, you're hopeless on your own.'

'Because I love you.'

'I know.'

They kissed, then looked up to see Rita beaming at them.

'It *is* good to see you back, Betty,' said Rita. 'You two are rocks on our shifting sands.'

'Rodney and I were talking the other day, Rita,' said Betty. 'Weren't we, Rodney?'

'Yes. Yes, we were.'

'You tell her.'

82

'Right. Tell her what?'

'What we were talking about.'

'Oh! Right!' Rodney thought hard. 'What were we talking about?'

'Offering her a job in our new health food complex and vegetarian restaurant.'

'Ah. Yes. Absolutely. Rita, will you come and work for me?'

'For us!'

'Us. Yes. Quite. Absolutely. What I meant. Us.'

'I'd love to!'

'Rita!' Betty leapt up and embraced Rita. The two women hugged each other. A golden, organic future stretched before them.

Even in the midst of so much happiness, Neville managed to find a mission of mercy.

'Carol looks lost,' he said.

'Neville!'

'I want this to be a great day, Liz. For everyone.'

Neville scurried off to Carol's conversational rescue.

Liz sighed.

'Carol, hello,' said Neville.

'Hello.'

Carol did indeed look lost. Her eyes were suspiciously moist.

'You look marvellous.' Neville beamed.

'Well, thank you very much.'

'No, you really do.'

'Well, you just said so.'

'No, what I mean is, sometimes one says these things without meaning them, but I do mean it. You really are . . . very lovely. Elvis is a lucky young man.'

'Isn't he?' Carol's eyes belied her smile. 'Isn't he just? Incredibly lucky.'

The edge in her voice escaped Neville completely. 'Named the day yet?' he asked innocently, pleasantly.

'No we sodding well haven't named the sodding day.' Carol stalked off, then returned almost immediately. She wasn't far from tears. 'I'm sorry. I shouldn't have said that. Not today. No scenes today. All smiles today. Happy day today.'

Neville looked deeply puzzled.

'Er . . . jolly good,' he said.

Rodney and Betty smiled at Ted and Corinna rather cautiously from their chairs.

'No doubt Rodney has told you, Betty. I can't imagine him overlooking anything so momentous and so gratifying to our many friends.' There was an irritatingly smug tone in Ted's voice. He knew that Rodney hadn't told Betty. 'Corinna and I are engaged.'

'No, Ted, he didn't.' Betty flashed Rodney the look of rebuke that Ted had hoped for. 'Congratulations! But what about . . . ?' Betty stopped in mid-sentence.

'More tea, anybody,' interrupted Sandra.

'Not for me, thanks,' said Ted.

'No, thank you,' said Rodney. 'Time to move on to something . . . '

'Weaker,' interrupted Betty hastily.

'Thank you, Sandra,' said Corinna, her composure utterly unruffled. 'I'll stick to champagne.'

'Right.' Sandra set off with her tea pot and milk jug, then stopped, between Ted and Corinna. 'Happy day, i'n't it? I love children, me.' She flashed an almost subliminal look at Ted. 'I'd like to have some of me own one day.' She moved off. An awkward silence followed, proving that, although she had found no takers for tea, Sandra's mission had not been in vain.

'So, how's Chez Edouard coming on?' asked Rodney eventually.

'Very well indeed.' Ted's face lit up. 'We chose the shade of dralon only yesterday. And what about you? What are you calling your great vegetarian emporium?'

'It's difficult,' said the former big wheel behind Cock-A-Doodle Chickens. 'We thought of amusing names like "Absolutely Nuts" and "Bags of Beans".'

'"Loadsalentils",' chortled Betty. '"Finger on the Pulses".'

Rodney and Betty chuckled.

Ted and Corinna didn't.

'Abandoning humour, we tried plain factual ones,' said Rodney. '"The Arbitration Road Natural Food Centre" etcetera. In the end we settled on just plain "Sillitoe's".'

'We think it has a ring to it,' said Betty.

'Arbitration Road?' said Ted. 'You're in Arbitration Road? What number?'

'182 to 184, if it's of any significance,' said Rodney.

'It is of some significance,' said Ted. 'Chez Edouard is at 186. We're going to be neighbours.'

'Well . . . ' It was unusual to find Betty lost for words.

'Sell up now,' said Ted.

'You what?' said Rodney.

'Next door to Chez Edouard. Wholefood vegetarian. In Yorkshire? You stand no chance. Do they, my petal?'

'No chance.' Corinna smiled lovingly at her fiancé. He basked in her agreement.

'Good luck, anyway,' said Ted.

As they walked away, Ted raised his eyebrows to Corinna. 'Poor deluded fools, I really am extremely sorry for them,' said Ted's thick, unkempt eyebrows.

'He called her "my petal",' said Betty.

'I'm going to have to lie down,' said Rodney, as if Ted's calling Corinna 'my petal' had been the final straw.

But before Rodney could lie down, he would have to stand up, and before he could stand up, the dapper, ageless Eric Siddall arrived.

'Sir, madam, your juices,' he announced.

'Thank you, Eric.' Betty Sillitoe, over-solicitous as usual, smiled warmly at Eric, for fear that he could see that his arrival was unwelcome to Rodney.

'You're surprised to see me here and not in my usual haunt,' began Eric, taking Betty's smile as an invitation to open his heart. 'I had . . . problems.'

Betty looked at Rodney, wondering whether to cut Eric short. But Rodney's curiosity overcame his discomfort.

'Problems?' he said.

'My . . . er . . . ' Eric lowered his voice. 'My proclivities . . . such as they are these days, but we won't go into . . . are not towards people of the opposite sex. Do you catch my drift?'

'We catch your drift,' said Betty.

'No one could ever say I've not been discreet. I've never advertised my . . . proclivities. But . . . well, let's say they were . . . known. A bookmaker who'd known me from my sea-going days passed a rather unfortunate remark after a mixed foursome. Mr Wintergreen made it clear that my continued presence, after years of good service, was no longer welcome. "Take any golfer you like," he said. "Nick Faldo, Bernhardt Langer, Jose-Maria Olafabal. Not a poofter among the whole caboosh." That's what he said. "Poofter". No thought for my feelings. "Go somewhere more suitable," he said. "A theatre bar. The Conservative Club. Start afresh, with a clean sheet. As it were." Well! I thought of going for unfair dismissal, but . . . my name in the papers, that just isn't me, I'm afraid, and with the climate we're moving back into . . . so, well, anyway, the manager here snapped me up. I think I know why, and I dread the day when . . . I'm sorry. I didn't mean to burden you with my . . . '

'Not at all,' said Betty. 'It was riveting. Well, not riveting exactly. More . . . sad.'

Rodney groaned.

'I really am going to have to lie down,' he said.

Betty hurried over to consult her hostess.

'He's not well,' she said. 'I want to lie him down. Could we use the bed in the room the babies are in?'

'Certainly,' said Liz. 'It's room 108. Out of the lift, turn right, third on the . . . or something like that, I was told. I haven't been there.'

Liz hurried off to break up a *tête-à-tête* that had developed between Neville and Rita.

'Rita's been telling me all about the imminent effect of her election on council policy,' said Neville.

'Riveting,' Liz was sorry that she had hurried off to break up the *tête-à-tête*.

'Little me, Rita Simcock, shifting the balance of power single-handed,' said Rita.

'So what exactly will be your first big issue?' said Neville, as if he hung on the answer.

'The inner relief ring road.'

Liz was no longer sorry that she had hurried off to break up the *tête-à-tête*.

'What about it?' she asked.

'There are two proposed routes.'

'Yes. We know. One of them passes near us.'

'Does it? Oh.' Rita didn't sound deeply surprised. 'Well, I

think the council would have voted for the inner inner relief ring road. Now, thanks to my election, we should be able to get the outer inner relief ring road through.'

'But that's the one that passes near us,' said Neville.

'Is it? Oh . . . well, the outer road destroys far less property, so, although it's more expensive, we have to go for it. There'll be under-passes beneath Crudgely Hill and the Alderman Potherbridge Memorial Park. The only properties it'll destroy will be one or two houses in Broadlands . . . '

'That's where we live, Rita.' Liz didn't attempt to hide how appalled she was.

'Is it? Oh. Well, yes, I suppose it is. And the odd, mainly rather clapped-out property in the Tunstall Road area and the top end of Arbitration Road. Well, I hope you won't be affected.'

'Do you, Rita?' Liz sounded sceptical.

'Well, of course I do. I've always been very fond of Neville.'

'Well, of course Rita does, Liz. She's always been very fond of me.' Neville had never lacked talent as an echo. 'Now, let's not argue. No clouds on silver linings today. More champagne!'

Rodney and Betty Sillitoe tip-toed into room 108, so as not to wake the sleeping infants. Rodney made a bee-line for the double bed, but Betty went briefly to look at little Thomas and little Josceleyn, breathing milkily in the cots provided by the management.

'Ah!' said Betty, over-sentimental as usual. 'Bless their little cotton socks.'

'Come and lie down and give me a quick cuddle,' said Rodney.

Betty crept quietly towards the very bed in which, nineteen months ago, Ted and Liz had conceived one of the two young boys now sleeping so peacefully in that very room.

The room had been refurbished since then. It was now safely, relentlessly beige. Amos Clissold no longer stared down from the wall above the bed, as he had once done from the wall above every bed. He had been removed after the under-manager at a DIY store had blamed the severity of his look for his inability, half-jokingly admitted to the receptionist, to consummate his marriage on the first night of his honeymoon. The receptionist had later joked that she hoped the honeymoon wouldn't be DIY throughout.

Above the bed there now hung a heavily romanticised, *faux-naïf* painting of a Northern industrial scene, very sub-Lowry, described by an art critic who had slept beneath it as, 'Dark satanic Mills and Boon.'

Below the painting, Rodney and Betty Sillitoe cuddled in exhausted contentment.

In the baby-free, champagne-bubbling Brontë Suite, the social chatter was intensifying, keeping the gloom of the outside world narrowly at bay. But Jenny's sharp maternal antennae could have picked up Thomas's cries if a baby link was plugged in on the opposite side of a runway at Heathrow, and she heard something now.

'Sssh everybody,' she said. 'I think I can hear something on the baby alarm.'

Only Liz heard Jenny's soft, diffident pleading.

'Sssh!' commanded Liz imperiously. 'Sssh!'

Her skeletal, ramrod uncle joined in the shushing. So did Graham Wintergreen and Neville. Soon there was absolute silence. All eyes were on Jenny, who was bending down, listening to the baby link.

The unmistakable voice of Rodney Sillitoe, still thick from past excesses, rang out.

'Rub it gently,' he said. 'There. Where it's sore. Aaah!'

'Rodney!' came Betty's reply. 'Two teetotal vegetarians cuddling in broad daylight!'

'Well, we can't deny ourselves every pleasure.'

Not a person moved in the Brontë Suite. Jenny, her hands only inches away from the power point, never even thought of switching the voices off.

After a brief silence Betty's voice came again. 'Careful, Rodney! I thought you were ill. You're squashing my breasts.'

Neville Badger was the first to recover the use of his limbs and voice.

'Yes, well, may as well switch it off, while there are adults up there,' he said.

'Oh yes. We don't want to eavesdrop on unseemly scenes in upstairs rooms,' said Ted, and he immediately wished he hadn't.

Neville switched the plug off, sparing the Sillitoes the broadcasting of any further indelicacies and sparing his guests from any further need to pretend that they weren't enjoying their eavesdropping.

Rodney and Betty became aware of low voices issuing from the bathroom of room 108. They clambered carefully, quietly off the bed. Carefully, quietly Rodney opened the bathroom door.

The bathroom had tiled walls, with the occasional Dutch windmill and sailing barge to break up the remorseless pink. The plastic three-quarter-length bath was green. The plastic washbasin was green. The plastic lavatory was green. On its plastic green seat cover sat Elvis Simcock, fully dressed. He was holding his head in his right hand in a pose reminiscent of that other great thinker, Rodin's. His left hand held a small tape recorder to which he was giving his complete attention.

Rodney and Betty stared in astonishment. As they eavesdropped on this strange scene, they were unaware that everybody in the Brontë Suite had so recently been eavesdropping on them.

'"Disappointed?"' came Rodney's voice from the tape recorder. '"Thought I was talking about *another woman?*"'

Betty raised her eyebrows.

Rodney controlled his anger.

'"No!"' came Elvis's reply. '"'Course not. Has it ever crossed your mind that when she's at Tadcaster Auntie Betty might be seeing *another man?*"'

'"It has crossed my mind, yes."' Betty looked horrified. '"Once. Just then, when you asked it."' Betty, standing incredulous at the door, relaxed. '"Of course it hasn't, Elvis. We have the perfect marriage."'

'Aaah!' whispered Betty.

'"'Course you do,"' came Elvis's sceptical reply on the tape recorder.

'Cynical young puppy,' whispered Betty.

'"So, Simon,"' came Elvis's voice, '"are you still planning to give up what it would anyway be an exaggeration to call your sex life?"'

The Sillitoes were riveted.

'"Too right. Today has confirmed that."'

89

'"What's so special about today?"'

'"The other godfather's wife was the woman in question."'

'"The pregnant one?"'

'"Precisely."'

'"Oh my God."'

'"Exactly."'

'We shouldn't be listening to this,' whispered Betty.

'No,' whispered Rodney. 'Sssh!'

'Right.'

'"What exactly went through your mind when you realised that the woman you'd made pregnant . . ."'

Rodney groaned as the gripes struck him again.

Elvis looked up, horrified. He switched the tape recorder off. He tried to stand, but slipped, falling into the tiny gap between bath and lavatory, cracking his bony backside against the toilet roll holder. He got to his feet. It was not a manoeuvre executed with dignity.

'What the . . . ?' he said.

'Sssh!' whispered Betty.

'Don't wake the little ones,' whispered Rodney.

'Rodney's not well,' whispered Betty. 'He came to lie down.'

'What the hell are you up to?' whispered Rodney.

'I'm practising interviewing techniques. For my career,' whispered Elvis.

'On the toilet?' whispered Betty.

'There's a baby-listening device in there. I didn't want anyone downstairs to hear.'

'Oh my God!' In his horror Rodney still remembered to whisper. 'You mean . . . ?'

'Oh Rodney!' whispered Betty. 'Oh Lord.'

'Wait a minute,' whispered Rodney indignantly. 'When you spoke to me downstairs, so full of concern, you were using me.'

'No, I wasn't.' Elvis forgot to whisper. The Sillitoes put their fingers to their lips. 'I was interested. A chat show host's no good if he doesn't have a genuine interest in people.'

'Chat show host?' whispered Betty.

'I'm going to have to lie down again,' whispered Rodney.

'Funny, us being friends now,' said Jenny Simcock, *née* Rodenhurst, hoisting her Bolivian bag further onto her shoulder.

'Hilarious,' said the long-haired Carol Fordingbridge.

'Oh, Carol.'

They'd been looking at the painting of Fountains Abbey, finding it easier than meeting each other's eyes. Now Carol looked Jenny in the face, forcing her to return the look.

'I'm right sorry about what I did with Paul, Jenny,' she said.

'Carol! It's over.'

'No. It isn't. It's only just begun. You said so yourself. The miasma of deception drifts across the plains of love and obscures everything that's good.'

'That sounds like me,' acknowledged Jenny ruefully.

'I'll never do anything like that again if I live to be a hundred.' Carol looked up at the ruined abbey. Perhaps she was wondering about the destructive effects of age. 'I'm not sure if I want to live to be a hundred.'

'You and Elvis'll be all right.'

'We won't. He's become ambitious. He's ashamed of me. He refuses to use my window.' After the closure of Cock-A-Doodle Chickens, Carol had got a job in the Midland Bank in Westgate, where Elvis banked. 'And I love him. Stupid, i'n't it?'

'It is rather.'

'I think he looks at me and thinks anybody stupid enough to love him is too stupid for him to love. What about you and Paul?'

'I can't talk about it, Carol. I might cry.'

'Don't start or I will.'

They avoided each other's eyes, gazing fixedly at Fountains Abbey. And suddenly, there, behind them, between them, was Neville Badger, awash with immaculate goodwill.

'How lovely you look,' he said. 'Two lovely young ladies, in love with two fine young brothers.'

Carol and Jenny tried not to look too aghast.

Neville ploughed on.

'Members of the younger generation, making a go of things. And upstairs, sleeping soundly, two innocent baby boys, a future generation. Today, at least, I feel, there's hope, there's a future. Thank you.'

Neville moved off, his job done.

'Sometimes I think I preferred him when he was miserable,' said Jenny.

Rarely in their lives could the Brontë sisters have witnessed such an apparently cheerful scene. Neville beamed at Caroline Ratchett, of the furniture Ratchetts, whose three putts on the last green in 1978 had given Neville's first wife Jane the last of her four ladies' individual championships. He beamed at Graham Wintergreen, who was enjoying a long discussion with her, on the subject of golf. He beamed at Angela Wintergreen, who was having a long discussion about corn dollies with Eric Siddall. Neville failed to realise that they were spinning out their conversation in the hope of sparking resentment in Graham's insensitive breast. Neville noticed nothing except laughter, smiles, champagne, beauty. The beauty of Liz. The beauty of the cake. The beauty of life.

He approached his wife, beaming.
'It's going well,' he said.
'I wonder what'll spoil it.'
'I'm going to make a speech.'
'I wonder no longer.'
'Ladies and gentlemen. Ladies and gentlemen.'
The Sillitoes returned.
Jenny switched on the baby link.
'Today is a happy day,' said Neville. 'Before we come to the cutting of the cake, I have an announcement. Will you please drink a toast to Ted Simcock and Corinna Price-Rodgerson, who have announced their engagement.'
Sandra dropped a pile of plates. They crashed spectacularly to the floor. None of them would carry cake that day or any other day.
'Oh hell,' she said.
She ran from the room.
'Oh Neville,' said Liz.
'Oh Lord,' said Neville.
'Oh heck,' said Ted.
He rushed out after Sandra.

As a badger to the sett, as a fox to the earth, as a catatonic to the womb, so Sandra made for the kitchen. There, dwarfed by the blackened ovens and the huge pots and pans, she turned and faced her foe.

Her foe entered breathlessly. It was a long while since Ted Simcock had run anywhere. He advanced diffidently, and stopped beside the ovens, as if frightened that his cornered ex-lover would tear him to pieces if he came too close.

'Sandra!' he said. 'Love!'

'So!' Sandra spat her words out. 'You're going to marry your tarty piece.'

'I came out here to . . . er . . . mend a few bridges, if I could. To build a few fences, to try to . . . I don't know.' Ted's words sounded hollow in the emptiness of the cold, lifeless kitchen. 'But, Sandra! Don't call her a tarty piece. Her father's a bishop.'

'He may be a bishop. She may be double-barrelled. Deep down, in her heart, where it matters, she's a tarty piece.'

'You never could judge character, could you?' said Ted sadly.

'No,' barked Sandra. 'I loved you.'

'Ouch!' Ted winced. 'Sandra! Love!'

'Why do you call me "love"? You don't love me.'

'No, I don't. And you don't love me.'

'No. Not now.'

'Love! You never did. We never did. Did we, love? We didn't. It was affection. Friendship. Desire. Lust. It was never love, love.'

'It was. Love curdles.' Sandra's tears began to flow again. Silent, reproachful tears. 'Love and hate are two sides of the same coin. That's what I reckon, anyroad. And I hate you.'

The empty kitchen of a great restaurant is a sad place. There is desolation in its temporary calm. In the calm of the kitchen of the Clissold Lodge Hotel there was no desolation. Emptiness seemed its natural state. Sandra's intensity rang strangely through this calm, cool place.

Still Ted found himself unable to move closer to this young animal that had been ripped open by life.

'I wanted to say . . . why I came out here was to say . . . you're a grand girl,' he said. 'A right smashing lass.'

'You must be an idiot to give me up, then.'

'Maybe I am, Sandra. Maybe I am. I didn't intend to,

love. I didn't want to, love. Then it burst upon me. Love, love.'

'You love her?' Sandra sounded incredulous.

'Oh yes.'

'She loves you?' Sandra sounded even more incredulous.

'Oh yes. I wanted to come in here . . . embarrassing though it is . . .'

'Big of you!' There wasn't a knife in the kitchen that could have cut as sharply as Sandra's scornful sarcasm.

Ted winced, but carried on. 'To say, I'll never forget you. You gave me something wonderful at a time of low ebb.'

'I warmed you up for her. 'Cos I haven't got a double-barrelled name and money and I keep dropping things, *which* I only do when you're around.'

Sandra began to sob again. Ted at last found the courage to move towards her, uttering the inappropriate words, 'Well, there you are, you see. We're best apart.'

A slightly-built, shinily-suited, middle-aged man entered. He had a toothbrush moustache and shiny black hair that had long ago been combed into submission. Had he been found with a speck of dust on his waistcoat, he wouldn't have slept for shame. He was Mr O'Mara, the duty manager.

Ted and Sandra hurriedly decided that they would indeed be best apart. They leapt apart.

'What's going on?' asked Mr O'Mara. Despite his name, there was no trace of Irish in his voice, which was slightly fruity, and just too large for him, like his suit.

Ted thought swiftly.

'I expressed a desire to see the kitchens of a great hotel,' he said. 'Your excellent, efficient, helpful waitress kindly obliged.'

'Yes.' Sandra was trying hard to hold back her tears. 'This is Ted Simcock, Mr O'Mara. Mr O'Mara, the duty manager.'

Ted and Mr O'Mara shook hands. Mr O'Mara's handshake was weary. He'd been shaking hands for seventeen years.

Sandra turned to Ted. 'These are the main ovens,' she sobbed. 'They can cook enough roasts to serve two hundred and fifty portions of meat at a sitting, which we often do, being known for our functions.'

'Yes,' said Ted with feeling. 'I know.'

'Why the tears?' said Mr O'Mara.

94

It was Sandra's turn to think quickly.

'I'm that proud, Mr O'Mara,' she said.

'What?'

'Of the kitchens. Of the hotel. It's that clean, that gleaming, that well-kept.' She struggled unavailingly against the flow of tears. 'I thought of when it's full and smoky and all the orders and all the cooking and all the satisfied customers and how we cope and I felt . . . right proud, Mr O'Mara.'

'That's wonderful, Sandra,' said the duty manager. He turned to Ted. 'Seventeen years in hotels, Mr Simcock. Given my life to the group.' Ted nodded numbly. 'Passed over for assistant manager five times.' Ted shook his head at the injustice of life. Mr O'Mara gave a tiny, bitter twitch. 'Outsiders brought in over my head.' Ted nodded his sad agreement at the ways of this harsh old world. 'Wondering, am I wasting my time? Here's my answer.' There was a tiny sob in Mr O'Mara's voice. He looked down at his shiny shoes, then straight into Ted's face. 'This is what makes it all worth while.' Ted nodded. Mr O'Mara turned to Sandra. 'Thank you, Sandra,' he sobbed. 'Oh Lord, I . . . ' He took out a tiny handkerchief and blew his shiny nose.

'Thank you, Mr O'Mara.' Sandra resumed her tear-ducted tour of the kitchen. 'This is the toast-making machine.'

The emotion was too much for Mr O'Mara. He fled, clutching his handkerchief. As he shut the door, Sandra's words rang in his ears.

'At peak breakfast times this can handle four hundred slices an hour.'

'Oh, Sandra.' There was a distinct tremor in Ted's voice. 'That was brilliant. Very clever. You're smashing. Oh, Sandra, I'm sorry.'

Ted also began to sob. The proud face that had launched a thousand boot scrapers crumpled with sorrow and shame.

The steady hum of conversation in the bright, busy Brontë Suite contrasted so startlingly with the echoing emptiness of the kitchen that Ted almost flinched. He had washed his face, and, because there were no towels, had bent down to dry it under the hand-dryer. This lack of dignity had pleased him, for he was honest enough to feel that he deserved it. He had stood on the steps in front of the hotel, and had felt only the clammy handshake of that foetid day. His poise had only been partially restored. He glanced uneasily towards his fiancée, wondering how she had taken his abrupt pursuit of Sandra. Before he could find out, he was accosted by his son.

'So, how are you feeling now you're engaged, Dad?'

'Very happy. Delighted.'

'And how do you feel about . . . about Mum?'

'What is this? *Panorama*?'

Elvis sounded hurt. 'It's your son showing an interest in his father, Dad. Do you regret what happened with Liz?'

' 'Course I do, son. And I regret it didn't work out with your mother. Bitterly. I mean . . . course I do. And now I must go to Corinna. She'll be upset.'

'She doesn't look upset.'

'Elvis! You know nothing about women.'

Ted grabbed a glass of champagne and drank without tasting it. He smiled at the bluff, egg-shaped Graham Wintergreen, but hardly saw him. He approached Corinna. She looked as calm as she was orange.

'Sorry about that,' he said, trying to sound as if it hadn't been important. 'Are you upset, my petal?'

'Of course not,' she said calmly. 'It's perfectly understandable. You wanted to try to help her retain some shreds of dignity.'

'You're an amazingly understanding woman.'

'My father's a bishop.'

Charlotte Ratchett was the first to see Sandra return. She carried a tray on which there were just two glasses of champagne. Charlotte Ratchett, whose tastes were as expensive as her furniture, tried to catch her eye, but Sandra had eyes only for Ted and Corinna. She thrust the tray under their noses, giving them a fixed, bright, dreadful smile.

'Champagne, sir? Madam? To celebrate your engagement?'

'Oh, thank you, Sandra,' said Ted. 'That's very . . . that's extremely . . . thank you.' He drained his glass rapidly, grimaced, put the empty glass on Sandra's tray, took the nearest full glass, realised that he hadn't shown good manners, and looked sheepish as Corinna took the remaining glass.

Sandra moved off, still smiling.

Ted raised his glass to Corinna, drank, and grimaced again.

'I don't like this very much,' he said.

'Oh!' said Corinna. 'I love it.'

'You're amazing,' said Ted. 'You don't seem jealous of Sandra at all.'

'Why should I be?' Corinna seemed astonished by the thought. 'It's over. I can tell that from the way you constantly cosset me. I might feel very much less secure if you stopped cosseting me.'

'We'll leave soon,' said Ted. 'I'm going to take you home and cosset you like the clappers.'

He took another hefty sip, and grimaced.

The immaculate Neville Badger took a delicate, immaculate sip, and beamed anxiously as he surveyed the progress of the party. At his side, seemingly inseparable from him as she had never been from Laurence, Liz watched with more acerbic, astringent eyes. She was a proud cockerel, and he the mother hen.

'Everybody's happy,' said Neville. 'Isn't it wonderful?'

'Jenny's very upset about Paul,' said Liz. 'Carol's very upset about Elvis, Ted's very upset about Sandra, Sandra's very upset about Corinna, Rodney and Betty are rather shocked to find their health food complex is next door to Chez Edouard, Simon is dreadfully scared about something, and I'm very upset that Rita's election will push through the outer inner relief ring road. Apart from that . . . as far as I know . . . people are ecstatic.'

Neville looked shattered.

'Will you speak to Rita, Neville?'

He leapt hurriedly into life. 'Of course,' he said decisively. 'Leave it to me.' Then he thought. 'What about?'

'The outer inner relief ring road.'

'Well, what can I . . . ? Yes, all right. I'll have a word with her some time.'

'Now.'

'Now?'

'Now.'

'Now.'

'Jenny?' said the former big wheel behind Cock-A-Doodle Chickens to the young lady with whom he had so often argued over the ethics of battery chicken farming. 'Would you at some time – after you've had your . . . er . . . of course – consider working for me?'

97

'For us!' Betty Sillitoe's indignation was marinaded in affection.

'Absolutely,' agreed Rodney hastily. 'Slip of the tongue. Old habits die hard. Us.'

'Well, I'd love to,' said Jenny, without enthusiasm. 'Thanks. Terrific.'

'Rita'll be working for us.' Betty could hardly contain her excitement at the prospect.

'Terrific,' said Jenny listlessly. 'It's all very exciting,' she added flatly. 'I feel . . . very excited.'

She drifted off. Rodney and Betty watched her with concern.

Neville was not approaching Rita with quite the dispatch that might have been expected. He stopped, with unprecedented eagerness, to listen to a golfing joke from Graham Wintergreen, to ask Mrs Wadebridge whether she'd had enough to eat, to begin to apologise to Mrs Wadebridge in case she construed his remark as a comment on her amplitude, and to stop in mid-apology in case the apology made matters worse. He exchanged polite nothings with Morris Wigmore with an intensity that suggested that a smile from Neville might ease the painful memory of his son's sticky end in Brisbane.

But all too soon he found himself confronting Rita. She was staring out of the window at her life.

He coughed. She jumped.

'I . . . hello, Rita,' he said. 'Liz is a little . . . not worried . . . a little concerned . . . and she's asked me to . . . to ask you . . . so here I am. If this isn't a good time, please forget it.'

'Please forget what?'

Neville hesitated only fractionally. 'The outer inner relief ring road.'

'Ah.'

'I wouldn't dream of asking you to . . . try to get us any special dispensation . . . to attempt to change the route in any way. . . . I know that you wouldn't . . . you couldn't . . . we . . . I understand that.'

'So what are you asking?'

'Ah.' In the absence of any alternative inspiration, Neville smiled. 'Well, I'm glad we've had this little chat.'

'Are you?' Rita was astounded. 'Good Lord.'

Neville walked off, quite swiftly at first, to get away from Rita, then much more slowly as he came closer to his wife.

He made a little detour, which took him, as it happened, past the table with the champagne, where the dapper, ageless Eric Siddall had been serving his former boss with an icy professional dignity which, he had hoped, would make Graham Wintergreen feel ashamed about sacking him, but which had made Graham wonder why he had put up with him for so long.

'There you go, sir. Tickety-boo,' said Eric to Neville. 'It's a pleasure to serve some people.'

Neville also paused briefly, to compliment Charlotte Ratchett on her appearance. She received his compliment, which consisted of the sentence, 'Charlotte, you're a model to us all on how to age gracefully,' with less delight than he had expected.

Now at last there was no escape from Liz.

'Well?' she said.

'I put our points. Very forcibly.'

'Good. Well done.'

'If obliquely.'

'What?'

'Sometimes, in politics, one needs to be oblique. I . . . left her in no doubt of what we were asking, though.'

'And?'

'She made no definite promises. She's too much of an old hand for that.'

'Old hand? She's only been elected two days. You should have twisted her round your little finger.'

'Yes, well, as Bing Crosby once said, I did it my way. And although she didn't say anything, I have no doubt what Rita will do.'

Liz looked as though she had no doubt either.

'You've given me back something I thought I'd lost forever.'

Corinna Price-Rodgerson looked pleased.

'Status.'

Corinna Price-Rodgerson looked less pleased.

'I thought you meant love,' she said coolly.

'Oh well. That too. That especially, of course, my petal. But also status. Reputation.' Ted leant forward to whisper, and almost lost his balance. 'Because there are people in this town who thought me a berk.'

'I find that hard to believe.'

'I know. It's barely credible, but it's true.' He swayed slightly. 'Anyroad, the last laugh's on me. Restaurateur. Marrying a bishop's daughter.'

Sandra approached them as before, smiling as before, with two widely-spaced glasses as before.

'More champagne?' she asked.

'Lovely.' Corinna gave her a flashing smile.

This time Ted remembered his manners and let Corinna take her glass first.

'Thank you very much indeed, Sandra,' he said, as he emptied his glass and replaced it with the one glass remaining on the tray.

Sandra moved off, still smiling.

'Where was I?' Ted asked Corinna.

'Having the last laugh. Is that why you're marrying me?'

'No! Love! 'Course not. But it's an enjoyable by-product.' Ted frowned. He could hardly get the words out. There was something wrong with his speech. And his head was swimming. He was ill.

'Are you drunk?'

'What?' He was indignant. 'On champagne? On French gnat's piss?' Several people turned their heads to seek out the source of this mild vulgarity. He suddenly remembered what he had thought it would be impossible for him to forget – that Corinna was a bishop's daughter. What was wrong with his brain? 'I feel odd, Corinna. Why should I feel odd? It's odd that I should feel odd. I never feel odd normally. Normally I feel absolutely normal.' *Was* he drunk? He couldn't be. And not so quickly. Not hard-headed, tough as old boots Ted Simcock. 'I can't be drunk. I haven't had much. Not much much, anyroad. Hardly at all much. If that.' His command of language was disintegrating. He was swaying. He *was* drunk. 'I'm drunk, Corinna. I mean, I am. How? Oh heck.'

Corinna took his drink, sniffed it, and sipped it.

'There's vodka in this,' she said.

'That's Sandra! Sandra!'

His legs were giving way. His head was swirling. Corinna had hold of him. He felt awful. She was guiding him into a chair. She was so strong. He felt wonderful.

Andrew Denton, husband of the pregnant Judy, approached the pregnant Jenny.

'Do you know what I said to the side of the church as I left?' he asked.

'No.'

'Aisle, be seeing you.'

'What?'

'Joke. The aisle is the side of the church, so I said, "aisle, be seeing you."'

'Ah.'

'Bit of a nave, aren't I?'

'Oh.'

'Aren't you font of my jokes? Are they an apse of taste?'

'What?'

'You looked sad. I'm cheering you up.'

'Ah. Thank you, Andrew.' Jenny tried to look cheered up. It was impossible. 'Terrific.'

Elvis approached them purposefully.

'Not interrupting, am I?' he asked.

'Yes. Terrific,' said Jenny, showing a flash of enthusiasm at last. 'Bye, Andrew.'

Elvis had placed two chairs facing each other across an occasional table. She allowed herself to be seated on one of them. Elvis sat opposite her. Between them was a rather cowed cactus. Elvis clasped his hands together as he searched for a telling and authoritative yet sensitive and sympathetic opening question. All around them people were chatting. Elvis Simcock, chat show host, was oblivious to all talk except his own and that of his interviewee.

'How are things really between you and Paul, Jenny?' he asked.

'Not very good. We're having terrible rows.'

'Would you mind telling me what your row this morning was about?'

'On the surface it was about boiled eggs.'

'M-hm.' Elvis shifted gear from chat show host to media psychiatrist. 'And what was it about under the surface?'

'Trust.'

Elvis's showbiz sheen fell away, revealing a rather gawky young Yorkshireman. 'You what?' said the rather gawky young Yorkshireman.

The words began to pour out. 'I'm finding it hard to trust him, after what he did with . . . and he says I'm not trying to trust him, and today, when all that's going on under the surface, we're arguing about boiled eggs and I'm crying and Thomas is upset because he's *very* sensitive and . . . oh, Elvis!'

Jenny's appeal wrung Elvis's heart-strings. He didn't see Rodney and Betty until they were almost on top of him.

'How's the interviewing technique coming on, Elvis?' asked Rodney, still smarting after discovering that he had been used.

'Rodney! Please!' pleaded Elvis frantically.

'Have I said something wrong?' said Rodney.

Elvis began to edge away from the scene of the crime. Jenny pursued him.

'What does he mean, "interviewing techniques"?' she asked.

'I've said something wrong.' Rodney realised that the revelation was going to hurt Jenny, his most recent recruit. He back-pedalled. 'Nothing, Jenny. Absolutely nothing.'

Elvis turned and faced Rodney.

'Tell her,' he said. 'I've nothing to be ashamed of.'

Rodney was doubtful about telling now, but Betty leapt in.

'He wasn't well,' she explained. 'I took him upstairs, laid him on the bed.'

'Yes, we heard,' said Jenny.

'Did you? Oh Lord.' Rodney tried not to think of all these people listening to their cuddling. 'We heard voices from the loo. Elvis was playing back conversations he'd secretly recorded with me and Simon. Hello, Simon.'

Nobody could have counted the number of times that Simon Rodenhurst had steamed merrily in on a group of people, molars flashing, and been sandbagged. Yet still he came back for more. Now he looked well and truly sandbagged. His smile died swiftly.

'With me?' he said to Rodney. To Elvis he said, 'You swine!' To the Sillitoes he said, 'And you listened?'

'We couldn't help it,' protested Betty. 'We tried not to.' It sounded unconvincing even to her.

'You swine, Elvis,' repeated Simon.

'I've done nothing I'm ashamed of,' said Elvis.

Simon erupted. 'Broadcasting to the Sillitoes that I got my fellow godfather's wife pregnant, and you're not ashamed!'

It was sheer bad luck that Andrew was leading his pregnant wife to the sandwiches for a little nibble at exactly that moment. The Dentons heard every word of Simon's eruption.

'*What?*' said Andrew, appalled.

'Simon!' reproached Judy desperately.

'Judy!' said Andrew accusingly.

'Oh, Andrew,' said Judy. 'I love you, Andrew. I do.'

She staggered towards a chair. It was occupied by Liz's skeletal, ramrod Uncle Hubert. He leapt up with an alacrity that belied his years. He was a man made by temperament and breeding for giving up his seat to women. In the long years out East he'd had few opportunities to exercise this talent, for he was also a man made by temperament and breeding for not giving up anything to the natives.

'Oh my God,' said Simon, watching them.

'I didn't know anyone was listening,' said Elvis.

'Nor did I!' said Simon.

Jenny found Elvis's tape recorder under the cactus. She hurled it furiously at him. He ducked. It sailed on towards Neville, and Liz. Neville, a keen cricketer in his day, caught it adeptly, and stared at it in bewilderment.

'So,' said Jenny angrily, while Rodney and Betty fluttered anxiously, and several people, alerted by the flying tape recorder, watched. 'Your questioning of me, Elvis, all that concern . . . '

' . . . was genuine. It has to be when interviewing people. You don't use people.'

'I didn't know it was an interview,' screamed Jenny. She tried to control her anger. People were listening. 'You used me,' she said more calmly, as Rita hurried over to see if she could be of help. 'Used the collapse of my marriage.'

'Collapse?' Rita was appalled.

'We're splitting up. Oh Lord. I didn't mean to tell you. Not today.' Jenny smiled. 'It's amicable.' She meant her smile to be encouraging and cheery. 'Quite happy really.' It only succeeded in looking bravely forlorn. 'Not at all sad. Sorry.'

'Oh, Jenny,' said Rita sadly. She turned on Elvis. 'Oh, Elvis!' She hugged Jenny.

Sandra swirled into the Brontë Suite, still vibrant with indignation and pride.

Ted tried to leap to his feet. It wasn't a success. He hadn't felt as drunk as this since he'd sampled every bottle on the top shelf of the Überwasser Bierhalle in Osnabruck when he was nineteen. Corinna tried to restrain him. He shook himself free and lurched towards Sandra.

'Sandra!' he said. 'You've been spiking my drinks.'

'Yeah,' said Sandra. ' 'Cos I hate you. I wanted her to see you drunk and pathetic. She has. I'm glad.'

Eric Siddall, barman supreme, scurried up to rescue Ted from his unprofessional colleague. 'Leave this to me, sir,' he said. 'No problem. All in hand. Can do.'

'Belt up, Eric,' said Sandra.

She gave Eric a fierce shove, fuelled by fury. He staggered backwards and fell to the floor. Morris Wigmore, deputy leader of the Conservatives, rushed to his rescue, tripped, and fell into the arms of Charlotte Ratchett. She smiled a champagne smile, kissed the top of his head, and said 'Morris. I never knew you cared.'

Neville and Liz watched the disintegration of the Christening Party with growing horror.

'Oh Lord!' said Liz.

Neville was speechless.

Sandra turned back to Ted, wiping her hands after disposing of Eric.

'Why did you have to come here, anyroad?' she yelled. 'Following me. Haunting me. Taunting me.'

'Sandra!' Ted raised his voice, to compete with hers. 'I wasn't.'

' 'Course you were,' yelled Sandra. 'Why else would you come?'

'Because they're Christening my baby,' shrieked Ted.

The room fell completely silent.

Neville and Liz gazed at the achingly still tableau with growing horror.

'Oh Lord!' said Neville.

Liz was speechless.

'Ted!' said Rita.

Nobody else spoke. Ted went white. He looked round the room and saw, mistily, his future wife, her face a shocked white buoy in an orange sea. He saw the blurred, horrified faces of his former wife, of the mother of his boy, of her second husband, of his ex-mistress Sandra, of his deeply embarrassed son, whose cynicism was proving so shallow, of his unhappy daughter-in-law, of Elvis's neglected fiancée, of his former good friends, the suddenly sober Sillitoes, of Eric Siddall, barman supreme. And beyond them, the shocked faces of people of the kind Ted had so often tried so hard to impress: Neville's partner, Matthew Wadebridge; the bluff, egg-shaped Graham Wintergreen, coarsely relishing the situation; his golfophobe wife Angela, her tight, whippy mouth wide open; Liz's skeletal, ramrod Uncle Hubert looking at Ted as an example of what happens to a nation when you let an empire go. The three ruined abbeys forgotten, the ruined buffet forgotten, the ruined cake forgotten, all of them gazing in horror at the ruined Ted Simcock.

He tried hard to retrieve the situation.

'Oh heck,' he said. 'I didn't really . . . I didn't mean . . . just a joke. In bad taste, I realise that now. You know what they say. In vino . . . in vino a load of absolute cobblers.' He tried to walk. 'Oh . . . I can't . . . my legs.' He had rubber legs. It was a nightmare. He wasn't really here. It was only a dream.

But the Sillitoes, grabbing him, lifting him up, they weren't part of a dream.

'Come on,' said Rodney.

'Soon have you off the premises,' said Betty.

'Man of your age, can't hold your drink,' said Rodney.

'Let go,' demanded Ted. 'I'm all right.'

They let go. For a few seconds he was all right. Then his legs buckled and he began to crumple backwards. Rodney and Betty grabbed him again.

'Leave it to us,' said Betty. 'We're the experts. Upsydaisy.'

Slowly, the Sillitoes lifted Ted into an upright position.

'Off we go,' said Rodney. 'Nice and quiet. Easy does it.'

Slowly, Betty and Rodney led him out of the Brontë Suite.

At the door, he turned.

'Sorry,' he told the stunned gathering. 'Sorry, everybody.' He tried to smile at Corinna. 'Sorry I lied, my honey bee.'

'I forgive you,' said Corinna Price-Rodgerson. 'Many wouldn't.'

'What a womanful wonder you are,' said her befuddled fiancé.

Corinna followed Ted out. At the door she turned, smiled graciously, said, 'Goodbye. Thank you for inviting us. We've had a simply marvellous time,' and made an exit that was, under the circumstances, a masterpiece of dignity.

Conversations began to break out all over the room. Charlotte Ratchett, of the furniture Ratchetts, bemoaned that the nation could no longer hold its drink. Hubert Ellsworth-Smythe spoke of rubber workers rendered mad by strong drink. Morris Wigmore, deputy leader of the Conservatives, felt it safe to smile again.

Could it be that the worst was over?

Not for Jenny. She burst into tears. Rita hurried over to comfort her.

'It wasn't amicable,' wailed Jenny. 'We've had a terrible row and split up. Today. Forever. Oh Lord. I shouldn't have told you. Not today.'

'Yes. You should,' said Rita. 'Oh, Jenny, how could he?'

'It's my fault as well. Always two sides.' Jenny flung a tiny glance in the direction of Liz. 'I expected too much from marriage, despite my mother.'

Rita hugged Jenny.

Elvis, who had been standing close by with Carol, hurried across to them.

'Paul has no idea how to treat a woman,' he said.

'Just like his brother,' muttered Carol.

'OK, Mum. Leave this to me. Please!' said Elvis decisively.

He put an arm round Jenny. Rita found herself obeying her suddenly masterful son.

'Jenny! Love!' said Elvis. 'I do care. I wasn't using you. I do. He's hopeless.'

He kissed his younger brother's wife tenderly.

'Oh, Elvis,' said the watching Rita. 'Oh, Paul. Oh, Jenny.'

'Just like his ruddy brother,' sobbed Carol.

'Oh, Carol,' said Rita. She hurried over to hug her. 'Oh Lord. Where did we go wrong with them? Was it my fault? And there's me, going into politics, thinking I can change the world.'

'Oh no,' wept Carol. 'You mustn't give up. You must change the world. Somebody must.'

White-faced, Neville and Liz Badger surveyed the wreckage of their elegant shindig. Their eyes went to Jenny and Elvis, crying in each other's arms, to Rita and Carol, holding each other tenderly and sobbing, to Andrew and Judy, weeping gently together.

'Oh Lord!' said Neville. 'I must go to . . . somebody.'

'Oh, Neville,' said Liz. 'How about me?'

'Are you upset?'

'Of course not! I'm having a simply wonderful afternoon.' Liz's body went taut. 'Sssh,' she said. 'Ssssh!' she repeated louder. 'I think I can hear the babies. Sssh everybody.'

'Sssh!' called out Neville urgently.

Conversations were swiftly dropped. Sobs were slowly stopped. Once again, complete silence fell upon the Brontë Suite.

Into that silence, over the baby link, there came the noise of two babies, crying.

'They learn so quickly, don't they?' said Rita.

Third Do

April:
The Grand Opening of Sillitoe's

'Nobody's going to come, are they?' asked Rodney Sillitoe, the joint big wheel behind Sillitoe's. He was standing in the middle of the bar area of what he hoped would become the most celebrated health food complex with wholefood vegetarian restaurant in Yorkshire. He was wearing green trousers, a green and yellow check shirt, a white apron emblazoned with the legend 'Sillitoe's' and a straw hat with a wide green sash.

Beside him stood Rita Simcock and her daughter-in-law Jenny. They were wearing green dresses, green and yellow check blouses and white aprons emblazoned with the legend 'Sillitoe's'.

Jenny had a glass of orange juice, Rita blackberry and apple, and Rodney carrot juice.

'Perhaps it was a mistake to advertise "mystery celebrity",' suggested Jenny.

'Jenny could be right,' said Rita. 'If it's somebody really impressive, perhaps you should have said who it is, Rodney.'

Rita invested the word 'Rodney' with a faintly questioning air. He didn't bite.

'Oh Lord,' he said. 'It's going to be a flop. Poor Betty! I can take it, but she gets so worked up, bless her.'

He looked round anxiously, as if hoping that Betty would materialise through the walls of exposed brick, which gave the room the air of a converted factory, which wasn't surprising, since it was a converted factory – it had made flanges – or that she would suddenly appear from under one of the stripped pine tables, which, with the stripped pine chairs and bare walls, gave the bar a rather antiseptic aura. This was not a bar where serious drinking was expected. It served only non-alcoholic drinks, as befitted an establishment owned by those reformed characters, the Sillitoes.

Behind Rodney a green tape hung across a large arch which separated the bar from the restaurant area, which was still in darkness. 'Where is she?' he repeated, moving off towards the restaurant, dipping under the tape.

'Men!' said Rita, as soon as he had disappeared into the darkness. '"She gets so worked up, bless her"! Who's getting worked up? He is. I expect she's as cool as a cucumber.'

Rita and Jenny shared a little laugh about the foolish ways of men.

Behind the bar, in front of his rows of non-alcoholic drinks, Eric Siddall sighed deeply. He was wearing green trousers, a green and yellow check shirt, a white apron emblazoned with the legend 'Sillitoe's' and a straw hat with a wide green sash. He did not look ecstatic.

In the centre of the bar area there was a large sculpture, a cross between a twisted pillar and a dead tree. It was the creation of a local sculptperson, Melissa Holdsworthy. Around its trunk there was a gnarled shelf on which drinks could be put.

Betty Sillitoe, the joint big wheel behind Sillitoe's, emerged out of the darkened restaurant, dipped under the tape, looked round the bar, and sighed.

'Oh Lord!' she said. 'Nobody here yet! Nobody's going to come, are they? It's going to be a fiasco.' She was wearing a green dress, a green and yellow check blouse, and a white apron emblazoned with the legend 'Sillitoe's'. She carried a glass of carrot juice.

'It said "from 7.30". It's only 7.36,' Rita pointed out.

'I don't mind so much for myself, but it's Rodney,' said Betty. 'He gets so het up, bless him. Oh! The apostrophe's wrong.'

Rodney emerged from the darkened restaurant, carrot juice in hand. He stepped under the tape, and sighed.

'Still nobody?'

'It's only 7.37,' said Jenny.

'Rodney,' said Betty urgently. 'The apostrophe's wrong. In 'Sillitoe's'. There are two of us. Two Sillitoes. So it should be s apostrophe. Not apostrophe s. Shouldn't it?'

'Oh Lord. I don't know,' said Rodney. He'd given the best part of his life to chickens. He didn't know about apostrophes.

'I don't want to be unpatriotic,' said Rita, 'but I'm not sure the nation understands the apostrophe any more. Oh, incidentally,

I should have told you, and perhaps I shouldn't have done it, but . . . I've invited a friend. Tonight.'

'Good!' said Betty. 'That'll make six of us.'

'Who is this friend?' asked Jenny.

'Oh, nobody special,' said Rita. 'Just a man I met in a pub. I don't expect he'll come, it was all very casual.' But how she hoped he would, and how they knew it.

The front door opened.

'Somebody!' said Rodney.

Liz and Neville Badger entered.

'Oh Lord!' said Rita.

A blast of cold air followed the Badgers into the warm bar. Liz was shivering. It was exceptionally cold for late April. A few unenthusiastic flakes of snow were drifting in the chill breeze that swept down Arbitration Road. Later, the Meteorological Office would announce that this was the coldest April day since 1907. That day, in fact, Dewsbury was colder than Rekjavik.

Liz had dipped her toes cautiously into the waters of ethnicity, and was wearing a black, tiered, strapless dress with white spots, and a black shawl top with large white spots and green ribbon edging. Neville's green tie bore no ecological clout. It was his rugby club tie.

'Betty! Hello! It all looks lovely,' enthused Liz, giving Betty an unprecedentedly warm kiss. There was a good old smacker for Rodney too. 'Rodney! A proud day!' For Jenny there was a flashing smile and another great kiss. 'Jenny! Darling!'

For Rita there was nothing. Liz walked straight past her.

'Oh Lord,' sighed Rita.

Neville stopped to speak to her briefly.

'I'm sorry,' he said, 'but she was very attached to that magnolia. Sorry.'

'Neville,' commanded Liz, as if she were Queen of England and he a naughty corgi.

With one last 'sorry', Neville was off to join his wife at the bar.

'Sir? Madam? What is your pleasure?' said Eric dispiritedly.

'Alcohol, but you haven't got any,' said Liz.

'What do you recommend, Eric?' asked Neville.

'Well, I don't know,' came the unenthusiastic reply. 'There's fruit squash, or bilberry-cocktail or home-made kiwi fruit, raspberry and cinnamon punch, but I can't speak for it personally. The Sillitoes enthuse over their carrot juice. It seems last year was a good year for carrots.'

'It all sounds most intriguing and inventive and original,' said Liz. 'Orange juice, please.'

'I'll have a go at that punch,' said Neville.

'Juice of the orange and one special punch, can do, no problem, tickety-boo,' said Eric, but his tone suggested that it was far from tickety-boo.

Jenny joined them. She looked like a young lady with a mission. She was.

'Mum? Can I have a word?' she said.

'Of course,' said Liz pleasantly.

The moment they were out of Neville's earshot, Jenny revealed her purpose.

'Mum. Don't you think you're being childish?'

'No. How are the children?'

'Fine.' Thomas and his six-week-old sister Steffie were sleeping, in the crèche area thoughtfully provided by these newly-enlightened Sillitoes. 'It isn't Rita's fault, Mum.'

'No? Little Steffie's cold better, is it?'

'Much better, they're both fine, can we stick to the point?'

'The point.' Liz spoke with low, controlled fury. 'Rita gets elected to the council, the council plump for the outer inner relief ring road, and, lo and behold, what a surprise, the route lops a great lump off our garden, destroying eighteen roses and a magnolia. That's the point, Jenny.'

'All over the world people are losing everything they possess in earthquakes, floods, hurricanes and avalanches. Billions never even possess anything to lose in the first place.'

'I know, and I'm sorry for them, and appalled, but I can only live my life, not the rest of the world's, and heaven forbid that I should ever be accused of being parochial but that is a magnificent magnolia.' Liz had been staring at the wall, whose exposed brickwork was broken only by a painting of a bowl of prunes. The artist had captured every wrinkle. But Liz, whose wrinkles were still mostly in the future, saw only her magnolia. Her anger grew colder still, as if ice could boil. 'Rita's done it deliberately, Jenny, and I will not speak to any member of the Simcock family, and I would urge you not to either.'

With her mission in tatters, Jenny lashed out bitterly. 'You must be thrilled I've split up with Paul then.'

'No!' Liz seemed immediately contrite. 'Of course not, Jenny. Children need their father. I'm sad. However, yes, it is true that out of all that sorry mess the one consolation I can find is that you are no longer in intimate association with a Simcock. Oh, Jenny, I hope you find somebody else soon. Somebody nice. Somebody of your own . . . class. Oh yes, because I'm not ashamed of being a snob.'

Another blast of cold air entered, along with a few flakes of unseasonal snow, and Ted Simcock.

'Oh Lord,' said Rodney. He was standing beside Betty and Rita. The three of them looked like a welcoming committee for refugees.

Ted surveyed the scene grandly, and came forward to shake Rodney's hand with dignity.

'Hello, Rodney. No hard feelings,' he said.

He kissed Betty affectionately.

'None of your doing, Betty, I realise that,' he said.

He looked straight through Rita, and moved off towards the bar.

'Oh Lord!' said Rita, hurrying after him.

The Mayor, Alderman Spigot, entered with his sister, Netta Ponsonby, the Mayoress. The Mayor was small and corpulent. The Mayoress was large and corpulent. They were extremely conscientious, very kind, and hardly pompous at all, and almost everybody made fun of them.

But not Betty Sillitoe. Over-deferential, as usual, she scurried across, made a small instinctive curtsey, and said, 'Hello, your worshipfulnesses.'

Rita caught up with Ted just before he reached the bar, which he was approaching quite slowly, as befitted one so unenthusiastic about its wares.

'Ted!' she said.

'I've no wish to speak to you, Rita.'

'Oh, Ted. I hate to see you letting yourself down by being small-minded in public.'

'Why should you care?'

'I know. Silly, isn't it, but I do. Maybe I still have some shred of affection for you. Some memories of happier times. Corinna all right?'

'Yes, just late as usual. She was twelve days late coming into the world, and she's never quite caught up.' Ted's face softened as he thought about Corinna. Then his expression changed abruptly. 'But, Rita . . . I mean . . . what do you expect? I mean . . . you get elected to the council and push through a route for the outer inner relief ring road which means demolition of your ex-husband's restaurant but leaves intact the nextdoor property, which just happens to be a vegetarian crank centre owned by his one-time best friend, where you are employed. In my book, that's tantamount to municipal corruption.'

'When I took the job I didn't know the exact route. I have no power to influence the exact route. I've done nothing wrong.' Rita was filled with the indignant frustration of one who is telling the truth but doesn't expect to be believed. 'I'm truly sorry about Chez Edouard, but you'll get compensation.'

'Oh, I know. Well, Corinna will, it's in her name, but it amounts to the same difference.' Ted's face softened again. He couldn't mention the woman without looking like a lovesick adolescent. He'd never looked like that with her. 'But it's nothing like what we'd get on the open market. It's daylight robbery.'

'It's democracy. We can't throw taxpayers' money around willy-nilly.'

'Politicians! When you're refusing to spend, you're saving taxpayers' money. When you're spending, you call it your money and pretend you're giving it away. You're hypocrites. I mean . . . you are.'

'It's the will of the people, Ted. Well, the will of the four people who gave me a majority in a 19.2 per cent turn out. Look, don't you think I'm embarrassed that my first influence on world politics loses you your restaurant and Liz and Neville eighteen rose bushes and a magnolia?'

'You what, Rita?'

'The route lops the end of their garden off.'

Ted gave a delighted laugh.

'Liz isn't speaking to me,' said Rita.

'What? How petty can you get? How small-minded these snobbish types can be.'

'Who's being hypocritical now?'

'What?'

'You weren't going to speak to me.'

'That's different.' Ted saw that Rita didn't believe him. 'It is! I mean . . . eighteen rose bushes and a magnolia, that's hardly concomitant with a temple of gastronomy as recommended by Egon Ronay, is it?'

'"As recommended by Egon Ronay"! You never even opened.'

'We would have been, with our cuisine.'

Ted thought wistfully of all the awards he would have won, the Michelin stars, the rave in the *Good Food Guide*, the popular TV series *Supper with Simcock*. Then his wistfulness was replaced by the soft absurdity of middle-aged infatuation. Following Ted's gaze, Rita saw Corinna Price-Rodgerson standing in the doorway, making an entrance. Where before she had been orange, all was now rust. Ploughing her way through the colours of autumn decay, thought Rita uncharitably.

'Here's Corinna,' said Ted unnecessarily. 'I'll be polite to you, but only so as not to show myself up in front of her for what I . . . well, not for what I am, but for what folk might wrongly think I was if I did. Hello, my petal.'

'Hello, darling.'

They kissed.

'Just chatting to dear old Rita here. No point in being petty.'

'Absolutely not.' Corinna flashed a dazzlingly insincere smile at Rita. 'Neither of us blame you personally, Rita. Goodbye, Rita.'

Corinna swept Ted on towards the bar and its array of green, red and purple drinks.

Eric Siddall wasn't looking as dapper or indeed as ageless as usual. There was in his face a pursed, wrinkled echo of the prunes in the painting. He hadn't even set his bow tie at its usual jaunty angle.

'Good evening, sir. Good evening, madam,' he droned. 'What can I do you for?'

'You're a ray of sunshine, Eric,' said Ted.

'Well . . . it just isn't me, isn't carrot juice,' said Eric Siddall, barman supreme.

Gradually, more guests began to arrive. Melissa Holdsworthy, the tall, handsome sculptperson, creator of the bar's central feature – who, despite a brief affair with the suave Doctor Spreckley, was said to be a lesbian on the slender evidence of her being both tall and unmarried – entered with James Whatmore, who wrote for children and had never hit the jackpot. Betty Sillitoe introduced Prunella Ransom, the parliamentary candidate for the Green Party, to the Mayor and Mayoress, who were too polite to say that they already knew her. Betty hurried over to greet the long-haired Carol Fordingbridge, who was looking very attractive in a navy cotton jersey cross-over balloon-style dress.

'Elvis not with you?' said Betty, kissing her warmly.

'He's hardly likely to be. We've split up,' said Carol.

'Oh, Carol. I'm sorry,' said Betty. 'We had no idea.'

Rodney emerged from the darkened restaurant, carrying his carrot juice. He dipped under the uncut green tape.

'Where've you been?' Betty asked him.

'Just checking the buffet. Everything's fine. Hello, Carol.' He kissed her warmly. 'Elvis not with you?'

'Rodney!' said Betty. 'Tact.'

'You what?'

'They've split up,' mouthed Betty.

'Oh Lord. I'd no idea.'

'I thought I'd come, anyroad,' said Carol. 'Why should I have to skulk around?'

'Absolutely. You, skulking? It's a contradiction in terms.'

'I've . . . er . . . well, thanks.' Carol acknowledged Rodney's compliment rather belatedly. 'I've . . . er . . . I suppose I shouldn't have, but . . . I've invited a friend.'

'Good. Why not?' Betty glanced round the half-empty room. 'The more the merrier.'

'He may not come, with it being vegetarian and non-alcoholic.' Carol looked mortified. 'Oh, I shouldn't have said that. Not today.' She recovered quickly. 'But I thought, no harm in letting Elvis see I've other nuts to fry.'

'You what?' Betty was puzzled.

'I'd have said other fish to fry, but you're vegetarian.'

'Very good. Very droll, Carol.' Rodney laughed. Betty joined in. 'Why Elvis should think you aren't clever enough for him is beyond me.'

'Rodney!'

'Well, I'll go and get a drink,' said Carol, but before she could fulfil her stated intention she was button-holed by Elvis, who had just walked in and had been horrified to see her.

'Carol! Are you here?' he exclaimed.

'That's an incredibly interesting question, Elvis.'

'You what?'

'A solipsist might say we could never know, because I might only exist in your imagination. I know that's not true, of course, but I don't know that you don't only exist in my imagination.'

'You what?'

'Because I'm not clever enough for you, before we split up, not knowing we were going to split up, I got these philosophy books from the mobile library, so I might be able to hold my own when you came out with incredibly intelligent questions like "Carol! Are you here?" I've got a question for you now. It's not exactly philosophical exactly, well, I suppose it is, sort of.'

'Fine.' Elvis bent down slightly, as if Carol's question would be easier to answer if they were on the same level. 'Well, fire away. I'll do my best.' He smiled slightly, as a teacher might smile at a pupil who deserved encouragement.

'OK,' said Carol. 'It's this: why don't you get stuffed?'

She swept off to the bar, where she plumped for a peach juice.

The smile froze on Elvis's face. Neville approached the bar and Elvis smiled again. Neville turned towards him, beaming with infinite good humour, saw who it was, wiped the smile from his face, and turned away. Elvis sauntered off, trying to look insouciant. Jenny approached him, and her smile didn't fade when she saw him.

'Have you ever had the feeling that it isn't your day?' he asked.

'What's wrong?'

'Nobody seems exactly pleased to see me.'

'I'm pleased to see you.'

Elvis was pleased that Jenny was pleased to see him. 'Well, I'm pleased to see you,' he said.

'Who wasn't pleased?'

'Well, Carol, obviously. And Neville just ignored me.'

'Mum is instigating a feud between the Simcocks and the Rodenhursts, because of the ring road.'

'Oh, I see.'

Simon Rodenhurst, of Trellis, Trellis, Openshaw and Finch, burst in from the chill of the street. He flashed his glorious molars and hurled an enviably uncomplicated 'Hello' in their direction.

'Simon!' commanded his mother imperiously from afar.

'Coming, Mother,' he called out. To Elvis he said, 'Talk with you in a moment,' as if offering the prospect of a treat.

'I wouldn't bet on it,' muttered Elvis.

'I know he sometimes seems a bit of a twit,' said Jenny, 'and it's a pity he's an estate agent, of course, but he'd never do anything deliberately to hurt me.'

'Why would his not talking to me hurt you?'

'Because I think I'm falling in love with you.'

'Jenny!'

Jenny seemed almost as astonished as Elvis by her words.

Simon burst insensitively upon their amazement.

'Hello, Jenny,' he said.

He gave Jenny a brotherly kiss and walked straight past Elvis.

'It gives me no pleasure at all to be proved right,' said Elvis.

'He doesn't know he's hurting me, because he doesn't know I'm falling in love with you, because I've only just found out myself,' said his brother's wife.

More people were arriving all the time. Rodney and Rita stood between the bar and the door and welcomed them. Where *was* Betty?

'I hope we haven't invited too many,' said Rodney.

'A few minutes ago you were worrying nobody would come.'

'I know. Aren't they silly things, nerves?'

Rodney was particularly pleased to see Gordon Trollope, whose butcher's shop in the Buttermarket was unrivalled. Gordon had taken the Sillitoes' conversion to vegetarianism hard. Betty had written him a lovely letter when his wife had died, and he had now decided that friendship was more important than principle. Where *was* Betty? She'd be thrilled to see their old friends, the abstemious Pilbeams. The Pilbeams, who had watched with disapproval the excessive consumption of hard liquor in the Crown and Walnut Angling Club, had become almost embarrassingly friendly since the Sillitoes had become teetotal.

Betty appeared at last, curtseying under the uncut tape, carrot juice in hand.

'Where've you been?' asked Rodney.

'Just checking the buffet.'

'I've just checked it.'

'Just checking to see you'd checked it thoroughly enough.' Yet more people hurried into the room, shivering. 'Good Lord! People are pouring in. It's going to be a success.'

'Yes. Incredible,' said Rodney. 'I mean, not that I ever . . . hello, Trevor.'

'Hello! My word, they don't look bad "in situ", do they?' said Trevor Coldwell, whose paintings of fruit and vegetables decorated the spartan walls.

'Very good,' said Betty.

Trevor Coldwell, who had a heavily lined face and a spectacularly unconvincing orange wig, which stirred occasionally like a dreaming cat, moved over to examine one of his works, 'The Peach'. Every tiny furry hair on the richly textured skin was clearly visible. 'I've done for the peach what Albrecht Dürer did for the hare,' thought Trevor Coldwell with an immodesty that he never allowed the world to suspect.

Rodney and Betty beamed at all these new arrivals. In their hearts there began to burn the glow of success.

'Rita?' said Rodney. 'Will you make a little speech about the raffle?'

'Me?'

'Well, it was your idea.'

'Oh Lord.'

'Rita!' Betty was amazed by Rita's reluctance. 'You do on the council.'

'You made a wonderful speech at your wedding,' said Rodney. 'I mean, your non-wedding.'

'Yes, it was very appropriate, Rita,' agreed Betty. 'Everyone said how appropriate it was.'

'Thank you, but this is different,' said Rita. 'It's still there, you know. I mean, sometimes I feel quite confident for minutes on end. Then back it comes.'

'Back what comes, Rita?' Betty was puzzled.

'My life. The long years of feeling inadequate. You don't lose it. Don't worry. I'll make the speech.'

Simon breezed up to them. 'Rodney, Betty, congratulations,' he beamed. If his father could have seen him, he'd have been proud of those teeth. He cast an uneasy glance towards Rita, then turned back to the Sillitoes and beamed again. 'A great night.'

Rita excused herself wryly. As soon as she'd gone, Simon said, 'It's embarrassing. I'm not allowed to talk to her.' He changed his tone, as if approaching dangerous but exciting waters. 'Look . . . er . . . I've . . . er . . . I've been a bit naughty.'

'Congratulations. Do we know her?' said Rodney.

'Rodney!' said Betty.

'I don't think you do, no,' said Simon.

'You what?' said Rodney.

'Know her. I've . . . er . . . I've met this friend. Well, I mean, she wasn't a friend when I met her, she couldn't be, I'd never met her, but then I did.'

'And you were naughty.'

'Betty!'

'Oh no. No, no. Not naughty in that . . . well, not yet. No, I mean, I . . . er . . . what was naughty was, I've invited her tonight.' Simon's eyes swept in wonderment round the juice drinkers, who were now thronging the bar. 'I shouldn't have. It's so full. But I never dreamt . . . she may not come, of course. Probably won't, it being me.'

'We're delighted you did, and we hope she does,' said Rodney.

When Simon had gone, the Sillitoes sipped their carrot juice reflectively.

'What sort of girl would fall for Simon?' said Rodney at last.

'A short-sighted estate agent?' suggested Betty.

The ravishing Liz Badger bore down on them ravishingly.

'I thought I ought to mention it,' she said. 'I've been a bit naughty.'

'Male or female?' enquired Rodney.

'What?'

'The person you've invited.'

'How on earth did you guess?'

'There seem to be about four hundred uninvited people invited,' said Rodney. 'If you see what I mean.'

'Oh Lord. But I never dreamt that so many . . . ' Liz didn't complete her sentence. She didn't need to.

Betty finished it for her. 'People would come? It's all right. Neither did we.'

'Male,' said Liz.

'What?' said Rodney.

'He's a he. My brother.'

'Brother?'

Betty echoed Rodney's astonishment. 'I didn't know you had a brother.'

'Oh yes. An elder brother.' Liz was enjoying their surprise. 'He's been abroad for twenty-two years. He's an anthropologist. He specialises in the social behaviour of primitive tribes.'

'He'll be in his element,' said Rodney drily.

'He may not come, of course. This may be too frightening after African headhunters.' Liz flashed them a soft smile that was as deadly as a blowpipe, and slid regally away.

'Cow,' said Betty.

'What?'

'Taking it on herself to invite people. And Simon. Typical Rodenhurst arrogance.'

'Rita and Carol did the same thing.'

'That's different.'

'What's different about it?'

Betty was briefly on the verge of being flummoxed.

'I like them,' she said.

'Time for the opening ceremony,' said Rodney, looking at his watch.

'But the mystery celebrity isn't here.'

'Oh yes she is.' Rodney was coyly mysterious.

Betty joined in the game. '"She"! Ah! Where?'

'Somewhere on the premises.' Rodney moved over to the long brick wall opposite the door to the street. In this wall there was another arch, which led to a corridor along which were the gleaming new toilets with their recycled toilet paper and soap from a firm which made no cosmetic experiments on animals.

Rodney stood, framed in the arch, with Trevor Coldwell's wrinkled prunes to his left and his masterly hairy peach to the right.

'Ladies and gentlemen,' he said. 'Thank you all for coming out, on this unseasonal night, to this bumper opening of Sillitoe's.' There was cheering. Rodney beamed. 'Thank you. You are already sampling our cornucopia of non-alcoholic drinks.' There was no cheering. Ted made a disgusted face. Rodney beamed. Despite his many weeks as a teetotaller, his face had its usual flushed, battered look, as if he'd been drinking bad wine in some hotel bar till two o'clock that morning. 'Shortly you will be confronted by the widest range of vegan and vegetarian foods in Yorkshire.' There was a soft murmur of approval. Prunella Ransom said, 'Hear hear.' Ted grimaced again. 'Don't all cheer at once. And there'll be folk singing from that popular Pennine group, the Hebden Bridge Griddlers.' There were cheers and applause, especially from those who had never heard the Hebden Bridge Griddlers. 'And I haven't finished yet! There will also be a raffle. A rather unusual raffle. To explain, I will call upon the brains behind the raffle, Councillor Rita Simcock.'

Rodney stepped to one side, and held out his hand towards Rita, inviting applause.

Rita stepped forward, shyly smiled her acknowledgement of the applause, and began. 'Well . . . hello – "the brains"! – Well, our raffle tonight . . . I mean, the proceeds from it, will go to a Third World charity.'

'Surprise surprise,' muttered Ted.

'Yes. And despite everything you've done to me, Ted, I'm glad you're well fed enough to find starvation boring,' snapped Rita.

Ted shrugged at Corinna. Her answering look was a mixture of coolness and warmth. 'Well, you did rather ask for that,' said her look.

'Tickets will be 25p each, or a pound for a strip of five. So that's one free if you buy five, or four is all you buy, in other words, so I hope you'll all have a strip.'

'Oooh! Sounds naughty!'

In his delight at his wit, Simon had forgotten that he wasn't supposed to be speaking to Rita. He was soon reminded.

'I'd heard rumours that the Rodenhursts weren't speaking to me,' said Rita. 'I'm glad it's not true. I'd hate to miss gems of that intellectual quality.'

Liz gave her son a furious glare. He looked suitably abashed.

'First prize,' continued Rita, 'is a First World hamper, i.e., containing the average calories, protein etcetera of the average Western adult daily diet, as per UN statistics.'

Betty produced, from a trolley concealed in the corridor, a wicker hamper, not very large, tied with green bows. She showed it to the gathering, turning the hamper to face all corners of the room, like a scantily-clad young lady on a television game show.

Ted yawned theatrically.

'Second prize is a Second World hamper, i.e., Iron Curtain rations.'

Betty showed the gathering a smaller wicker hamper.

'Third prize is a Third World hamper, the average daily diet of the Third World.'

Betty showed a still smaller, almost square wicker hamper, tied with a large green bow. The size of this hamper had been a subject of great debate. It had been suggested that it should be the largest, since the Third World diet was all bulk and no protein, but this had been overruled on grounds of symbolism if not of accuracy.

'Everyone who buys a ticket guarantees if they win to eat on their nominated day their diet and nothing else.'

Jenny looked as if she might cry. She clutched Elvis's hand for support. He looked down at her hand, wonderingly.

'A tiny little gesture.' Rita's voice began to crack. 'A symbol of our concern for those less fortunate than ourselves. I'm sorry. This is silly. Sorry. Thank you.'

Rita almost ran off, to hide among the guests.

Rodney led the enthusiastic applause. Ted was astounded to see that Corinna's eyes were moist. Even Eric Siddall, barman supreme, wiped the corner of his eye when nobody was looking.

'Splendid,' said Rodney. 'Well done, Rita. And now, our mystery celebrity.'

Betty, who had been carefully replacing the prize hampers on the trolley, backed slowly into view, eager to learn the identity of the celebrity.

'It's somebody I've admired more than anybody in the world,' continued her husband. 'The mystery is why she puts up with me.'

Realisation dawned slowly on Betty's face. Slowly, her mouth opened in disbelief.

'Yes, it's the only celebrity in my life, my wife Betty.'

'Oooh!' cried Betty.

There was warm applause. A few people cheered. Even Ted smiled.

Betty made her way through the excited throng to the green tape. Rodney followed, carrying a large pair of scissors.

Betty turned to face her audience. Beside her, a young couple with Friends of the Earth badges and hole-studded jeans kissed in their excitement. Everyone was excited. Elvis and Jenny forgot not to clasp hands. Even Liz couldn't find a fittingly caustic expression.

'Well!' said Betty. 'Well! Oooh! Rodney, what a . . . ladies and . . . oh dear. I'm overcome. I am. I'm overcome. Oooh, what a lovely . . . what a total . . . so now, without further ado . . . I don't know what to say, I'm knocked all of a . . . so without further ado . . . I feel like a queen. I do. I feel like a queen. Ladies and gentlemen, I name this health food complex and wholefood vegetarian restaurant "Sillitoe's". God bless her and all who eat in her. Oooh!'

She had a moment of panic as she realised that she had no scissors.

Rodney handed her the scissors. She laughed with relief.

She snipped the tape. Its two green arms fell lifeless to the ground.

Beyond the arch, all the lights came up, revealing an Aladdin's cave of stripped pine, exposed brick, and tasteful paintings of vegetables. At the far end of the room, which looked slightly like an aircraft hangar, there was a long counter, laden with many dishes of hot and cold food. Beyond the counter, two waitresses waited for the rush. But the guests, sobered more by thoughts of the Third World than by lack of alcohol, filtered only slowly through into the larger room.

126

The Hebden Bridge Griddlers tuned up briefly and began to play. There were two male griddlers. One of them looked like an ageing hippy and moved every part of his anatomy as he sang. The other one was tall and grizzled, and looked as if he could have been a sergeant in the marines. He was very cool and laid back. Between them the lady griddler smiled and swayed, flashed her dark eyes, tossed her dark hair, heaved her fine bosom and tried to look as if she had gipsy blood in her veins. In this she was surprisingly successful, considering that she was a chiropodist's daughter from Batley.

'Well, this is ridiculous. Somebody must try the food,' said Melissa Holdsworthy, the tall, handsome sculptperson with the prematurely greying hair and the belatedly growing reputation. Unhonoured in Britain, she had recently held major exhibitions in Bremen and Seville. She strode athletically to the counter and gazed with astonishment at the food. 'Bloody hell,' she said, 'I think this place might be the real McCoy.'

Once the ice was broken the tables soon began to fill with eager diners.

Others, the natural holders-back, the ones who never queued to get off ferries, or hurried at airports, decided to examine the contents of the shop first.

You will not be surprised to learn that the third and final part of the complex had walls of exposed brick, bare save for Trevor Coldwell's matching studies of globe and Jerusalem artichokes. An arch led to the restaurant, and through it there could be heard the strains of 'Barnyard of Dalghaty', from the Hebden Bridge Griddlers.

Neville found Rita escorting some guests round the well-stocked shelves.

'Ah! There you are, Rita!' he said.

'Feel free to browse,' Rita told the guests. 'And if you find you've found anything that you can't find, let us know. Excuse me.' She hurried over to Neville. 'Neville! You're talking to me!'

'No. I'm afraid not.'

'What?'

'I'm not talking to you, but I wanted you to know that I'm only not talking to you because Liz isn't talking to you.' Neville was frowning with concentration as he sought to identify his position accurately. 'I'm not not talking to you really.'

'Well, thanks, Neville.' Rita decided to try to reason with this eminently reasonable man. 'Look, I know it's a very nice magnolia, but in the context of the rain forests being cut down at the rate of two football pitches a minute . . . '

'I don't want to talk about it.'

'That's a squash court every 0.7 seconds.'

But Neville's face had become yet another brick wall on that evening of brick walls.

'I must get back to her,' he said.

In the restaurant all was noise and bustle. The Hebden Bridge Griddlers were bashing out 'Prickly Eye Bush'. Behind the counter Jenny was helping the waitresses. The quiches and salads were proving popular, but so were the more unusual dishes: the walnut and mushroom bake with dark orange sauce and red cabbage, and the aubergine and butter bean biryani. Rodney and Betty Sillitoe could scarcely hide their excitement as they clinked their glasses of carrot juice.

At one table Melissa Holdsworthy raved to the abstemious Pilbeams about the spicy, saffrony Rata Marseillaise. 'It's bouillabaisse without the fish,' she told them. They smiled abstemiously, and said the quiche was nice. Melissa 'real sculptpersons don't eat quiche' Holdsworthy sighed and hoped Rodney and Betty weren't going to be too adventurous for local tastes. She sipped her damson and dandelion cocktail and sighed again, wishing it was rich red Burgundy.

At another table, Prunella Ransom found the Mayor and Mayoress making a bee-line for her, bearing trays of spinach cannelloni and salad. Being shy, they were thrilled to find somebody they knew. She'd nothing against them, they were dear souls, but she had a feeling that tonight she'd meet an interesting unmarried man, and the Mayor with his three cats and his budgie certainly wasn't that.

At a third table, Corinna Price-Rodgerson was eating her biryani with enthusiasm. Beside her, Ted Simcock chewed his walnut and mushroom bake as if it were polystyrene.

'Great food, isn't it?' said Elvis, plonking himself into the empty chair beside his father.

'Delicious, if you happen to be a squirrel,' said Ted, nibbling sourly.

'I'm going to give this place a rave report in my "Gosh, what nosh" spot that you've no doubt heard me do on early morning extra,' said Elvis.

'No,' said Ted dismissively.

'Ted!' Corinna gave Elvis a real Bramah of an impending stepmother smile and said, 'I'm interested in your local radio career, anyway, Elvis. How's it going?'

Resentment for Corinna fought briefly with pride in his career. Pride won easily. 'Not too bad at all. I'm not really interested in reporting, of course, but you can't expect to become a chat show host straightaway.'

'Chat show host?' Ted was astounded.

'That's my ultimate goal. Why not? I've got the name for it. A name with that showbiz ring.'

'Oh, I see,' said Corinna. 'Yes. "Elvis".'

'No. "Simcock",' said Elvis.

'"Simcock"?' said Ted.

'It sounds good, don't you think? Tonight "Simcock", with Sue Lawley. Because they get fabulous holidays, chat show hosts.' Elvis turned to Ted, seeking, perhaps suddenly needing, his father's approval. 'Won't you be proud, Dad, when the family name's a household word?'

'Absolutely,' said Ted, who had so recently dreamt of his own cookery show. 'It'll be a great thrill as I pick my way through the rubble to which council JCBs have reduced *my* life's dream.'

'Darling!' Corinna's reproof of his bitterness was gentleness itself. 'Think positive. We regard this little setback as an opportunity.'

'Oh yes, yes,' said Ted. 'We do. An opportunity, Elvis.'

'An open sesame to wider horizons.'

'An open sesame to wider horizons, Elvis.'

'Good,' said Elvis airily. 'I'm glad.'

He moved away to chat to Jenny across the food counter.

'Patronising berk!' said Ted. 'What opportunity, love? What open sesame to what wider horizons?'

'I have an idea,' said Corinna. 'I've travelled almost every inch of East Africa, with my father. It's a rapidly expanding area for Brits. What ain't they got? They ain't got good British cooking.'

There was a smattering of applause. The Hebden Bridge Griddlers had finished their rendition of 'Prickly Eye Bush'. They went into a huddle, as if their programme were spontaneous and sensitive to the individual demands of the evening, although it had all been decided in advance. It was the programme they always did.

'You mean we . . . ' Ted was staggered at the scope of the idea, at the scale of its implications. 'East Africa! But that's . . . in Africa. You mean we go and live in East Africa?'

'Why not?'

The Hebden Bridge Griddlers launched themselves into 'Wild Rover'. Wild Rover! Why not?

'Why not indeed?' His enthusiasm was so sudden that it took Corinna aback. 'Chat show host! If he thinks he's the only one with wide horizons, he's got another think coming. I mean, he has.'

Rita approached her elder son, who was mouthing sweet nothings to his brother's wife across the *chile sin carne*.

'Elvis?' said Rita, and there was an ominous pleading tone in her voice. 'Can I have a word?'

Elvis moved off with his mother. They stood in a corner, underneath 'Root Vegetable Medley', by Trevor Coldwell. 'Wild Rover' continued in the background, half ignored. Rita spoke so earnestly, so secretively, that several people stopped to wonder what it was all about. Others knew.

'We must have a talk.'

'Not now, Mum. It isn't the time.'

'It's never the time with you, is it? This is worse than the Rodenhursts.'

'What?'

'You and I don't talk to each other, not because we aren't talking to each other but because we can't find anything to talk about even though we *are* talking to each other. Elvis, I want to talk about Carol.'

'Mum, there's nothing to talk about.'

Jenny was watching them from behind the food counter, straining to catch their every expression. They were both aware of her eyes upon them, though neither of them looked in her direction.

'She's a lovely girl. I don't like to see her hurt.'

'I always thought you didn't like her.'

'I've warmed to her. Mothers never like their sons' girl-friends at first.'

'I don't want to see her hurt either. But it didn't work out. It was lust, not love. There is a difference.'

'Thanks. A useful hint. Where's my diary, I must make a note of it.'

Rita pretended to search in the non-existent pockets of her Sillitoe's uniform. Jenny, seeing the gesture, was puzzled.

'Mum! Besides, Jenny's a lovely girl too, and she's having to look after two kids on her own, and I don't like to see her hurt, and our Paul hurt her.'

'I know, but that's not your responsibility.'

'Yes, it is. I love her.'

Elvis moved off, out of range of Rita's eyes. Rita stood stock still, struck dumb. Slowly she turned to look at Jenny.

Jenny gave her mother-in-law a hopeful little smile.

Rita tried to respond.

The Hebden Bridge Griddlers continued to strum, and sing, and smile, and sway, and shake.

'You talked to Rita, didn't you?'

Neville carefully finished his mouthful before speaking. He ate immaculately.

'If anybody'd told me that I'd enjoy a cashew nut moussaka, I wouldn't have believed them,' he said.

Liz ignored his evasion contemptuously. 'You talked to Rita, didn't you?' she repeated.

'No. No! Well, yes, but . . . no.'

'What on earth does *that* mean?'

Neville shifted uncomfortably in his stripped pine chair.

'It means I talked to Rita purely to tell her I wasn't talking to her.' He speared some more moussaka and raised it halfway to his mouth. 'I said you weren't talking to her, so I wasn't talking to her because . . . you weren't talking to her.'

'Oh, Neville, what on earth is the point of not talking to people if you tell them why you're not talking to them? Why must you be so nice all the time?'

131

'You miss Laurence, don't you? His barbs. His sarcasm. His icy retorts.'

'I don't miss Laurence. I do miss the cut and thrust. A bit. But I want it to be your cut and thrust.'

'So sorry I'm sarcastically inadequate.' Neville's face suddenly contorted with sarcastic fury. 'So sorry I suffer from brewer's droop in the icy retorts department.'

'That's better,' said Liz admiringly.

In a far corner of the now-deserted shop, behind bags of millet and bulgar wheat, Elvis Simcock and his younger brother's wife explored each other's mouth and lips.

'This is fantastic, Jenny,' said Elvis softly, without a trace of cynicism. 'I didn't know such happiness existed.'

'Elvis?' Jenny's voice had a diffident but unmistakably searching tone, as if she was about to tread on dangerous ground. Before she could do so, a door marked 'Store room. Private' opened. The young lovers stepped away from each other. Betty Sillitoe emerged, clutching an almost full glass of carrot juice.

'Had a dreadful thought,' she said. 'We ordered organic rhubarb. I couldn't remember seeing it. It's there.'

She moved off towards the restaurant, seemingly oblivious to the nature of Elvis and Jenny's meeting.

'Elvis?' said Jenny. 'I've always liked you . . . admired you. The philosopher. The rebel.' There was a catch in her voice. It was the shyness of new love. But there was also a frown. 'It worries me that you're becoming so ambitious.'

'It's not ambition for its own sake, Jenny,' explained Elvis earnestly. 'I only want to become famous in order to gain the influence to have my controversial and highly socially relevant and innately rebellious philosophical thoughts taken notice of.'

'I can't tell you how happy it makes me feel to hear you say that.' Jenny kissed Elvis warmly. Then a further worry darkened her brow. 'What controversial and highly socially relevant and innately rebellious thoughts?'

'The ones I'll have when I'm famous.'

Jenny looked somewhat sceptical still. Elvis began to kiss her again. He pressed her gently against a shelf of polyunsaturated fats. He held his hard body against hers and drove the scepticism out. He became aware that somebody was in the shop. He let go of her and swung round.

His mother was watching them gravely.

They could think of nothing to say. Jenny's hand clasped his. Far away, on a distant planet, the musicians griddled remorselessly.

'I wanted to say to you,' said Rita. 'It's none of my business I suppose, these days, but . . . I love you both, you see, so . . . I wanted to say . . . are you really serious?'

'Yeah. 'Course we are, Mum,' said Elvis with a decisiveness that would have been more impressive if he hadn't looked anxiously at Jenny for confirmation.

'I really think we are, Rita.' Jenny's confirmation was all the more convincing for being so quietly and carefully expressed.

'Well in that case . . . for what it's worth . . . ' said Rita, ' . . . you have my blessing . . . I suppose.'

'Thanks,' said Jenny. 'I don't think we'll get Mum's blessing.'

'Oh Lord!' Rita snorted with mirth. 'Not that that thought gives me any pleasure whatsoever.'

The snow turned rapidly to slush on the streets of the dim, unpeopled town. The lines of cars swished grimly down Arbitration Road. The lights burned wastefully in the windows of the shops near its junction with Westgate. There were few pedestrians about on that filthy night, and not many of them stopped to gaze at the absurdly expensive dresses in the boutiques that failed each year, to be replaced by even more expensive boutiques, which failed even quicker.

Towards the top end of the street, beyond the Gadd Garage, beyond the Chinese take-away with its dimly-lit waiting room, where the few customers sat uneasily like nervous patients – 'I'm still having trouble with my squid in black bean sauce, doc, can't seem to shake it off' – beyond the gloomy Arbitration Arms and the marginally less gloomy Jubilee Tavern with its upstairs disco with your resident host, Deke Ramsbottom, beyond the turf accountant's and the pet shop and the empty, failed greengrocer's, beyond the antique shop full of huge, hideous gilt eagles and the grimy video shop packed with grimy videos, there were signs of incipient gentrification: a bistro at number 167, named, imaginatively, 167, Arbitration Road; a kitchenware shop called The Cook Boutique; an up-market antique shop, without a gilt eagle in sight; an arts materials shop offering framing and restoration; and, newest of all, the flagship of this frail, brave navy, Sillitoe's; and beyond that, blackness. Planning blight. Dereliction. The dead hand of what would, one brave new rainswept dawn, be the outer inner relief ring road, carved as by the knife of a mad surgeon through the delicate intestines of the town.

In the Good Ship Sillitoe, the first evening at least was turning into a real success. Perhaps the absence of alcohol was a source of some regret. Possibly a perfectionist might have cavilled at the gloomy expression on the face of Eric Siddall, barman supreme. Maybe a musicologist might have noted a slight lack of variety in the repertoire of the Hebden Bridge Griddlers – who had moved on from 'Wild Rover' to 'Gipsy Rover' – but the lights were bright, the juices were tasty, the food was superb, the talk was lively, and a hostile world was splendidly if briefly defied.

Rodney and Betty basked in their success like unpolluted seals. Not only would they receive a rave report from Elvis in his 'Gosh, what nosh' spot, but Ginny Fenwick, ace reporter from the *Argus*, had come, had seen, had eaten, and had been conquered. As Marjorie Boon, cookery editor, Ginny had recently been starring a series of articles by the distinguished cookery writer Delia Brown, who was also Ginny Fenwick. Delia Brown, Ginny had assured the basking Sillitoes, would give this place top marks.

The Sillitoes tried not to look too pleased with themselves as they watched Ted Simcock approach across the bar. Little did they know that he was now a gipsy rover to whom Chez Edouard in Arbitration Road would have been small beer indeed.

'Well, it's all going very well, to say there's no meat, fish or alcohol,' he said. 'The omens are good.'

'Nice of you to say so, Ted.' Rodney tried not to sound surprised.

'I'm delighted you've taken that attitude,' said Betty.

'Life's too short to be petty, Betty.'

'Rodney!' Betty prompted her husband.

'I know,' said Rodney. 'Ted, we're very sorry about nextdoor, truly, but . . . one man's loss is another man's opportunity, as they . . . will you come and work for me?'

'For us!' corrected Betty indignantly.

'Oh Lord. Us. Sorry. Takes some getting used to. Ted, will you work for us?'

'No.'

'What?' said Betty. 'Oh, Ted. Let bygones . . . '

'It's not the bygones. They've gone by. They have! Did Rodney buy my premises when my foundry went bankrupt? I can't remember.' Ted couldn't help showing his satisfaction at this linguistic device, which enabled him to air his grievances while claiming to have forgotten them. 'Is your business going to flourish next to my pile of rubble? I forget. But.'

'But what?' The response was dragged out of Rodney by Ted's silence.

'I wouldn't work for you if you were the last tea in China.'

'Oh, Ted.' Betty sounded hurt. 'Why?'

'Because, in the words of your barman tonight, "It just isn't me, isn't carrot juice."'

Eric Siddall wouldn't have been flattered if he'd heard Ted's impression.

'Eric said that?' said Rodney. 'When we asked for him specially, as a favour? After he'd said he'd be delighted to rearrange his week so as to make himself available?'

'All right.' Ted began to reveal the resentment that he claimed not to feel. 'You've found a bandwagon and you've climbed aboard. Fair enough. Good luck to you.'

'It's not a bandwagon,' said Betty rather haughtily. 'It's a sincerely held belief.'

'All right. But it's not my belief. In my book, with respect, it's trendy, overpriced garbage, and I wouldn't touch it with a bargepole even if I didn't have plans of my own.'

'Plans of your own?' Rodney was tactlessly amazed.

'The concept of the Yorkshire pudding is a closed book on the dark continent.'

'You what, Ted?' Betty was frankly bemused.

'Africa. Yorkshire pudding. They don't have it. Same difference with fish and chips. Batter as we understand the term is unknown from Mozambique to Mogadishu.'

'You what, Ted?' This time, the bemusement was Rodney's.

'I'm telling you about my business expansion plans, and all you can say is, "You what, Ted?" You've become insular. We're an insular nation. I expect it's with being an island.'

'You what, Ted?'

'Corinna was talking about how tourism has increased in East Africa. Her father's a bishop there, I don't know if you know that. And . . . well, if you have an eye for a business opportunity you never lose it, it's like se . . . ' Ted glanced at Betty and found himself unable to talk about sex, ' . . . riding a bicycle. I saw our chance immediately. I've persuaded her to open a chain of English restaurants in East Africa. You're impressed, I can see.'

'Impressed' was not perhaps the first word that a casual watcher would have applied to the faces of Rodney and Betty Sillitoe.

'Well . . . ' said Rodney, recovering slowly.

'Good luck,' said Betty.

'Thanks. And thank you for your offer. I don't doubt it was kindly meant,' said the embryonic East African entrepreneur patronisingly.

Ted set off towards the restaurant, from which the strains of 'When I Was Single' were now emerging. But before he could get there he was collared by Neville.

'I want your advice, Ted. A man's advice.'

'Neville!' Ted was flattered. 'Well . . . absolutely . . . I'm your man. What's the problem? You can tell me. These things happen to the best of us.'

'It's nothing like that. It's Liz and me.'

'Well, yes, I assumed it was.'

'I irritate her. It gets on her nerves that I'm so nice all the time. I thought of you immediately.'

'Really?' Ted was pleased.

'I want to learn how to become nasty.'

'You what, Neville?' Ted was no longer pleased.

'Not very nasty. Somewhat nasty. Less nice.'

'Neville? Why have you come to me?' Ted was becoming indignant. 'Do you regard me as nasty? Or less nice? Am I the acknowledged local expert on obnoxiousness?'

'No. Of course not. In no way.'

'So, I repeat, and I'd like an answer, why the hell come to me?'

'I'm sorry I did now.'

'So am I, Neville.' Ted's anger was rising steadily. 'So am I.'

'But there you are, you see. You really are rather good at being angry.'

'Why don't you get stuffed?' Ted was almost shouting now. He stalked off hurriedly towards Corinna.

Betty Sillitoe, the joint big wheel behind Sillitoe's, stood near the end of the food counter with her employee and good friend, Rita Simcock, and surveyed the scene.

At a nearby table, Trevor Coldwell sat gazing at James Whatmore and, beyond James Whatmore, at his own painting, entitled 'The Prize Marrow'. You could almost taste the juice.

Beyond them, Prunella Ransom was talking earnestly with Ginny Fenwick. As the Green Party candidate she lost no opportunity of publicising her cause. Mock not, gentle reader. If everybody stole every suit of clothes you produced, you'd feel the need to publicise yourself.

'So far so good,' said Betty.

'Very much so, Betty.' A sigh took Rita unawares. Betty looked at her questioningly. She found she wanted to explain. 'Well, it doesn't look as though my man's going to come. I never really thought he would.'

'There's still time, Rita.'

'It was just an hour in a pub, I suppose. It was just that we seemed to . . . click. He said he thought I was . . . ' Rita couldn't say it.

'Beautiful?'

'Well, yes. How did you . . . ? And I was thinking, "Is it it this time?" and he was thinking, "This isn't a bad way of filling up an hour. M'm! This ham roll's nice."'

Simon entered the restaurant with a bespectacled, rather primly dressed young lady. They stopped to talk with Neville and Liz. Betty was riveted.

'The silly thing is,' continued Rita, 'it's not as if I feel the need of a man. Will I ever learn, Betty? Or is this sort of thing going to happen all the time?'

'M'm? Oh. Fourteen minutes to nine,' said Betty, looking at her watch.

137

'My love life is incredibly boring, I agree,' said Rita.

'No. That was fascinating,' said Betty. 'Utterly fascinating, Rita. I expect. But I just wasn't listening. I was watching. Simon's friend has arrived.'

Simon brought his friend over to them. She wore glasses. She looked demure in a pale grey Prince of Wales check suit with a blue silk blouse, but she might, Betty felt, have hidden depths.

'Hello, Betty,' said Simon. 'This is Lucinda Snellmarsh. Betty Sillitoe, our hostess.'

They shook hands and Lucinda said 'Hello.' There followed a lacuna, as Lucinda waited to be introduced to Rita.

'It's rather awkward,' said Simon to Lucinda. His voice, though lowered, was loud enough for Rita to hear. 'I can't introduce you to the other person. We're having a feud.'

'Goodness,' said Lucinda. 'What fun!' She turned to Betty. 'Sorry I'm so late. I had to show a client round a house.' She looked in the direction of the food. 'Is that the food?' She went to peer closely at the remains of the hot dishes. Simon followed her. 'Mm! It looks super.'

'She *is* a short-sighted estate agent,' said Betty to Rita.

'What?'

'We wondered what sort of girl-friend Simon would have. I said, a short-sighted estate agent.'

'I think that's very cruel and rather unfair,' said Rita.

'But it's true.'

'That makes it all the more cruel and unfair.'

Rodney joined them, clutching his carrot juice.

'Ah! There you are,' said Betty.

'Here I am,' said Rodney cheerfully. 'I'm going to go and beard Eric in his den.'

'I've just got to check something in the store room,' said Betty.

Rodney and Betty went off in opposite directions, clutching their carrot juices. Simon and Lucinda were also moving off, Lucinda peering anxiously, protecting her tray of food from dimly-seen terrors. Rita felt that she had been abandoned. She felt suddenly tired. Tired of this feud. Tired of trouble. Tired of challenges. She closed her eyes. This wouldn't do. She opened them and saw Simon and Lucinda talking with Carol

138

Fordingbridge. She stood and watched and tried to regain her strength.

'Yours turned up?' Simon asked.

'Has he heck?' said Carol wryly.

Simon shook his head in mystification. 'I don't understand it,' he said. 'I simply don't understand it, Carol.'

'You what?'

'A beautiful girl like you. She is beautiful, isn't she, Lucinda?'

The short-sighted Lucinda Snellmarsh peered closely at the long-haired Carol Fordingbridge.

'Yes,' she said.

Simon smiled. He had introduced two attractive young women to each other. He was handling their meeting well. He was sophisticated. Life was good.

'Highly desirable?' he said.

'I'd have thought so,' said Lucinda, somewhat drily, though Simon didn't notice.

'I'm a woman, Simon, not a house,' protested Carol.

Simon did notice *her* dryness. He strove to deal with it. 'A very attractive woman. A beautiful woman. A gorgeous woman. Wouldn't you say so, Lucinda?'

'Well . . . attractive.'

Simon did realise now that Lucinda was getting somewhat miffed at his praise of Carol. But she could handle it, unlike Carol, who, though lovely, wasn't out of the top drawer. So it was Carol he strove to placate.

'Absolutely,' he said. 'So where are the men with taste?'

'Thank you, Simon,' said Carol bitterly, and she stomped off.

Simon was hurt. 'I thought I was being extremely complimentary,' he said. His lips curled scornfully. 'Women!' He noticed Lucinda's expression. 'Apart from you, of course.'

'Eric. A word.'

'Certainly, sir,' said Eric Siddall without enthusiasm. 'Can do. Tickety-boo. We have a lull.'

'Erm . . . ' began Rodney. 'A little bird has told me that you earlier uttered the words "it just isn't me, isn't carrot juice".'

'I know what you're going to say, and you're right.'

'You what?'

'You were going to say, "Eric," you were going to say, "I have not employed you on this important night to be lukewarm over your beverages," you were going to say.'

'Well, yes.'

'The rebuke is merited,' said Eric Siddall, barman supreme. 'I have served, during what I like to think of as a modestly distinguished career behind the pumps, four years on the Cunarders, head barman in the cocktail bar of the Savoy Hotel . . . Hunstanton, eighteen years stewardship of the golf club, until . . . well, we won't go into that. I've smiled through streaming colds, gout and a trapped disc. I've endured, with stoic fortitude, heavy seas, leaking roofs, golfers' anecdotes, and the lager playing me up. I have to say that your drinks have depressed me, and I've shown it. I've let you down. I've let meself down. All I can say is, I'm very, very disappointed in meself.'

'Yes, well,' said Rodney, 'I just wanted to say, "Never mind, Eric. Keep at it." Jolly good.'

It would have been difficult to say which man was closer to tears.

'Hello, Mum,' said Jenny, smiling bravely. 'Hello . . . Neville.'

'Hello,' said Liz warily.

'I've something to . . . er . . . ' began Jenny. She was determined to tell them before they found out. 'Earlier, Mum, you said you hoped I'd find somebody soon.'

'Yes,' said her mother even more warily.

'Well, I have.'

'That *was* soon,' said Neville.

'Yes. You said you hoped he'd be nice. He is nice.'

'That's nice,' said Liz and Neville.

'Yes. You said you hoped he'd be of my – I can hardly use the word, I find the concept so distasteful – class.'

'Well, I did, yes,' said Liz.

'Yes, well, I suppose he, although I don't think in those terms any more, but if I did think in those terms any more I'd have to say, isn't.'

Neville smiled with vague alarm, and left the conversation entirely to the women.

'Yes, well, I suppose I might have guessed he wouldn't be,' said Liz. 'Especially as I was so foolish as to suggest he should be. Will parents never learn?'

'He . . . er . . . I'm afraid he may disappoint your hopes pretty considerably in one particular respect.'

'What?'

'I'm afraid he fails, utterly and totally fails, the criterion of . . . er . . . oh Lord . . . of . . . er . . . not being a Simcock.'

Neville looked puzzled, as if mentally checking through a long list of possible Simcocks.

Liz was quicker.

'*Elvis?*'

The Hebden Bridge Griddlers were cheerfully instructing the guests to 'Look at the Coffin'. Lucinda was on to her dessert. The decaffeinated coffee was flowing. Rita and Jenny were busily selling raffle tickets.

Gordon Trollope, the bewildered butcher, told them that last Sunday, over at Thirsk, when asked to recite a nursery rhyme, his vegetarian two-year-old grand-daughter had said, 'This little piggy went to market, this little piggy stayed at home, this little piggy had lentils, this little piggy had none.' They laughed. Jenny said, 'Terrific,' and Rita said, 'Oh, that's beautiful.' It was the wrong response. Gordon Trollope only bought one ticket.

While Jenny sold raffle tickets, Elvis chatted to Ginny Fenwick about media matters. He told her that he planned to become a TV personality. She didn't tell him that, more than thirty years ago, she'd dreamt of becoming a famous war correspondent. He told her that he was in love and it was the real thing. She didn't tell him that she had twice believed it to be the real thing, and it hadn't been either time. When he wandered off, she began to think of those old times, on that other *Argus*. Where were they now, those two men, Ted Plunkett and Gordon Carstairs, neither of whom had been the real thing? Where were kind, effete Denzil Ackerman and podgy Henry Pratt?

It was no use looking back.

Rita hovered beside Trevor Coldwell and James Whatmore. They were in high good humour. No matter tonight that Trevor's exquisite paintings were barely known outside his home town.

No matter tonight that all James Whatmore's good ideas had come just too late and been just wrong – his BBC puppet idea, *The Magic Ferris Wheel*, his book for older children, *The Tiger, the Witch and the Cupboard*, his great character for younger children, Milkman Mike. Tonight, they were kings, as they laughed at success and scorned Metropolitan society, and all the temporary gods who were made and destroyed by fashion. They rejoiced that, in a world full of false values, they had not achieved the success that proves one's worthlessness. They were happy because, in a warm, genuine corner of their untalented and self-deceptive souls, they really did put a low value on worldly riches. When at last Rita managed to attract their attention they bought ten strips of tickets each, and their old bloodshot eyes grew moist for the Third World, and they counted themselves lucky.

Jenny hovered beside Prunella Ransom and the Mayor and Mayoress. The Mayor waxed eloquent about his cats, who were called Edward Heath, Nigel Lawson and Geoffrey Howe. Prunella, having abandoned her hopes of finding a suitable man tonight, was happy to listen. She almost said that having one of the Mayor's cats named after you seemed to be a recipe for political extinction, but she resisted. She had long ago learnt that few men liked clever women.

Jenny sold Prunella three strips. The Mayor and Mayoress could hardly buy less.

The sale of raffle tickets was complete. It was time for the draw. Everyone moved into the restaurant, even Eric Siddall. An air of excitement and tension sat suddenly on that room of brick and pine, an atmosphere altogether out of scale with the size of the little event. Some people wanted to win very much. Others were hoping, equally fervently, that they wouldn't. Some of the massed vegetarians and conservationists felt moved by the knowledge that they would be raising money for the Third World. Others felt embarrassed by the utter insignificance of the likely sum. Some felt uneasy at making any kind of excitement, having any element of fun, about problems and miseries that were so vast.

Rita wondered why she kept letting herself in for things that were so embarrassing. She stood facing the gathered guests, smiling glassily. On a table in front of her were the three wicker hampers. Behind her sat the Hebden Bridge Griddlers, glad to rest their feet. Normally they kept their energies going with pints of bitter. Whortleberry juice was no substitute.

She gave the cardboard box containing the tickets a vigorous shake and held it out to the small, corpulent Mayor. He shook his head and indicated that the large, corpulent Mayoress should draw the first ticket. 'Ladies first,' he muttered shyly.

Netta Ponsonby dived deep into the box and brought out a yellow ticket.

Rita took the ticket and read out the number. 'First prize! The First World hamper. Yellow ticket number 127. Oh no! That's me!'

There were some cheers, a few groans, and a cry of 'Fix' from an embarrassed Elvis.

'Better put it back,' said Rita. 'It's not right I should win.'

'Rubbish,' called out Rodney. 'You entered. You paid.'

'But I don't want it. I won't enjoy it,' said Rita. 'I'll feel guilty.'

'I thought that was the idea.' Heads turned to see who had spoken. Ted tried to look as though it hadn't been him.

'Oh well . . . ' said Rita. 'It's a bit embarrassing though. Oh well. Let's hope I don't win the second prize too.'

Rita shook the box again and presented it to the Mayor. He drew a blue ticket and handed it to her.

'Blue ticket number 141,' she announced.

Nobody spoke. There was much hunting in pockets, and checking and rechecking.

'That could be you, Liz,' said Neville, not without a trace of unbadgerly excitement. 'You were just before me, and I'm 151 to 160.'

'Shut up,' hissed Liz. 'Don't be so stupid.'

'Oooh. It's me,' said the lady griddler. 'Oooh! I've never won anything before.'

There was relief all round. In the safety of the applause, Neville said, 'Maybe I'm being stupid, but why did you say I was stupid?'

'Because I don't want to have to smile at Rita, and I'd have looked a bit of a bitch if I hadn't smiled at her, stupid.'

Neville still looked puzzled.

'Now the third prize,' said Rita. 'Isn't this exciting?' She wished she hadn't said that. It was wrong to be excited.

She shook the box and held it out to the Mayor. He again indicated the Mayoress. Nothing became the Mayor and Mayoress more than their love for each other. He was proud of the honour only for her. She was proud of it only for him.

The Mayoress drew another blue ticket and handed it to Rita.

'Blue ticket again, number 84,' she announced.

'Good Lord!' said Corinna.

'Oh heck!' said Ted.

There were gasps. It seemed so wrong, and therefore so right, that of all people in that room the Third World hamper should go to Ted Simcock.

Ted looked thoroughly discomfited. He was damned if he'd go and get the bloody thing. Rita could bring it to him.

The moment she realised that Ted wasn't going to move, Rita hurried over to him, clutching the tiny, the absurd, the tragic hamper.

Ex-husband and ex-wife stared at each other, he grumpily, she embarrassed but also a little amused.

'Congratulations, Ted,' she said.

'What do you mean, congratulations?' said Ted, falling to the occasion. 'Have I to live a whole day on this?'

'No, darling, on half of it. I'll share it with you,' said Corinna.

'Whose side are you on?' grumbled Ted.

'I didn't realise there were sides,' said Corinna.

'It's a stupid idea,' said Ted.

'I don't think so.' Corinna smiled at Rita so sweetly that Rita felt like murdering her. 'I think Rita hoped it might go to somebody who needed to have their eyes opened to their greed and complacency.'

'It has,' said Rita.

The evening resumed its steady course. Some people went to the bar. One or two left to go to the pub. Others wanted to, but hadn't the nerve. Some wanted more of the delicious food, but didn't like to take any, after the business with the hampers. Others decided that, in a world short of food, waste was the real crime, so they piled their plates high. The Griddlers went into a huddle, pretending to debate about the next number, but actually sharing a joke about a nun and a traction engine. Alderman Spigot confessed to the worrying possibility that Nigel Lawson might have worms. Jenny disappeared briefly, to breast-feed Steffie. Ted talked to his fiancée, his vision in rust, his Corinna.

'I know people haven't got enough to eat,' he said. 'I don't need this.'

'My father would say that you know it intellectually and this is your chance to know it physically. My father would say, use this to dedicate yourself to being a better human being. My father would say, be thankful for what you've got.'

'What have I got?'

'Me, for a start.'

'Oh. Right. Granted. You. Absolutely,' said Ted hastily. 'But . . . I mean . . . what else?'

'Aren't I enough?'

' 'Course you are, love. More than enough. You're everything to me.' Corinna waited for Ted's 'but'. 'But.'

'But what?'

'You aren't a career. You're me evenings.' Ted leered. 'Me nights. Where's me nine to five? Me job?'

'Don't you believe in my East Africa idea?'

'Well . . . I don't know . . . I mean, it's so far off. I mean, will it really work?'

The Hebden Bridge Griddlers, their huddle completed, launched themselves into 'Old Flames'.

'I know that country,' said Corinna decisively. 'I believe it will. A new life. A new adventure, in a new world. Accept that you're a lucky man, Ted, and learn to be at peace with yourself.'

'I am at peace with myself, Corinna. I mean . . . I am.'

'Are you? You're resentful of Rita. You're guilty about Sandra. You have almost no relationship with your sons.'

'I'm disappointed in them.'

'Maybe you wouldn't be if you helped them more. They need you, Ted. So don't be embarrassed about winning this. Use it. Make your peace with everybody. Start now. With Rita. Now.'

'Hell's bells, Corinna. You aren't half pushing me around.'

'Only because I want you to be happy,' said Corinna, so quietly that Ted had to lean forward to hear her over the music. 'Because I love you so very, very much, my darling.'

Ted gulped.

'Corinna Price-Rodgerson, you are one extraordinary woman,' said the former toasting fork tycoon.

'I know,' said Corinna Price-Rodgerson.

'There you go, sir,' said the dapper, ageless Eric Siddall, barman supreme. He handed Rodney a fresh glass of carrot juice. 'One juice of the carrot *au naturel*! They can't touch you for it.' He leant forward, to whisper, 'I've regained my professional pride.'

'Well done, Eric.' Rodney tried to walk off. His legs buckled. 'Oops! Odd. Floor's moving.' He looked round the bar. Nobody seemed to have noticed. 'Where's that wife of mine gone?'

He moved off very carefully.

Warmed by Corinna's words, Ted found the strength to admit to himself that his past behaviour had often been unworthy of his true nature, of that better, nicer Ted Simcock who had never fully expressed himself.

Backed by the music of the Hebden Bridge Griddlers, he approached his ex-wife nervously. She was wiping a table on which natural yoghurt had been spilt.

'Rita! Hello!' he said.

'Hello, Ted.' She turned to face him.

'Hello.'

They stood smiling at each other. Rita was kneading her yoghurty dishcloth tensely.

'Well, we can't go on saying hello forever,' she said. 'We'll have to think of something else.'

'Yes. Rita, I've come to . . . er . . . I've been a bit of a prat.'

'We're all bits of prats sometimes, Ted.'

'I realise now that it was none of your doing. The route for the road smashing Chez Edouard. I was stupid to think it was.'

'Well . . . I understand, because I understand how disappointed you must have felt. Will you open a restaurant somewhere else?'

'Yes. Nairobi.'

'You what?'

'We're going away. We're going to be married in East Africa and live there. You'll be shot of me.' Rita turned away, and resumed her wiping of the table. 'No more keeping bumping into each other embarrassingly at do's. You never need see me again. Great news, isn't it?'

'It should be.'

'You what?'

She turned away from the table again to look him full in the face.

'Aren't we stupid?' she said.

'Who?'

'Folk. People. This is ridiculous. I feel quite sad. At the thought . . . I'll never see you again. I feel . . . oooh . . . all . . . well, I hope you'll be very happy.'

'We will be.'

'And successful.'

'Most probably. We'll have a farewell party before we go. A real classy do.'

'Lovely.'

'Good idea, that raffle, Rita. Imaginative. Caring. Great.'

'Ted!'

Ted kissed his ex-wife tenderly and moved off before she could see the embarrassing moisture in his macho Yorkshire eyes.

'Ted!'

She rubbed the table top blindly.

There was nobody in the shop to hear the words of 'Hernando's Hide-Away' being hummed with blurry imprecision. There was nobody to see Rodney Sillitoe as he searched for his elusive spouse.

Behind him the door of the store room opened and Betty emerged carefully, clutching a glass of carrot juice. They circled slowly round each other, not seeing each other. At last Rodney saw her.

'Betty! There you are.'

Betty hiccuped.

'Hiccups?'

'Lentils.'

147

'I beg your pardon?'

'I ate a bit of lentil and aubergine bake rather too fast.' Betty's words were slurred.

'Betty!' Rodney was appalled. 'Are you drunk? On carrot juice?'

Betty became conspiratorial, as if the shop were crammed with customers.

'I have a confession to make. Because I was so nervous, because I wanted tonight to be a success, because it's important, because I love you, I . . . hid a bottle of vodka in the store room. Dark in there, but with all the carrot juice I could see quite well!'

She gave a peal of laughter.

'Sssh!' said Rodney urgently. 'We mustn't let anybody realise or we'll totally destroy our crebidility.'

'Crebidility? Rodney, are you drunk too?'

'I have had a bit. Topped it up a bit. Vodka. In the office. Because I was nervous, because I . . . what you said.'

'And, because we haven't drunk anything for ages . . . '

'Longer than that. Very ages.'

'It's gone straight to our heads.'

'It mustn't leak out. We'll be a laughing stock if we're known as the only two people in the history of the . . . the thingummyjig . . . big round thing . . . '

'The world.'

'That's it! To get drunk on carrot juice.'

'While preaching teetotal . . . itarianism. What are we going to do?'

'Sober up. Walk slowly, with dignity. Drink ginuine . . . genuine carrot juice. Eat a lot.'

'Use very short words.'

'Yes.'

'Good.'

'Right.'

They set off, slowly, carefully, into the restaurant. Slowly, carefully they made their way towards the food counter. They were stopped by Rita. They smiled at her slowly, carefully.

'I've been thinking,' she said. 'There's going to be an awful lot of clearing up to be done. We could stay late and do it all tonight or come in early and do it all tomorrow or do it half and half. What do you think?'

'Yes,' said Rodney and Betty Sillitoe.

They floated on towards the food counter, slowly, carefully, like two swans on a placid river.

Rita hurried over to consult Jenny, who was chatting, surprise surprise, with Elvis.

'Jenny? Can I have a word?' she said. 'In private.'

'Mum!' Elvis was hurt.

'Sorry, Elvis, but this is shop. Shop shop.'

Rita pushed Elvis. He moved away, slowly, reluctantly, indignantly, towards the bar, turning several times to look back at the two most important women in his life, his mother and his lover.

'You can trust Elvis,' said Jenny.

'Can I? He's the media.'

'He's your son.'

'He's a professional. I don't want to give him a good story that he might have a crisis of conscience as to whether to use or not.'

'Good story? Nothing's wrong, is it?'

'Not really.'

'I feel great.' Jenny's words tumbled out enthusiastically. 'I've eaten only organic food and drunk only organic drink and I feel . . . well . . . really organic.'

'Yes, well, I'm afraid Rodney and Betty are as organic as newts.'

The Sillitoes turned away from the food counter, their trays piled high with food. They made their way towards the nearest table, swaying and lurching as if on a ship in a gale.

In the bar, while Elvis searched grumpily for something drinkable, Ted tackled Neville and Liz. With Corinna's words floating sexily through his bloodstream, he was warming to his mission of peace. His heart was filled with *glasnost*. He would tear down every Berlin Wall in his life.

'You aren't not speaking to *me*, are you?' he asked.

'Good Lord, no,' said Liz. 'You're a fellow victim of Rita. A fellow compulsory purchasee.'

'Speak to her. There's no point not.'

'When I intend to appoint you as my spiritual adviser, Ted, I'll let you know.'

Ted smiled. 'Your sarcasm can't wound me now, Liz. It's water off a duck's back. Give it up. Learn to be at peace with yourself,' said his eloquent smile.

Ted himself, less eloquently, said, 'Yes . . . well . . . I . . . I want to . . . apologise.'

'What?' said Liz.

'Good Lord!' said Neville.

'No need to sound so surprised,' said Ted. 'I am human.'

'Apologise for what, Ted?' said Neville.

'For . . . what I did at the Christening. I mean . . . telling everyone . . . ' he dropped his voice to a whisper, ' . . . that he's my baby.'

'It's a bit late for whispering now, Ted,' pointed out Liz.

'Most people knew anyway,' said Neville.

'Yes, but while they didn't know that everybody else knew they could pretend they didn't know.'

'Anyway, thank you,' said Neville. 'A handsome apology.'

'Happily accepted.' Liz smiled.

'How is he?' Ted asked.

'Marvellous. Bright as a button,' said Neville proudly.

'Aaah! Just like his . . . ' Ted glanced at Liz, and narrowly avoided a return to tactlessness, ' . . . mother.'

'Neville's so proud. Such a good father. He changes his nappies almost as much as I do.'

'Liz!'

'What?'

'I have a position to keep up.'

'What?'

'Senior partner in Badger, Badger, Fox and Badger. Tough, unyielding, determined. A scourge of the criminal fraternity. I don't want it noised abroad that I change nappies.'

'Corinna and I'll be going away soon. To Africa.' Ted made the 'Africa' sound very casual, as if he'd said 'Torquay'.

'Good Lord!' said Liz, and this time Ted was pleased that she was surprised.

'May I take this opportunity . . . ' he lowered his voice to a whisper again, ' . . . of wishing nothing but the best for the lad.'

'There's no need to whisper, Ted.' For some reason best known to herself Liz was also whispering.

'I know,' whispered Ted, 'but I prefer it. And of wishing you
oth many years of happiness.'

They stared reflectively at Ted's departing back.

'Good Lord!' said Liz.

'Liz!' said Neville. 'I must speak out. Abandon this feud!' It
as almost an order. 'Stop behaving in a way that makes it
ifficult for me to admire you and look up to you as much as
want to.'

'I don't want to be admired and looked up to, Neville. I want
o be loved.'

'You are. I love you.'

Neville kissed her as he had never kissed her in pub-
c before.

'Neville!'

s Elvis strolled away from the bar with his loganberry and tonic,
e came face to face with Carol, who was attempting to slip out
ithout anybody noticing.

'Carol! Are you going?' he said.

'Another deep, philosophical question from the same great
rain that gave the world "are you here?".'

'Carol!'

'Let's see if my *little* brain can cope with it. Think logi-
ally. There's the door. I'm walking towards it. Yes, I think I
m going.'

'He didn't . . . '

'Turn up, then? I'm getting the hang of your style. No, he
idn't. He rang. I'm meeting him in the pub. Well, he's a
it of a lager lout, and you don't get carrot juice louts,
o you?'

'You, with a lager lout?'

'Yeah. He's dead ignorant. He's great.'

'You're just trying to annoy me.'

'Bye, Elvis.' Carol walked briskly to the door. Without turning
ound, she said, 'I'm no longer there, therefore I've gone,' and
he stepped out into the windy, slushy night.

Elvis turned away and found himself face to face again, this
ime with Simon.

'Simon!' he said. 'I see you have a companion tonight.'

Simon didn't reply.

'Ah. We're not speaking. What an improvement on our previous conversations.'

Simon didn't reply.

'Really?' said Elvis. 'Hey, you were at such pains to tell me you'd given up sex forever, does she know she's wasting her time?'

Simon waited long enough to show that he wasn't giving even a flicker of response, and strode off to the bar counter.

'Terrific,' said Elvis.

He entered the restaurant, where the Griddlers were still griddling, the Sillitoes were still eating, Trevor Coldwell and James Whatmore were still demolishing with feline delight the entire artistic and literary establishments and the Mayor and Mayoress were worrying because Geoffrey Howe was off his milk.

'Psst! Son?' called out Ted.

Elvis approached his father cautiously, fearing further social blows. Imagine his astonishment when Ted's first words were, 'I thought a chat would be nice.'

'Good God!"

'Am I that inhuman? Have we drifted that far apart?'

'No. No, Dad.'

'I'd like to get closer, Son. I mean . . . I would. Much closer. Much much closer.'

'Well, so would I.'

'I'll be going away soon.'

'Where?'

'Nairobi.'

'I don't want to quibble, Dad, but won't that prove a slight obstacle to our getting closer?'

'I hope not. I hope you'll visit. With Jenny.'

'Oh. You've heard.'

'Yes.'

'And?'

'I don't have the right to express any views, do I, the cock-up I've made of my . . . until now, of course. I hope you'll come to see Corinna as a, as a new mother . . . '

Rita smiled at them warmly as she passed with camomile teas for the Mayor and Mayoress.

'Without – hello, Rita – without losing your old mother as . . . an old mother.'

Jenny scurried up, smiling. Little Steffie had dropped off again. She was a happy baby and didn't miss her father because she didn't know she was supposed to have one.

'Hello, Jenny darling.' Ted had a big, affectionate kiss for his daughter-in-law, who looked as if she might become his ex-daughter-in-law, in order to pave the way for becoming his daughter-in-law again. 'I hope you'll be very happy and visit us regularly in Nairobi.'

Ted hurried off, lest Jenny might see that his eyes were moist.

'Good Lord!' said Elvis.

'I know!' said Jenny. 'Nairobi!'

'I meant me dad being so nice to me,' said Elvis.

Conversation was buzzing, the Griddlers were huddling and griddling, the Mayor was anxiously discussing the texture of Edward Heath's stools, and Eric Siddall was in danger of becoming positively enthusiastic about his non-alcoholic cornucopia.

Rodney and Betty, their vast meals safely stowed away, walked slowly and carefully through to the bar, acknowledging the congratulations of their guests with carefully enunciated thank you's.

Ted and Corinna, sipping their peach juices, watched them enter with fond amusement.

Elvis and Jenny, happy in their new-found love, watched them with indulgent smiles.

Neville and Liz, keeping their own counsel in their chosen corner of the bar, watched everybody watching each other.

Rita joined Elvis and Jenny, and Liz stiffened like a cat.

'Liz!' said Neville. 'I'd like you to go and talk to Rita.'

'Neville!' Surprise fought with remonstration in Liz's voice.

'Hatred is so destructive. Political hatred. Religious hatred. Racial hatred. Sexual hatred. All hatred.' Liz would have been open-mouthed in her astonishment if she hadn't known that she didn't look at her best open-mouthed. She had never heard Neville speak like this. 'Mouths that hate grow hard and ugly. Eyes that hate reveal how self-destructive hatred is. Life is so short, and people waste so much of it on hate. I'll love you however you behave, but for your sake, darling, I beg you, make

153

peace with Rita.' He kissed her on the forehead. 'More fruit juice needed.'

Liz stood stock still, as if in shock.

At the bar, not quite believing, himself, that he had actually said what he had just said, Neville smiled at the Sillitoes, who were leaning on the counter for support as they drank their unadulterated carrot juices.

'It's extraordinary,' he said. 'No alcohol has been served, nobody has had a drop . . . ' The Sillitoes had the grace to look uncomfortable. 'Yet the buzz has grown louder, the chat more cheery, inhibitions have begun to break down, as if perhaps being sociable is itself an intoxicant. What do you think? What's your explanation?'

'Yes,' said Rodney and Betty.

And Liz stood stock still, looking inwards, thinking. Then she glanced irresolutely towards Rita.

Rita felt a tingling right down her spine.

'I think your mother is thinking of coming over and talking to me,' she said.

'Oh, I hope so,' said Jenny.

Liz took a first step, as though she still hadn't quite decided.

'Oh Lord,' said Rita. 'Should I go to meet her or what? I feel like a jelly.'

'Go on, Mum,' said Elvis.

Rita stepped towards Liz.

Liz continued to walk towards Rita.

'They're going to talk,' said Corinna.

'Great,' said Ted. 'I mean that. No . . . I do.'

'But?'

'No buts at all, my cherry blossom.'

Rita and Liz walked right up to each other, and stopped. All eyes in the bar were upon them.

They faced each other in silence, not smiling, not hostile, not quite sure whether to speak first or what to say.

A good-looking man with greying hair and a luxuriant grey beard entered on a blast of cold air from Arbitration Road. He wore a light grey suit and a dark Crombie overcoat. His smile revealed none of the agonising which he had endured before finally deciding to come.

Rita saw him first.

'You came!' she said.

He spread his hands in a gesture of helplessness, of capitulation to destiny.

'How could I not?' he said. 'How could I not, Rita?' He turned to Liz, who was staring at him in horror. 'Hello, Liz.'

'You know Liz?' said Rita.

'I'm her brother.'

'Oh!' Rita's hand went to her mouth, as if to hide the beginning of a smile.

Liz fainted. Nobody moved as she crashed to the ground.

'Oh my God!' said Ted and Corinna together.

Neville Badger turned away from the bar, with their drinks in his hand, a good-natured smile relaxing his sometimes anxious face. The smile gave way to puzzlement, and then to consternation as he saw his wife lying unconscious on the floor.

'Oh Lord!' he said.

'Oh heavens,' said Rodney and Betty Sillitoe, and they collapsed into great chortling, trilling peals of tipsy laughter.

All heads in the restaurant turned towards the bar. Even the Griddlers wavered momentarily in their griddling.

Fourth Do

June:
The Farewell Party

The midsummer wind howled in frustration as it hurled itself
impotently against the rain-dribbled concrete of the Grand Universal Hotel. Its fury grew as it failed to batter down the wide,
treble-glazed windows of the gleaming, patriotic Royalty Suite.

Ted Simcock surveyed the empty, air-conditioned suite. All
was calm and quiet, order and confidence. The elements were
derided. Mankind was king here. 'You futile wind, all you're
doing is making us feel smug,' purred the man-made Royalty
Suite. 'My day will come,' wailed the wild and wicked wind.

If mankind was king here, Ted Simcock was emperor. He
seemed confident, excited, even cocky. And he was dressed as
Napoleon.

To his right, as he admired his kingdom, was the bar. To
his left stretched the flexible multi-purpose function room.
The rooms were joined by a panelled wall, which was set
half open, allowing the bar a separate identity, but within an
integrated whole.

The walls were white, the carpets red, the wide square arm-
chairs blue, with chrome arms. The chrome ashtrays revolved
when pressed and could mash cigars into small pieces. In the
flexible, multi-purpose function room the chairs and tables were
set round the walls, affording a spacious dance floor in the centre.
At the far end, on a platform reached by two inappropriately
pretty curved little stairways, sat four musical instruments. On
the big drum, in large letters, were the words 'The Dale Monsal
Quartet'. Below the platform a long table smirked with food.
Beside the buffet there were bottles of champagne, two of them
in ice buckets.

Ted examined all this, and saw that it was good. He struck
a Napoleonic pose and said grandly, 'Not tonight, Josephine.'

He didn't see the approach of the head barman, and jumped out of his imperial skin when that worthy thrust a plate under his nose and said, 'Olive, sir?'

Ted returned slowly to reality. Josephine disappeared. His army vanished. He found himself gazing at the dark, intense Alec Skiddaw, thirty-seven and still beset by boils. Alec was dressed as a Bavarian peasant, with green hat and braces, and *Lederhosen* shorts. He had spindly, prematurely varicosed legs. The costume was chafing the boil on his scarred neck.

'Would you like some stuffed olives before the rush?' he asked.

'No thanks, Alec,' said Ted. 'Look at that buffet, Alec. Smoked salmon, fresh salmon, wild asparagus, caviare.' Alec Skiddaw examined the buffet table without interest. Food wasn't his province. Drink, women, boils and the narration of interminable family anecdotes were his provinces. 'Not that I rate caviare, me. In my book, it's just like fish roe.'

'*I'm* writing a book,' said Alec Skiddaw. 'An autobiography. It'll be about me and my life.'

'It's going to be a right classy do,' continued Ted. 'Some folk are going to have to revise their opinion of Ted Simcock, posthumously.'

'All the biographies you get are about famous people. You know about them buggers already. I'm writing about me and my family, what nobody knows owt about. That's more interesting. It's forced to be.'

'Well, not posthumously, but you know what I mean. When I've gone.'

Ted marched off to inspect the bar.

'That's right,' grumbled Alec Skiddaw. 'Don't listen to a word I say. Ignorant pig.'

The wind howled, and his boil throbbed. He began to distribute his olives.

'Elvis! It's fancy dress!'

Ted's elder son examined the patriotic decor cynically, thinking back to the last time he'd been here, when Carol Fordingbridge, now his ex-fiancée, had failed to be elected Miss Frozen Chicken (UK). He was wearing his usual grey-green suit.

'Yes, well, I'm afraid it just isn't me, Dad, isn't fancy dress,' he said.

'Oh heck,' said his father. 'It's my glittering, sophisticated farewell. So what do my sons do? One only says he *may* be able to get here, the other doesn't even bother to dress up. I mean! Really! Elvis!'

'Yes, well,' said Elvis. 'I just can't see Jean-Paul Sartre making a berk of himself by going to a party dressed as Napoleon.'

A nun walked through from the bar, cradling a pint of bitter in her gnarled fist. She smiled at Ted.

'Love it,' he said.

The nun moved on towards the buffet. She was followed by a frogman, taking long, absurd steps with his great webbed feet.

'Good. Well done,' said Ted.

Next came a penguin, which waved its flippers, spilling half its beer.

'Well done. Terrific,' said Napoleon, inspecting this absurd march past. 'Look at that,' he said to Elvis. 'If the lads from the Halifax Building Society aren't too proud to let their hair down, what's so special about Jean-Paul ruddy Sartre?' He scurried over to the new arrivals. 'Lads! Welcome to my humble party.'

'Champagne, sir?'

'I'd prefer a pint of bitter.'

'Certainly, sir.'

They set off towards the bar. The dark, intense Alec Skiddaw lowered his voice. 'I wish I'd got the courage to come dressed like you.'

Elvis glanced at Alec Skiddaw's Bavarian costume.

'I wish I'd got the courage to come dressed like you,' he said.

Three leggy waitresses took up their positions. They were dressed as French maids, with short black skirts and fishnet stockings.

From Ted and Corinna's new local, the Stag and Garter, there came an arab, Sherlock Holmes, and a nurse. From his bank, the listening bank, there came, appropriately, Big Ears, accompanied by Noddy and Alice-in-Wonderland.

The ravishing Liz Badger made a bold, sweeping entrance. She was magnificently dressed as Queen Elizabeth the First, with wide ruff and flaming red wig.

Ted scuttled towards her, making absurdly short steps in his stiff, painful boots. His spurs tinkled. He expected to see, in Liz's regal wake, an immaculate Sir Walter Raleigh. Imagine his surprise when Neville, who had come to Ted's Angling Club Christmas Party as Henry the Eighth, drifted in dressed as a police officer, his round, good-natured, eager-to-please face looking utterly incongruous under a helmet.

'Hello, hello, hello,' Neville began, in a funny policeman voice, bending his incipiently arthritic knees, 'I'm afraid I'm going to have to ask you a few questions, sir.'

'Yes, yes. Amazingly amusing. Incredibly inventive,' said Ted. 'They aren't exactly integrated costumes, though, are they? I mean . . . what's wrong with Raleigh?'

The immaculate Neville Badger, of Badger, Badger, Fox and Badger, looked as if he might be going to burst into tears. He excused himself and hurried off.

'Neville and Jane were Elizabeth and Raleigh,' explained Liz. 'They were Antony and Cleopatra. They were every romantic pair in history. "Jane loved fancy dress." It brings it all back. His perfect first marriage. I feel about two feet high, Ted.'

'You? Never!'

'Never before. A painful experience. Are you pleased? Liz's come-uppance?'

'Liz! 'Course I'm not! Really! You look grand, anyroad. You look right regal.' Liz accepted the compliment as her due. 'Liz?' Ted's tone changed abruptly, became confidential. 'Tonight may be the last time you and I see each other before I go to Nairobi. That means – well, it might be, mightn't it? – the last time we ever see each other again ever. Liz?' His face was close to his former lover's as he made his appeal. 'Will you do something really special for me tonight?'

'Ted!'

'Not that! How could you think that? And how could you of all people be outraged even if you did think it? No, what it is is . . . will you suspend your feud with Rita, for tonight at any rate? For Corinna and me? As a personal favour?'

'Rita is deliberately humiliating me, Ted. Lopping a lump off

162

our garden with her ring road. Destroying my magnolia and eighteen roses.'

Ted abandoned his request in the face of Liz's white-hot tirade. 'Enough said,' he said. 'Now come and meet the lads from the Halifax Building Society.'

Napoleon led Queen Elizabeth over to the nun, the frogman and the penguin. 'Lads,' he announced. 'This is Liz Badger.'

He left her to it and hurried over to Neville. Behind him, a party from Allied Dunbar entered, dressed as a Viking, a polar bear, Carmen Miranda and a French onion seller.

The wide windows of the Royalty Suite, being on the first floor of the hotel, afforded an excellent view over the ring road to a twee, red-brick executive housing estate, which appeared to have been built for very small executives with dwarf families and vast cars. Outside the hotel, facing the ring road, the flags of the major nations were the gale's playthings. The road was busy with French and German juggernauts and sad, defeated caravans returning early from wrecked holidays, swinging alarmingly in the wind. Later, the Meteorological Office would announce that this was the windiest June day since 1886. That day, in fact, Northallerton was windier than Cape Horn.

What did Neville see, as he gazed at this inspiring view? His dead wife, in her six handicap hey-day? The scene when this road, which would be known as the outer ring road when the outer inner relief ring road was built, was itself built, and beautiful women who were now in old people's homes had complained about the destruction of their magnolias? We will never know. Neville's eyes were faithful watch dogs, guarding his emotions.

'Neville!' said Ted.

Neville dragged himself away from the window. 'I know,' he said. 'I love Liz, Ted, but my love can't erase all memory of Jane. Every now and then something brings it back. And my heart and stomach burst.'

'I know,' said Ted. 'And in your time you and Jane dressed up as every pair in history.'

'Every pair except Joseph and Mary. But there are people in this town who'd be very offended if Liz came as the Virgin Mary.'

'I see their point. Neville? I've sown the seed. In Liz. Will you water that seed?'

'I beg your pardon?'

'I've asked her to end her feud with Rita, at least for . . . oh no!'

Rita stood in the doorway. She was magnificently dressed as Queen Elizabeth the First, with wide ruff and flaming red wig. Beside her stood Sir Walter Raleigh. Geoffrey Ellsworth-Smythe, Liz's brother, looking every inch the discoverer of tobacco, laid his cloak on the floor of the multi-purpose function room. Rita stepped regally across it. Geoffrey swung the cloak back onto his shoulders. And Rita saw Liz.

The two Queen Elizabeths stared at each other in horror. A transvestite who had hoped to create a sensation entered quite unnoticed.

Liz flounced across to Neville.

'Take me home,' she commanded.

'No, no. Look . . . Liz . . . oh Lord . . . let's . . . er . . . in the bar, quick.'

Neville hurried Liz into the bar.

Napoleon scuttled over to Rita and Geoffrey.

'Rita!' he said. 'Hello, Geoffrey. Rita! What on earth possessed you to come as Queen Elizabeth?'

'How like a man to blame his ex-wife rather than his ex-mistress for the unfortunate coincidence.'

'No, but . . . I mean . . . it isn't you, is it, isn't absolute monarchy? It isn't. Is it? I mean, you're a socialist councillor.'

'I'm also a woman.'

'And how!' said Geoffrey Ellsworth-Smythe. 'Oh sorry, Ted. I didn't mean to embarrass you.'

'Oh no,' said Ted. 'No, no, Rita and I are . . . '

'Yesterday's cold potatoes?' said Rita.

'Yes. No! Well, yes, in a . . . I mean, we're both in . . . well, I'm in love again, anyroad, and you . . . I mean . . . ' Ted abandoned this un-Napoleonic floundering.

'Where is Corinna?' asked Rita.

'Taking an age to get into her costume. It's her athlete's heel, is time. But, Rita, why not somebody more suitable? Florence Nightingale? Mrs Pankhurst? Germaine Greer? Why Elizabeth?'

'Because I thought I'd look magnificent.'

A monk and a spotty schoolgirl, both from Ted and Corinna's new local, waved their greeting. Ted nodded back.

'I rather hoped you might say I do,' said Rita drily.

'What? Oh, you do. You do. Magnificent.'

'Too late. And also we were lent our costumes by the Operatic. They've just done *Merrie England*. I'm sorry, Ted. I didn't mean to upset Liz tonight.'

'No, well, it can't be helped. You're very quiet, Geoffrey.'

'I think you rather lose the art of small talk, Ted, when you've spent twenty-two years among primitive tribes who don't speak a word of English.' Geoffrey's soft, luxuriant, greying beard lent authenticity to his Raleigh. Facial hair grows now much as it did then. His soft voice seemed gentle and courteous, yet it clearly riled Ted.

'You won't annoy me, Geoffrey,' said the former king of the boot scrapers. 'The great anthropologist won't get under my skin with his "I've seen the world" routine.'

The insulted emperor stalked off.

'I wasn't meaning anything like that,' said Geoffrey.

'I know. You wouldn't,' said Rita.

'I've never been anywhere where you have to be as careful what you say as you do here. When you've spent twenty-two years among . . . oh Lord. There I go again. The great anthropologist'll be upsetting you next.'

'I don't believe you could ever upset me, Geoffrey.'

'You're an extraordinary woman, Rita.'

'It's beginning to look that way. Odd, isn't it?'

'If you go home, everyone'll remember it as the time you both came as Queen Elizabeth and she stayed and you ran away.'

Liz contemplated the inevitable disdainfully.

'I haven't much choice, have I?' she said at last.

'I don't think so. Brazen it out. Show a bit of style.'

'It's a deliberate campaign to ridicule me.'

'If it is, and I don't say that I agree that it is, then by rising above it you'll make her look ridiculous.'

They were talking in low voices, even though they were quite a way from the bar counter, where Alec Skiddaw was serving a vampire and a pearly king and queen. The pearly king and queen were George and Iris Spooner, Ted's new neighbours in the flats. The vampire was a representative from the Bridlington Mercantile Credit Company.

Neville tried to shift his square, blue, aggressively modern chair closer to Liz. But it was fixed. It was intimacy-proof as well as fire-proof. He leant across, as best he could, and said, 'Darling? Do you remember what happened last time we came to this hotel?'

'We got engaged.'

'Yes. I love you . . . Liz.'

It was only for a split second that the panic-stricken doyen of the town's lawyers stumbled for his wife's name, but it was too long.

'You almost called me Jane, then.' Liz stood up, looking every inch a Queen of England. 'I wonder how many times you'll call me Jane before the evening's out.'

'No! I didn't. I couldn't. There's no . . . '

Liz finished it for him. 'No comparison?' And she swept out.

In the flexible, multi-purpose function room, the Dale Monsal Quartet were tuning up excruciatingly. They comprised piano, drums, saxophone and clarinet. The eponymous Dale Monsal, on sax, was a gloomy, withdrawn man with a long, sad face. The pianist was male, black, wiry, and all smiles. The drummer was male, white, huge and fierce. The clarinettist was female, white and mature. Normally she wore her hair in a severe bun which contrasted dramatically with her low-cut evening dresses. Today, she had sacrificed her bun and her bosom. The musicians were dressed as a barber's shop quartet, with striped jackets, bow ties and straw boaters.

Liz strode regally across the room, noticing nothing, not even seeing Geoffrey and Rita until, as she passed their table, Geoffrey called out, 'Liz!'

'Tell her how you used to pull my hair, Geoffrey.' Liz threw the words over her shoulder, barely checking her queenly stride.

'Did you?' said Rita.

'Not every day. I *was* pretty horrid to her. But then she was *extremely* horrid to me. She cut the squeak out of my favourite teddy. This'll be the final straw.'

'What will?'

'My loving you.'

'Ladies and gentlemen.' Dale Monsal intruded on their conversation. His slow, world-weary voice was as dry as a desert, as flat as a prairie. 'Ladies and gentlemen, my name is Dale Monsal, and this is my quartet.' He gestured limply towards his colleagues. 'Music is our business, and delight is our aim. Let us therefore plunge headlong, metaphorically speaking, into that mythically blue river which watered the fertile fields of the Austro-Hungarian Empire.' He half-turned towards his musicians. 'One, two, three.'

The Dale Monsal Quartet plunged headlong, metaphorically speaking, into something very similar to the familiar strains of 'The Blue Danube'.

'Is that why you love me?' Rita took up the conversation as if the interruption hadn't occurred. 'Because it'll be the final straw for Liz?'

'Of course not,' protested Geoffrey. 'It does add a twist of pepper to the stew, though.'

'The stew! What a romantic image. Not even a casserole.'

'I can't promise you romantic images, Rita. When you've been twenty-two years . . . oh my God! I must stop saying that!' Geoffrey's voice took on a gentle intensity. 'What I can promise you, my darling, is that I really will try never to say anything remotely hurtful to you. Good Lord! Who are those idiots?'

The much-travelled anthropologist was staring towards the door, as if he had seen something more extraordinary than anything his tribal rituals had ever afforded. Perhaps he had. Rodney and Betty and Jenny, dressed as huge peppers, stood side by side in the doorway.

'My two best friends and my daughter-in-law,' said Rita.

'Sorry!' said Geoffrey Ellsworth-Smythe.

Ted clanked across the dance floor towards the new arrivals. Rodney, Betty and Jenny had come, respectively, as red, green and yellow peppers. Their costumes were huge, brightly coloured, pepper-shaped bags with padded, ribbed, peppery shoulders. Their hands and lower arms protruded from holes. On their heads they wore flat hats, red, yellow and green, with upturned, incipiently drooping stalks. The hats were shaped like the bits that you cut out of peppers before you remove the pith and seeds. Careful thought had gone into these costumes. The three peppers smiled with modest self-satisfaction, awaiting Ted's compliments. They were somewhat disappointed to hear him say, 'What are you – a set of traffic lights?'

'Peppers,' said Rodney with as much dignity as he could muster.

'You what?'

'Symbolic of our vegetarian restaurant,' said Betty.

'Advertising your business, even at our farewell do?'

'There's no room for shrinking violets in business, Ted,' said Rodney.

'Rodney! Look!' Betty gave an un-pepperlike whoop. 'Rita and Liz have both come as Queen Elizabeth!'

'Betty! Dignity! As befits joint managing directors of Sillitoe's.' But Rodney's eyes followed Betty's. 'Oooh! Yes! They look identical!'

'Oh Lord,' said Jenny. 'I must go to . . . whichever of them I decide I feel sorriest for most.'

Jenny edged past Betty. So large were their costumes that both women had to turn sideways before she could get through. She hurried round the side of the dance floor, where the onion seller was getting on very well with Alice-in-Wonderland, Dick Whittington was waltzing sedately with his cat, and Punch, alias Larry Benson, of fitted kitchen fame, was tripping round with Judy, alias his lady wife, who was actually no lady.

Jenny found herself on collision course with the cynical Elvis, her brother-in-law, her lover. His expression owed more to his cynicism than his love.

'I know,' said Jenny. 'Simone de Beauvoir wouldn't have been seen dead dressed as a green pepper.'

'I didn't say anything.'

'Haven't you come as anything?'

'Can't. I might get bleeped.'

'What?'

'The news desk has given us bleepers. I mean, I couldn't go on a big story dressed as a parsnip, could I?'

'You wouldn't go during Ted's farewell party, would you?'

'I might have to. Your true radio reporter's never off duty. I mean, it might be a big ecological disaster – every fish in the Gadd poisoned by leaking drums of cyanide. Couldn't stuff myself on smoked salmon while those poor silver-bellied fish are gasping for life, could I?'

'Of course you couldn't. I shouldn't have . . . oh, Elvis.' Jenny kissed him. Her eyes filled with tears. In the pools of her eyes, fish thrashed in frenzy before sinking lifeless beneath the rancorous, foamy waters. 'Oh Lord. Those poor fish. I think I'm going to cry.'

She rushed off as fast as her costume allowed, to the sound of muted applause from the oddly-garbed dancers. She fought back her tears. The dark, intense Alec Skiddaw, smiling darkly, intensely, offered her champagne. She accepted. One glass wouldn't upset her milk too much.

'How's that husband of yours?' enquired Alec Skiddaw solicitously.

'Fine. Great.' She gave a watery smile.

'I'll never forget how worried you both were because you felt you hadn't treated me as a social equal.'

'Oh . . . well . . . yes . . . silly.' Please change the subject, Alec.

'I said to myself, they may have problems but they'll pull through. I know,' said Alec Skiddaw with ghastly encouragement. 'Well, I have this slight psychic gift inherited from a great aunt who married a chiropodist in Skegness.'

'Oh, stuff your . . . ' Jenny's green stalk wobbled with her distress. 'Oh, I'm sorry, Alec. Oh, Alec.'

'Never mind, madam. It's all in a day's work,' said Alec Skiddaw. He sounded calm and resigned, but his boil pulsated with hurt fury. Pity not Alec Skiddaw for his boils, gentle reader. They were the device whereby the poison of his dark intensity escaped.

Ted hadn't yet offered the Sillitoes a drink. It was a delicate subject, after their behaviour at the grand opening.

'Er . . . champagne?' he said. 'Or are you still . . . ?'

'You may not have noticed,' said Rodney, 'but – '

'At the grand opening of Sillitoes,' interrupted Betty.

'We both got – '

'Slightly inebriated.'

'It showed us the error of our ways.'

'You've given up drink for good.' Ted nodded his simulated approval.

'No!' said Betty. 'We've got a full licence.'

'You don't have to be miserable to be a vegetarian,' said Rodney.

Behind them, the dance floor was steadily filling. Arab danced with squaw, teddy boy with drum majorette, vicar with belly dancer. A can-can girl waltzed sedately to the Dale Monsal Quartet's unintentionally original rendition of Strauss's 'Rose from the South'. Ted Simcock, secure in the success of his glittering party, felt that it was time to take a magnanimous interest in the Sillitoes' business.

'How's business?' he asked.

'Good,' said Rodney.

'Very good,' said Betty.

'Well . . . good. No, I mean that . . . that's good.'

'Good,' said Rodney. 'I'm glad you mean it, Ted.'

'No, I do,' said Ted. 'I really do mean it.'

'Well, yes, we believe you,' said Rodney.

'Good. Because I mean it. No, I really do. Our prospects are good, too. Corinna has made a flying visit to Nairobi. She's already negotiated for four prime sites for our restaurants. She says the prospects are very good.'

'Good.'

'Very good.'

Betty looked round the dance floor. She searched the tables. She glanced towards the bar.

'Where is Corinna?' she asked.

'Where indeed?' Ted sighed. He straightened his great Napoleonic hat nervously. 'It's the rift in the diamond. The flaw in the lute.'

'What is?' Rodney was puzzled.

'Corinna's timekeeping. Excuse me. That penguin's eating all the salmon.'

Rodney and Betty watched Ted as he scampered towards the laden tables.

'I do hope nothing's wrong,' said Betty thoughtfully.

170

'Oh, so do I,' agreed Rodney fervently. 'So do I. No, I really do.'

'Good.'

Simon Rodenhurst, of Trellis, Trellis, Openshaw and Finch, arrived arm-in-arm with his girl-friend, the short-sighted Lucinda Snellmarsh, of Peacock, Tester and Devine. Simon was wearing a long dressing gown, and carried a cigarette holder. His hair was smoothed back. Lucinda wore a low-cut black dress with a silver stole. She also carried a cigarette holder.

'Hello, Simon. Hello, Lucinda.' Bathing in his triumph, Ted welcomed them like old friends.

'I'm Noël Coward,' said Simon.

'Of course you are.'

'I'm Mae West.'

Ted cast an unflattering, chauvinistic glance towards Lucinda's bosom.

There was an awkward pause.

'Quite a few people already,' said Simon.

'You'll have to do a bit better than that,' said Ted.

'Sorry?'

'As Noël Coward. Be a bit more sparkling.'

'Oh. Yes. Right. Absolutely.'

There was another awkward pause.

'Well come on, Lucinda,' said Ted, abandoning Simon as a dead loss. 'Say something outrageously provocative and sexy.'

Lucinda thought hard. 'Oh lorks!' she said. 'I don't think I can.'

The two young estate agents moved on into the swirling party. The cynical Elvis Simcock slouched towards them.

'Hello, Noël,' he said. 'Say something amazingly witty, then.'

'Oh belt up, you stupid twit,' quipped Noël Coward.

'Very good. Such elegance,' said Elvis with mock elegance. 'Anyone got a pencil? I must write that down.'

'I'm beginning to wonder if this was such a good idea,' confessed Simon Rodenhurst, of Trellis, Trellis, Openshaw and Finch to Lucinda Snellmarsh, of Peacock, Tester and Devine.

The self-satisfaction brought on by Elvis's rout of Noël Coward lasted 2.17 seconds. Then he came face to face with Carol

Fordingbridge. Carol was wearing a striped low-cut Victorian dress with a large bustle. Elvis knew straightaway that she was supposed to be a woman from the past. Beyond that he hadn't a clue.

'Hello, Carol,' he said. 'You look . . . '

'Ridiculous?'

'No. Great.' She did. 'Who are you?'

'Marie Lloyd.'

'Ah! Right. Who?'

'She was a legendary comedienne and singer of music hall songs. My dad had this thing about her, so I've sort of grown up with her.'

'Oh. Right. Well, terrific.'

'I like your outfit,' said Carol. 'Very imaginative.'

Carol left Elvis wishing just for a moment that he had come in fancy dress.

Ted recognised Carol instantly.

'Hello, Carol.' He kissed her. 'Fantastic! You've got Vesta Tilley off to a tee.'

'I'm Marie Lloyd.'

'Absolutely. There's champagne, caviare, asparagus, wild salmon, Dale Monsal. Enjoy yourself.'

'By heck, it sounds quite a classy do,' said Carol.

'Don't sound so surprised,' said Ted. 'He's quite a classy fellow, Ted Simcock.'

There was applause as the Dale Monsal Quartet reached the end of 'Rose from the South' without any major disaster. Ted strolled round the edge of the floor, inspecting his absurd troops. He smiled at a Roman, beamed at a clown, nodded approval of a witch. He passed a man covered from head to foot in bandages. He had tiny slits round his eyes and mouth and was trying to drink champagne through a straw.

'Don't tell me,' said Ted. 'The invisible man!' He chuckled. 'And you're sweating in there and wondering why the hell you chose it.'

The invisible man nodded, and grimaced invisibly.

A man dressed as a police sergeant appeared in the doorway. Ted intercepted him, still smiling at the invisible man's discomfiture.

'Bad luck,' he said. 'We've got a policeman already.'

'Mr Simcock?' said the man, who had ginger hair and freckles.

Ted nodded, thinking, 'You shouldn't have come as a policeman. It doesn't go with ginger hair.'

'I'm afraid I'm going to have to ask you some questions,' continued the newcomer.

'Yes, yes, you've got all the chat,' said Ted. 'Champagne?'

They both had this routine off to a tee.

'I don't when I'm on duty,' they said in unison.

'Very good,' said Ted. 'Brilliantly original. Well done.'

'No, sir. I really am a police officer.' The man showed Ted his identification. 'Sergeant Mallet, B Division. Do you know a woman called Jessica Mardenborough?'

'No.' But Ted's smile wobbled. His face was a half-set jelly.

'Also known as Fiona Benbow-Jones,' said the man who called himself Sergeant Mallet. 'Also known as Corinna Price-Rodgerson.'

The jelly set rapidly. 'If this is a joke . . . ' began Ted uncertainly.

'I'm afraid it isn't a joke, sir.' Sergeant Mallet spoke quietly, deferentially. Respect for authority had been branded into him, and it was difficult to speak other than deferentially to a man dressed as Napoleon. 'The woman, whose real name, incidentally, is Mavis Stant, has been arrested at the airport. She was trying to leave on a false passport.'

'If this *is* a joke, you're in trouble, pal.'

'It's no joke, sir. She's a con artist and bigamist. I'm sorry, sir.'

There was a tiny twitch on Ted's face. Just a quiver on the lips, as if the jelly had been poked with a feather.

'Oh,' he said. 'Oh heck. Oh utter and confounded heck.'

Neville Badger appeared between them, smiling with vaguely bold roguishness. 'Hello hello hello,' he said, in his funny-policeman voice. He smiled at Sergeant Mallet, including him in the jape. 'I'm going to have to ask you to accompany us to the station.'

'Oh, belt up, you twerp,' said Ted savagely.

Ted rushed out into the corridor. The Dale Monsal Quartet

ground out 'Hello, Dolly' remorselessly. The real policeman glared at the false policeman and hurried out after Ted.

The Dale Monsal Quartet played 'All I Do Is Dream of You' in their own style, which had more than once been described as inimitable. Marie Lloyd danced with Batman, a kilted Scotsman attempted a Scottish dance he didn't know with a crimson-cheeked cowgirl who didn't know it either, and a green pepper refused on moral grounds to dance with a bullfighter. People toyed with smoked salmon and indulged in asparagus. Some ate caviare with enjoyment. Others pretended to eat caviare with enjoyment. One Queen Elizabeth talked happily with Sir Walter Raleigh. The other Queen Elizabeth talked not quite so happily with a police officer. Noël Coward cracked an elegant *bon mot* to a gangster's moll. The moll didn't laugh.

The music ceased. Mild applause spattered out. Dale Monsal leant forward and spoke. His voice was like a bulb field in November.

'The word "gay" has developed conurbations which make it impossible to use in its original meaning,' he announced. 'I can't talk today about "Gay Paree". Nevertheless, it is to the elegant capital of "La Belle France" that we turn next for our musical inspiration. Take it away, maestros. *Un, deux, trois.*'

The maestros took it away. Strains of 'The Skater's Waltz' filled the room.

Ted returned to face his public. He tried to smile at the vicar, who was actually Sid Crabtree from the wet fish shop in Tannergate, where they shopped for fish of a Saturday because Corinna liked . . . Corinna!

The vicar smiled back, so Ted's smile must have worked. He smiled at the vicar's partner, the spotty schoolgirl from the Stag and Garter, Ted and Corinna's new . . . Corinna! They'd just begun to find their feet in the Stag and Garter, which had been called the Star and Garter until an elderly signwriter had made an error and a soft-hearted brewery official had allowed the mistake to stand – in olden days, when there were horse-drawn cabs and brewers with soft hearts.

The spotty schoolgirl with her jolly-hockey-sticks garb and the stick-on spots from the joke shop in Arbitration Road smiled back. His smile *was* working! Amazing. Arbitration

Road! Where he and Corinna had planned . . . Corinna! All roads led to her. All thoughts ended with her. Smile at the polar bear. 'Hello, Dave, all right?' Smile at Mrs Fortescue from Flat 3, dressed as a horrible baby . . . silly old . . . Flat 3. The flats. Corinna.

This wouldn't do. He must at least simulate normality, if he was to survive. He set off across the crowded floor towards that incongruous couple, the policeman and Queen Elizabeth the First. He threw little remarks at the throng as he passed. 'Enjoying yourselves? Good. Well done. Love your outfit. Keep at it.' To his amazement his voice sounded quite normal, as if his world hadn't ended.

'Ted's bearing down on us,' said the policeman. 'Let's dance.'

'No,' said Queen Elizabeth. 'If you won't dance with me because it reminds you of Jane, I won't dance with you just to avoid . . . hello, Ted.'

'I wanted a word with Neville,' said Ted.

'Nothing's private in our marriage, Ted,' said Liz. 'Remember what our children said. Marriage is a totality of shared experience.'

'Pompous know-all pipsqueaks, fat lot of good it did them. Well . . . all right, then. You needn't go, Liz.'

'Thank you, sir.' Liz gave a mock salute.

'It's just that . . . ' the emperor gulped, ' . . . I find apologising difficult.'

'I'd have thought you'd get enough practice.'

'You see why I wanted to talk to Neville alone.'

'Sorry.'

Ted turned to Neville. Behind them Judy, alias Larry Benson's lady wife, was touching Sherlock Holmes in ways that no lady should attempt with a man who is not her husband to so demure a tune as 'The Skater's Waltz'. Even Doctor Watson would have deduced that she was dancing on thin ice.

'I'm . . . er . . . sorry if I was a trifle . . . angry and rude earlier,' began Ted pawkily.

'Don't worry, Ted,' said Neville. 'I'm used to it. I try to be pleasant to everybody and then I think, "Oh Lord. They're going to be rude to me." And they are! It gives me a certain grim satisfaction at my accurate prediction.'

'It's just that – you dressed as a policeman, and there being a real policeman here – I – '

'Why *was* the real policeman here?' asked Liz.

'Ah. Er . . . ' He couldn't bring himself to admit the ghastly truth, as if making it public would make it irrevocable. 'They'd had a message from Corinna. She . . . can't come. Touch of flu.'

'And she rang the police?'

'Forgot the name of the hotel. Not herself, poor darling. Semi-delirious.'

'And the police came to tell you?' The lawyer in Neville was outraged. 'And they claim they're grossly under-manned!'

'So . . . er . . . I was that disappointed – about Corinna – that I flew off the . . . sorry.'

Ted fled, smiled with excruciating brightness at a Mexican who was clinking champagne glasses with a flapper, said, 'Having a good time? Great. Don't stint. There's plenty more where that came from,' and blundered on, going nowhere.

Rita pursued him.

'What's wrong?' she said.

'Wrong? Why should anything be wrong? You can't believe things can go right for me, can you? Well, they can go right and they have gone right, and nothing's wrong. All right?'

'You don't live with someone for twenty-five years without getting to know them. And I know that something is wrong.'

Ted opened his mouth indignantly, intending to voice an unequivocal denial. He heard himself, as from a great distance, say, 'Want to gloat, do you?'

'What a small-minded prat you can be, Ted.'

'Rita!'

'I do not want to gloat. Maybe the sort of person I was would have gloated. The sort of person I find I can be doesn't want to gloat. What's wrong, Ted?'

'It's Corinna.' His voice was so low that passing onion sellers and transvestites couldn't possibly hear, and even Queen Elizabeth the First had to lean forward to catch his whisper. 'She's gone.'

'Gone?'

'Gone. None of it was true, Rita. Her name even. I've been

conned. Me, Ted Simcock, man of the world, blunt no-nonsense Yorkshireman, shrewd businessman, conned. Because of love.'

'Oh, Ted. Did you ever really . . . no.'

'Did I ever really what?'

'Well . . . oh Lord . . . I can't say it.'

Ted was indignant. 'I'm a mature businessman with a strong character and personality,' he said. 'So don't patronise me, Rita. All right?'

'All right. Well . . . I mean . . . didn't it strike you as rather unbelievable that a beautiful . . . elegant . . . sophisticated . . . wealthy . . . virgin should fall head over heels in love with you on sight?'

Ted opened his mouth desperately, like a poisoned fish in the polluted Gadd. No sound emerged.

'Well . . . didn't it?'

'Well, yes. Yes, of course. I was right suspicious from the word go. I mean . . . I was.' Ted's lie began to gather pace as it rolled unstoppably downhill, like his life. 'Right from the start I thought, "Hey up, Ted. What's this one's game?" "Double-barrelled?" I thought. "Give over. Father a bishop? Whole family conveniently far away in Africa? Pull the other one. She's a . . . tarty piece underneath."' Ted's eyes filled with wonderment, as he realised that he was echoing Sandra's words. Wonderment, and just a tear or two. 'But.'

'But?'

'Love, Rita. I loved her.'

'Oh, Ted. Forget her.'

'How can I? The cow's gone off with all my money.'

'What? What money? I thought you didn't have any.'

'Rodney gave me quite a whack for the foundry.' He smiled mechanically as Big Ears and Noddy passed. 'It was a prime site.'

'But you went bankrupt. Didn't it all go to the creditors?'

'Rita! You don't give it all. You keep some back. I stashed some away in a secret account in Jersey. What do you think I am – naïve?'

'Perhaps slightly naïve if you gave it all to Corinna.' Rita spoke gently, as if embarrassed to be given the chance of making such an overwhelming reply. 'Especially as you say you knew she wasn't what she said she was.'

'She showed me the deeds. A hotel restaurant in Nairobi. A prime corner site in Mogadishu. It all looked so legal, I never dreamt. . . . Oh, Rita. Love is blind. I mean, you know what sexual passion is like.'

'I do now, yes.'

'Rita!'

'Sorry,' Rita was contrite. 'Oh, I'm sorry, Ted. I didn't mean . . . but, you see, what I've found with Geoffrey is so unexpected, so utterly . . . ' she searched for a word that would express the strength of it without sounding boastful ' . . . good, that I feel the need to shout about it. I'm only human.'

'So, I've got very little left. Just enough to pay for all this. Perhaps. I'm ruined, Rita.'

'What'll you do?'

'Tomorrow? Cry. Today? Have a wonderful party.'

Ted rubbed his hands together and strode boldly round the edge of the dance floor towards the Sillitoes. The Dale Monsal Quartet, still in mercilessly Gallic vein, were giving their unique version of 'Clopin Clopant'.

The joint big wheels behind Sillitoe's were sitting watching the dancing and sipping champagne with a contentment that almost purred.

'Hello, Rodney,' said Ted jovially. 'Hello, Betty. Friendship – you can't whack it.'

'What's happened, Ted?' asked Rodney.

'Happened? Does something have to have happened before I tell you how much I value your friendship?'

'No! 'Course not!' said Betty. 'Don't be ridiculous. What's happened?'

'Nothing's happened, for God's sake. Sorry. No, I just thought, seeing you two sitting there, making utter prats of yourselves, I felt a surge of warmth for you both.'

'What do you mean, "making utter prats of ourselves"?' Rodney seemed greatly puzzled.

'Dressed as peppers.'

'Oh Lord!' Betty glanced at the great yellow pepper which encased her. 'I forgot. But what do you mean – "prats"?'

'Well . . . I just meant . . . everybody dressed as Napoleon, Noël Coward, Queen Elizabeth, two Queen Elizabeths . . . '

'Yes!' Rodney and Betty laughed.

178

'And you, peppers. You look ridiculous.'

'I see!' said Betty with as much hurt dignity as a pepper could muster.

'I see nothing ridiculous in coming as peppers,' said the red-faced, red-capped, red pepper at her side. 'It's a little less pretentious than identifying with Napoleon.'

'Well said, Rodney. It needed to be said.'

'Our costumes symbolise not only our business.'

'That's unimportant, comparatively.'

'They symbolise healthy eating, organic eating. We've come as organic peppers, incidentally, with no pesticides.'

'They symbolise the environment.'

'Red for danger, because it's in danger.'

'Green for . . . green, because that's the solution.'

'And yellow?'

Ted's question staunched the flow of rhetoric completely. Betty looked down at her yellow costume, and looked to Rodney for an answer. Came there none. The Sillitoes were two distinctly nonplussed peppers.

Then inspiration, that occasional visitor, knocked on Rodney's brain.

'Birth control,' he said.

'Absolutely. Bir . . . you what, Rodney?' said Betty.

'Yellow for fighting the menace of the population explosion. Because one in three people in the world is born Chinese.'

'Aaaah! That's clever, Rodney.' Betty leant across and kissed him, no mean feat when they were both wearing peppery bell-tents. 'I love him,' she said proudly to Ted.

'And I love her,' echoed Rodney.

'Thank you, Ted,' said Betty.

'What for?'

'For being happy with Corinna. Because, because you're happy, we don't have to hide how happy we are for fear of seeming smug, which we did have to do, while you weren't happy.'

'So we're happy that you're happy.'

'Very happy.'

'Where is Corinna?'

'Er . . . ill.'

'Ted!'

179

'Nothing serious.' Ted smiled, trying to look calm, trying to allay Betty's intuitive alarm. 'Touch of the dreaded lurgies.'

He adjusted his Napoleonic hat and sauntered off, attempting not entirely successfully to look a picture of insouciance.

'Ladies and gentlemen,' said Dale Monsal, whose face would have made the Stag at Bay look insouciant. He had abandoned his boater. His hair was slicked wispily and shinily onto his pate. 'Next, in more modern vein, a tune forever associated with a star long dead, but still shining brightly in the showbiz constellation. Or is he dead? Rumours that he has been sighted are rife. Of whom do I speak? I'll give you a clue. It isn't Hitler.'

Dale Monsal gave a series of deep, pneumatic wheezes. They were to laughter what his quartet was to music.

'Yes,' he announced, almost dramatically. 'You've guessed it. It's Elvis.'

The Dale Monsal Quartet wound themselves up into 'Blue Suede Shoes'. And Elvis Simcock glowered.

'Ignore it, Elvis,' said his lover.

'I was ignoring it till you said "ignore it".'

'Don't let's row. We mustn't ever row. I couldn't bear it. Come on, dance. Show people that you don't mind being called Elvis.'

'I do mind.'

'All the more reason for showing that you don't, then.'

So, the great communicator danced grumpily with his pepper. Vicar and schoolgirl, Robin Hood and squaw, transvestite and nun tried to relive their youth. And Ted Simcock approached his ex-wife, who was watching peacefully with her bearded anthropologist.

'May I borrow Rita, Geoffrey?' asked Ted.

'She isn't a library book,' said Geoffrey.

'Thanks, Geoffrey,' said Rita, but she allowed herself to be led away by Ted. 'You asking me to dance?' she asked her ex-husband in astonishment.

'They're playing my music, Rita.'

Neville beamed bottomlessly at the happiness of his fellow men. Liz gave a snort of irritation and slipped across to buttonhole her brother before Rita returned.

'You don't really find her attractive, do you?' she said, indicating the other Queen of England with a tiny movement of her flaming head.

'Yes, I do,' said Geoffrey softly. 'Very much. Do you disapprove?'

'Of course.'

'Why "of course"?'

'She isn't one of us, Geoffrey. She isn't our class.'

'Oh. Of course! How dim of me.'

'You may mock, but this is England.'

'Surely that doesn't matter today, even in England?'

'It's still important to some people. Not everything this country once stood for has been lost along with my magnolia. Rita's father was a common little man who talked in public about . . . breaking wind, but he didn't use those words, he used a – what's the opposite of a euphemism? A malphemism, I suppose.'

'Good heavens.' Her brother's reply was silkily sarcastic. 'And the vulgarity will come out in Rita, who will start behaving like a common fishwife, a phrase which I have always thought very unfair to fishwives, who aren't common at all; they're extremely rare.' The Dale Monsal Quartet were playing 'Rock Around the Clock' now. Liz was annoyed to find herself leaning forward to hear Geoffrey's outwardly gentle words, even though she knew that she would hate what she heard. 'You're worried that when I take her to the anthropologists' dinner she'll ask all the other anthropologists how often they fart.'

They were back in the nursery, in times long forgotten.

'You've always hated me, haven't you?' said Liz.

'Yes.'

Geoffrey Ellsworth-Smythe smiled.

Napoleon rocked, Queen Elizabeth rolled, Dale Monsal almost smiled, Dick Whittington goosed his cat, the can-can dancer phoned the baby-sitter, Sir Walter Raleigh smiled deep in his courtly beard, and only Ted and Rita knew Ted's dreadful secret.

Neville Badger, carrying his helmet, smiling innocently, like a man who has never falsified anybody's confession, hurried to the social rescue of Carol Fordingbridge.

'Hello. Lovely,' he announced.

'Thank you.'

'I wish I could have *seen* Gertie Gitana.'

'So do I, but I'm Marie Lloyd.'

'I wish I could have seen Marie Lloyd. Men were men then.'

'You what?'

'I'd have expected young men to swarm round you like bees round a honeypot. If I was a young man I would.'

'You'd look ridiculous.'

'I beg your pardon?'

'Swarming, on your own. For the record, Neville, not that it's any of your business, but I was asked out tonight by a physics teacher, a welder and a quality control supervisor at the biscuit factory. I turned all three down because I wanted to be at Ted's farewell.'

'I always try to say the right thing.' Neville was truly bewildered. 'Why do I always end up putting my foot in it.'

'Because you always try to say the right thing,' said Carol Fordingbridge. 'It's a right daft basis for conversation, is that.'

She moved off, only to return instantly.

'I'm sorry,' she said. She kissed his bemused cheek. 'You mean to be kind.'

The rock and roll came to an end. The middle-aged clapped wildly, to preserve their youth for a few more seconds.

In the bar, Elvis and Jenny found Simon and Lucinda united by long cigarette holders and silence.

'Enjoying yourselves?' asked Elvis unnecessarily.

'No.' In his embarrassment, Simon had forgotten that he wasn't supposed to be speaking to Elvis. 'Coming as Noël Coward has been the biggest mistake of my life. It's shown me what a dimwit I am.'

At the counter, Alec Skiddaw was telling a long story to Larry Benson, who wasn't listening. He was thinking about his lady wife, and about how she was no lady.

'The brains we inherit are a matter of luck, Simon,' said Jenny, 'so if you find you're . . . well, not thick exactly . . . '

'Oh, charming. Who'd have sisters?'

182

In his indignation, Simon raised his voice. The onion seller, who was chatting up Alice-in-Wonderland and finding that she wasn't taking him seriously because of his strings of onions, gave him a brief glance before returning to his lost cause.

'Well you called yourself a dimwit,' said Jenny.

'It's all right for Simon to say it,' said Lucinda. 'It's not all right for anyone else to say it.'

'Right! No risk in you being called thick,' said Simon admiringly.

'No. Just wet.'

'You what?' said Elvis.

'Coming as Mae West has shown me how crabby and inhibited and English I am,' said Lucinda. 'I've been going out with Simon for weeks and I haven't once said . . . ' She embarked on an impression of Mae West without conviction, "Come up and see me some time." Nor has he. Said to me to come up and see him some time.'

'No,' said Simon. 'I want to save . . . '

'Save what?'

'All that.'

'You see. Passion. Sex . . . '

'Lucinda!'

'Our writhing, intertwined bodies . . . '

'*Lucinda!*'

'What does Simon call it? "All that"! He's as bad as me.'

There was a supercilious smile on Elvis's thrusting media man face, but Jenny was listening with steadily dawning delight.

'But, sweetybonce,' Simon continued, 'if I'd gone on after that, what do you think I'd have said? "I want to save 'all that' . . . ?"'

'Until?'

'Until what?'

'Until . . . we're married?'

'Yes.'

'Is this a proposal?' Lucinda sounded almost incredulous.

Simon looked almost appalled at this unexpected turn in the conversation.

'Well, yes,' he said, as if moved by logic rather than emotion, 'I suppose it is. Will you marry me?'

'Well, yes, I suppose I will.'

183

They tried to shift their fixed, intimacy-proof chairs. They leant across the chrome arms and kissed. Their kiss, though uncomfortable, was long.

'Congratulations!' said Elvis, watching them with an air of disbelief. 'A union of true estate agents.'

'Elvis!' Jenny's outrage was softened by affection.

'Simon may be thick,' persisted the cynical Elvis Simcock, 'Lucinda may be wet, but between them they ought to be able to find a really nice house to be thick and wet in.'

'Elvis! Don't be stupid,' said Jenny.

'But he *is* stupid,' said her brother ferociously.

Gentle applause filtered in from the function room.

'Well at least I'm clever enough not to come in fancy dress,' said Elvis. 'A Noël Coward who can't be witty, a Mae West who can't be sexy, a Marie Lloyd who can't sing.' He shook his head, sadly, regretting the infinite folly of the rest of humankind.

'Ladies and gentlemen,' said Dale Monsal, with the animation of a constipated walrus, 'a lovely young lady, Miss Carol Fordingbridge, alias the legendary Miss Marie Lloyd, will now transport you back, across the great prairies of time, to the vintage years of the music hall.'

The long-haired Marie Lloyd flounced prettily onto the stage, just as her ex-fiancé entered from the bar with his lover.

There was warm applause. Carol began with a pretty little bustle-bouncing dance. Elvis's half opened mouth looked a quarter cynical, a quarter astonished, and half baked.

All eyes were on Carol as she began to sing.

'I'm very fond of ruins, ruins I love to scan.'

Her voice was confident and charming, if not expert.

'You'd say I'm very fond of ruins if you saw my old man.'

Her cockney accent was quite adequate. Ted watched her wistfully.

'I went out in the country for a stroll the other day.'

She was capturing the style and spirit of Marie Lloyd. The invisible man nodded his bandaged head in time with the music. Elvis gawped. Jenny, seeing Elvis gawping, frowned.

'I love to study history and the pubs along the way.'

Jenny linked arms with Elvis.

'I came across an abbey that was crumbling all to bits.'

'You do still love me, don't you?' asked Jenny.

'Fool,' said Elvis.

Alec Skiddaw was surprised to see Ted Simcock enter the bar at that magical moment, when all his guests were held in a time warp by Carol Fordingbridge.

'Pint of Guinness, please,' said Ted flatly.

'My ex-brother-in-law – well, he's my brother-in-law again now – he likes his Guinness,' said Alec Skiddaw as he poured Ted's pint. 'His first wife, my sister, who's now his third wife, she drinks Courvoisier.' He handed Ted the dark bitter brew with its milk-white top.

Ted held his pint up and stared at it. 'That's better,' he said. 'As black as my mood.'

'I beg your pardon, sir?' said Alec Skiddaw.

'I was watching that girl. Carol. Pretty, Lively. Bright.' Carol's lively, bright voice floated prettily in from the function room. 'Life ahead of her. And I was thinking of my life, behind me. A mess, Alec.'

'A mess, sir? You? I find that hard to believe. You're a man of substance.' There was an indignant edge to Alec Skiddaw's voice, as if his own life was so much worse that Ted had no right to complain.

'An utter and total mess, Alec.'

Ted spoke so darkly, so intensely, that all the wind was knocked out of Alec Skiddaw's sails. He searched hard for a suitable reply.

'That was what broke their marriage up, first time round,' he said. 'She poured her Courvoisier in his Guinness, and he poured it all over her new perm.'

Carol was thundering towards the end of her song.

'Outside the Oliver Cromwell last Saturday night.'

Ted slid back in with his Guinness, and stood at the back of the crowd.

'I was one of the ruins that Cromwell knocked about a bit.'

There was warm applause. Elvis clapped as in a dream. Carol took a brief curtsey. Neville whispered to Dale Monsal. Dale Monsal nodded gravely.

'Ladies and gentlemen,' he said, as if announcing the outbreak of war. 'It's time to silence the strings and put the lid on the ivories for a few moments. Mr Neville Badger would like to address a few words to your host.'

Rita shivered. 'Oh dear,' she said.

Neville climbed onto the platform, and Elvis's bleeper went. 'News desk!' he said excitedly.

'Not now!' said Jenny, but already Elvis was gone.

'Hello, hello, hello,' began Neville. He produced a police whistle and blew it enthusiastically. 'It's a fair cop.'

'Oh, Neville,' said Liz to herself.

'Ladies and gentlemen, penguins, peppers and polar bears,' continued her husband. 'This is a sad day.'

'You can say that again,' thought Ted.

'A sad day,' said Neville again. 'Ted Simcock is leaving us. Nairobi's gain is our loss. Many of us here today, and not gone tomorrow, though he will be, may never see that loved and trusted face again.'

'Don't overdo it,' thought Rita.

'Tonight, Ted has laid on a fabulous do. The champagne has flowed. The caviare has gone down like . . . ' Neville searched for a suitable simile.

'A lead balloon,' suggested Rodney to himself.

Neville found his simile. 'Like caviare. We've had music.'

'Almost,' thought Betty.

'We've had dancing. Sadly, one important person has missed our junketings. Her name is Corinna Price-Rodgerson.'

'Oh no it isn't,' thought Rita.

'Why is she not here?' asked Neville rhetorically.

'Should I tell them?' thought Ted.

'Because she is indisposed. Never mind. I don't mean, never mind that she's indisposed; we all mind.'

'Oh, Neville,' groaned Liz silently.

'I mean, we will continue to enjoy ourselves.'

'Speak for yourself,' thought Simon.

'We will enjoy ourselves, despite her sad absence, which make the heart grow fonder, and so say all of us. This isn't the time for speeches.'

'Well shut up, then,' implored Geoffrey secretly.

'So I want to end . . . '

'Hooray,' thought Jenny.

' . . . by asking you all . . . ' Neville beamed with the innocence of a man who has never raised a truncheon in anger, ' . . . to join me . . . '

'Oh no!' thought Rita.

' . . . in singing . . . '

'Oh Lord!' thought Liz.

' . . . "For He's a Jolly Good Fellow".'

'Oh heck!' thought Ted.

Neville led the singing. All Ted's guests joined in. Witch and vampire, polar bear and nun, yellow pepper and Noël Coward, all sang enthusiastically.

Ted stepped onto the platform. He faced his guests and adjusted his hat. His complexion was pale.

'Ladies and gentlemen,' he said. 'I . . . ' his voice was shaky, 'I'm overcome. I am. I'm overcome. The way you sang that song. The revelation of how you feel about me. It was . . . a revelation. Ladies and gentlemen, don't regard this as "goodbye" – more "*au revoir*". I will probably see you all again sooner than you think.'

'Hooray!' cried Neville.

'Shut up!' hissed Liz.

'So . . . no sadness, eh?' But Ted's voice was breaking. 'Oh Lord. What a sentimental old fool I am. Thank you.'

Ted hurried off the platform. There was loud applause.

As Ted blundered blindly through the gathered guests towards the exit, Elvis rushed in, his media-hound face weighty with exciting news.

Jenny and Rita scurried over to hear it.

'It's our Paul,' said Elvis. 'He's been arrested.'

'Arrested? What for?' said Ted, just as Neville reached them, his face alive with concern.

'There's been a big demonstration. He threw an egg at the Prime Minister.'

'Did it hit?' asked Rita.

'Was it free range?' asked Jenny.

'Was it infected with salmonella?' asked Neville.

'Belt up!' screamed Ted. 'Belt up, the lot of you.'

It was a long time since any cord had been wained in Cordwainer's Road. One side of the street was occupied by the back of the crisis-torn Whincliff Centre, that rusting off-white elephant, that stained concrete cathedral of consumerism, through whose bright nave unholy music tinkled. On the other side stood a building site, where two sandwich bars and a pub had been. A huge sign announced that the Probert McEwan Group regretted any inconvenience, as if the building site was an accident they hadn't been able to avoid. Beyond the construction site stood the police station, three-storied, modern, flat-roofed, with three rows of straight, disciplined windows; a dull, obedient building, unprovocative but unavoidable.

The summer wind complained bitterly as it attempted to destroy the Whincliff Centre. It tore a poster of a wanted man from the front of the police station. Empty chip bags bowled along the pavement beside the scurrying feet of Queen Elizabeth the First and Sir Walter Raleigh.

Napoleon was already in the police station, standing in the reception area at a long window of double thickness. Behind the window there stood a police sergeant, who had raised one eyebrow a quarter of a millimetre at the sight of the angry old Corsican.

The small reception area was bleak enough to be inhospitable without seeming so unwelcoming as to arouse hostility. Along both walls were uninviting benches. There were two pairs of cheap hard chairs at either side of the entrance.

'Do you realise who I am?' said Ted. 'Ted Simcock,' he added hastily, in case the sergeant was thinking of saying Napoleon.

The sergeant looked blank.

'One time owner of the Jupiter Foundry.'

The sergeant continued to look blank.

'Latterly *chef de cuisine* at the Restaurant Chez Albert.'

The sergeant discovered new depths of blankness.

'I have friends who are masons,' said Ted. 'If you don't let me in there, you're on your way out, matey.'

Rita and Geoffrey entered. The sergeant raised half of one eyebrow at their costumes.

Ted clanked over to Rita with un-Napoleonic haste.

'That puffed-up petty Hitler behind his reinforced glass won't let us see our son,' he said.

'You've put his back up, haven't you?' said Rita. 'You've got to treat people right.'

188

Geoffrey took in the details of this unfamiliar room with quiet astonishment, as if witnessing a tribal rite of which he had no knowledge.

Rita walked quietly, unthreateningly towards the sergeant. He awaited her without expression. She turned on a smile that made her feel vaguely uneasy: a winning smile, a politician's smile, a smile with which one might kiss a baby before reintroducing hanging.

'Good evening, officer,' she said.

The sergeant smiled minimally.

'My name's Rita Simcock. Councillor Rita Simcock. I know this is an extremely busy time for you, a weekend evening, but I'm very concerned about my son, and I would very much appreciate it if I could possibly see him for just a few moments.'

The sergeant smiled. 'No,' he said.

Ted almost laughed. Geoffrey squeezed Rita's arm.

'I'm very sorry, madam,' said the sergeant, 'but at present we have nobody to supervise a visit. We have this student demonstration, two road accidents, one armed robbery and the usual tribal warfare between lager louts.'

'Interesting,' said Geoffrey. 'I must study that.'

'I'll wait,' said Rita.

'By all means, madam, but I can make no guarantees,' said the sergeant.

Liz swept in, with Neville following as if attached to her by an invisible tow-rope.

The sergeant raised half an eyebrow at Liz's costume and a whole one at Neville's.

'We were at a fancy dress party,' said Rita.

'I'd guessed,' said the sergeant drily. 'The level of intelligence in the force isn't quite as low as it's sometimes painted.' He didn't even deign to raise half an eyebrow at the entry of Elvis and his green pepper.

Rita and Geoffrey waited beneath a hideous identikit picture of a wanted man. On the opposite bench, defiantly alone, beneath a warning against drinking and driving, sat Ted. Neville and Liz stood. Elvis and Jenny sat on the chairs to the right of the doorway.

'What's the point of your seeing him?' said Elvis.

'He needs me.'

189

'Jenny!'

'Not in that way. Trust me. But he is still the father of m[y] children. And he needs our support. Including yours. And I fee[l] ashamed of how wrong I was. I thought after we'd split up he'[d] end up as the great wet slob he was before we met.'

'You approve of what he's done, don't you?' Elvis spoke ver[y] quietly, trying not to look as if they were having an argument[.]

'Don't *you*?' said Jenny. 'I thought you were committedl[y] anti-establishment.'

'Do you know what Aristotle, Nietzsche, Kant, Bertran[d] Russell and Jean-Paul Sartre had in common?' said Elvis wit[h] lofty maturity. 'None of them splattered their opponents wit[h] eggs. You win with arguments, Jenny, not eggs.'

'I must have a word with Ted,' said Neville.

'Must you?' said Liz.

Neville strode off purposefully. The abandoned Queen o[f] England sat down angrily on one of the chairs to the left o[f] the entrance, beneath a notice exhorting the public not to d[o] the burglar's job for him.

Neville plonked himself on the bench beside Ted.

'I hope you appreciated my little speech, Ted,' he said.

'No.'

'Oh good. What?'

'I wanted to strangle you. I might yet.'

'There are times when I'm glad you're going to Nairobi,' sai[d] Neville with the sadness of a man disappointed by huma[n] nature.

'Oh belt up about Nairobi,' said Ted. 'You know nothing.'

Neville strode back to his smouldering wife. He was puzzle[d] and hurt.

'He insulted me,' he said.

'What did you expect?' snorted Liz.

She stormed off, and made Geoffrey move up so that sh[e] could sit beside him.

A middle-aged lady with a worried face entered the blea[k] reception area. She stared with disbelief at Napoleon. Sh[e] stared with even greater disbelief at Elvis and the green pepper[.] Her astonishment grew as she saw Sir Walter Raleigh sittin[g] between two Queen Elizabeths. Small wonder that she battene[d]

190

with huge relief upon the policeman seated in the corner, with the round, puzzled, but reassuring face of a man who has never knee'd a suspect in the groin.

'Ah!' she said.

Neville stood up politely.

'Have a seat, madam,' he said.

'Oh, thank you,' she said, only slightly puzzled by this unexpected solicitude. She sat, and sighed. 'It's my son.'

'I beg your pardon?'

'My eldest. He's disappeared.'

'Oh no. Oh I am sorry.' Neville sat beside her and asked gently, 'When did this happen?'

The words gushed out. 'He didn't come home last night, but I didn't think owt about it, he stays with his friend sometimes, you know young people, so I wasn't right bothered, but his friend hasn't seen him.'

'Oh dear! Was he . . . did he seem unhappy at home?'

'It's difficult to tell.' Their faces were close, hers worried, his deeply concerned. 'He hasn't talked much lately, not to say talk. But he used to talk, when he did talk, about what a dump this place is. He hankered after London. Well, they do, don't they?'

'I fear so. They hanker away. Awfully worrying for you, though. Oh, I am sorry.'

'Well, thank you.' She was too absorbed in her worry to be more than vaguely surprised by the man in blue's concern. 'So, what are you going to do about it?'

'What do you mean, "what are you going to do about it?"?' Neville's bewilderment was total.

So was the worried mother's. 'What do you mean, "what do you mean, 'what are you going to do about it?'?"?' she said. 'I mean, "what are you going to do about it?"'

'I'm not going to do anything about it. Why should I do anything about it?'

'Well, you're a policeman.'

'Oh. Oh Lord!' Neville glanced down at his uniform, appalled. 'Yes. No.'

'You what?'

'I'm not a policeman. I'm at a fancy dress party. I mean, I was. I'm here now. My wife's daughter by her first marriage's husband has thrown an egg at the Prime Minister.'

'So why did you ask me all them questions?' asked the worried mother indignantly.

'I thought you wanted to talk about it. I was being kind.'

'You great twassock!'

Everyone turned to look at Neville. He tried to look unruffled. The worried mother stormed over to the sergeant's window.

Rita leant across Geoffrey to say to Liz, 'It's absurd, not talking at a time like this. Absurd. Tell her, Geoffrey.'

'Don't start using Geoffrey as a mediator, Rita,' said Liz, and Sir Walter Raleigh found himself looking from one Queen Elizabeth to the other, as if watching a long rally at real tennis. 'He isn't exactly neutral. Exposure to tropical weather has unhinged his mind. He hates me and loves you.'

'Liz! You spoke to me,' said Rita. 'Hardly honeyed words, but it's a start.'

The identikit face of the ghastly criminal stared expressionlessly, inhumanly at these exchanges.

'I'll speak to you briefly, Rita, just to say that I never thought I'd find myself in one of these places.' Liz was sailing on a rising tide of fury. 'This is the most humiliating moment of my life.'

'I know. Contact with real life. Absolutely remarkable.'

'So this is where it's led to, the disastrous mingling of our two families.'

'If you so hate the disastrous mingling of our two families, perhaps you shouldn't have mingled so disastrously with Ted at our children's wedding.'

Liz could find no instant reply. Geoffrey seized on his chance to speak.

'I think I may go back to study the head-hunters of Borneo,' he said. 'I need a bit of peace and quiet.'

'Now listen,' said the sergeant, when he'd heard the mother's story. 'We've got another major incident – a suspected murder – it's going to be one of those nights, there's only me to deal with this lady whose son has disappeared, your son has not disappeared, so I really do suggest that you all go home and leave us to try and stem the collapse of Western civilisation.'

For a moment nobody spoke or moved. Then Ted stood up.

'Well . . . it's back to the glittering party, then,' he said.

In the bleak, unlovely street, the wind still howled, and the chip bags still ran their infernal race, pale greasy little chaps without legs or arms or eyes, bowling along on their moth-like bodies, visitors from an environment even more inhospitable than Cordwainer's Road.

And how the party glittered, in the flexible, multi-purpose function room, in the Royalty Suite of the Grand Universal Hotel. It's true that Punch, alias Larry Benson, of fitted kitchen fame, and Judy, alias Larry Benson's lady wife, who was no lady, had carried their disguises a little too far, and a large knobbly pepper mill is a dangerous instrument with which to belabour your partner's head. It's true that no memorable witticisms had issued from 'The Master's' lips, nor any seductive boldness from Mae West's. It's true that the invisible man was suffering from a fierce heat rash. It's true that the music of the Dale Monsal Quartet failed entirely to make up in vitality what it lacked in accuracy. It's true that the absence for more than an hour of the host, both Queen Elizabeths, Sir Walter Raleigh, the policeman, the green pepper and the only person not in fancy dress had not passed entirely unnoticed. But these were minor flaws. The room was pulsating to the rhythms of 'Brazil'. The vicar was still cavorting with the schoolgirl. The nun whirled the pearly queen around. The Viking held Alice-in-Wonderland in his horny embrace. And Rodney and Betty Sillitoe were dancing the samba with as much style as it has ever been danced . . . by a red pepper and a yellow pepper.

The two Queen Elizabeths and Sir Walter Raleigh tried to enter unobtrusively. In vain!

'Rodney! They're back!' said Betty.

'Don't look.'

'No. Right.'

The two peppers danced on, swirled round stylishly, and approached each other again, stalks bobbing in time with the music.

'It isn't stylish, isn't curiosity,' said Rodney.

'No. Right.'

'It's not concomitant with our status as leading business people . . . ' Rodney paused as they went out of earshot, then resumed as they swung round and approached each other again,

' . . . who are living proof that profit and the environment can go together.'

'Absolutely. Something's happened, though.'

'Oh, I know.'

Elvis and Jenny made an attempt at an inconspicuous entrance. To no avail!

'Elvis and Jenny are back too!' said Rodney. 'Go and pump Rita, tactfully, without seeming to pump her.'

'Good idea.'

Betty danced off in search of Rita.

The doors slid open, sibilantly. Napoleon entered from the windswept forecourt just as Sandra was crossing the vast foyer with the duty manager's dinner.

'Sandra!'

Sandra's tray crashed onto the thick pile carpet. The piped music tinkled on.

'Oh Sandra!'

'I only do that when you're around,' said Sandra indignantly. 'I've only broken one cup in the last six weeks.'

'Are you working here now?' said Ted foolishly, kneeling to talk to his former lover.

'No. It's my day off. I come in as a hobby.' Sandra scraped œufs Benedict and carpet fluff into a slightly broken bowl. 'I got sacked at the Clissold Lodge.'

Ted managed to stop himself saying, 'I'm not surprised.' Instead, he said quietly, 'Sandra! You were right.'

'You what?' Sandra spooned fluffy kidneys Turbigo on top of the œufs.'

'About Corinna. You were right.'

'Oh?'

'She *was* a tarty piece.'

'I know. "Was"?'

'Yes. Was.'

'Oh! Well!'

'Yes. She . . . er . . . she's conned me out of all me money and disappeared off the face of the earth.'

Sandra stood up. Ted stood too. They rose together.

'You should have stayed with me, shouldn't yer?'

'Yes, Sandra, I . . . '

But Sandra had gone, striding off towards the kitchens with the duty manager's wrecked dinner.

'I should,' he finished to nobody.

Ted walked slowly towards the lift, which would transport him to the first floor, to the Royalty Suite, to his glittering farewell.

A large yellow pepper approached Queen Elizabeth the First.

Rita was picking at the remains of the buffet. The Dale Monsal Quartet were playing 'Spanish Eyes'.

'Hello, Rita,' said Betty. 'You've . . . er . . . I haven't . . . er . . . well, seen you around for an hour or so.'

'No.'

There was a pause. It became clear that Rita wasn't going to break it.

'Nor Ted.'

'He's over there.'

'I know, but before he was over there he wasn't over anywhere for ages. And I . . . er . . . we . . . er . . . couldn't help wondering if . . . well . . . something had happened.'

'Yes. Something has happened.'

'Oh.'

'And something else has happened as well.'

'Oh! Oh dear! I mean . . . unless they were pleasant.'

'One of them was rather unpleasant.'

'Oh dear.'

'But the other one was much worse.'

'Oh dear.'

There was another pause.

'It's none of our business, of course,' said Betty at last.

'That's right.'

'But . . . as your friends . . . and your employers . . . if you ever felt the need to . . . confide in us, we wouldn't mind. We'd always be prepared to listen.'

'I'm sure you would. Thank you, Betty. If I ever want to confide in you, I will.'

'Well, thank you.'

'I love you dearly, Betty. I love working at Sillitoe's. But if I ever wanted anything publicised in this town, what I'd do would be, I'd tell you, and I'd tell you it was a secret.'

Betty smiled modestly, as if pooh-poohing some undeserved flattery. Then Rita's meaning sank in, and her smile imploded.

'Rita!' she said.

She threaded her way carefully through the dancers towards Elvis and Jenny, in order to pump them. Just as she reached them she heard Elvis say, 'You do still love me, don't you?'

'Fool!' said Jenny affectionately.

Betty hurried off, before they saw her.

'Good party, isn't it?' said Simon, slipping into the seat beside his stepfather.

Neville Badger still looked immaculate, on an evening in the course of which he had been called a twerp, a fool and a great twassock.

'Yes,' he said.

'I can't decide whether the Halifax Building Society lot or the Allied Dunbar mob take the palm for inventiveness.'

'No.'

There was an uncomfortable little silence between the two men.

'Ted certainly seems to be moving in financial circles these days,' said Simon.

'Yes. Round and round.'

The little conversational flurry died.

'Is something wrong, Neville?'

'Some men can't ride horses, Simon. Other men can't swim. I can't converse.'

'I don't understand.'

'Precisely. Conversation. I can't manage it. I'm considered a pretty good lawyer down at Badger, Badger, Fox and Badger. I'm considered a pretty social sort of fellow on the golf course. At do's I'm a nightmare, best avoided.'

'Snap.'

'Pardon?'

'Coming as Noël Coward's brought it home to me. No wit.' Applause greeted the moment when, almost in unison, the Dale Monsal Quartet completed their rendition of 'Spanish Eyes'. Simon leant forward to speak more intimately. 'Neville? I . . . I must have loved my father, in a funny sort of way, because I missed him after he died. I resented your marrying my mother. But I think it's working out surprisingly well . . . well, not surprisingly . . . '

'Yes. Yes, I think it is, Simon.'

The Dale Monsal Quartet embarked upon 'Arrivederci, Roma'.

'I wonder if you'd mind,' continued Simon, 'or think it absurd, if I . . . tried calling you "Father".'

'Good Lord!' Neville was moved. 'Good Lord, no. No. Not if I can . . . try calling you "Son" . . . Son.'

'Not a bad conversation from two chaps who're no good at it, Father.'

'Pretty good, Son.' Neville clapped Simon awkwardly on the shoulder. 'I'd kiss you if we were French. I might even though we aren't if you weren't dressed as Noël Coward.'

Neville hurried off to speak to Liz. Seeing the unusual urgency in his step, she peeled away from the Allied Dunbar mob, with whom she'd been discussing what life insurance premiums would have needed to be in the first Elizabethan age.

'Darling, I'm very happy,' he announced.

'Neville!'

Liz kissed him.

'Simon called me Father.

'For a delicious, absurd moment I thought you meant you were happy with me.'

'I did. I am. That's the whole point. Simon called me Father because he knows we're happy.'

'We are? What excellent news.'

'I was dreading tonight. But I needn't have. I've enjoyed it as much as I ever did with Jane.'

Neville's cheery beam faded as he saw Liz's expression.

'I've spoilt it, haven't I?' he said. 'I've ruined the moment.'

Liz gave him a brittle, bitter smile. 'Trampled all over the carpet of life with your great muddy boots,' she said.

'It's conversation. I'm such a mug at it,' said Neville.

He turned away and found himself walking towards Carol Fordingbridge. She, finding herself walking towards him, turned away and found herself walking towards Jenny.

'Carol?' said Jenny uncertainly.

'Yes.'

'I hope you don't resent me for taking Elvis. Well, not taking him. Because it was over between you and him before he and I . . .'

'Yes, well, if I was going to resent you I should never have started, should I?'

'How do you mean?'

'Having my one night stand with Paul.'

'I'm not going with Elvis to get back at you for going with Paul, Carol. I love him.'

'If you spent less time worrying about sex and fellers, Jenny, you might have more time for the important things in life, like animal rights and the Third World and the ozone layer and feminism, 'cos they're a dead loss, Jenny, sex and fellers.'

Jenny was stunned, stunned to have this said to her of all people. And by Carol of all people. And by Carol dressed as Marie Lloyd of all people.

She realised that Ted was speaking to her.

'Jenny!' he was saying. 'The very person. You've always believed in telling the truth, haven't you?'

'Well . . . yes, Ted.'

'If you don't, it'll follow you, chase you relentlessly?'

'Well . . . yes, Ted.'

'If it's going to come out, best to let it out yourself.'

'Well . . . yes, Ted.'

Ted kissed her.

'Wise words, Jenny. Thanks. I'm going to take your advice.'

Ted pushed through his guests, towards the Dale Monsal Quartet, just as they finished their interpretation of 'Arrividerci, Roma'.

Dale Monsal leant forward to caress the microphone with his flat tones. He didn't see Ted signalling.

'Whose soul is so dull that he is not excited by Italy?' he said dully. 'However, it's time to leave the sunshine and spaghetti and whisk ourselves over the great Alpine ranges to the thunder and dumplings of Germany. Yes, it's *arrividerci, Roma*, and *guten Tag, Schwarzwald*.'

He began to turn, to address his musicians, demure in their barber's shop outfits. But before he could say, '*Eins, zwei, drei*,' he noticed Ted's increasingly furious hand signals.

'But wait,' said Dale Monsal. 'Our host wishes to have a

word. Our walk in the Black Forest must be briefly postponed.'

Napoleon mounted the platform and faced not an army in uniform, but a ragbag of revellers in multiform.

'Thank you, Dale,' he said. 'Ladies and gentlemen, this evening has been held as a farewell for myself and Corinna. But there is . . . er . . . there is to be no farewell, because . . . there is no Corinna. Ladies and gentlemen, I . . . er . . . I have been conned. I have. Me, conned. Corinna was a conwoman, or a conperson as the feminists among you would say.'

He laughed. Nobody else did, not squaw nor monk nor Dracula nor Noël Coward nor Sherlock Holmes nor witch. Not a titter among the whole bang shoot.

'You see, I can still laugh, even if none of you can. I, a Yorkshireman, one time premier maker of door knockers in the County of the White Rose, have been conned. But.' He paused. 'I felt sad. I felt wretched. I no longer do. I feel happy. I do.' His lower lip quivered. 'No. I mean it. I do. Because.' He paused again. 'Because why? Because, ladies and gentlemen, I will be staying here, among my friends, because tonight . . . ' He scanned their faces. What did he see? Friends? Where were his colleagues from the Crown and Walnut Angling Club? His former associates at the Jupiter Foundry? His school chums? Where were all those with whom he'd discussed girls, caught roach, bemoaned the demise of the toasting fork, chewed the nostalgic fat? 'No, I mean it, I really have . . . I have realised that you, my friends . . . ' What friends? The Sillitoes, whose omnipresence rivalled that of their Maker. But who else? Relatives. Acquaintances. Rentachum. Financial contacts. People from the flats and the Stag and Garter, barely known. 'You, my friends, are the people who matter to me, and I'm staying with you, and I'm glad. No, I am. I'm glad. Thank you. You may now walk in the Black Forest.'

'A brave speech,' cried out Neville. 'Come on. All together.' He began to sing, 'For he's a jolly good . . . '

'Oh, not again, you steaming great pillock,' screamed Ted.

Ted hurried off, going he knew not where. The ravishing Liz Badger blocked his path.

'That was a brave speech, Ted,' she said. 'I almost understood again what it was I once saw in you.'

'When you say things like that, I totally fail to see what I once saw in you,' said Ted.

He stumbled on and found himself confronted by the immaculate Neville Badger.

'Don't say anything,' he warned.

'Oh no. Don't worry,' said Neville. 'I won't. My lips are sealed. My conversational days are over. I shall embarrass you no more. From now on I'm going to make Trappist monks sound like compulsive gossips.'

'Do shut up, Neville,' said Ted.

And Neville did. The man who'd been called a twerp, a fool, a great twassock and a steaming great pillock had finally had enough.

And Ted moved blindly on. And there was Rita.

'Well spoken, Ted,' she said. 'Very well done indeed.'

'Thank you, Rita. Well . . . I'll never trust a woman again.'

From behind them there came the familiar strains of 'A Walk in the Black Forest'. The party was swinging on.

'No, Ted,' said Rita. 'Don't be stupid. Don't judge all women by her. There are women you can trust and women you can't trust. Just as there are men you can trust and men you can't trust, except there aren't as many men you can trust.'

'Trust you to fling that in.'

'I'm one you could have trusted, Ted. I'm happy now and I'd like you to be happy too. Find a woman you can trust, Ted. And trust her.'

Rita patted his arm and moved off to rescue Geoffrey, who was finding very little in common with the penguin.

Ted looked at Rita, looked at the door, and thought. He thought hard. He hurried from the room, suddenly full of purpose.

'Where's he going now?' asked Rodney.

Betty shook her peppered head, as if to say, 'It isn't stylish, isn't curiosity.'

Ted stood by the reception desk in the great tinkling foyer, drumming his fingers nervously on the counter.

At last Sandra arrived. How fetching she looked in her black and white outfit.

'You wanted me,' she said.

'Yes, I . . . er . . . ' Ted gulped. 'I wanted you, Sandra. I . . er . . . '

'You . . . er . . . what?'

The receptionist made great play with not listening to them, so they knew that she was hanging on their words. It didn't matter.

'I . . . er . . . Sandra, I was wondering . . . erm . . . '

'Yes, Ted. What were you wondering . . . erm . . . ?'

'I was wondering . . . erm . . . Sandra? What say we go out one evening?'

'Get knotted.'

Ted set off towards the lifts, then turned and walked slowly away, away from the lifts, away from the Halifax Building Society lot and the Allied Dunbar mob, away from the champagne and caviare, away from his ex-wife and his ex-lover, away from his glittering party. He walked slowly out into the stormy detritus of an unsummery evening. He was an emperor without an army. He was a man without a friend.

Fifth Do

August:
The Inauguration of the Outer Inner Relief Ring Road

'So, what chance there being a Yorkshireman in the touring team this winter?' enquired Councillor Mirfield.

'I'm afraid I know very little about cricket,' said Geoffrey Ellsworth-Smythe, seeming not one whit afraid.

'Having spent his adult life abroad, in non-English speaking countries,' explained Councillor Rita Simcock.

'Ah,' said Councillor Mirfield.

They were standing just below the platform, at one end of the Gadd Room, on the first floor of the grandiose Town Hall. The two men were wearing sober suits. Rita was wearing a pale pink long jacket and skirt, with pink camisole top, and pink and gold earrings.

'I'm an anthropologist,' explained Geoffrey at last.

'Ah,' said Councillor Mirfield.

'Oh Lord,' said Rita. 'Here comes sympathy. Excuse me.'

The Sillitoes sailed up to Rita, oozing sympathy. Rodney wore a crumpled suit, which bore traces of an errant bean goulash. Betty looked over-dressed as usual in a turquoise knitted bodice, with turquoise, pink and blue silk sleeves, a matching skirt and a large bow on her left hip.

Councillor Mirfield, who had never admitted to himself that he disliked women, gave her a sour look and found himself thinking, 'Put a matching cap on her and she'll find herself riding at Wetherby.'

'Rita!' said Betty sympathetically. 'We've just heard! Oh Rita!'

'Absolutely,' said Rodney. His right shoulder was damp where rain had got in under their shared golfing umbrella.

'I said, "We must come and . . ." but Rodney said, "No, best not, she'll be . . ." but I said, "Rodney! We're her employers, and, above all, her friends." I mean, what are friends for?'

'Thank you,' said Rita, 'but I'd rather not talk about it.'

'Of course,' said Betty. 'Of course. We understand. We wouldn't dream. Would we, Rodney?'

'Absolutely not.'

Rita led them to a long table on which two exhibits stood side by side. There were many exhibits dotted around the room, which regularly hosted exhibitions. When Labour was in control these tended towards art produced by the handicapped. Under the Conservatives they tended towards opportunities offered to the powerful.

'Well, this is it,' said Rita. 'The outer inner relief ring road. And there's the inner inner relief ring road, so you can compare them and see why we're plumping for the outer inner relief ring road . . . rather than the inner inner relief ring road.'

Rodney and Betty looked at the models of the proposed routes for both roads. Then they looked at each other. It was clear from their looks that they had failed to see why the council were plumping for the outer inner relief ring road . . . rather than the inner inner relief ring road.

'Very unsettled for the time of year,' said Councillor Mirfield.

'I suppose so,' said Geoffrey. 'I hardly remember what the climate's supposed to be like.'

'I suppose not.'

Councillor Mirfield gazed round the room, searching for inspiration. He prided himself on being good with people. He had an uneasy feeling that everyone was looking at him, witnessing his discomfiture. Why did he still get these uneasy feelings, when he was so clearly a success?

'It must be a very interesting life, being an anthropologist,' he said.

'Yes,' said Geoffrey.

Councillor Mirfield was beginning to think that chat show hosts earned their corn.

'Have you converted to unleaded petrol yet?' he asked.

'Yes.'

'Me too. Well, where would we be if we didn't have the environment?'

Perhaps not surprisingly, Geoffrey didn't answer. Councillor Mirfield decided to take the bull by the horns.

'You and Councillor Simcock are pretty close friends, aren't you?' he asked.

This at least provoked a reply. 'I rather think that's our business, Councillor Mirfield.'

Councillor Mirfield glanced round the room again.

'Really exceptionally unsettled,' he said. 'It's playing havoc with me runner beans.'

Rodney and Betty Sillitoe were still trying to come to terms with the two models.

'Doesn't it look small, Rodney?' said Betty.

'Well of course it does,' said Rodney. 'It's to scale.'

'I meant our premises. Sillitoe's.'

'Well, looked at one road it is small, Betty. Looked at another road it's the widest selection of vegetarian produce in Yorkshire. Looked at one road, you're a minute earwig crawling across a vast parched continent for one brief blip in eternity. Looked at another road, you're my whole life. It's the paradox of existence, is that.'

Betty gave Rodney an astounded look, then turned abruptly to Rita.

'Well anyway, Rita, it's very interesting,' she said, 'but what a shame. Little you . . . I mean, little you as we'd once have thought of you, but big you now – your election virtually changing the face of the town single-handed, your great night, and then this has to happen.'

'Betty!' said Rodney. 'I thought we weren't mentioning it.'

'Oh, I won't,' said Betty, over-emphatic as usual. 'I wouldn't dream. But I mean . . . what are friends for?'

'Excuse me,' said Rita, rather more abruptly than was strictly necessary.

Rodney and Betty, abandoned in mid-sympathy, made their way to the drinks table, took glasses of wine which the dapper, ageless Eric Siddall found impossible to refuse them, and sallied forth to be bemused by further exhibits.

Rita's greeting to Elvis and Jenny was not perhaps quite as warm as they would have liked.

'Who invited you?' she said.

'I'm the media, Mum.' Elvis looked like a drowned rat, having been told that raincoats were not trendy wear for up-and-coming media men. 'This is a propaganda exercise.'

'It's not.' The councillor in Rita was indignant. 'It's the process of public consultation by your user friendly council.'

'To persuade the users to be friendly towards what you've decided,' said the cynical Elvis Simcock.

Rita turned her attention to Jenny, who had adopted a rather Chinese appearance. She was wearing a pale grey and blue large-check, mandarin-style jacket, with short baggy navy cotton trousers, and decidedly ethnic earrings.

'Elvis takes me with him whenever he can,' she said. 'Any objections?'

'Well, no. Well, yes. Well, you know why. The very day Paul gets six months, and here you are . . . ' She couldn't say it.

'Flaunting our love?'

'Well, no. Well, yes.'

'Paul and I'd split up before he went to prison. Elvis isn't a marriage breaker.'

'I know. I just think of Paul behind bars.'

'Do you think I don't?'

Jenny stalked off indignantly. Elvis gave his mother a sad, reproving look, which infuriated her. Then he hurried after Jenny, catching up with her just as she met Simon and Lucinda. They looked so trim, Simon in his dark suit, Lucinda in a black and apricot jacket, with apricot skirt and top, that Elvis suddenly wished he hadn't got so wet.

'We're awfully sorry to hear about Paul, Elvis,' said Simon.

'You must both be very upset,' said Lucinda.

'There's no need to sound so disapproving,' said Jenny. 'We are.'

'There's no need to be so defensive,' said Lucinda. 'We know.'

'What are you doing here anyway?' asked Elvis, going onto the attack the moment his lover was accused of being defensive.

'New roads affect a lot of our properties,' said Simon.

'And a lot of business gets secretly and irregularly put your way.'

'This is yet another slur on our profession.'

'No, it's yet another slur on you.'

Simon Rodenhurst, of Trellis, Trellis, Openshaw and Finch, looked more than somewhat hurt. But now he had Lucinda Snellmarsh, of Peacock, Tester and Devine, to soothe him. 'Don't let him get under your skin, sugar plum,' she said.

'Oh, I won't, sugar plum. Don't you worry! Elvis get under my skin? Some chance!' Simon glowered at Elvis and delivered his devastating *coup de grace*, which turned out to be, 'Huh!'

'Well, have a nice day, sugar plums,' said Jenny.

'Jenny!'

Simon was astounded by his sister's uncharacteristic bitterness.

Rita stood alone for a moment, smiling vaguely, hoping to keep people at arm's length without offending them. She gazed round the huge Gadd Room, dark-panelled, decorated only by a relief map of the Gadd Valley on the wall opposite the platform and a painting of the exterior of the town hall, of its extravagant curved gables and off-centre tower, reminiscent of, but sadly not of the same quality as, the Palazzo Vecchio in Florence. Today, scaffolding encased the building, hiding its façade, which one architectural critic had called 'a Baroque Gothic Victorian extravaganza, a rare piece of nineteenth-century frippery in stone' and another had described as 'a pig's breakfast'.

And now there were graphs of traffic flows, models of road plans, photographs of derelict areas through which the outer inner relief ring road would pass, photographs of sweet corners that would be destroyed by the inner inner relief ring road. All this because her election had swayed the balance of power. All this to say, not 'You, the public, will decide,' but, 'We're right, aren't we?' The workings of a semi-democracy, an almost free society.

Rita felt dreadful about Paul being in prison. Dreadful about Elvis being here tonight while Paul was in prison. And dreadful about something else, something which she couldn't isolate from her general unease.

So she was quite pleased when Eric Siddall, barman supreme,

who was giving up his night off because she had asked for him, appeared beside her with a tray of glasses.

'A glass of wine, madam?' he said. 'Help you put the whole sad business out of your mind on your great night? 'Cos I know you're upset, you're forced to be – headlines plastered all over the town, court makes an example of newest councillor's son – 'cos you're a mother, and I've always had this empathy with mothers, me, always been able to get right under their . . . I've red or sweet or medium-dry white.'

'I'll have a medium-dry white, please.'

'Can do. No problem. There you go, madam. Tickety-boo.'

'Thanks. And Eric? Thanks for helping me put the whole sad business out of my mind.'

'No problem, madam. All in a day's . . . ' Eric's smile and his words dried up as Rita's gentle sarcasm dawned on him.

Rita took a sip of her wine and wished that the council didn't feel quite so strong a need not to waste public money.

And then she saw him.

'Ted!'

'I'm touched that so much affection still lingers.'

'No, I meant . . . I was surprised, that's all. I mean . . . who invited you?'

'Well . . . I'm unemployed. I've made a fool of myself with a conwoman. And now me son's a cause celebrated of street protest. Who do you think would invite me?' Rita was at a loss. 'Precisely. No bugger.'

'Ted!'

Rita was a little ashamed, after all she had achieved, to find herself looking round anxiously for fear somebody might have heard her ex-husband using bad language. But we aren't snakes. We can't slough off old skins.

'It's true,' said Ted, who was wearing a decent suit and looked fairly respectable apart from his wet hair, for he regarded umbrellas as evidence of softness. 'When you're down, the whole world queues up to kick you in the cobblers.'

'So . . . how did you get in?'

Rita knew how difficult it was for the uninvited to make their way undetected across the vast, gloomy, forbidding foyer, past the human Rottweiler on the desk, and up the long, curved, self-important staircase, onto the dark, first-floor corridor, whose brown gloom was broken only by the occasional scarlet fire extinguisher.

'Simple. By saying, "I am Councillor Simcock's husband." They all know you.'

'Ted!'

'Well . . . all right . . . I left out the "ex-". What are two letters and a hyphen among friends? But . . . I mean . . . Rita . . . I hoped you might be pleased that I wanted to be with you on your great night.'

'It's not my great night. Our son is in prison.'

'I know. Dreadful. You feed them. You educate them. What do they do? Turn round and kick you in the crutch.'

'Is that how you feel? No sympathy?'

'He broke the law.'

'He got over-excited about things he feels very strongly about. He got carried away.'

'Yes, by three policemen.' A touch of pride flitted across Ted's face. 'It took three, I'll give him that.'

'Ted! Our son, the . . . ' Rita hesitated as two councillors' wives walked past. One of them gave her a frosty smile which contained bottomless hostility towards women who didn't know their place.

'Fruit of our loins?' said Ted.

'Well, yes. Though it sounds right silly saying that now . . . locked up, because he couldn't control his warm heart. Are you ashamed of him? Don't you love him?'

' 'Course I do, Rita. 'Course I love him. I mean . . . I do. But.'

'But what?'

'It's not very nice, is it? Your name plastered all over the papers.'

'It wasn't your name. It was mine.'

'I know. And how do you think I felt about that? No mention of ex-foundry owner's son. No mention of ex-toasting fork magnate's son. I don't exist any more, Rita. I'm a nothing.' A drop of rainwater slid off his hair onto his nose. He brushed it off hurriedly, in case Rita might mistake it for a tear of self-pity.

'Is that what worries you most, today of all days?' said Rita.

'Rita! 'Course it isn't. Our Paul worries me. But it isn't very nice walking in here, being a nobody. It isn't, Rita.'

'So why have you come?'

'You call yourselves the user friendly council. I'm a user. I came to be friendly.'

'What's your real reason?'

'I'm interested. I'm a responsible citizen, deeply concerned about town planning.' Rita looked sceptical. Ted tried to stare her out. 'I am. And I thought, I must come, even on such a foul night.'

It was indeed a foul night. Later, the Meteorological Office would announce that it had been the wettest August day since 1809, in the wettest August since 1792. That month, in fact, Otley had more rain than Tierra del Fuego.

'What's your real reason?' repeated Rita.

'Because, Rita, I've no alternative. What do I do? Slip down back alleys every time I see old friends? Drink in the public bar because folk who once queued to buy my quality door knockers are supping in the lounge? I'm not going to run, Rita. There's nowhere to run to. I'm not going to hide, Rita. There's nothing I need hide from.'

Sandra approached with a plate of quartered sausage rolls.

'Well, almost nothing.'

He fled.

'Sausage roll, madam?' said the cake-loving Sandra Pickersgill.

'I'm a vegetarian,' said Rita.

'These are from the Vale of York Bakery,' said Sandra. 'I know how little meat goes in them.'

Sandra bore her gastronomical delights onwards. Rita was astounded to see Liz and Neville arrive.

'Good Lord!' she said. 'I didn't expect you here.'

'In my time . . . ' began the immaculate Neville Badger.

'Don't answer her, Neville,' commanded his ravishing wife.

'Sorry, Rita,' said Neville.

'Don't apologise to her, Neville,' commanded Liz.

'Sorry, darling.'

'Oh, Neville, don't apologise to me either.'

'Sorry,' said Neville, apologising for apologising. 'Sorry,' he added, apologising for saying sorry.

'Oh, Neville!'

Liz marched on, as though she were still dressed as Queen Elizabeth. In fact she was wearing black silk trousers and a silk camisole top, with a pink, blue and black cummerbund, a petrol blue silk jacket, large black and gold earrings and a gold neck chain; yet, to many women's chagrin, she managed not to look ostentatious.

Neville caught up with her by the model of the route of the outer inner relief ring road.

'No, but, Liz, please, listen,' he said. 'I must speak to you.'

'Neville! Are you being masterful?'

'Yes. Sorry. I mean . . . yes! I understand your reasons for refusing to talk to Rita, but please, Liz, today Rita is a mother in torment.'

'Do you think I'm not? My daughter's road sweeper husband is in prison. My daughter's name is being dragged through the mud.' Liz bent down to examine the model. 'And what is she doing, my daughter? Carrying on in public with her husband's brother, who, from which I suppose I should glean a tiny crumb of comfort, is not a road sweeper. My association with the Simcock family has been a total and unmitigated . . . Neville! Look!'

'What?'

'That's our house.' Liz pointed at the tiny cube which represented their marital home. 'Look at our garden.'

Neville peered at the model.

'I can't see our garden,' he said.

'Precisely.'

'What?'

'It isn't there. It's gone.'

'Gone? Gone where?'

'Are you being deliberately obtuse? It's gone into the ring road. We're not losing twenty yards of garden. We're losing all our garden. This is what the woman you used to take to dinner and can't stop apologising to has done.'

Neville took another close look at the model, as if he hoped that this time the evidence would be different. He faced the same stark picture: their home. On three sides, greenery. On the fourth, touching their home, the silver snake that represented the outer inner relief ring road.

'The model may not be accurate,' he said, straightening up with some difficulty.

'Well go and ask her.'

213

'You now want me to speak to Rita?'

'Yes.'

'Right.'

'Forcefully.'

'Right.'

'Coldly but politely, with icy dignity.'

'Right.'

'Without the remotest hint of apology.'

'Right.'

'Well go on.'

'Right.'

Neville set off reluctantly, and returned instantly.

'You don't think there's a risk that in having refused to talk to Rita, and then talking to her two minutes later, I'll make myself look rather . . . er . . . indecisive . . . er . . . a bit of a dog's-body doing your dirty work, enabling you to maintain your uncompromising position of total isolation while I make myself look a . . . slight . . . total idiot?'

'No.'

'Right.'

Neville set off again on his reluctant mission. Jenny approached Liz, who was staring at the model as if she could shame it into changing its route.

'Hello, Mum,' said Jenny, smiling.

Liz didn't speak or move a muscle.

'Mum! Aren't you speaking to me?' Jenny's frail smile ended its mayfly life.

Liz didn't speak or move a muscle.

'Oh Mum!'

Liz turned on her daughter. Jenny flinched as if she'd been hit.

'You have allied yourself totally with the Simcocks,' said Liz with cold fury. 'And not even the same one all the time.'

'Mum!' said Jenny, quivering on the verge of tears.

Neville's journey towards Rita was proving a social minefield. He found himself forced into polite small talk with Alderman Spigot, the small corpulent Mayor, his sister Netta Ponsonby, the large corpulent Mayoress, Craig Welting, the Australian managing

214

director of Radio Gadd – who believed that everybody, including his wife, regarded him as the poor man's Rupert Murdoch – and Dr Andrew Millard, the anaesthetist, who had just told a story which appeared to have reduced Alderman Spigot, Netta Ponsonby and Craig Welting to anaesthesia. Welcomed as a distraction, Neville had to stay for a few moments. Yes, what an awful summer. It's the holiday makers I'm sorry for. No, can't stand caravans, I like my creature comforts. Have you heard the new scare? Brown bread. Gall stones. Well, we wouldn't eat anything, would we? And all the time, boring into his bored back, Liz's eyes, accusing him of deliberate delaying tactics.

At last he reached Rita, who was chatting with Councillor Wendy Bullock, a left-winger of passion and integrity who had unreservedly welcomed the arrival of this new sister among the brothers.

Rita excused herself with a raised eyebrow that said, 'Sorry. Neurotic male on the horizon.'

'A word, Rita,' said Neville.

'Neville!'

'Yes, I know. I'm speaking to you. But . . . er . . . ' Neville became masterful. 'Now the thing is . . . ' His masterfulness proved short-lived. 'Incidentally, the reason we're invited is because I've done a bit of legal work for the council.'

'Yes, I realised after I'd asked.'

'Now this plan for the outer inner relief ring road . . . ' again, Neville's masterfulness proved short-lived, ' . . . incidentally, I'm so sorry about Paul. It's all very well having scapegoats in theory, but it seems very unfair when one actually knows the goat that's being scaped.'

'Thank you, Neville.'

'Now on this plan, I have to tell you, Rita . . . ' It didn't prove third time lucky, so far as Neville's masterfulness was concerned. 'I mean I imagine there's a perfectly good explanation, but there's no sign of our garden at all. Liz is worried we're going to lose it all. And so am I.'

'Oh, Neville! We can't show every blade of grass. Of course you're not going to lose your whole garden.'

'Do I have your unequivocal assurance? Nothing less will do . . . or some kind of assurance. I can't go back empty-handed.'

'You have my unequivocal assurance.'

'Thank you, Rita. And I *am* sorry about Paul.'

'Get off with you before I cry.'

'Right.'

Neville managed to return to Liz without serious social mishap.

'We're not going to lose the whole garden,' he said. 'I wormed an assurance out of her.'

'"Wormed an assurance"! You apologised for not talking to her.'

'I did not. Well, only a bit.'

'You said you were sorry about Paul.'

'How do you know what I said? You couldn't hear me.'

'I saw you. I know your body language. I saw those shoulders saying you were sorry.'

'Well I may have done a bit.'

'You're still attracted to her a bit.'

'No. Of course not.'

'Two can play at that game.'

'Liz!'

The lighting was just too dim, on that gloomy August evening, for the exhibits to be clearly seen without peering. The room was just too large for the number of people who had braved the elements. The Conservatives had criticised the holding of this public consultation exercise in August, when so many of the public were away. The Socialists had retorted that the Conservatives wouldn't have consulted the public at all, and suggested that more Socialists than Conservatives took holidays in August, since the privileged could choose off-peak times. The truth was that no politicians really wanted to consult the public, because the public weren't experts, so how could they know best? And it seems that the public agreed, since barely half those invited had turned up.

The joint big wheels behind Sillitoe's crossed the uncrowded room purposefully. They had something to say to the one uninvited guest who had turned up.

'Ted!' said Betty. 'Bra . . . well, not brave of you . . . '

'Betty means it's good to see you,' said Rodney.

'Absolutely. How's things, Ted?'

'Very good. Fine. On me own, me own master again. Eat

what I want when I want, pop down the pub, no rush home. I'm loving it.'

'Good,' said Rodney. 'Any . . . er . . . plans?'

'Plans?'

'Occupational prospects,' said Betty.

'Ah. Jobs. Well, there are irons in fires. Feelers in the right places.'

'What sort of irons and feelers, Ted?' asked Betty.

'Ah well. Discretion, eh?' Ted tapped his nose. 'Folk are sounding me out. I have to weigh up the pros and cons. Early days. No rush.'

'So, there wouldn't be any point in my . . . ' Rodney caught Betty's look, ' . . . in *our* sounding you out, then?'

'What for?'

Betty grew rather coy. 'A certain something that might have cropped up that we might think you might feel might suit you.'

'Well . . . one more iron, one more feeler. . . . You have somebody in mind, some business contact who's told you he's looking for a man of my calibre?'

'No!' said Betty. 'It's us, Ted.'

'You! Me, work for you?'

'I know I've . . . *we've* asked you before, but circumstances have changed. Why not, Ted?'

'Why not? Because you've become crackpot lunatic fringe animal rights trendy health food freaky nut nuts, and even if I did swallow me pride and me nut cutlets and work for you there'd be no point, you'll be bankrupt by Christmas. This is Yorkshire, not Shangri sodding La. That's why not.'

Ted moved off, leaving Rodney and Betty staring in stunned disbelief that anyone, let alone an old friend, could describe their business in those terms. They were still staring in stunned disbelief when he sidled awkwardly back to them.

'I'm sorry,' he said.

'You what, Ted?' said Betty faintly.

'I think I may have been slightly rude.'

'Slightly!' exploded Rodney.

'Slightly ungracious. It's kind of you. It's much appreciated . . . but . . . I'm a man.' Betty raised her eyebrows. 'A macho man.' Betty lowered her eyes. 'A Yorkshire man. A man's man.

217

Well, and a ladies' man too. A hairs-on-the-chest man. A red meat man. A black pudding man. Me, a vegetarian man? I'd be a laughing stock.'

Ted moved off again, leaving Rodney and Betty staring in stunned disbelief, so that, if his purpose in returning had been to clear the stunned disbelief from their faces, it was difficult not to conclude that his return had been a mistake.

'Well, stuff him then,' said Betty.

'Absolutely. Drink?'

'Definitely.'

Rodney set off for the table where Eric was dispensing his cheap wines, his beers and ciders, his array of low alcohol drinks with the placard announcing 'For the motorist!' But before he could recharge their glasses, he was waylaid by Liz.

'Trouble with Ted?' she said quietly.

'We offered him a job. He was horrified. He's a macho man.'

'And you aren't?'

'You what, Liz?'

Liz stood very close to him, and spoke softly. 'I think you're a very attractive man, improving, like a good wine, with age.'

'You what, Liz?'

'Oh, come on, Rodney. It must have been said before.'

'Well . . . yes.' Rodney couldn't help looking flattered. 'Well . . . yes . . . of course.'

'And now it's been said again,' said Liz very softly.

'Oh Lord,' said Rodney.

The rain ceased to patter against the high sash windows of the Gadd Room. Perversely, as night drew near, the sky lightened.

The beer and the cheap wine flowed. The sausage rolls were supplemented by pieces of cheese and tinned pineapple on cocktail sticks.

The guests felt obliged to spend a few minutes examining the models and graphs, the maps and photographs. Mrs Bellamy, wife of old Gordon Bellamy the town clerk, examined a photograph of a picturesque corner that would be destroyed by the inner inner relief ring road and said, 'Look at those straggly roses. A bit of hard pruning wouldn't have come amiss.'

Councillor Desmond Filbert, overhearing this, tut-tutted at the magpie minds of women. Yet later, when he and Councillor Laurie Penfold were examining the model of the outer inner relief ring road, and Councillor Penfold said, 'There's where the old Rose and Crown used to be,' Councillor Filbert didn't tut-tut at the magpie minds of men, he said, 'Now that *was* a pub, when Archie Huggett had it.'

Elvis was examining a graph with every appearance of deep wisdom. Jenny, although she appeared to be looking at its green, yellow and red lines, was miles away.

'I see,' said Elvis. 'Those green lines are the estimated traffic flow in certain streets if they adopt, which of course they will – democracy? Excuse me if I puke – the outer inner relief . . . ' He became aware that Jenny wasn't listening. 'You aren't listening,' he said. 'You're thinking.'

'Sorry? What?' said Jenny. 'I wasn't listening. I was thinking.'

'I said you weren't listening. You were thinking. What were you thinking?'

'I was wondering what he had for tea.'

'Who?'

'*Who?* Who do you think? The assistant keeper at the Eddystone Lighthouse? Paul. Your brother.'

'Ah. Yes, of course.'

'Aren't you sorry for him, locked in a damp, dripping cell? Aren't you thinking of him at all?

' 'Course I am. All the time. Practically. But I don't want you to.'

'Well, I have to. I mean . . . he's still . . . ' It was as if Jenny didn't like to finish her sentence, for fear of hurting Elvis.

'The father of your children.'

'Yes. Well, he is. Don't you see how much it proves I love you?'

'Sorry. That's too clever for me. I'm only a philosophy graduate.'

'Well, if I wasn't certain of my love for you, I wouldn't dare to even begin to think of Paul.'

She smiled at Elvis and kissed him.

'I wonder what time they have lights out,' she said.

Rodney sensed Liz's arrival at his side. His heart, that imperfect old friend, began to beat irregularly and alarmingly. He stared at the exhibit with desperate concentration.

'It's a breakdown of the socio-economic groups who'd be rendered homeless by the inner inner relief ring road,' he said.

'Come outside in a few minutes,' said Liz softly.

'In socio-economic groups D, CD, C and . . . you what? You what, Liz?'

'Come outside in a few minutes.'

Rodney gulped.

'It's stopped raining,' said Liz.

'Liz!' he said. 'I'm a happily married man.'

'That's one of the reasons I've chosen you.'

There was silence between them. Liz let it hang there, in a threatening void. Rodney felt obliged to speak.

'In socio-economic groups A, AB and . . . '

'Don't change the subject.'

'I'm not. That *is* the subject. It's you what's changing the subject.'

'I don't want to break up your marriage,' explained Liz intently. 'I want to cement mine. All I want is a little harmless flirtatious chat. To make Neville fume with jealousy. To make him realise how much I mean to him. To make him commit himself. That's all.'

'I see,' said Rodney. 'Well, what a . . . well, not a relief exactly. I mean, you're still a . . . ' He took a swig of his wine, closing his eyes as the taste hit him. 'It's just that . . . Betty. I love her. I know that sounds ridiculous these days after all these years, but, no, I do. You see.'

The object of Rodney's love was watching him in the company of the long-haired Carol Fordingbridge, who was wearing a navy skirt, and a blue, grey, green and cream chiffon top, with a navy suede belt. How the women shone, in the great gloomy room, on that dark August evening, amid all the sober suits.

'Carol?' said Betty. 'Do you feel anything? Jealousy, anger . . . anything, looking at Elvis now? I mean, if it's not a painful subject.'

'No. I don't care about Elvis any more,' said his ex-fiancée.

'Something funny's going on between Rodney and Liz. I'm

used to his chatting women up. He doesn't mean anything by it. Young women. He just . . . likes them. I wouldn't be surprised if he chatted you up.'

'Betty!'

'No. I wouldn't. And I wouldn't mind, because . . . '

'I'm a fluffy, empty-headed young thing.'

'No. You aren't, Carol.'

'Elvis thinks I am.'

'I thought you didn't care any more.'

'Well!'

'I know. No, I just meant, because you're so much younger, and he'd never be a dirty old man, wouldn't Rodney. He's got too much pride. Just an innocent flirt. But Liz! He wouldn't flirt with her. I don't like it.'

'Maybe this talk'll be enough,' Liz was saying. 'Maybe he's fuming with jealousy now. If not, I'll go outside in about ten minutes. If I do, will you follow?'

'Oh Liz!' said Rodney, who was only too aware that Betty was watching him.

'I know what Laurence would have done. Ignored it. I just have to know that history isn't repeating itself. I can't let my life go down the lines it did with Laurence. Will you, Rodney?'

Rodney knew that he must look her full in the face and say, 'Sorry, Liz. No.' Half the plan worked well. He did look her full in the face. Then things went wrong. He heard the words, 'Well, yes, all right,' emerge from his throat.

'Thank you,' said Liz. 'Thank you very much. If I was looking for . . . ' Rodney gave a tiny yelp, as if a beagle pup was being strangled somewhere near his uvula. 'Don't be so alarmed. I'm not. But if I was, I wouldn't need to look any further than . . . ' Rodney was turned to stone. 'Don't look so frightened. I'm not.'

The joint big wheel behind Sillitoe's managed to wrench his face out of Liz's magnetic field.

'Whereas the outer inner relief ring road only displaces thirty-six people in groups D, CD and C, you see.'

The heavy clouds were clearing from the west, allowing the setting sun to hint at what might have been. The clouds above the town were briefly bruised with purple.

Ginny Fenwick sipped her wine, grimaced, and told Elvis how she'd describe it in the column that she wrote under the soubriquet of 'The Imbiber'. Elvis saw Janet Turnbull from BBC Radio leaving the room with Councillor Mirfield. She was going to interview him! He should be interviewing people! Ginny Fenwick sighed and remembered the days when men had listened to her.

Ted Simcock, unemployed caterer, was struggling to find something in common with the new man in his ex-wife's life.

'I was in Middlesbrough the other day,' he said. 'It's very sad that the whole of the North East . . . if you include Middlesbrough in the North East, which I do . . . hasn't got a single first division team next season.'

'Yes,' said Geoffrey Ellsworth-Smythe.

There was a pause. It could not be described as comfortable.

'Not interested in football?' said Ted.

'No,' said Geoffrey. 'Sorry.'

There was a pause. It could not be described as companionable.

'Cricket?' said Ted at last.

'Sorry. I never was interested in organised sport. Loner, you see. My trouble is, I have no small talk. That's probably why I've spent so much of my life so happily among people who don't speak a word of English.'

'You and Rita must have a lively time.'

'You don't need small talk when you're in love. Sorry.'

'What?'

'I seem to keep telling you how much I love your ex-wife.'

'Geoffrey! Do you think I'm small-minded or summat? Rita and I *were* married. Now we aren't. She's happy. Terrific! Great!'

Suddenly Geoffrey revealed real animation. He smiled. 'Oh, I'm so glad, Ted,' he said. 'Because we are happy. Sometimes we just sit by the fire, or in the garden on warm nights, listening to the sounds, not saying a word.'

'It sounds riveting,' said Ted. 'All that sitting. Terrific.'

'And yet, at other times . . . ' Geoffrey failed to notice Ted's dry tone, ' . . . well I don't need to tell you . . . you know what a passionate woman she is.'

'*What?* Oh. Yes. Yes! Well, terrific, Geoffrey. Thank you.'

This time Geoffrey did notice Ted's dry tone. It puzzled him. 'What?' he said.

'I'm so thrilled for you. Tell me more about your idyll. Then I'll have the complete picture of your domestic bliss as I sit in my dingy furnished room opening tins of corned beef and baked beans for my solitary tea before I pop down to the pub for me ritual three pints and pretend I'm living.'

'This is another thing I find difficult about English life after being away for so long,' said Geoffrey Ellsworth-Smythe. 'I keep thinking people mean what they say.'

After his conversation with Liz, Rodney had replenished his glass – each glass of wine seemed fractionally less odious than its predecessor – and had made a bee-line for his old sparring partner, Councillor Alf Noddington. Alf Noddington wore his Socialism on his sleeve, which had a leather patch and was attached to a very old sports jacket. To have worn a suit would have been to kowtow to capitalism. Alf Noddington had once told the Tory leader of the council to 'bugger off'. He was an embarrassment to some of the new, smooth Socialists. Rodney liked him. They discussed pipes, pigeons and snooker, and Rodney waves his arms about a lot.

When Rodney reached Betty, he hoped she would ask him what all the excitement had been about, *vis à vis* Alf Noddington.

'Nice conversation with Liz?' said Betty.

Rodney looked at her in astonishment. 'Are you jealous?' he said.

'Well . . . no . . . but . . . '

'You're never jealous. Neither of us is. We don't need to be.'

'I know,' said Betty. 'But before we've just been dealing with the rest of the human race. Now it's . . . '

'Liz.'

'Yes.

'She wants me to pretend to be . . . planning a – I can't even say it, it sounds so ridiculous – to make Neville jealous.'

Betty stared at her glass as if amazed to find that there was still wine in it. She said nothing.

'Don't you believe me?' said Rodney. 'Hell's bells, Betty.

She's trying to make Neville jealous and she makes you jealous.'

'Let's hope she's equally successful with Neville,' said Betty.

Liz had also taken her time before rejoining Neville, not in the hope that he would have forgotten her meeting with Rodney, but in the belief that he might become more suspicious if she appeared to be trying to hide its significance from him.

'There you are,' he said, when she finally returned.

'Yes. Here I am. Have you missed me?'

'Well you haven't exactly been crossing the Sahara. I assumed you'd come back when you'd finished your little chat with Rodney.'

'Ah. You saw.'

'Well, yes. You were looking at the graphs and things. You seemed . . . rather intense. As if . . . which rather surprised me, frankly, because . . . '

'As if what, which rather surprised you frankly, because . . . ?'

'As if you found them interesting, which rather surprised me, frankly, because I don't.'

'We weren't talking about the graphs and things.' Liz tried to invest her words with a significance beyond their meaning. 'We were talking about life and things.'

'Ah.'

'Rodney's a very interesting man. I like him.'

Liz gave a little private smile at the memory of her conversation with Rodney. It was intended to infuriate Neville without making him suspect that it had been intended to infuriate him. It was a subtle smile, exquisitely judged. It was a total failure.

'Well, so do I,' said Neville.

'Oh Neville!'

The senior partner in Badger, Badger, Fox and Badger was puzzled.

'What did I say?' he said to Liz's departing back. 'I didn't say anything!'

The light was fading again as Elvis hurried back to Jenny. His interview with Councillor Wendy Bullock had been disappointing. Common sense didn't make for controversy.

'Sorry about that,' he said. 'Have you missed me?'

224

'I wonder what sort of person he's sharing a cell with,' said Jenny.

'Jenny!'

'Well, I can't believe he's got one to himself. Not with all the overcrowding there is. Probably there's three of them.'

'Jenny!'

'Three might be better than two, in case the other one was a real psychopathic brute. Unless they were both psychopathic brutes. I mean, I'm not one of those people who think all prisoners are psychopathic brutes, heavens no! Lots of them are just mixed up and misunderstood victims of a cruel society. But I'm not naïve. Some *are* psychopathic brutes. And with Paul's luck . . . '

'You seem to be thinking of him almost all the time,' said Elvis.

'I suppose I am rather, tonight.'

'I didn't realise you loved me that much!'

'But I do!'

Jenny kissed him warmly.

The first either of them knew of the approach of Simon and Lucinda was when they heard Simon say, 'How distasteful!' They sprang apart with a haste that they regretted instantly.

'What?' said Jenny.

'Kissing,' said Simon.'

'Oh yes,' said Elvis. 'Filthy habit. Glad to hear Simon doesn't do filthy things like that to you, Lucinda.' He wrinkled his face into a parody of puritan disgust. 'Kiss kiss. Ugh! Horrid! Wet! Messy!'

'Elvis? Do me a favour. Shut up,' said Lucinda.

'Well said, darling,' said her fiancé admiringly.

'Yes. Immensely witty,' said Elvis.

'Simon didn't mean kissing is distasteful,' explained Lucinda unnecessarily. 'He meant you two kissing today is distasteful.'

'Your husband's in prison, Jenny, or had you forgotten?' said Simon with the scorn of an elder brother whose sister expects a relationship based on equality and not on protectiveness.

'No, she hasn't quite forgotten,' said Elvis.

'Don't start giving me moral lectures, Simon,' said the ungrateful younger sister, 'or I'll start to resent you. Are you and Lucinda so morally pure yourselves?'

'Yes,' said Lucinda.

'Simon!' said Elvis.

'Apart from Simon's isolated lapse, which he's told me all about and I've forgiven,' said Lucinda smugly.

'No lapses at all in your past, Lucinda?' said Jenny.

'Unfashionably for this day and age, no. In fifty-seven days Simon will become the first person in the world to know my body.'

'We were planning to invite you both,' said Simon hastily.

'I'll watch with interest,' said Elvis. 'I may even be able to give you a tip or two.'

A person who has suddenly seen the light needs disciples. A person who has made a painful climb towards maturity and fulfilment hunts, more modestly, for a protégé. Councillor Rita Simcock, former housewife and grey smudge, hadn't realised that she had been hunting for a protégé and hadn't realised that she had found one. She began to realise it now in the surge of warm affection which she felt as she approached Carol Fordingbridge, former beauty queen.

'Enjoying the exhibition?' Rita asked.

'Well . . . roads. They aren't really me. But thank you for inviting me on your great . . . on what would have been your great . . . '

'Well, I – '

Rita broke off as she saw Liz making a rather strange exit on the far side of the room. Liz gave Rodney a meaningful look. Rodney pretended to ignore it. Betty didn't. Neville, watching, frowned. Rita, watching Neville watching and frowning, frowned.

'Good Lord!' she said. 'What's . . . ?' She stopped.

'Liz up to?' said Carol.

'No. Well, none of my . . . How *are* you, Carol?' It was a meaningful question. The unspoken sub-text was, 'After your typically disgusting treatment at the hands of a man, my son.' Carol understood the sub-text and said, 'I'm fine, Mrs Simcock. Honestly.'

Mrs Simcock! Didn't Carol realise that she was Rita's protégé? 'Mrs Simcock!' reproved Rita. 'I'm not your boy-friend's mother any more. Call me Rita.'

'Are you so much more friendly to me now because I'm not your son's fiancée?' asked Carol.

'I suppose I became sympathetic to you because of how he treated you. And then I realised how much I . . . how much I . . .'

Rita broke off again as she saw Rodney attempt to make an unobtrusively obtrusive exit. He made his way to the door with painfully studied nonchalance, walking with slow soft steps, as if hoping to sound as if he was hoping not to be heard, and with hunched shoulders, as if hoping to look as if he was hoping not to be seen. Neville, watching, frowned again. Rita caught Betty's eye and didn't know how to respond. She turned back to Carol.

'Sorry,' she said. 'Where was I?'

'I'm not quite sure. You said you realised how much you . . . and then you went into a kind of trance.'

'Sorry. I just wondered what . . .'

'Rodney's up to.'

'No. Well, none of my . . . No, I realised how much more there is to you than my wretched boy realised. Look, I'd love to have a chat with you about life and things. Why don't you come to supper one night?'

Elvis, scurrying past them in the hope of beating Jane Turnbull to his next interviewee, said, 'What are you two plotting?'

'My exciting future without you,' said Carol.

'Oh God!' said Elvis, hurtling onwards to nab his man.

'I will,' Carol told Rita. 'He's talked me into it.'

'Sandra!' said Ted. 'Can I have a word? Please.'

'I can't just drop everything,' said Sandra, who was carrying a plate of water biscuits spread with cream cheese.'

'Why not? You usually do.' Ted winced. 'Sorry. Tasteless joke, bitterly regretted. No, I . . . er . . . what are you doing here, anyroad?'

'Unlike some people, your ex-wife is loyal to her friends.'

Ted winced again.

'She asked me if I'd be free if she recommended me, and I said, "Yes, I can always change with Antonio. He's terrific about things like that. Well, having no ties over here it doesn't make much difference to him."'

Ted found himself having unpleasant thoughts about other things about which Antonio with no ties might be terrific.

'Please, Sandra,' he said. 'I must talk to you.'

'Can't live without me?'

'Something of the sort.'

'We *had* better talk then.'

'We don't want tongues wagging,' said Ted. 'I'll go first. You follow. Meet you in the store cupboard opposite the top of the stairs.'

Ted hurried off before Sandra could ask him how he knew about the store cupboard. He didn't want to admit that not an hour earlier he had steeled himself to face a crowded room of local bigwigs, and found himself smiling at rows of cheap, folding chairs.

'Would you like to come to my yoga class some time?' said Carol eagerly.

'Sorry. I missed that,' admitted Rita. 'I was just wondering what . . . ' She stopped.

'Ted was doing.'

'No. Well, it's none of my . . . '

It was Sandra's turn to attempt an unobtrusive exit.

'Now we know,' said Carol.

'You don't miss much, do you?' said Rita.

'Not a lot. Nor do you.'

'I miss nothing. It's awful.'

In the store cupboard, which was lit by one bare bulb, there were rows of folding chairs, two tea urns that had known better days, a selection of environmentally unsound cleaning fluids, banished now that the council had gone green, a bronze griffin presented by the City of Namur at a twinning ceremony, and a series of cruel framed cartoons lampooning councillors long forgotten and, to judge from the lampoons, deservedly so.

In this unlikely setting, Ted Simcock faced the unemployed bakery assistant he had met at the DHSS, and with whom he had fallen so rapidly in and out of love. He looked embarrassed. The cake-loving Sandra Pickersgill looked almost serene as she waited, plate of water biscuits in hand, for Ted to speak.

'Sandra?' he began without confidence. 'I just wanted to say . . . '

'There's no point,' said Sandra firmly.

'All right. All right. But I want to say it anyway. All right?'

'Yeah, but make it quick.'

'Right. I'll make it quick.' He searched for the words. 'Oh heck.'

'Was that it – "Oh heck"?'

'You know it wasn't. Would I get you in here just to say "Oh heck". I mean . . . would I?'

'Well hurry up. I've work to do.'

'Right. Right.' Ted tried to smile. Sandra waited impatiently. 'Sandra?' Words failed him again. 'Oh heck.' Sandra looked at her watch. 'Sandra? I . . . ' Ted couldn't meet her eye. He looked away, met the griffin's eye, and looked back hurriedly. 'I treated you very badly over . . . that woman, and everything, because . . . I had false values. I worshipped false shibboleths. I abased myself before empty icons.'

'You what?'

'I craved for success, money, respect among my peers, fame.'

'Fame?' Sandra sounded incredulous.

'In my small pond. I wanted to be a big fish. I was seduced by glamour, charm, elegance, sophistication.'

'All the things I haven't got.'

'Yes. No! Yes. All the things you don't need, because . . . you're Sandra. You're yourself. You're honest . . . you're fun . . . you're beautiful. Yes, Sandra. Beautiful.'

'I didn't argue.'

'No. Why should you? Because you are. No, I mean it.' Ted gulped. He was absurdly aware of the griffin. 'I love you. I did before, and I didn't realise it, and I've treated you right badly, and it'll serve me right if you ignore me, but I don't care about any of those things any more – fame and image and credit rating and the latest car registration and all that cobblers. If you have me back, which I won't blame you if you won't, but if you will, I'll love you for the rest of your life . . . my life.'

Ted's words echoed into silence. Sandra stood as still as the folding chairs, as unyielding as the tea urns, as fierce as the griffin.

'Thanks,' she said. 'Can I go now?'

'What?' said Ted. 'Oh. Yes. Yes. There's no . . . no pressure. No, go. Go. Right.'

Sandra went.

'Oh heck,' said Ted.

More than half an hour had passed since Rodney's unobtrusively obtrusive exit. The sky had no colour left in it. Sandra had returned, followed by Ted. The deputy housing officer had choked on a water biscuit. Rodney made an unobtrusively obtrusive entrance, dripping with innocence.

'Nice time?' enquired Betty sharply.

'No. Let's just hope it works.'

'Oh yes. *Awful* if you had to do it again.'

'Yes. Yes! It would be, Betty. Betty!'

'Sorry. I trust you.' She tried to smile. 'I don't trust her. And I don't quite trust you . . . not to be defeated by her.'

'I think I'd better go and have a word with Neville,' said Rodney. 'I don't want this dragging on.'

He hurried over to Neville, who excused himself from a numbing conversation with the anaesthetist. Neville's face, usually so eager to please, was a state archive. 'Hello, Rodney,' he said. 'Been outside?'

'Yes. I fancied a bit of . . . '

'A bit of what?'

'Air. A bit of air.'

'Ah. Air. See anybody else out there, fancying a bit of air?'

'Yes. Funnily enough. Liz. Funnily enough.'

'Ah.'

'I think I can claim a bit of insight into psychology, Neville, and it seems to me that Liz is – how can I put it? – trying to cement your marriage by having a little flirtatious chat with me, to make you fume with jealousy.'

'Ah.'

'To make you commit yourself. As I see it, Liz knows what Laurence would have done – ignored it. She just has to know that history isn't repeating itself. She can't let her life go down the lines it did with Laurence. She's hoping that you'll make a scene, sweep her off her feet, take her home and make mad, passionate love to her.'

'What, tonight?'

'Yes.'

'What, make a scene tonight, in front of everyone here tonight, tonight?'

'Yes.'

'Oh Lord.'

Ted was flattered to be spoken to with such interest by the Labour leader, even though the conversation was about his ex-wife. Councillor Mirfield had the knack of seeming to be interested in you alone, so that it was only afterwards you realised that he had been using you. A self-important man, an ambitious man, but not an evil man. A man genuinely dedicated to helping the weak against the strong, but flawed by vanity and dislike of women.

'You were married to Councillor Simcock, our rising new star, for quite a while, weren't you?' he asked.

'Quarter of a century.'

'Rita must have been devastated when you . . . ' Councillor Mirfield stopped, as if sparing Ted from the need to feel guilty.

'Well . . . yes. She's put a brave face on it. Got a job. Gone into politics. Got engaged.'

'Failed to turn up at the wedding.'

'That's right.'

'And now she's . . . er . . . I believe.'

'That's right. She is.

'With Liz Badger's brother?'

'Not running her down,' said Ted, 'but the reason she's throwing herself on unsuitable men is to fill the chasm caused by our bust-up. It's sad. I'm very sad for her.'

'Will there be wedding bells there, do you think?'

'I doubt it.' Ted, so close to being a social outcast, felt a man of the world again, being asked his views on matters of such delicacy by such a worldly man. 'I think Rita feels she can get what she wants without marriage.'

'What does she want?'

'You know. Companionship. Happiness. Intellectual and emotional fulfilment. Nooky.'

'They sleep together?'

'Conversations I've had recently with Geoffrey and Rita render that conclusion unavoidable.' Ted was pleased with the dignified sentence. Then it struck him that he might be painting himself in rather a prying light, so he added hastily, 'I mean, not that I care. Why should I?'

'Quite,' said Councillor Mirfield. 'Thank you, Ted.'

Councillor Mirfield moved on, leaving Ted rather puzzled.

'Thank you?' he said to himself. 'What for?'

Elvis approached, carrying a beer and a glass of white wine.

'Dad?' he said. 'Will you do an in-depth interview with me? The torment of the father.'

Ted was outraged. 'You mean you intend to use your brother's misfortune to further your career?' he said. 'You selfish unprincipled swine.'

'I just thought, as a prominent ex-foundry owner, given a public platform – 'cos a lot of people listen – if they heard you making an impressive defence of the values you believe in, a moving analysis of the clash between your parental love and your respect for law and order . . . you never know . . . it might further *your* career.'

'Eleven o'clock tomorrow suit you?'

'Right.'

Elvis took Jenny her glass of wine.

'Thanks,' she said. 'Do you think he'll have "facilities"? It must be awful having to slop out.'

'Stop thinking about him,' said Elvis. 'I'm not worthy of such constant love.' Rita was approaching, smiling. 'Please, Jenny,' he implored hurriedly. 'If thinking about Paul could get him out of prison, I'd think about him all night.' He turned to Rita. 'Mum! You look cheerful.'

'Don't I?' said Rita. 'I'm doing my best.'

'It's a very interesting exhibition,' said Jenny. 'And all because you got elected. This really is your great night.'

'If one more person calls it my great night, I'll scream. My son, your children's father, is in prison. Or had you forgotten?'

Elvis hurried after his mother, leaving Jenny staring with her mouth open, like a trout that has heard bad news.

'Mum!' Elvis's cloak of cynicism was ripped from him by the tide of events. 'Jenny's been talking about nothing but Paul all night and I begged her to stop and that's the only reason she wasn't and you shouldn't have said that. Not today.'

'Oh Lord.' Rita returned to Jenny, full of contrition. 'Jenny! I'm sorry. I'm all on edge.'

'Me too.' Jenny managed one of her watery little smiles. 'You see, Elvis, it just isn't any use trying not to think about Paul tonight.'

'As we are thinking about him,' said Elvis, 'how about doing an in-depth interview with me tomorrow, Mum? The torment of the mother.'

'Elvis!'

'Your mother doesn't want to exploit Paul's predicament for your career, Elvis,' said Jenny.

'Thanks, Jenny,' said Rita, with just a slight edge to her voice. She didn't quite feel that it had been necessary for Jenny to spell this out.

'Hell's bells,' said Elvis. 'Women!'

'I know,' said Carol, passing by with withering timing. 'They do get in the way of your meteoric rise to fame, don't they?'

Elvis looked at his ex-fiancée, and then at his mother, and then at his lover, and felt hard done by.

The last of those who had made unobtrusive exits made her obtrusively unobtrusive entrance. Liz Badger, a woman not known for her unobtrusiveness, approached her husband with a carefully casual air.

Neville greeted her with a carefully neutral smile.

'You look better after your spot of air,' he said. 'There's a touch of colour in your cheeks. Almost one could mistake it for . . . a flush of excitement.'

'The wind, I expect. I walked across those little gardens that lead down to the river. Rather pleasant. Lots of salvia and roses. Everything steaming after the rain. And a gash of colour in the Western sky.'

'Very picturesque. And the Gadd, was it romantic?'

'It was muddy and swollen.'

'Did you see . . . Rodney out there . . . at all?'

'Rodney?' Liz widened her eyes in simulated amazement. 'Why on earth should I have?'

'Well . . . he popped out just after you popped out, and he popped back in just before you popped back in, and he looked as if he . . . had a flush of excitement.'

'The wind, I expect,' they said in unison.

'I did see a shadowy figure,' said Liz reflectively. 'I heard . . . grunts. I thought it was either an escaped pig, or two people being passionate.'

'Rodney and someone?'

'It's possible, I suppose.'

'Wouldn't they have got rather damp?'

'They might have had a rug.'

'They might, mightn't they?' Neville paused. He hoped it was a dramatic pause. 'So you didn't yourself actually see Rodney yourself . . . at all?'

'Neville!' Liz sounded as if the thought had just crossed her mind for the first time. What a leading lady the Gadd Players had lost, because she was too snobbish to join an amateur group. 'You don't think Rodney and I . . . Neville!'

'Liz?' said Neville decisively.

'Yes?' Liz was excited by his decisiveness.

'I . . . would you like another drink?'

Liz's head sank onto Neville's shoulder in disappointment. Neville looked puzzled.

Ted approached Rodney diffidently, regretting the extent of his earlier rudeness. He noticed that Rodney was swaying slightly. Perhaps he'd have forgotten.

'Hello, Rodney,' he said. 'You seem to be chatting to Liz a lot tonight. I mean . . . not that I've . . . but you can't help . . . '

'I dream about it every night.'

'With Liz? Rodney!'

'Meat.'

'Meat?'

'Pork chops. Steak. Even saveloys. Last night I dreamt it was Christmas. We didn't have paper chains. We decorated the house with chains of black puddings. We didn't have an angel on top of the tree. We had a rissole. No fairy lights. Illuminated faggots.'

'But I thought you were totally committed to vegetarianism.'

'Betty is. And I didn't like all that factory farming. But things that aren't factory farmed, and game, and fish, and . . . more fish. All my employees, and specially Rita and Jenny – and my Betty – they all think I'm a born-again vegetarian. A fundalentilist.' Rodney paused briefly, to admire his incredible cleverness. 'I'm not. I'm a businessman. It's profitable. I identified a gap in the market. I filled it.'

Ted hesitated. Was Rodney in the right state to be receptive? But the cue was too good to miss.

'Is that offer of a job still open?'

Rodney was amazed, if rather slowly. 'But you were very offensive.'

'Only in fun,' said Ted hastily. 'Well . . . I mean . . . I thought you were on a moral crusade. Shrewd business venture, that's more my line.'

'You were very rude, Ted. So I suggest you stuff yourself up your own backside, boil yourself for two hours over a moderate heat, and serve yourself with noodles and a tossed salad.' He laughed, loudly, slowly, several times, with deep, rich satisfaction at his immense wit.

He moved on, still laughing, put his empty glass on Eric's table, took a full glass and lurched towards Carol.

'Carol!' he said. 'You look lovely.' He attempted a gracious smile. It came out as a bit of a leer.

'Thank you,' said Carol.

'I'm very happily sliced . . . ' Rodney looked puzzled. 'No, not sliced, that's meat . . . honey-roasted ham, juicy rare beef, glistening with blood . . . happily spliced. If I was younger, I'd – and unspliced – I'd . . . but other, younger people are, and I hope one of them will.'

'Thank you very much,' said Carol drily.

Sandra was serving coffee, that gesture of apparent hospitality which is actually a hint that it's almost time to leave.

Councillor Mirfield sprang into action. He approached Rita with a sense of urgency.

'High time I made a little speech, Rita,' he said. 'Nothing formal. Er, it has been suggested that since this is, er . . . in a way . . . your . . . '

'Great night?' It wasn't quite as painful saying it as listening to it.

'Well . . . yes.' Councillor Mirfield was put out. He didn't like being interrupted. 'That you should make a little speech. You don't want to make a speech, do you?'

'Heavens, no.'

'Good. That's settled.'

'I will, though.'

'You what?'

'You wouldn't want me to disappoint my public, would you?' Rita smiled. Councillor Mirfield tried not to look too obviously sour. 'Right, then. That's settled. I'll just have a word with Geoffrey. I'd like to give him the chance of escaping before I make my speech, in case it embarrasses him.'

'He can't be much of a . . . ' Councillor Mirfield realised that his annoyance with Rita was making him indiscreet.

'Of a what?'

Councillor Mirfield found himself forced to explain, against his wishes, despite all his experience.

'Well, whatever he is to you,' he said. 'Lover, as I'm led to believe.'

'I see. And who's led you to believe that?'

'Your ex-husband.' Councillor Mirfield gave a grim smile. He didn't mind landing Ted in it now that the subject had been broached. But he didn't expect his answer to galvanise Rita to quite the extent that it did. He said, 'Rita! Time is pressing,' but he said it to her departing back.

Rita's anger swept her towards Ted, through groups of small-town big-wigs, who scattered before her like guillemots before a liner. But Ted was deep in conversation with an attractive, dark-haired lady in her thirties, and a lifetime's careful practice of good manners proved stronger than Rita's spurt of fury. She stood watching, waiting, fuming, while her ex-husband chatted up this younger woman.

'I used to run the Jupiter Foundry,' Ted was saying. 'You may have heard of it.'

'Yes.'

'Well, we made . . . you have?'

'Yes.'

Ted tried to hide his surprise.

'In fact, I bought a poker off you,' said the dark-haired lady. Her brown eyes were twinkling.

'Good Lord!' said Ted. His eyes strayed to Sandra, standing beside a display of photographs of urban dereliction, gripping her tray of coffee cups with whitened knuckles. She turned away

236

sharply. As his eyes followed her, he saw Rita, watching, fuming. He forced his eyes back onto this rather sultry, youngish woman with the gently twinkling eyes. 'Good Lord!' he repeated. He must concentrate on her. This was the chance of a lifetime. 'It's a small world! Fancy that. You and me, linked by a poker.'

'Amazing.'

'Absolutely. Is it a sign, I wonder?'

The brown eyes twinkled even more. 'Not a happy sign, if it was. The knob kept falling off.'

'Oh heck.' Could it be that she was laughing at him? And what did Rita want? And what did Sandra think? Why, suddenly, in the emotional desert that his life had become, all these women, and all so difficult to handle? He heard his voice chuntering on. 'We did have design problems at one . . . ' He turned towards Rita and, holding his hand beside his back, made a frantic signal to her to go away. He turned back to the dark-haired lady, looked deep into her twinkling eyes and said, 'Anyroad, changing the subject from pokers, would you like to . . . ?' and at that moment Rita could stand it no longer.

'I'm sorry,' she said. 'Ted, I have to have a word.'

'Rita!' said Ted angrily.

The dark-haired lady scuttled off almost as if making an escape.

'Rita!' repeated Ted. 'I was talking to that young lady. We were having a very interesting chat. Establishing social rapport. I was on the point of cracking it.'

'Well if you don't want to be interrupted while you're cracking it you shouldn't go round gabbing about me and Geoffrey.'

'Rita! I don't gab. I mean . . . I don't. I don't know what you and Geoffrey get up to, anyroad. Maybe you make love. Maybe he ties you to a totem pole and worships you and sacrifices live chickens to you. Just don't tell Jenny if he does. Or maybe you just play scrabble. I don't know. I don't care. I'm not interested. I mean it. I'm not.'

Anger is hard to sustain, and Rita felt hers slipping away. She felt, instead, a subtler desire, to tease Ted. He had given her the perfect opening.

'We do,' she said. 'Regularly. Almost every night.' Ted tried not to look upset. 'Geoffrey loves scrabble.'

237

'Ah.' Ted tried to hide his relief. 'Good. I'm very pleased to hear it.'

'And then we make love.'

Ted tried not to look as if he'd been hit by a juggernaut. 'Good,' he said. 'Very good. Terrific. For a moment there you had me worrying that he was . . . you know . . . all scrabble and no trousers. I'm very relieved. But has it ever occurred to you that maybe I'd like to make love to somebody too, and not be interrupted in the middle of cha . . . well, not chatting them up, that sounds crude . . . in the middle of establishing social, emotional and cultural rapport?'

'How dare you gab about my private life to Councillor Mirfield?'

'Rita! I didn't.' Ted had all the indignation of a deeply wronged man. 'He cross-examined me. Wormed it out of me. It's true, Rita. I mean . . . have I ever lied to you?'

'Yes. Often.'

'Yes. Often. What? No. Well, yes, it's true, I have. Sometimes. But not this time. I didn't even realise he was cross-examining me till he said "Thank you", and I didn't know what he was saying "Thank you" for. It's true, Rita. It . . . '

But Rita had gone. She knew that it was true. Once again she was striding angrily past little knots of talkers, creating worry on the faces of Councillor Wendy Bullock and Councillor Alf Noddington, and amused speculation on the faces of Mrs Bellows, the town clerk's wife, and Morris Wigmore, the deputy leader of the Conservatives, whose son had met a sticky end in Brisbane.

Councillor Mirfield excused himself from the Medical Officer of Health and Mrs Barraclough, when he saw the expression on Rita's face.

'Did you systematically question Ted about my private life?' hissed Rita.

Councillor Mirfield smiled an appeaser's smile. 'You've made an excellent start as a councillor,' he said. 'Already you've proved yourself an invaluable committee man . . . woman . . . person.'

'You didn't answer,' said Rita, unappeased. 'That means you did. I'm learning about politics fast. There's no need to be evasive with me, Councillor Mirfield. I'm not a TV interviewer, just an obscure local councillor.'

238

'Obscure?' Councillor Mirfield twitched. 'Hardly obscure. You hardly habitually keep a low profile, social life-wise. The actions of your son plastered all over the papers, overshadowing this launch.'

'You're jealous of me.'

Councillor Mirfield was too old a hand not to be able to respond to a direct accusation with a fine-sounding phrase.

'There's no such thing as a private life in public life, Councillor Simcock,' he thundered.

'Come on, Councillor Mirfield. Let's make those speeches. Time is pressing,' said Rita.

'Are you all right?' said Betty Sillitoe anxiously.

'Never been lesser righter in my life.'

'Oh, Rodney.'

'I'm a sham. No, I am. I'm a sham. It's a shame, but I'm a sham. Do you see what I'm driving at?'

'You're a sham.'

'So you've realised it too!'

Rodney staggered off. Liz buttonholed him, and Betty wasn't going to demean herself by making a scene, so she stood and watched, nervously.

'Oh, bloody hell,' said Rodney. 'Not you again.'

A strange noise, like a pigeon crashing into a wall, floated across the room. Councillor Mirfield was testing the microphone.

'Look, nothing personal, Liz,' slurred Rodney, 'but . . . I wouldn't touch you if you were the last bargepole in China.'

'I don't want you to touch me. Just talk to me.'

At last Neville strode up to his wife's rescue. There was a hard, hurt look on his normally good-natured face.

'This has gone on long enough,' he said firmly.

'Absolutely,' agreed Rodney.

'Neville!' said Liz.

'You're drunk, so I'll speak slowly,' said Neville.

On the platform, Councillor Mirfield, satisfied with the microphone, held up an authoritative hand, silently demanding silence.

'Good idea,' said Rodney. 'Because I'm drunk, so if you speak slowly I'll have a better chance of understanding. That's clever.'

Several people, seeing Councillor Mirfield holding up his hand, began to ask for silence. Their cries of 'Sssh!' and 'Quiet!' drowned the beginning of Neville's stern, slow warning to Rodney.

'If . . . you . . . so . . . much . . . as . . . glance . . . at . . . my . . . wife . . . again . . . '

Silence fell rapidly. Those nearest turned to listen to Neville.

'I . . . will . . . put . . . my . . . dignity . . . at . . . risk . . . and . . . '

By now the silence was complete. More and more people turned to listen to Neville. Councillor Mirfield found himself facing a sea of backs.

'Visibly . . . thrash . . . you . . . to . . . within . . . an . . . inch . . . of . . . your . . . life.'

Rodney considered Neville's words carefully. 'Terrific,' he said. 'Isn't that terrific, Liz? What a terrific idea.'

'Come on, Liz,' said Neville. 'We're going home. I insist.'

'Oh, Neville!' said Liz delightedly.

'Have you quite finished?' called out Councillor Mirfield drily.

Neville looked towards Councillor Mirfield and saw the whole gathering of big-wigs staring at him.

'Oh Lord!' he said, his new assertiveness draining out of him. 'You mean everyone's . . . oh Lord!'

'I don't care,' said Liz. 'Come on.'

She led Neville towards the great double doors of the Gadd Room.

'He's taking me home,' she told the gathering. 'He insists.'

'Yes, I'm taking her home. I insist,' echoed Neville, as Liz pulled him out of the room.

'Can I begin?' said Councillor Mirfield.

Slowly, almost reluctantly, as if the climax of the evening's entertainment had already passed, the assembled guests turned towards Councillor Mirfield.

'Ladies and gentlemen,' said Councillor Mirfield. 'Tonight is a great night.'

Rita squirmed.

'A great night,' repeated Councillor Mirfield. 'Soon our traffic congestion . . . '

A young man, scruffily dressed in jeans and a dirty T-shirt, burst in, drinking from a can of lager and shouting, 'Here we go, here we go, here we go.'

'Oh my God!' The dapper, ageless Eric Siddall turned pale, as the lager lout weaved towards the bar.

'Out!' said Eric, confronting him. 'This is a private party. O U T, out.'

'You what?' said the lager lout.

'O U T spells "Out". L O U T spells "lout". Out, lout!'

The lager lout thought hard.

'Are you calling me a lout?' he said.

'Yes. Want to make something of it?'

Eric grabbled the lager lout in a half-Nelson and frog-marched him to the doors.

'There's ladies present,' he said, 'and we don't want trouble, and we don't want bad language, so piss off.'

He threw the intruder out of the double doors and turned back to face a fish tank of open mouths.

'No problem!' he said, wiping his hands. 'Interruption over. Everything's tickety-boo. Carry on with your speech, councillor. We're all agog.'

Again, the guests turned reluctantly towards Councillor Mirfield, who was just about to open his mouth to speak when Eric added, 'In fact, I personally have rarely been agogger.'

Councillor Mirfield fixed upon Eric a glare which would have quelled a lesser man. But this was Eric Siddall, barman supreme, who had served perfect dry Martinis in a force eleven gale off Biscay, but had never had an opportunity of showing himself to the town in his true colours. This man, of whom any golf club could be proud, smiled back, very unquelled indeed.

'No more interruptions?' said Councillor Mirfield. 'Amazing. As I say, a great night.'

Rita squirmed again.

'And all made possible by the election of Rita Simcock.'

There was loud and prolonged applause. Councillor Mirfield held up his hand for silence.

'Thank you. That's enough,' he said. 'Because time is pressing. And I'm sure you'd like Councillor Simcock to say a *few* words. Councillor Simcock?'

Councillor Mirfield was happy to stand down. His love of his own voice had been destroyed so far as that night was concerned.

But, as Rita stepped to the microphone, he stood quite close to her, to hint that her election was in a way a triumph for him.

'"A great night", says Councillor Mirfield,' said Rita. 'Not for me, because . . . well, you all know . . . and I wouldn't be his mother if I didn't worry. I know that in public life we're supposed to . . . but I don't think I can do that. Anyroad, it's because of my by-election victory that this exhibition . . . '

Rita looked down on the Mayor and Mayoress, on Geoffrey, who loved her, on Ted, with whom she had lived for twenty-five years, on her elder son and his lover, on her employers, on her protégé, on her fellow councillors and council officials and their partners, and they all looked up at her anxiously, because she was pausing for far too long, and the words that she knew she must speak formed themselves as if unbidden.

'I've got to say it,' she said. 'Things like what's happened help you get things in proportion.' She paused again, but this was a controlled pause, well-judged. She felt as if she had made the speech before. She knew what was coming next. The sombre Gadd Room seemed to retreat and approach, retreat and approach, as in a dream, and yet this was no dream. She felt very solid; a woman, a mother. 'Outer inner relief ring road. Inner inner relief ring road. Outer outer relief ring road. Inner outer relief ring road. It'd be a great relief to me if we didn't have a ring road at all. Clogged motorways. Look at the M25. Simcock's Law. Traffic expands to fill the roads available. Too many people rushing to look at places which are being ruined because too many people are rushing to look at them. I think we should stop before we let our town be destroyed by machines. Give it back to pedestrians before there's nothing left to give. A great night? Sorry, Councillor Mirfield.'

Rita stepped down hurriedly. Some people applauded enthusiastically, others in embarrassment, others not at all. There was even a jeer or two.

People hurried up to her from all sides.

'That was unbelievable,' said Councillor Mirfield.

'Oh, thank you very much,' said Rita.

'That was amazing, Rita,' said Geoffrey.

'I was worried you might be embarrassed.'

'Of course not. I love you.' He began to kiss her, then became aware of Ted. 'Sorry, Ted,' he said. 'I've done it again.'

'No, no,' said Ted. 'No, no. Be my guest. I mean . . . '

'We have to go,' said Jenny. 'The baby-sitter's unproven.'

'And I've got work to do. That was great copy, Mum.' Elvis turned to Councillor Mirfield. '"Newest councillor's sensational outburst against road plan". Great stuff.'

Councillor Mirfield glowered. Rita saw him glowering and said, 'Oh Elvis – I will do that interview for you. A mother in torment. One o'clock suit you?'

'Great. I'm doing a father in torment at eleven. Bye. See you both.'

Jenny kissed Rita. 'Even if there are "facilities",' she said, 'I don't expect they're allowed to go during the night.'

Elvis's bleeper bleeped.

'News desk! Next scoop!' He hurried out, followed by Jenny.

'I hoped I might influence you, Rita, profile-wise,' said Councillor Mirfield.

'Oh, but you have,' said Rita. 'I wouldn't have agreed to do the interview but for you.'

'Are you trying to sabotage your political career?'

'No. Just telling you I won't be playing by your rules.'

Councillor Mirfield gave Rita a final sour, disillusioned look, and stomped off.

'He's bitten off more than he can chew with you, Rita,' said Ted.

'Thank you, Ted.'

'It wasn't a compliment.'

'I liked it, though.'

The Gadd Room was buzzing with discussion and debate. Councillor Rita Simcock, who had set the cat among the pigeons, stood in momentary silence with her lover and her ex-husband.

'You're very quiet, Geoffrey,' said Ted. 'Are you wondering what you've let yourself in for?'

Geoffrey gave Ted one of his gentle smiles, which were disconcerting, because the sarcastic ones were so difficult to tell from the affectionate ones.

'Sorry to disappoint you, Ted,' he said, 'but, no, I'm pretty good at chewing. Our mother taught us to chew everything thirty-two times.'

Ted gave Geoffrey up as a bad job. 'No, but . . . I mean . . .
Rita . . . do you think you're cut out for politics?'

'Listen. I care about the world's problems, and I want to be
of some use, and not entirely waste my life, and I want to be
honest and open, and I want, if I make mistakes – and I will
– to admit them.'

'This is what I say. Do you think you're cut out for politics?'

Eric, dapper in his white jacket and bow-tie, brought a tray
of glasses.

'More wine, anybody?' he enquired.

Rita took a glass and thanked him.

'Eric!' said Ted. 'What you did just then . . . I mean . . .
wasn't it? Amazing.'

'Amazing, sir? Why?'

'Well . . . I mean . . . you're . . . aren't you?'

'Ted!' said Rita and Geoffrey.

'Well, he is.'

'With respect, sir, that's stereotyped thinking,' said Eric. 'My
fellow barman Alec Skiddaw – I don't know if you know him,
he's the only barman in this town I've any respect for – he told
me that his great-uncle from Hereford was as bent as a nine
pound note and undefeated in thirty-two fights. Only knocked
down once, and that wasn't in the ring, it was in a fracas at
chucking out time in Leominster after an auctioneer's runner
had called him a nancy boy.'

Ted stared at Eric in amazement, partly that anybody could
listen to one of Alec's stories with sufficient attention to remember it, and partly because of the contrast between his behaviour
tonight and his performance at the Christening.

'Yes . . . but . . . I mean . . . ' he said, ' . . . Sandra knocked
you down.'

'Call me a male chauvinist pig if you like,' said Eric, 'but I'd
never hit a woman. Not in me. But tonight, well, my job is
serving alcohol. Alcohol is a civilised pleasure. Abuse of that
civilised pleasure is abuse of my professional standing. So, I
stand up and am counted. Tickety-boo.'

Eric moved on to offer drinks to the Registrar of Births and
Deaths and Mrs Fradley.

It was a stunned little group that Simon and Lucinda
joined.

'Simon wants to know if you can get the ring road plan scrapped,' said Lucinda to Rita.

'Hasn't he got the courage to ask me himself?' said Rita to Lucinda.

'Haven't you got the courage to ask her yourself?' said Lucinda to Simon.

'Of course I have,' said Simon to Lucinda, 'but, unlike some of my mother's close relatives . . . ' he flung a resentful glance at Geoffrey, 'I care about her.'

'Of course he has,' said Lucinda to Rita, 'but, unlike some of his mother's close relatives . . . ' she flung a resentful glance at Geoffrey, 'he cares about her.'

'I wonder who he has in mind?' said Geoffrey.

'Tell him, "No, I can't get it scrapped,"' said Rita to Lucinda.

'No, she can't get it scrapped,' said Lucinda to Simon.

'Damn!' said Simon to Lucinda.

'Damn!' said Lucinda to Rita.

'Simon? Thanks,' said Ted.

'What on earth for?' said Simon.

'Every time I meet you, I think, maybe my sons aren't such berks after all.'

Simon and Lucinda flounced off.

Ted had noticed Rita's look and said gently, 'Sorry, Rita, I just can't resist that Simon. I don't really think they're berks. I mean, not . . . er . . . and, I mean, I do love them.'

'Ted!' Rita became quite gentle too. 'Sorry I interrupted you with that woman.'

'Oh, don't worry about that,' said Ted. 'The affair was doomed from the start. The knob fell off her poker.'

He moved off. Before Rita could say 'Poor Ted' he'd returned.

'And don't pity me,' he said, as if he could read her mind. 'There's no need. I still have me moments. Women still occasionally make me offers I can't refuse.'

On Sandra's face there was a proud, purposeful, even serene expression. She walked up to Ted and smiled, as if she might be about to make him an offer he couldn't refuse.

'Sausage roll, sir?' she said.

'Thank you, Sandra,' said Ted with dignity. He took a

quartered sausage roll, shoved it in his mouth, and shrugged his shoulders at Rita.

Rodney stumbled into the room, pursued by Betty.

'No! Rodney!' she pleaded.

'No, Betty. It must be said,' he said.

He tacked his way into the middle of the room, narrowly missing crashing into several people. All conversation had stopped.

'Rita!' he said. 'You've had problems. Son in prison and other son carrying on with the son in prison's wife and your ex-husband's ex-lover's husband who is the stepfather of the son in prison's wife dragging her away in the middle of speeches, and I want to show that great twat-arse Councillor Thingummy that you have some friends who know how to behave.'

He tried to smile at Rita, who stared back in horror. He lurched, tripped, tried to regain his balance, failed, and fell spectacularly backwards onto the model of the outer inner relief ring road. The table overturned, and Rodney and the model fell to the ground in a heap. The model buckled and cracked. Rodney lay there, legs in the air, head half in the Gadd and half in the fractured remains of Commercial Street, buttocks jammed in a ravine where the abbey and Tannergate had been.

He looked up at Rita, his employee, his friend.

'So,' he slurred, 'just wanted to say, thank you very much for inviting me. It's been a privilege to witness your great night.'

Rita screamed.

Sixth Do

September:
The Funeral

On a day as grey as the face of a dying man . . . no. Too obvious. After weeks of mellow, golden sunshine, a pall of dark cloud hung over the old abbey, as if the universe itself were in mourning . . . no. More like a weather report than a piece of memorable broadcasting.

'Hello.'

The long-haired Carol Fordingbridge's greeting filtered slowly into Elvis's brain. He looked up in some surprise.

'Are you here?' he said. 'Oh Lord. I've given you another chance to be sarcastic about my deeply searching philosophical questions.'

'I wouldn't. Not today.' Carol was wearing a navy, two-piece suit, with a lime-green skirt. The effect was tasteful, restrained, yet attractive.

'What I meant was,' explained Elvis, 'I'm surprised you've been invited, since you aren't family.'

'I haven't. I've come because I felt I must. Sorry, was I interrupting something?'

'No. No.'

He couldn't tell her that while he'd been sitting on a bench beneath the abbey, he'd been imagining that he was honing a colour piece on the funeral of a world leader for this week's 'Letter From Yorkshire'.

Rita greeted them with quick kisses and silent speculation. She was dressed soberly, but not entirely in black. Her pleated skirt was black, but her cross-over jacket had a large floral pattern, in green and cream as well as black.

'It's all right, Mum,' said Elvis. 'Nothing's happened. We aren't together again.'

'I wasn't even thinking you might be.' She was telling more

little social lies, and telling them with greater smoothness, now that she was a councillor. That would have to be watched. In the meantime she might as well round off her little lie. 'It's hardly the time for idle speculation.'

'I'd have thought Carol and I being together again, if we were, which we aren't, would be too important to be described as "idle speculation".'

'Oh Elvis! Don't say that today of all days the great philosopher is discovering a talent for linguistic analysis.'

'Mum!'

'Sorry. It's nerves. Well, it's all very well saying, "It's not to be a sad occasion. It's to be the celebration of a life, not the mourning of a death," but it puts us all in a very awkward position. If you do care, you're so sad you can't smile. If you don't care, you're so anxious to look as though you do that you daren't smile.'

'I think everybody today will care,' said Carol.

'True.'

'I feel so . . . you know . . . ' said Carol, ' . . . some of the things I said . . . I feel awful.'

Elvis gave her a quick kiss.

'Oooh! Rodney!' said Betty Sillitoe, over-excited as usual. 'Elvis just kissed Carol.'

Betty had come to an abrupt halt, forcing Rodney, who was holding her arm, to stop also.

'Don't be so inquisitive,' said Rodney. 'It isn't appropriate at a funeral, isn't curiosity.' He was wearing a crumpled suit. His tie was sober, but not black.

They moved on slowly, arms linked, between the grave-stones.

'No, I know,' said Betty, 'but . . . I was looking for crumbs of comfort.'

Now Rodney stopped dead, forcing Betty to do so also.

'Crumbs of comfort?' he said. 'Elvis and Jenny are in love. Elvis kissing Carol isn't a crumb of comfort. It's a slice of trouble.'

'No, but . . . I mean . . . ' Betty's dress and hat were black, but her top had a large flower pattern in fuchsia, yellow and blue, and she had a gold chain round her neck. 'If Elvis went back to Carol, then when Paul came out of prison, maybe he and Jenny . . . I mean, Paul is still the father of her children. And I like Carol. Well, I like them all.'

'Well, we can't just stand here all day, liking everybody. Come on. Best foot forward.'

They set off again, slowly. The graveyard had recently been mown. The cuttings smelt of expiring life.

'And smile,' said Rodney.

'You what?'

'They said it was to be a happy day. He would have wanted it. Not that I imagine they had riotous joy in mind. So smile a bit, but not too much.'

'Oh Lord.'

They glided towards their friends, smiling a bit, but not too much.

'Hello,' said Betty to Rita, brightly, but not too brightly. 'Hello,' she said to Elvis, vivaciously, but not too vivaciously. 'Hello, Carol,' she added, inquisitively, but not too inquisitively.

'Oh, we haven't got together again, Betty,' said Carol. 'We just ran into each other.'

'You make it sound like a traffic accident,' said Elvis.

The cynical Elvis Simcock closed his eyes in uncynical horror. The thrusting media man was submerged beneath a tidal wave of gaucherie.

'The first tactless remark of the day,' said Rita, and she immediately wished that she hadn't.

'Well, it saved me,' said Rodney. 'I was just going to make the first tactless remark of the day.'

'What?' said Betty, eagerly, but not too eagerly.

'Well, it's tactless. If I make it now it'll be the second tactless remark of the day.'

'You can't not now. Not after you've . . . well, not whetted our appetites exactly, we don't have such insensitive appetites that they'd be whetted by tactless remarks on such a sad occasion,' said Betty, over-garrulous as usual. 'But if you don't tell us we'll be wondering, I mean, we're only human, thinking it might be something even more tactless than what it is.'

'Well, all right, then. I was going to say, "Fancy this happening to Ted of all people. He's always prided himself so much on his safe driving."'

'Well, there you are,' said Betty. 'That's life.'

'Hardly life, exactly, in this case,' said Rita.

'I think that's the trouble with funerals.' Carol leapt into the conversation. It was as if they all felt that a moment of silence would be unbearable. 'Everything you say . . . the circumstances seem to blow it up out of all proportion. If you say, "We've gorra nice day for it," it seems heartless. If you say, "We've gorra rotten day for it," it seems depressing.'

'Best to shut up really,' said Elvis.

'Elvis!' said Rita.

'Oh, I didn't mean it personally, Carol. Oh Lord. I just meant . . . it's awful standing around jabbering like this when . . . oh heck.' Elvis, on the verge of tears, hurried off along the side of the church, like a hamster staying close to a wall for protection.

Carol looked as if she felt that she ought to go to him.

'No. I'll go,' said Rita.

'Thanks,' said Carol gratefully.

'If you go, certain people in this gossip-mad town will talk.'

'Rita!' said Betty. 'As if anybody would, today.'

Rita hurried off towards Elvis, smiling at a group of mourners, which included Graham Wintergreen and his golfophobic wife, Angela. Councillor Morris Wigmore, Deputy Leader of the Conservatives, smiled back. Rita realised that she shouldn't be smiling, and stopped smiling hurriedly, looking almost as gauche as she had in the grey smudge days. Councillor Wigmore stopped smiling too, perhaps because the funeral was reminding him of his son, who had come to a sticky end in Brisbane.

'Are you all right?' Rita asked her elder son.

'Yes. Sorry, Mum. This is stupid.'

'There's nothing stupid in showing grief.'

'I was just thinking . . . it just came home to me . . . poor Dad.'

'I know. I know. It seems wrong to say it, today, but . . . since I can't help thinking it, I may as well say it.'

'I'll say it for you. Whatever Rodney may say about Dad's driving, you're amazed he's never been in an accident before.'

'Well, yes, I am, frankly. Well, better get in the church.'

Groups of mourners were moving slowly towards the abbey, like wading birds forced up a beach by the tide. For all the uneasiness of their conversations in that sombre churchyard, nobody wanted to enter the church and admit the finality of death.

Rita found herself beside Betty as they approached the West Door.

'I didn't know what to wear,' said Betty.

'I know,' said Rita. 'I mean, if it's black, at least you know where you are.'

'I know. I kept saying to myself, "What does it matter what I wear?"'

'I know. But it does.'

'I know. I mean, I agree in theory. About celebrating a life, not mourning a death. But . . . where does it leave us?'

'I vowed a long while ago not to worry about stupid social niceties like that any more.'

'I know. But you still do.'

'I know.'

'Good God!'

The cause of the astonishment hobbled slowly round the corner of the church and stood there, beside the vast buttress, resting on his crutch, staring defiantly. Ted's right leg was encased in plaster, his left arm was in a sling, he had a neck brace, and a large bandage on his forehead, inelegantly held in place by two lengths of Band Aid, only partially hid a great purple and mauve bruise.

'Ted!' said Rita.

'Dad!' said Elvis.

'Ten out of ten for recognition,' said Ted. 'Well, this is a rum do.'

There was an awkward silence. Carol Fordingbridge broke it.

'How are you, Mr Simcock?' she asked.

Ted gave her a searching look, seeking sarcasm where there was only unself-conscious concern.

'Alive, Carol,' he said. 'I'm alive.'

He hobbled towards the porch.

'I'll go and help him sit down,' said Carol.

'Thanks, Carol,' said Rita.

Carol took his sound arm gently.

'I don't know why I should say "thanks",' said Rita. 'It isn't my responsibility. I'm not married to him any more.'

'It's because you have a warm heart, Rita,' said Betty, 'and you know how Ted's suffering. There's nothing more painful than guilt.'

'Not even a broken leg and a broken arm?' said Rodney.

'No. Probably not even that.'

They all turned to look, as the hearse and four silent, tactful limousines drove slowly towards the church. Not a squeak came from any of their brakes as they slid to a halt beyond the unshapely ash, beneath which Gerry Lansdown had addressed his wedding guests eight months ago.

The four silent, tactful drivers of the four silent, tactful limousines moved round their cars to open the doors in unison.

Out of the first car stepped the ravishing Liz Badger, twice a widow. Her skirt was black, but her worsted top had a large flower and dot pattern in white, blue, green and pink. With her were her two children, Simon in his dark suit and Jenny with an ethnic look, in a burgundy cross-over bodice top, a maroon patterned skirt, maroon tights, and maroon suede shoes.

From the second car there stepped Liz's brother, Geoffrey Ellsworth-Smythe, Neville's brother, Arthur, and Arthur's wife Glenys, who was Welsh.

From the third car there emerged Liz's skeletal, ramrod uncle Hubert, Neville's Cousin Edith from Morpeth, who loathed being called a Geordie, and his nephew, Arthur's elder son Mark, who taught.

From the fourth car came Lucinda, demure in a grey and cream spotted dress with pleated skirt, navy jacket and a navy straw hat. She was escorting two obscure relations, long lost except at times of disaster.

The majority of the family mourners were as sombrely dressed as it was possible to be without flouting Neville's wish that they should not wear mourning.

'Don't say it,' said Rodney, watching from the porch between Rita and Betty.

'Don't say what, Rodney?' said Betty.

'What you're both thinking.'

'How do you know what we're thinking, Rodney?' said Rita.

'Because I can see it in your eyes.'

'What can you see in our eyes, Rodney?' said Betty.

'What you're thinking.'

'What are we thinking, Rodney?' said Rita.

'"Look at what she's wearing!"'

'Well . . . look at it,' said Betty.

'Exactly,' said Rita.

'It's up to her, isn't it?' said Rodney. 'To interpret what Neville would have wanted in the way she thinks fit. . . . Come on. Let's get in that church.'

They entered the church. Behind them, Liz addressed the family mourners.

'Well come on,' she said. 'Don't all look so miserable. It's not what he'd have wanted.'

The funeral service was almost perfect. Dignified but not solemn. The new young vicar had done his homework. His address went off almost perfectly. When he said, 'He didn't have an enemy in the world,' everybody thought, 'That's usually a cliché, but in this case it really is true,' and he said, 'I know you're thinking that's a cliché, but in this case it really is true.' That was just before it happened. Just as it happened, Rita was thinking, rather sorrowfully, that the new young vicar seemed more at ease with death than with life. When it happened, he was thrown only briefly out of his stride. He even told a little joke, about Neville's absent-mindedness, about how, after a hard spell of Latin revision, he'd gone to the station and asked for a third person singular to York. It produced a gentle, affectionate laugh, which wasn't quite swallowed up in the vastness of the dark church. There was a rousing rendition of Neville's favourite hymn, 'Onward Christian Soldiers'. Many eyes were moist. Rita and Ted fumed. Jenny was in turmoil. There was a short prayer, and it was over.

Elvis was waiting outside, pacing nervously.

The moment they came out of the church, Ted and Rita made a bee-line for him. Ted hobbled his way through the mourners at astonishing speed, wielding his crutch furiously.

'Well, I was mortified,' he shouted. 'Mortified.'

'Don't raise your voice, Ted,' pleaded Rita breathlessly. 'Let's not have a family row. It'd hardly be appropriate.'

'"Hardly be appropriate", the woman says!' shouted Ted. He was heaving for breath after his exertions, but his anger was unabated. 'What's appropriate about being bleeped in the middle of a funeral oration? I couldn't believe it. Solemn moment. Bleep bleep bleep. Solemn moment straight down the pan.'

'I didn't even know I was going to be bleeped.' Elvis was raising his voice too, in his indignation.

'You should have switched it off,' said Rita.

'I'd regard that as dereliction of duty. Your true reporter never sleeps.'

'Do you keep it on while you're at it?' said Ted.

'There's no need to be crude, Ted Simcock,' said Rita, turning her anger onto Ted. She couldn't help glancing towards the other mourners, but they seemed to be ignoring this public row with a studied tact which mortified her all the more. They were Neville and Liz's friends and relations. They knew how to behave.

'I mean . . . ' said Ted, ' . . . walking out in the middle of a funeral oration. I was. I was mortified.'

'I had to. I could hardly talk to my news desk in the middle of a funeral oration.'

'What was so important that it couldn't wait, anyroad?' enquired his mother.

'An ongoing enquiry into professional corruption involving a guest at this funeral do.' Elvis was beginning to regain his professional *sang-froid*.

'What?' said Rita.

'Who?' said Ted.

'I'm not at liberty to reveal,' said Elvis rather grandly.

'You aren't going to start in-depth interviewing at this time of solemnity?' said Rita.

' 'Course not. Do you think I don't know how to behave?'

'Yes!' said Rita and Ted, momentarily united by the behaviour of their son.

Liz approached them, smiling strangely. Elvis legged it unashamedly.

'We are sorry, Liz,' said Rita.

'We're mortified,' said Ted.

'Oh please. Don't worry,' said Liz. 'I think Neville would have rather enjoyed it.'

She moved on, doing her social round with every appearance of composure.

'Is that woman made of ice?' said Rita.

'I didn't think so once,' said Ted.

'I hardly wanted to be reminded of that!' Rita turned away in fury and found herself face to face with Geoffrey.

'I love you,' said Geoffrey. 'I want you.'

'Geoffrey! Shut up!' whispered Rita. 'It's not appropriate.'

'Grief is an aphrodisiac,' said Geoffrey Ellsworth-Smythe softly.

'Well!' said Simon Rodenhurst, of Trellis, Trellis, Openshaw and Finch, contemptuously. 'I think that was despicable, and so does Lucinda.'

'No sign of Andrew Denton and his wife and your child?' said the cynical Elvis.

'Don't change the subject, you worm,' said Simon. 'I think your behaviour today has been absolutely disgusting, and so does Lucinda.'

'It was very important that the news desk contact me before the do at the house,' said Elvis.

'Why?'

'They want to interview somebody who's been involved in widespread corruption and dishonesty.'

'You're going to interview this corrupt person at my . . . mother's husband's funeral?' Simon swept a gaze round the mourners, some of whom were moving towards their cars, while others were held captive in shared embarrassment. 'I think you're a reptile, Elvis, and so does Lucinda.'

'No,' said Elvis, 'I'm going to arrange to see this corrupt person at a time which suits this corrupt person. What time does suit you?'

'Me?'

'You.'

'Oh my God.'

'Yes.'

Wharfedale Road was an oasis of moderate wealth, surrounded at an almost discreet distance by estates of moderate poverty. Its houses were separated by large, well-wooded gardens, although two houses had already been replaced by luxury executive flats, and 'The Elms' had become a retirement home. One of its residents had taken to roaming the streets in a raincoat three sizes too large and shouting. Otherwise all was peace, except for the noisy exhausts of the vans of the carpet cleaning contractors and the burglar alarm installers.

On this sullen September day, when no twigs stirred and even the chaffinches were listless, the cars of the mourners slid apologetically to a halt beside the privet hedge that protected 'Antibes' from prying eyes. The Badgers' home was a well-mannered, immaculate red-brick house, tastefully proportioned, built in 1928 in the Georgian style. Not for it the excesses of its neighbours, the pseudo-Dutch gables, green-tiled roofs and mock-Tudor facing. These houses shouted, 'We're rich!' Neville's house whispered, 'It's not my fault if I'm privileged.'

Liz stood by the door of what Neville had called the drawing room. She called it the sitting room. Jenny called it the living room. Simon called it the main reception room. Rita and Ted called it the lounge. It was a pleasant room, divided by an arch into two sections. In the front section there were a three piece suite in discreet oatmeal and four antique hard chairs which Simon, in the nearest he ever came to wit, described as Brown Windsor. The back section sported a small mahogany dining table which was never used for dining, and a bookcase which contained a complete set of Dickens and a variety of legal tomes. Paperbacks were kept upstairs, out of sight. The room was dotted with ornaments, including several tall Japanese vases. The effect was of a gathering together of things that didn't clash rather than a positive expression of personal taste.

'What a nice name – "Antibes",' said Mrs Wadebridge, who was big in the Red Cross, and fairly big in the Badgers' living room.

'It was named after Neville's first honeymoon,' said Liz, and Mrs Wadebridge blushed blotchily. 'We went there for our honeymoon too. I felt it better to be under Jane's shadow for a fortnight rather than for the rest of our life together. I didn't realise then how short that would be.'

Mrs Wadebridge hurried off, thoroughly discomfited. Liz greeted the Sillitoes brightly.

'Hello, Rodney. Hello, Betty. Thank you for coming.'

Liz's brightness made Rodney and Betty uneasy. They exchanged anxious looks, uncertain how to respond.

'Er . . . lovely service,' said Betty.

'Just what he would have wanted,' said Rodney.

'I think so,' said Liz. 'How's business?'

'Well . . . it hardly seems right to say it today,' said Betty, 'but . . . it's going very well.'

'Up 7.3% across the whole spectrum last month.'

'Rodney!'

'No,' said Liz. 'Please. Neville specifically wanted this to be a happy occasion. And 7.3% across the whole spectrum! That makes me very happy. Now there's champagne. Please don't hold back, from some sense of social propriety. Indulge yourselves just this once. For Neville. Ted!'

Liz had turned her smile onto the next arrivals. The Sillitoes, anxious to escape from this discomfiting conversation, found themselves even more discomfited by their abrupt dismissal. They slid on into the room, trying not to look as if they were searching for the champagne.

Ted hobbled in, helped by Carol Fordingbridge.

'Are you coping, Ted?' Liz enquired.

'Carol is being very helpful.'

'Thank you for inviting me back, Mrs . . . Liz,' said Carol. 'I didn't expect it.'

'I know,' said Liz. 'And if I thought you had, I wouldn't have invited you.' Carol found herself dismissed. 'Simon! Lucinda!'

Ted hobbled off on Carol's arm, and Simon tried not to look for Elvis.

'So!' said Liz. 'Six weeks to go!'

'Mother, I think we should put back the wedding,' said Simon. 'And so does Lucinda.'

'I don't think there's any alternative,' said Lucinda.

'I won't hear of it,' said Liz. 'Neville would be most upset.'

'Besides . . . ' Lucinda hesitated, 'we . . . er . . . I . . . er . . . '

'Yes?'

'I don't want any shadow hanging over my great day.'

'Me neither. Over my great day.' Simon tried not to look as sick as he was feeling. There already was a shadow over his great day. Elvis had put it there.

'Isn't that a little selfish of you?' said Liz. 'Think of Neville. He thought of everybody's happiness all the time. Think of me.

259

I want a wedding. I'm going to need some fun. Now off you go, stop worrying, and have some champagne.'

'Champagne?' Well-bred though Lucinda was, she couldn't hide her astonishment.

'To celebrate.'

'Celebrate?' Simon looked puzzled.

'Neville specifically asked for champagne in his will, Simon. To celebrate his life. His happy life. His long, idyllic first marriage. His short, idyllic second marriage. His life. Mr Perkins! Good to see you. And Mrs Perkins! What a charming little hat!'

It was Simon and Lucinda's turn to feel dismissed. They turned to watch Liz give a dazzling smile to Neville's old schoolfriend, now the manager of Travelorama in Tannergate, a slightly less dazzling smile to his wife Barbara, and a totally undazzling smile to her charming little hat.

'Thanks. You're a great girl,' said Ted, as Carol eased his bandaged right foot onto a frilly velvet pouf placed there by her for just such a purpose. 'My son's a fool.' He saw Jenny approach. 'Well, not a fool. I mean, how could . . . ?'

'I'll go and find you some food,' said Carol.

'No, Jenny,' said Ted, as soon as Carol had gone. 'I was just saying . . . nobody could say anybody was a fool to fall in love with you.'

'Thanks, Ted,' said Jenny. 'Neville wanted today to be normal and there you are putting your foot in it as normal.'

'Jenny!'

'I'm sorry. I shouldn't have said that. Not today.'

'Yes you should, according to your argument, because you normally say things like that.'

'Ted!' Jenny's face looked as if it was about to crumple into tears.

'Oh, I'm sorry, Jenny. It's the pain. I'm finding it hard to be my usual sunny, jovial, generous self.'

'No, it's me as well, Ted. I'm finding it awful, trying to be normal when I want to cry my eyes out. I . . . all of us really . . . we used to be quite rude to Neville at times, and he was such a lovely man. Why are we all so selfish, Ted?'

'Because we're human, Jenny.'

'Oh!'

Jenny gasped, and hurried off in distress.

Ted stared up at the ceiling. 'Because we're human,' he repeated, in case God hadn't heard. 'I rather like that.'

'I beg your pardon, sir?' said the dark, intense Alec Skiddaw, looming with a tray of champagne. He was a man with a talent for looming.

'Oh, nothing, Alec. Just . . . nothing.'

'Champagne, sir?'

'I don't know that I should, in my . . . ' Alec Skiddaw began to remove his tray. 'Well, I'd better, I suppose.' Ted grabbed a glass. 'He'd have wanted me to.'

Ted smiled at Alec Skiddaw, suddenly feeling pity for his dark intensity, for the sadness in his eyes. He wasn't to know that Alec was feeling fighting fit, being between boils, and was trying to hide his rare, inexplicable, inappropriate feeling of *joie de vivre* behind a curtain of professional gravity.

Alec Skiddaw took Ted's smile to be a brave attempt at concealing his physical and mental anguish, and decided to reward him with an anecdote about his family.

'This takes me back to my grandmother's funeral,' he said.

'Ah.'

'What a character she was. Do you know what she asked for on her eightieth birthday?'

'No.

'Well, how could you? A ride on a motorbike.'

'Good Lord!' Ted hated listening to interesting stories. You felt such a pillock making bored expressions of surprise.

'And she did. Pillion. Eighteen miles. And it was snowing. And icy.'

'Good Lord!'

'And me Cousin Percy, the one with the budgies, I don't know if I ever told you about him . . . '

'Yes,' said Ted hurriedly, in case he did.

'Oh.' Alec sounded disappointed, but rallied. 'Well, this furniture van came in the opposite direction – it was near Nuneaton, I forget exactly where – and Percy skidded.'

'Good Lord! And . . . so . . . she was . . . killed?'

'No. He regained control, and when they got home – well,

261

where they were staying, with me auntie – she said, "That was grand. Specially the skid!" What a woman!'

'But . . . the funeral?'

'She died peacefully in her sleep, when she was ninety-four.'

Rita met Liz in the hall, which had brown panelled doors, walls the colour of digestive biscuits, and a brown carpet running up the stairs with their dark brown varnished banisters. It was as if they'd decorated the hall last, and run out of colours before they'd come to it.

As Rita had been striding purposefully across the brown carpet towards the brown panelled door of the dining room, it wasn't any use pretending.

'I was just going to . . . er . . . look for the . . . er . . . food,' she said. 'Not that I'm hungry, but . . . ' Her voice trailed away in embarrassment.

'Why shouldn't you be hungry?' said Liz. 'Most people are. Tension makes them hungry. Come and have a look at the garden.'

'What?'

'I'd like to get out of it all for a moment. Please.'

'Yes. Yes, of course.'

The garden wasn't particularly wide, but it was long. It was terraced, on three levels. The lawns were well-kept, the flower beds immaculate. It was a garden where nettles died of shame.

There wasn't a breath of wind. There wasn't a trace of moisture. There was no feeling of heat or cold. The day was still, neutral, grey. The world was waiting . . . but for what?

The garden wasn't at its best that September. The best of the flowers were over, and even those that were sometimes splendid, like the hybrid tea roses, were disappointing. What had been drenched in mid-August had become too dry by mid-September. Later, the Meteorological Office would announce that it had been the driest September since 1776. That month, in fact, Mexborough had been drier than Marrakesh.

They walked slowly across the lawn that dominated the top level of the garden.

'Liz, I . . . ' began Rita.

'Please! Before you say something you regret . . . ' interrupted Liz.

'No, no. No, no. I was going to say something nice.'

'Precisely.'

'You what?'

'Before you say something nice, which you'll regret, I think I ought to make it clear that I'm not burying the hatchet.'

'I see.'

A short-sighted bee examined Liz's floral top. She whooshed it away imperiously. It obeyed.

'I'm talking to you today, and today only, because Neville would have wished it, and today his wishes are paramount.'

'I see. Well . . . yes . . . yes, of course.'

They were on the second level now, approaching a flower bed given over to lupins and roses.

'This little corner was Neville's pride and joy.'

'Ah. Well, it's . . . very nice.'

Liz moved on. Rita, the obedient guest, followed.

'That's a lovely clematis,' said Rita, as they passed the purple-blue of a tall clematis jackmanii.

'I prefer the Nellie Moser,' said Liz.

They sauntered on. Rita kept silent, after what she took to be a rebuff.

'Neville and I had separate beds,' said Liz.

'Ah. Well . . . I . . . er . . . I don't think I really want the details of . . . '

'In the garden. I was speaking of the garden, Rita.'

'Oh. Well . . . of course. As if you'd . . . I mean . . . well, anyway, it's none of my . . . sorry.'

It was becoming a nightmare for Rita, this slow passage through the autumn garden on this grey, empty day. They were on the lowest level now. Liz led her to a border where dahlias and phlox and begonias were in bloom.

'This was my area, over here.'

'Ah. It's very . . . "was"? Will you move?'

'I haven't thought yet. Will I be able to sell, with your ring road being built at the bottom of my garden?'

'Ah.'

Rita found herself imagining juggernauts roaring through this third level, and through the narrow strip of woodland

263

beyond, which screened these houses from the Dalton Wood Estate.

'And here is the magnolia. The fateful magnolia.'

'Ah.'

It was not, in truth, a particularly splendid example, but then it wasn't in flower. Rita felt that Liz was angry with it for not being in flower, as if it had let her down. But maybe the anger was for her, its destroyer. It sat, motionless, flowerless, in a circular bed studded with miniature roses.

'How naïve of me not to realise where we were heading.'

'Yes. I was surprised. Beautiful, isn't it?'

'Beautiful.'

'Soon to be no more.'

'Er . . . no.'

'I must go back. Do my duty. Thank you, Rita.'

'What for?'

'This little talk. This little walk. They've made me feel better.'

Liz set off back to the house, briskly.

Rita followed her, slowly.

Several minutes later Rita was standing in the brown hall with a plate of food, which she couldn't remember selecting. Sometimes, when driving, she would pass through a village without noticing it, yet apparently drive with perfect safety. And now she seemed to have chosen her food quite consciously, for everything on her plate was vegetarian. But this gap in her memory, here today, was an unpleasant shock.

The drone of conversation in the living room was more animated than when she had left. She was reminded of those times, in the bad old days, when she'd gone to make tea or coffee, and had heard merry laughter from their lounge, and had believed that the world was a jollier place when she was absent. Now, although all that was over, she felt once again the sheer dread of entering a room full of people.

But there was a difference now. Geoffrey Ellsworth-Smythe was in that room.

She tried not to meet anybody's eyes. Not Betty's slightly bloodshot eyes, for that would make her cry. Not the unsmiling eyes in Morris Wigmore's smiling face, for he would button-hole her and discuss committees and agendas. Not Matthew Wadehurst's grave legal eyes, for he would feel obliged to say something to her; all sorts of people spoke to her now that she was a councillor, now that she was somebody.

Geoffrey was standing by the unlit fireplace. She squeezed his arm and said, 'Hello,' but her tone suggested that she meant, 'Thank God.'

Geoffrey understood and said, 'Rita!' as if he were saying, 'What a wonderful stroke of luck. It's you, the person I most want to see in the whole world,' causing Rita to say, in a low voice, 'You aren't going to tell me that you want me again, are you?' Geoffrey, in a voice even lower than usual, said, 'Not if it upsets you.' He gave her a close look, and said, 'You are upset, aren't you?'

'It's Liz.'

'Snap.'

'She showed me the magnolia.'

'Ah.'

'It's become an obsession with her. Sometimes, which is an awful thing to say, I wonder if she cares more for that magnolia than . . . what do you mean, "snap"?'

'I'm upset about Liz. I'm dreadfully ashamed.'

'What about?'

'My dislike of her. When I left England she was a selfish, spoilt girl. I suppose I assumed she couldn't change and hadn't changed.'

'Has she changed?' Rita was surprised.

'Well, I certainly didn't think her capable of the courage she's shown.'

'Courage?' Rita was very surprised.

'Hiding her grief so bravely.'

'Hiding her grief?' Rita was very, very surprised.

'Excuse me. Be back soon.'

'Where are you going?'

'Big brother is going to be supportive for the first time in his life.'

And Geoffrey was gone. And Rita, reeling but no longer able to cope, found that her legs had decided to take her past the oatmeal settee towards the front window, past a dimly seen man in an oatmeal armchair, who said, 'Don't speak to me, then.'

'Oh. Sorry, Ted,' she said. 'I didn't realise it was you.'

'There *are* lots of people encased in plaster, aren't there?'

'Sorry.' His face was grey with pain. She pulled up a Windsor chair and sat beside him. 'How are you?' she asked.

Ted smiled bravely. 'I'll recover,' he said. 'The scars will heal.'

'And . . . the mental scars?'

'Healed. Almost. Forgotten she ever existed. Almost.'

'She? Oh, Corinna! No, I meant . . . the accident . . . the . . . '

Ted leant forward, to speak yet more confidentially. His left arm, the one in the sling, was almost digging into Rita's bust.

'Rita,' he said. 'You're a woman.'

'Ten out of ten for recognition.'

'I suppose this isn't really the time or place. But.'

'But?'

'Is it possible, Rita, for a woman to entirely . . . utterly . . . fool a man over experiencing . . . sexual ecstasy?'

'You what, Ted?'

'Incidentally, I'm . . . er . . . luckily under the . . . I'm . . . er . . . undamaged in . . . ' Ted glanced down, as if making a final check that everything was still there, ' . . . those areas.'

'Oh good. I'm relieved to hear it. I speak disinterestedly, of course.'

'Oh yes. I realise that. Those days are . . . but . . . I mean . . . sexual ecstasy . . . can it be simulated?'

Rita glanced round the room, full of respectable people, dressed quite sombrely, and a few, who hadn't known of Neville's wishes, wearing black.

'Should we be discussing this here today?' she said.

'No. No. I agree. Not the . . . er . . . at all.' Ted lowered his voice a further notch. 'But . . . I mean . . . Corinna conned me in business. Could she have conned me in . . . er . . . well . . . bed? I mean, she . . . regularly made . . . ' he searched for a description that might not be too unseemly for a funeral, ' . . . movements consistent with gratification. She regularly . . . uttered cries indicative of ecstasy. I mean, she must have liked me a bit, mustn't she?'

266

'Oh, Ted. This really isn't the time or place.'

'No, no. I know. Right. Let's change the . . . but I mean you sometimes . . . in our marriage . . . '

'Made movements consistent with gratification?'

'Well . . . yes. Well . . . you did.'

'Uttered cries indicative of ecstasy?'

'Well . . . yes. Well . . . you did. I mean . . . were they . . . ?'

'Sometimes.'

'You what?'

'Sometimes they were genuine. Sometimes I was . . . giving you what I thought you wanted to hear.'

'Rita!'

'I really think we ought to change the subject.'

'Oh yes. Yes. Right. You see, I don't think I could ever again trust a woman in . . . if I . . . if I felt . . . I mean, Corinna couldn't have found me utterly repulsive, could she?'

'No, Ted, I daresay she couldn't have found you utterly repulsive. Oh Ted!'

'Thanks, Rita.' Ted's voice went through a gear change, as if it was entirely his idea to change the subject. 'I . . . er . . . I see Liz is talking to you.'

'Only for today. After that, it's back to silence.'

'That's pathetic.'

'Rather inconvenient, too, as I'm in love with her brother.'

'I like your clothes.'

Big brother's support of Liz was taking place near the back window, beside the unused dining table, far from Rita and Ted.

'Good heavens.'

'Why "Good heavens"?'

'"Good heavens, Geoffrey is making small talk." "Good heavens, Geoffrey has said something nice to me," and, "Good heavens, Geoffrey likes my clothes, because everyone else disapproves.'

Geoffrey Ellsworth-Smythe tried not to look too rueful. His beard was a great help in this deception. He hadn't really noticed Liz's clothes. He wasn't a man for noticing clothes. It had just been a random throw in his awkward attempt to find a comfortable conversational level with his sister. Once started, however, it was as good a subject as any.

'I didn't mean these particularly,' he said. 'I meant . . . all your clothes. I like your dress sense.'

'Good heavens.'

'Once again, why "Good heavens"?'

'"Good heavens, a member of the male sex has noticed my clothes." "Good heavens, the great anthropologist, who's spent a lifetime studying people who run around in the buff, can appreciate dress sense," and, "Good heavens, Geoffrey has now said two nice things to me," making, when you include all the childhood years, the grand total of . . . two.'

Alec Skiddaw, the great loomer, loomed.

'More champagne, madam?' he said.

'Thanks. Tickety-bloody-boo.'

Alec Skiddaw looked somewhat surprised by this remark, and Liz realised that it was Eric Siddall who said 'tickety-boo' and that when she'd asked Geoffrey to ask Alec to serve the drinks today, she'd meant Eric. And so she displayed, briefly, a condition rarely seen on the face of the ravishing Liz Badger. She displayed social confusion.

Alec Skiddaw, also socially confused, scampered off.

Geoffrey, single-mindedly bent on offering his support, hadn't listened to this brief exchange. He waited until it was over. Now he resumed his mission.

'Well . . . ' he said, 'I've missed you all these years I've been abroad.'

'Good heavens. Meaning, "I hadn't the faintest idea."'

'Nor had I really till now. Silly, isn't it? Look, anything you need, Liz – help, support, a roof, a shoulder to lean on.'

'You can help me now.'

'At your service.' Geoffrey, pleased, made a tiny mock bow, and adopted an eager-to-please expression.

'Here comes Ted. I think I know what he wants to talk about. You can make yourself scarce and leave us alone.'

'Oh.' Geoffrey tried not to look too disappointed. 'Well, that was hardly . . . well, all right.'

He moved off, reluctantly.

Ted hobbled slowly towards Liz, negotiating with slight difficulty the small step which separated the two areas of the room.

The mourners pretended that they hadn't seen him, since they didn't know what to say to him, but it was clear that they had seen him, since they moved away to make room for him. Ted therefore approached Liz through a wide tunnel formed by two rows of backs. Liz stood at the end of the tunnel, waiting, as if she was still dressed as Queen Elizabeth the First.

'Hello, Ted,' she said, when at last her injured serf had reached her. 'I'm flattered.'

'You what?'

'You, struggling all the way over to speak to me.'

'Well . . . since you didn't even move an inch towards me . . . '

'Oh Lord. I never thought.'

'Not your strong point.'

'Thank you very much.'

'Oh heck. Not a good start.'

'On what?'

'Diplomacy. I'm not very good at it.'

'Not having had much practice.'

'Ouch. No, but, Liz, doesn't it? A thing like this. Put everything in proportion.'

'Yes.'

'So . . . '

'No.'

'What?'

'The answer's "no", Ted.'

'I haven't asked the question yet.'

'The question is, will I end my feud with Rita forever? Become friends. You were going to say that I'm going to need friends and shouldn't be petty.'

'Oh heck.'

'Nicely put, Ted, but the answer's "no".'

'Why, Liz?'

'I can't do it. I don't know how to.'

'I'm sorry for you.'

'Spare me your pity and go.'

'Right. Right.'

Ted hobbled off, banging his crutch unnecessarily hard in frustration at the total failure of his mission.

•

269

Simon Rodenhurst decided that it was time to show his mettle. He strode briskly across the spacious main reception room. He had no eyes for the exceptionally attractive arch, for the pleasant views afforded by the double-glazed windows, for the six power points, or for Ted Simcock, struggling in the opposite direction, as if Simon were going with the tide and wind and Ted straight into them. He had eyes only for Elvis.

'How much do you know?' he demanded.

'About what?' said Elvis.

There was a pause.

'Nothing,' said Simon. 'I've done nothing wrong.'

'Why did you say, "How much do you know?" then?'

'Because I'm not very good at this sort of thing.'

'What sort of thing do you think this sort of thing is?'

There was another pause.

'Hounding innocent people. Making false allegations. The media. All right, let me put it another way. What exactly do you falsely and ludicrously claim I've done?' said Simon Rodenhurst, of Trellis, Trellis, Openshaw and Finch.

'I can't talk about it here, Simon. It's not the time or place,' said the cynical, almost smirking Elvis Simcock.

Having replenished his glass – 'He'd have wanted me to' – Ted struggled towards Rita, who was still sitting on the same chair, trying not to look as though she was enjoying her food.

'Thank you for not coming to meet me,' said Ted.

'I know how much you enjoy feeling hard done by,' said Rita.

'I see,' said Ted, in his feeling-hard-done-by voice. 'So this is my reward for trying to help.'

'Trying to help?'

'I begged Liz to be friends with you.'

'Ted! Why?'

'I don't know. Maybe I wanted you to remember me with some affection.'

'Oh.' Since Ted showed no sign of sitting down, Rita felt it incumbent upon her to stand up, in gratitude for his efforts. 'Thanks, Ted.'

'No. I failed. She said, "I can't do it. I don't know how to."'

'I'm sorry for her.'

'That's what I said. She wasn't thrilled.'

'Oh, Ted. Well, thanks, anyway.'

Rita smiled at her ex-husband. He didn't quite smile back, but nodded, as if acknowledging that Rita's smile had been the correct response. He hobbled off, making a slow bee-line for the Sillitoes, who were remaining close to each other and the champagne.

'Ted! Love! How are you?' said Betty, her voice over-effusive as usual.

'Terrific. Limping's my hobby.' Ted paused, to let the full weight of his sarcasm sink in, then changed his tone abruptly. 'I realise this isn't the time or place, but how's business?'

'Well,' said Rodney, trying to look lugubrious, 'if it wasn't that on an occasion like this it would seem rather insensitive to say so, I'd say, "extremely satisfactory".'

'Up 7.3% across the whole spectrum,' said Betty.

'Betty!' said Rodney.

'Well, if you did say that,' said Ted, 'I might say, perhaps equally insensitively, "any chance of your reconsidering the possibility of my working for you?"'

'If you did say that,' said Rodney, 'I might well reply, not only insensitively but extremely bluntly, that you described us as "crackpot lunatic fringe animal rights trendy health food freaky nut nuts".'

'Well, folk exaggerate, don't they?' said Ted. 'No, I've had time to think, and reappraise my ideas *vis-à-vis* other offers I've been considering, and . . . well . . . frankly, I was . . . well . . . wrong. That's all there is to it.'

He gave an apologetic little smile. He looked, at that moment, as dignified as it is possible for a man to look when he has one foot in plaster, an arm in a sling, a neck brace, and a large bandage on his bruised forehead.

'Well, under the circumstances, I feel . . . ' Betty smiled warmly at Ted. 'Don't we, Rodney?'

'Yes, Betty, we do.' The former big wheel behind Cock-A-Doodle Chickens also smiled warmly at Ted. 'We have a vacancy for an experienced person to supervise our rapidly expanding fruit and vegetable buying operation.'

'Incorporating nuts, grains and spices,' put in the joint big wheel behind Sillitoe's.

'Well, thanks. Thanks. I . . . er . . . I like the sound of it.' Ted tried to look deeply excited. He must have known that he'd failed, since he felt it necessary to emphasise the point. 'No. I mean it. I really do. But.'

'But?'

'I foresee one possible snag. Rita works for you.'

'So?'

'Well, Rita and I have reached a . . . a plateau of peace. I'd hate to embarrass her by having her working under me.'

'Oh no,' said Rodney. 'There'd be nothing like that.'

'Oh good.'

'You'd be working under Rita, Ted,' said Betty.

'You can stuff your organic fruit and vegetables,' said Ted.

Simon tried to make his approach to Arthur Badger, Neville's slightly less charming and immaculate elder brother, appear totally casual. They discussed the loss to the community, and the impossibility of putting into words adequately what they were failing to put into words adequately.

'Incidentally,' said Simon, as if he'd just thought of it, 'Why are Andrew and Judy not here?'

'We couldn't contact them. They're touring in France. They're determined not to let the little one hamstring their life-style.'

'Ah. How are they?'

'Blooming.'

'And . . . the little one?'

'Excellent. She's a real little flirt already.'

'Terrific. Terrific.' Simon searched for something else to say, but couldn't find anything. 'Terrific.'

'You should see her,' said Arthur Badger. 'I guarantee it'll make you start to want to have babies of your own.'

'Yes. I must. Terrific.'

Did Arthur Badger know?

'What's happening this weekend, about visiting Paul?' asked Jenny.

They were sitting on the oatmeal settee. Elvis put his arm round her as he said, 'Oh, love, it isn't the time or place.'

272

'It never is with you, is it?'

'Yes, it is, but this isn't.'

'Well, I'd like to see him.'

'We'll go together. And tell him . . . about us.'

'We can't tell him while he's in prison. He's got enough to contend with.'

'It's all very well for you, Jenny. You were his wife, now you aren't. I was his brother and still am.'

'He's still the father of my children.'

'He's the father of my children too.' Elvis was a little upset that his remark seemed to surprise Jenny. 'Well, that's what I think of them as, now. I think we should go on Sunday, together, and I should say, "Hello, Paul. I know you're very worried about Jenny since your marriage broke up because of what you did, but you needn't worry, she's found another feller and a good home for your children and you'll be given full access because you know the feller. In fact, you're related to him. In fact, it's me."'

Even as he spoke, Elvis realised the impracticability of the suggested scenario, so he wasn't surprised, and in fact was rather relieved, though he would never have admitted it, to hear Jenny say, 'This isn't the time or place.' He patted her left thigh with his right arm, stood up abruptly, and sighed. Then he forced himself to tackle her mother.

'I'm sorry about my bleeper,' he said.

'No. Please.' Liz smiled at him. 'Neville wanted everything to be normal.'

'Yes, but . . . a funeral isn't normal.'

'You must understand. My husband was a certain type of Englishman who believed that you don't show emotion. All the misery he revealed after his first wife died was a source of great shame to him. To see us overcome with grief today would horrify him. We must respect his wishes. And you did that. Thank you.' Liz moved off towards the hall. Elvis stared after her, somewhat dumbfounded. He tried not to look quite so dumbfounded. She came back. 'We all must die. You know that. You're the philosopher.' Elvis was failing in his effort not to look quite so dumbfounded. 'If death is unpleasant, then life becomes a journey towards something unpleasant, so death cannot be unpleasant. Neville was happy for much of his life. And he went quickly. So, please, none of you grieve for him. And as for me, I don't have any feelings, do I? I'm inhuman.'

She strode out into the hall, leaving Elvis even more dumbfounded than before.

Liz had no idea where she was going. Her sole aim had been to leave. Since she was facing the door of the dining room, she walked towards it, less because she wanted food than because she had no other need which might have caused her to change course.

As she passed the foot of the stairs, she felt a tingle all down her spine. She felt as if her hair was standing on end, and hundreds of tiny insects were scampering across her scalp. She stopped dead in her tracks. She knew that she wasn't alone in that brown hall.

She turned her head very slowly, half knowing what she would see; half frightened of seeing it, half frightened of not seeing it.

She saw her dead husband, Neville Badger, of Badger, Badger, Fox and Badger. She saw him sitting at the top of the stairs, with his feet on the second stair down, and his face silhouetted against the inappropriately dim light from the landing window. She saw that he was wearing a light, immaculate, grey suit, with grey shoes, grey socks, a grey shirt and a grey tie. She saw that he had a small harp across his knee. She saw that his face was not happy, not sad, but serene. She heard him say, firmly, clearly, one word. It was, 'Sorry.'

She felt a lesser tingling of the spine, a lesser crawling of the scalp, a lesser bristling of the hair. She became aware that she was being watched. She turned her head and saw Rita standing at the door of the living room.

She turned away and looked up the stairs again. There was nobody there.

Rita knocked on the door of what she guessed was the master bedroom.

'Yes?'

'Are you all right?'

It seemed an age before Liz said, 'Come in.'

It was a restful room, with cream walls and a blue carpet.

Liz sat, hunched up, almost foetal, on the crumpled pillows of the double bed, with her stockinged feet on the silvery, quilted counterpane. Well, no, not her stockinged feet. She wore tights. Rita wondered how you described such feet. You couldn't say 'her tighted feet'. Then she met Liz's glistening eyes, and all foolish thoughts vanished from her mind, and she felt what she wouldn't have believed she could ever have felt: she felt warmth and compassion for Liz.

'Liz!' she said. 'I saw.'

Beside the bed, on a mahogany bedside table, there was an expensive alarm clock, a glass of water and a box of pills. On the other bedside table there was only a lamp. No water, no pills. No need.

'You saw what?' said Liz at last. All her reactions seemed delayed.

'In the hall.'

'Neville?' Liz was astounded, suddenly alert.

'Neville?'

'I thought I saw him. At the top of the stairs. Complete with harp.'

'I know. I saw. Well, not Neville and the harp. I saw you thinking you saw him. I saw . . . ' Why was it so difficult to say? 'I saw how much you loved him.'

'Well, yes. Yes, I did.'

Liz made a small gesture, indicating that Rita should sit on the bed. Rita sat, awkwardly. She felt a shyness at this proximity.

'I never realised,' she said.

'No, nor did he.'

'What?'

'I never told him. Not properly. Not the depth of it.' Liz gave a sob of pure grief. 'You always think there's time.' Another sob.

'I know,' said Rita, with feeling, remembering the death of her father on the dance floor. She was crying too, and this embarrassed her. She had no right to feel as unhappy as Liz. Not today. Yet how could she not feel for Liz? How, for all the power of human imagination, can one know what someone else feels unless one has felt it oneself? How, therefore, when knowing, could Rita not remember how she knew? How, therefore, could she not weep?

'The other Sunday,' said Liz, smiling through her tears, fighting to avoid a moment of desperate shared emotion that she would perhaps come to regret, 'at Sunday lunch, all the family were there, Simon and Lucinda and Jenny and the children . . . and Elvis . . . and I longed to say, "I love you, Neville, with all my heart," but I looked at Simon and Lucinda and Jenny and the children . . . and Elvis . . . and I said, "Would you like some more horseradish, darling?" instead. I tried to make it sound like, "I love you with all my heart," but I don't think he picked up on the sub-text.'

'Neville wasn't strong on sub-texts.'

'No. He said, "No, thanks. I'm not actually the most tremendous horseradish freak." I think if he'd known what I meant he'd just have said "yes". Neville always wanted to do the right thing, make people happy, not be a nuisance, and he's ended up being the most enormous nuisance to me.'

'What on earth do you mean?'

'Not wanting any unseemly grief.'

They became aware of the whining of a micro-light aircraft as it passed over the house like a huge disgruntled hornet. They both seemed slightly astonished that there was still a world outside this hothouse.

'Forcing me, in consideration of his wishes,' continued Liz, 'to come in bright clothes, enduring universal disapproval.'

'No one disapproves, Liz.'

A touch of the tartness returned. 'In politics less than a year, and lying in your teeth already.'

'All right. People do disapprove, but only because they don't understand. So . . . explain.'

'What? And demean myself to that rabble? Arrogant, aren't I? Well, arrogant, naughty, unfaithful Liz learns her lesson and is given her come-uppance. A cruelly moral lady, Dame Fortune.'

Liz tried another smile. It wasn't a success, so Rita knew that the attempt had been sincere.

'Shall we end this stupid feud?' said Liz.

'Yes, please,' said Rita.

'Peace?'

'Peace.'

•

At the moment when Liz and Rita were concluding their emotional exchange in Liz's bedroom, Simon was concluding a rather less emotional exchange on the telephone in the hall.

'A hundred and eighty-two thousand. Not a penny less,' he was saying. He saw Elvis emerge from the living room, looking for him, and said hurriedly, 'Look, must rush. Bye.' He smiled uneasily at Elvis, hoping that he hadn't heard.

But Elvis had heard. 'Carrying on business at your step-father's funeral!' he said. 'I think that's disrespectful, and so will Jenny.'

'It was urgent, and Neville wanted everything to be normal.'

'I'm sure he hoped that human greed could be suspended for an hour or two. Well, in that case, if you're showing no respect, I'll tell you what I know about you. You are involved, up to your badly-washed neck, in arranging phoney mortgages for ruthless property speculators to whom the council is giving hundreds of thousands of taxpayers' money to provide squalid bed and breakfast accommodation for the many homeless it can't afford to house because it's spending so much money on these phoney mortgages you are helping to finance.'

'How much?' said Simon, who had gone pale.

'That's typical of your sort,' said Elvis scornfully. 'Straight to the cheque book. It won't work, Simon.'

'Mother will be very upset to hear what you're doing,' said Simon. 'And so will Jenny.'

'Oh Lord,' said Elvis.

'Oh Lord!' said Simon and Elvis.

They were being approached, the moment they returned to the room, by Jenny and Lucinda.

'What's going on?' said Jenny.

She led Elvis away, behind the oatmeal settee, where they were separated from Simon and Lucinda by Graham Wintergreen, the manager of the golf club, who was talking about golf to Mrs Wadebridge, who was talking about the Red Cross to Graham Wintergreen, and by Barbara Perkins, who was listening to the gallantry and randiness of Liz's skeletal, ramrod uncle, Hubert Ellsworth-Smythe, who dared not sit down lest he be forced by good manners to offer his seat to a lady, who would humiliate him by refusing to accept it because he looked at death's door.

'What's going on?' repeated Jenny.

'Nothing, love.'

'Are you sure? What have you and Simon been talking about?'

'Nothing, love. Nothing to do with . . . anything to do with you.'

'What are Simon and Lucinda talking about?'

'Nothing. Nothing to do with anything to do with anything to do with you, love.'

'If you were telling the truth, you'd have said you didn't know what they were talking about.'

'I don't. And since I don't I assume it's nothing to do with anything to do with anything to do with anything to do with you.'

'I hope you're telling the truth. I couldn't bear it if you lied to me.'

'Oh heck,' thought Elvis.

On the far side of Hubert Ellsworth-Smythe, who had an enormous interest in Barbara Perkins, who had no interest in him, and of Mrs Wadebridge, who had no interest in golf or Graham Wintergreen, who had no interest in the Red Cross or the enormous Mrs Wadebridge, Simon and Lucinda were showing an enormous interest in Elvis and Jenny.

'If it's nothing important,' Lucinda was saying, 'why is Jenny so interested?'

'She's always been like that. It doesn't mean anything. Don't you trust me?'

'Yes, of course. I trust you utterly.'

'Do you? Ah.'

'I shouldn't be saying this, on an occasion like this.' Lucinda lowered her voice to a primly naughty undertone. 'I can barely wait for our wedding night, when you take my body.'

'Well . . . er . . . terrific.' Simon gulped. 'I . . . terrific.'

'You may not be the subtlest person in the world . . . '

'I see!'

'You aren't exactly a genius, you aren't exceptionally good-looking . . . ' Lucinda peered at Simon through her thick glasses,

'. . . fairly good-looking, but not exceptionally . . . but I've never met a man I feel I can trust as I feel I can trust you.' She kissed him.

'And . . . er . . . this is why you can hardly wait for our wedding night?'

'Yes.'

'Oh Lord!' thought Simon, who had not yet known her body.

The atmosphere in 'Antibes' was becoming more animated. More than one person, uneasy about this, found consolation in remarks such as 'He'd have enjoyed this' and 'This is the way he'd have wanted it.'

Morris Wigmore, Deputy Leader of the Conservatives, whose son came to a sticky end in Brisbane, felt aroused by Angela Wintergreen's tense mouth and unhappy eyes. What safe subject could he broach? Of course!

'What about Ballasteros on Sunday?' he said. 'Incredible. Who else could get a birdie via the car park?'

'Excuse me,' said Angela Wintergreen grimly.

She found herself on collision course with Ted, and turned away, unable to cope.

Ted was oblivious to Angela Wintergreen. He had other fish to fry. He was steeling himself for a difficult encounter with Rodney and Betty Sillitoe.

'I've been thinking,' he said. 'These . . . er . . . these other offers that I've been . . . er . . . offered. They're . . . er . . . '

'Non-existent,' said Betty.

'Betty!' said Rodney.

'I had been going to say they were unexciting,' said Ted. 'Unenticing. Oh, what the hell? You're right. They're non-existent.'

Ted laughed. So did Rodney and Betty. Rodney's laugh was a quiet growl, but Betty's was a shrill peal, a memory of a distant foolish youth.

Betty stopped laughing abruptly. 'Oh Lord!' she said. 'Folk'll think we don't care.'

'They know we care,' said Rodney. 'Sorry, Ted, you were saying?'

'Yes. Yes, I was. I've been thinking, and I think it'd be wrong

279

of me to refuse to work for you just because I'd be working under Rita. I'm a bigger man than that.'

'Much bigger,' said Rodney.

'Much, much bigger,' said Betty.

Rita stood by the unlit fireplace with Geoffrey. It seemed to be their corner as of right. Well, he was Liz's brother.

'I'm ashamed I didn't see what you saw, that Liz is putting on a big, brave act,' said Rita.

'Well perhaps this is the first time she's experienced real emotion for anyone other than herself.' Geoffrey's voice might have been made for crowded rooms. Even when they were on their own he talked as if there were fifty people in the next room who mustn't overhear him. 'Perhaps this late awakening of love is a characteristic of us Ellsworth-Smythes.'

'Don't talk about love,' said Rita. 'I find our joy indecent today.'

'Hello, Rita. Hello, Geoffrey,' said Ted, and they jumped. They'd been so involved with each other that they hadn't noticed his slow approach. 'I bring you good news, Rita. I'm going to be working under you.'

'What?'

'I knew you'd be pleased. I'm going to work for the Sillitoes. It'll be right cosy being close to each other again, won't it? Working with a person like me who spreads such joy and happiness around.'

He limped off. Rita called after him.

'Don't be too hard on yourself, Ted.'

'You what?'

'Blaming yourself for Neville's death.'

'I don't. I blame the design of cars.'

Ted resumed his painful progress. Rita was still wondering what he meant when Geoffrey said, 'Marry me,' so it took a moment to sink in.

'You what?'

'Marry me, Rita.'

'What a time to propose!'

'I studied the sexual stimulation of grief among primitive peoples. I never thought I'd experience it myself.'

'Are you feeling grief?'

'Yes. For Neville. For Liz. For myself, for not recognising that my hostility to her was thwarted brotherly love. And, grieving for her, I'm filled with love and desire for the person whom my marrying will hurt Liz most in the whole world. Awkward syntax for an awkward situation.'

'We can't get engaged today.'

'Not publicly, no, but just between the two of us, will you marry me?'

'Oh Lord.'

'Oh Lord?'

'Very much so.'

'Oh Lord.'

Rita took a quick look round the room. Nobody was taking any notice of them. There was no excuse for delaying this important conversation.

'Why should I marry?' she said. 'I'm not incomplete without a man. I love you, but do I want to enter into a male-dominated institution and change my name to Ellsworth-Smythe?'

'I'll change mine.'

'To Simcock?'

Geoffrey paused fractionally. 'Hopefully not, but if you insist. But why not your maiden name?'

'Spragg?'

'Why not? You loved your parents.'

'Would you?'

'Women change their names without a second thought. Why shouldn't I? Anyway, I rather like it.' He tried it on for size. 'Geoffrey Spragg. Blunt. Honest. Down to earth. We were Smiths before some social-climbing twit Ellsworth and Smythed us. I've never felt double-barrelled.'

'This proposal – the discovery that Ted's going to be working in close proximity wouldn't have anything to do with it, would it?'

'Absolutely.'

'What?'

'In all the films that I really like, a man arrives at a small town, alone, by train or on horseback. There's trouble. He sorts it out. He leaves, alone, by train or on horseback. I've been that man all my life. The last few weeks I've begun, rather timidly, to wonder if I want to be alone any more. Suddenly, just then,

I felt a magnificent shaft of naked jealousy. Marry me, Rita. I'm not leaving town on the *Santa Fe*.'

'I'll let you know.'

'That would be very kind.'

Rita reeled away, and came face to face with Alec Skiddaw before she was ready for further human contact.

'Champagne, madam?' he said.

'Thank you.'

'My sister-in-law's uncle fell off some scaffolding at the age of ninety-three,' he said, filling her glass.

'Good Lord!'

'Yes! And you're forced to wonder. Because he was a member of the Plymouth Brethren, and ascribed his longevity to right-eousness and abstinence, but my sister-in-law's uncle drank like a fish, not that I think fish do, they're fed up to the back teeth with water, if you ask me. Anyroad, he was in the pub crib team till he was eighty-eight, and he only pretended he was resigning because of failing eyesight. The real reason was his girl-friend. She was eighty-five, and she wanted him to meet her from her pottery class, because she was frightened of being mugged, and he didn't want the lads in the crib team to think he was hen-pecked. And that was in Ross-on-Wye, not Chicago.'

'What?'

Alec Skiddaw gave Rita a slow, dark, intense stare. If he'd had a boil, it would have throbbed.

'Sorry,' she said. 'That was rude of me, Alec. Your stories are always absolutely riveting, but I was thinking. I have a difficult decision to make.'

She moved off.

'Whether to have a vol-au-vent or a tortilla chip, no doubt,' mumbled Alec Skiddaw bitterly when she had gone.

As she came slowly down the stairs and heard the rumble of chatter from her sitting room, Liz felt sick. They were all still here. She'd known they would be, of course. She knew that it would be worse when they'd gone, of course. But that didn't make it any easier, or any pleasanter, to walk back into that room.

She pretended that Neville was watching her. Smile in place. Best foot forward. You can do it, darling. There. Well done, darling.

Rita raised her eyebrows and mouthed, 'Are you all right?'
Liz nodded, smiled slightly, and shrugged. 'As well as can be
expected,' said her shrug.

Neither woman wanted to seem to snub the other so soon after
their declaration of peace. Yet neither wanted to talk further, for
further talk could add nothing to that moment, and might well
begin to rub the gloss off it.

It was Carol Fordingbridge who came to the rescue, button-
holing Rita and leaving Liz free to stroll casually into a room
from which her absence, she realised with a touch of her normal
asperity, had only been noticed by a few.

'I've been trying not to tell you, because it doesn't seem right
to be pleased about anything today,' said Carol, with suppressed
excitement, 'but I've done it, and I feel terrific.'

'You've done what, Carol?'

'I've enrolled for three "A" levels. I've taken the first tentative
steps up the ladder to self-fulfilment.'

'Well, that's great, Carol.' Rita hugged her protégé. 'Great!
Well done.'

'Who knows where it'll end? The poly, university. Wouldn't
it be a laugh if I got a better degree than Elvis? And it's all
thanks to your encouragement. I've given men up completely.
They only want one thing. Yesterday this fitter with two tattoos
asked me out, and I thought, "Simone de Beauvoir never went
out with a fitter with two tattoos."'

'Don't become a snob, Carol, whatever you do.'

'Oh, it wasn't because he was a fitter, or because of the two
tattoos. But, I mean, they're all the same, men, aren't they?'

'Perhaps not all men, Carol.'

'You what?'

'Geoffrey's proposed to me.' Rita tried desperately not to seem
remotely coy in front of her protégé.

'You've turned him down?' It was only just a question.

'Well . . . not in so many words. It isn't as simple as that.'

'Would you say it isn't as simple as that if he wasn't a successful
anthropologist, but a fitter with two tattoos?'

The protégé stomped off. The teacher looked rueful.

The return of Liz had led some people to wonder if it was time to make a move. Nobody wanted to leave, except Angela Winter-green. The champagne was excellent, the food was pleasant, the house was nice, and they were an agreeable, select bunch. Chide them not, gentle reader. While they remained there, connected to each other through Neville Badger, there was a sense in which he seemed to be there. When at last they went their separate ways, into the Neville-less town, then they would feel the awful irreversibility of loss.

For the moment the problem was solved. They couldn't take their leave. Liz was talking with Ted.

'I've been thinking,' Ted was saying. 'One of the many sad aspects of this sad affair is that my son, our son, is now without a father for the second time.'

'You aren't suggesting that you and I . . . ?'

'No. Bloody hell, no. I mean . . . no. Not that I . . . but no. I mean, it's over. I mean, it is. But when he's grown up, he won't remember Neville. I mean . . . he won't. I'm offering, Liz, to visit him, take him to the zoo, fill a gap in his psyche, that kind of thing.'

'Are you saying all this because you feel so guilty?'

Ted looked puzzled. He might have scratched his head, if one arm wasn't in a sling and the other clutching a crutch. 'Guilty? What do you mean?'

'Well, if you hadn't offered to take him fishing . . . '

'If you think like that you'd never offer to do anything. "I would have asked you out to dinner. Better not, in case a meteorite falls on your head."' Ted had been surprised, in fact, that Neville had accepted his impulsive offer.

'And you must have thought, "If only I hadn't accepted when he offered to drive for a bit."'

'You can't deal in "if onlys" in life. I don't blame myself. I blame the design of cars. He tried to indicate right, but he got the windscreen wipers instead. This car hit us broadsides. They should put these things in the same place in every car. Look, we'll talk about it some other time, eh? About little . . . ' He could hardly bring himself to utter the hated name. 'Josceleyn. 'Cos I'd like to have one son I could be proud of. Hello, Elvis. All right?' Elvis, passing on his way to get champagne, nodded. 'Good.' He turned back to Liz. 'I mean not that my lads are bad lads.' Ted's face took on a soft, almost gentle expression.

With his bandaged forehead, his bruising and his neck brace, he suddenly looked very vulnerable, almost a baby, a great, tired, creased, haggard baby. 'Liz?' he said, very gently. 'About Neville. It was quick. He knew nothing about it.'

'Thank you.'

'Look on the bright side, love. Where he is . . . ' Ted looked up at the ceiling, 'well . . . who knows? We don't, do we? We can't. Maybe he's happy.' He smiled, trying to sell the idea of Neville's happiness. 'Maybe he's reunited with Jane.' His smile died. He realised his *faux pas* even as he was uttering it.

'It would stretch a point for me to regard that prospect as looking on the bright side,' said Liz.

She swept off, looking momentarily too fearsome to be approached by any leave-takers.

Betty Sillitoe emerged, glass in hand, from the dining room, where she'd demolished a drumstick in secret, just as Ted limped sideways through the door of the living room, holding his injured arm carefully away from the door and the wall.

'Where are you going?' she asked.

'You know.'

She offered to help him. He accepted politely, although he didn't really need help.

The downstairs lavatory was at the back of the hall, beneath the stairs. Betty took Ted's arm and began to lead him towards it, very slowly.

'Ted,' she said, and she put her left hand firmly on the crutch, where it fitted onto his right arm, making it impossible for him to move. She leant forward and turned to look into his face. 'It's going to be lovely having you working for us. Lovely.'

'Thanks.'

She removed her hand. Ted tried to hurry towards the lavatory. His need was increasing in relation to its proximity.

'No, I really mean it,' said Betty, putting her hand over the crutch again for emphasis. She gazed into his face. 'It's going to be lovely.'

'Thanks.'

She removed her hand. Ted hobbled a couple of steps hurriedly. Down came the hand again.

'All right, you said we'd be bankrupt by Christmas, but that's forgotten.'

'Thanks.'

Off came the hand. Ted set off like an injured greyhound. On went the hand.

'OK, you called us freaky creaky nut cutlet folk, but that's forgiven. Because – and this is the point – it's going to be lovely having you working for us.'

'Thanks.'

'Even if you are a stubborn, opinionated sod.'

'Thank you, Betty,' said Ted desperately. Her hand came off the crutch again, and he hobbled hurriedly to the door. 'You can't come any further.'

'Are you sure? I mean, if you need help . . . No need to be coy.'

'I'm not coy, but I can manage.'

Betty was holding the lavatory door now. 'Nothing to be coy about,' she said. 'We've all got them. Well, no, women haven't, but they've got other things. We've all got parts of the body, of various peculiar kinds, and I've seen it all before. I was a nurse before I met Rodney.'

'Thank you very much, Betty, but I'm all right.'

'Right. Message received. You're coy. Understood.'

She let go of the door at last.

'Betty, I am not coy, but I can manage,' he repeated, and he shut the door in her face.

'If you get into difficulties,' shouted Betty, as if he were miles away, 'shout "nurse".'

She drained her glass and put it behind a rubber plant. She found another glass hidden behind the rubber plant. It was half full. She sniffed it, then sipped it.

Rodney knew that he ought to be concentrating on what Alec Skiddaw was saying, and did manage to pick out the occasional word so that he could comment and appear to be listening, but where was she? 'Alice Springs! Good Lord, Alec. A bit different from Daventry.' How would he cope if she died, when he hated it if she even left the room? 'In the bedroom! Good Lord! I hate snakes.' It wasn't *his* death that he feared. He wouldn't be around to suffer. It was hers. 'Ayers Rock! Amazing!' They'd done everything together. People warned them how dangerous it was to be everything to each other. 'To jump? Good Lord!' Let's hope I go first. No! Can't let the dear old duck down. Betty on her own, without me – unthinkable. 'Well, I suppose there aren't many places to jump from in the outback.' Let's hope we go together. Unlikely. Possible. Shanghai flu? Plane crash? Maybe we ought to have a suicide pact. Pills. Shouldn't be too hard. Or something more spectacular, a grand gesture. Knaresborough. Nice thought, if a trifle morbid. 'We might just do that.'

'I beg your pardon, sir?' said Alec Skiddaw.

'Sorry. I was thinking,' said Rodney. 'Morbid, in a way. Yet, in a way, not. About jumping. Betty and me. When we're old. Off the viaduct in Knaresborough, maybe, hand in hand, together, into the Nidd. Sorry. It was your friend who jumped off Ayers Rock that set me off.'

'But he didn't. That's the point.'

'You what?'

'My cousin persuaded him not to. Because he was from Daventry, too, and they found friends in common. That was the whole point of the story.'

'Yes. Yes, of course. I . . . er . . . didn't quite catch every word of it, I'm afraid. Fascinating, though, Alec. Fascinating.'

Where was she?

When Ted emerged from the lavatory he didn't see Betty at first, and he jumped when she suddenly stepped into his path and said, 'All right?'

'Yes.'

'Have you ever loved someone, Ted, and been too shy to tell them?'

'No, I . . . shyness, that's never been a . . . '

'I have.' Betty stood in front of him, staring into his face, swaying only slightly. 'I have met a man, and loved him for many years, and said nothing. Met him regularly, and said nothing. I don't think I need tell you who that man is.'

'You mean . . . ?' Ted could hardly bring himself to believe it. 'You mean . . . ?'

'Precisely. Someone not a million miles from this spot on which I'm standing on. Then the time came when I realised

I had to admit my secret love, so my secret love would be no secret any more.' Betty looked puzzled. 'That sounds familiar. Is it Shakespeare?'

Ted tried to think, but it wouldn't come. He wasn't that familiar with Shakespeare.

Betty gave up the hunt. 'I realised that the time had come to say, "I love you with all my heart."'

'Betty!'

Ted launched himself at her.

'Not you!' she shrieked. 'Ted! Ted!'

She pushed him off her. He lost his balance, tried to regain it with his crutch. The crutch slipped. He fell towards Betty. She tried to get out of the way and slipped. They fell together. Ted gave a screech of agony as his broken limbs crashed to the ground.

Rodney rushed into the hall, closely followed by Rita and Geoffrey. Elvis and Jenny weren't far behind.

They gazed down on Ted and Betty, entwined and gasping on the carpet by the bottom of the stairs.

'What's happened?' said Rodney.

'He attacked me,' said Betty.

'Ted!' said Rita.

'He made advances upon my person.'

'With an arm and a leg in plaster? That must be some kind of record,' said Rita.

'She told me she loved me,' said Ted.

'I didn't, Rodney,' said Betty desperately. 'I told him I loved you.'

'Oh Betty!' The dreadful realisation dawned on Ted. 'You mean . . . ? Oh heck. Oh, Betty. I'm . . . oh, Betty.' He tried to get up, raising his head and chest slowly. He failed. His head crashed onto the brown carpet. He gave a cry of pain.

By now Simon and Lucinda and Liz and Carol were among those who had come out to see what was happening.

Rita and Geoffrey tried to lift Ted up.

Rodney tried to lift Betty up.

'Help us, somebody,' said Rita, so urgently that Rodney hurried to her aid, dropping Betty like a sack of coal.

'Rodney!' cried Betty.

Rodney swung back to Betty's aid. Morris Wigmore and

Elvis helped Rita, and Simon and Liz helped Rodney with Betty.

At last Betty and Ted were on their feet again, and Ted was reunited with his crutch. Betty was shaken, and Ted very shaken.

'I told him how I'd been a nurse,' Betty explained to Rodney, 'and how when I first met you, when I was a nurse, when you were in hospital with . . . well, I won't tell them what you had . . . and how shy we were, and all those years before we realised we loved each other. You do believe me, don't you?'

' 'Course I do,' said Rodney. ' 'Course I do, love.' He turned to Ted. 'All right, Ted?'

'I think so.'

'No more bones broken?'

'I don't think so.'

'Good. You're sacked.'

'You what?'

'Thinking Betty and I are like everyone else, playing around . . . ' Rodney looked uneasily at Rita, and Liz, and Elvis and Jenny, and Simon, and Carol. 'Well, not everyone else . . . So conceited you think every woman loves you. You're sacked.'

'I haven't even started work yet.'

'You're still sacked. Two hundred pounds a week down the drain.'

'Two hundred pounds a week! I had more like four hundred in mind.'

'You can have it. You're sacked. Four hundred pounds a week down the drain.'

Betty gave a shriek of laughter.

'Come on, old girl,' said Rodney. 'Home.'

He led Betty towards the front door. People began to drift back to the living room.

Liz held the front door open, perhaps out of politeness, perhaps to make sure they went through it.

'It's been a lovely party, Liz,' said Betty. 'Most enjoyable.'

'Betty!' said Rodney.

'Well, not enjoyable. Awful. Well, not awful. What I mean is, you made the best of a bad job. Well, not a bad job. A . . . I . . . good night. Well, not night. Afternoon.'

Betty blundered out, into the front garden.

'I'm sorry, Liz,' said Rodney. 'It's the emotion. I'm so sorry.'

'It's all right,' said Liz. 'Really.'

Rodney hurried after Betty.

Liz closed the door. Only Ted and Rita remained in the hall. Rita had helped Ted to the door of the living room.

'I'm sorry, Liz,' said Ted.

'It's all right,' said Liz. 'I think the dear man would have seen the funny side, don't you, Rita?'

'Yes, I rather think he would, Liz,' said Rita.

Ted struggled sideways through the door into the living room.

'I think it would have tickled Neville pink,' said Liz.

The two women gave each other long, wondering looks.

'Oh, Liz,' said Rita.

She returned to the living room.

Liz, still the hostess, went to clear a dirty plate which had been left on a small table by the dining room door. As she passed the foot of the stairs, she stopped. Her spine was tingling again.

She hardly dared look up the stairs. She could hardly breathe. She forced herself to look.

'Wouldn't it, my love?' she said.

There was nobody there.

She sighed. Then she cleared away the dirty plate.

Seventh Do

October:
The Civil Wedding

Geoffrey Ellsworth-Smythe's nostrils twitched as the light
October wind bore exotic spices along Commercial Street.
His sister sniffed the wind more warily, her nose wrinkled in
disapproval. She had never been inside either the good Indian
restaurant or the bad Indian restaurant. They weren't her style.

The forecourt of the council offices was steaming, as warm
sunshine dried off the effects of a recent shower. The tempera-
ture was average for the time of year. So were the rainfall, the
sunshine and the wind speed. Yorkshire was experiencing that
extreme rarity, an average day. Later, the Meteorological Office
would state that it had been the most average day since 1678.

But for Geoffrey Ellsworth-Smythe this most average day was
the most extraordinary day of his life. It was his wedding day.
He looked up at the solid, squat council offices, which housed
the social services department, the housing department, the
planning department and the register office. He sniffed the
scents of turmeric and fenugreek, cumin, chillies and garam
masala, garlic and ginger, cardamon and coriander, saffron,
mace and cinnamon. He recalled palmed paradises, dark rain
forests, deep jungle clearings, crocodile rivers, cathedrals black
with vultures, bare bodies, painted bodies, ritually scarred bodies,
grinning teeth, decaying teeth, and mouths with no teeth at all.
Now he was to become a husband and live in England. He took
his sister's arm and escorted her between the cars of the heads
and deputy heads of departments, neatly parked in their reserved
spaces in this neat, reserved corner of the world, and entered the
council offices.

They blinked in the dark interior. Gradually, they became
able to see dark, panelled walls, studded with doors, one of
which bore the legend 'Register Office'. There were benches

293

around the walls. Double doors led to the social services department, and a wide staircase led up to the housing and planning departments.

'Oh Lord!' sighed Liz.

'What?' said Geoffrey.

'Nothing.' She paced the unlovely hall, a caged tigress.

'No, please. Tell me. We mustn't start drifting apart again. I need you today, Liz. I'm scared.'

Surprise halted the tigress. 'Scared? The great anthropologist, who's faced head hunters, witch doctors and poisoned blowpipes?'

'The great bachelor. The great wanderer. The great loner. Terrified.'

'Terrified she may not turn up?'

'Good heavens, no. She wouldn't do that . . . twice. Would you be happy if she didn't turn up?'

'Really, Geoffrey! What a thing to ask! Of course I would. I'd be ecstatic.'

'Oh, Liz! I thought you were friends again.'

'I was very emotional at Neville's funeral. I said some foolish things I bitterly regret.'

'Such as?'

'Such as, "Shall we end this stupid feud, Rita?" Whereupon she marries my brother, and her son exposes my son and loses him his job. Damnable Simcocks!'

'You still haven't told me why you said "Oh Lord!"'

'The last time I stood here, *I* was getting married.'

'Oh Lord.'

'Sorry. I don't want to cast a pall over your great day.'

'Liz?' Geoffrey put his hands on her shoulders, as if blessing her. 'Rita and I both want you to be a frequent and regular guest at our house.'

'Watching you touching each other?' She wriggled free of his touch. 'Enviously listening to your creaking bed-springs? Terrific. I can't wait.'

Liz went to study a notice board which contained information on where to go if you needed marriage guidance, had VD, or needed advice about alcoholism or AIDS.'

Simon Rodenhurst, no longer of Trellis, Trellis, Openshaw and Finch, came in rather shyly.

'Hello,' he beamed.

'Hello, Simon.' Geoffrey nodded towards Liz. 'Fragile. Handle with care.'

'Oh Lord!' Simon went up to his mother, smiled hugely, and kissed her. 'You look fantastic.' Liz was wearing a green, large-collared jacket, green skirt, and a black tricorn hat with green and white squiggles. 'Everyone'll think you're the bride.'

'Not this time, Simon.'

'Oh Lord! Crunch! Thud! Sacked estate agent drops brick. Sorry, Mother.'

Liz turned on him. 'A minor indiscretion compared to your recent efforts. I can just forgive you for being dishonest, Simon. But for being stupid enough to be found out by Elvis, never.'

She stalked off, plonked herself on a bench, and stared resolutely into space.

'Phew!' said Simon, letting out the tension like air from a taut tyre.

'Bad luck,' said Geoffrey. 'Lucinda all right?'

'Oh yes. The wedding isn't off. It's just postponed till I find myself a job.'

There she was, in the doorway. For her third wedding day, and her second wedding, Rita had chosen a grey and cream tiered dress with a wide grey suede belt, a corsage of turquoise orchids, a double-row pearl bracelet and a large turquoise straw hat.

Was there relief in Geoffrey's eyes and disappointment in Liz's?

Rita gave Geoffrey a curiously shy, self-conscious little kiss. 'Well, I've turned up,' she said. She looked round the gloomy hall, whose only natural light came from a grimy skylight five stories up. 'Unlike most other people, it seems. Elvis rang. The little swine's been bleeped. Emergency. He'll meet me here. Who'd have sons? Monsters.'

'Paul?'

Rita gave Simon a look. Even he couldn't fail to understand that she didn't want to talk about Paul in front of him. 'Oh, I'll just slope off, tactfully,' he said.

'Thank you, Simon,' said Geoffrey. 'Do it tactfully enough, without a word, we won't even notice.'

Simon sloped off, tactfully, to read the notice board and wonder why he regretted having led such a sheltered life.

'He's gone fishing,' said Rita.

'*Fishing?*' said Geoffrey.

'He's finding it difficult to cope with life outside prison. Crowded rooms make him panic. And I don't imagine he'd have relished facing Elvis. He phoned, though. Cried a bit. Sent us his love and blessing.'

'But . . . fishing, today! And him a vegetarian!'

'No Jenny yet?'

'Not a sign. Nor Carol.'

'Yes, well . . . I'm afraid marrying you is making me a traitor to the cause to which I've recruited Carol. Even you changing your name to mine hasn't mollified her. No Rodney and Betty either. That's odd.'

Rita noticed Liz for the first time, and raised an eyebrow.

'Fuming,' whispered Geoffrey. 'Back to square one.'

'Oh dear.'

The dapper, ageless Eric Siddall entered enthusiastically. He was wearing an ordinary tie, instead of his bow-tie, in order not to look like a barman.

'Thank you so much for inviting me, Mrs . . . well, it's still Simcock, isn't it? For a few minutes.'

'Please. Call me Rita.'

'In my career I've done twenty-seven nuptials, Mrs . . . Rita! Twenty-seven!'

'Amazing.'

'Well, no, what I . . . well, I suppose it's not a bad tribute, I'd never really . . . but what I mean is . . . you're the first one ever to invite me to the ceremony. I'm . . . I . . . '

'Eric!'

Rita kissed him.

'Oooh!' he said. 'I won't wash for a month! I've checked everything at the hotel, Mr Ellsworth-Smythe. It's all . . . well . . . '

'Tickety-boo,' prompted Geoffrey.

'Incredible. You've taken the very words out of my mouth. You must be psychic. You're one in a million, Mrs . . . Rita. You've seen through the barman to the human being underneath. I'll never forget that.' Eric moved away, in case he was outstaying his welcome. He found himself looking at the door of the register office, just as it opened. 'Oooh!' he said, pointing excitedly.

It was indeed a surprising sight. Rita was distinctly surprised to see her ex-husband emerging from the register office, arm in arm with the cake-loving Sandra Pickersgill. She was surprised to see that for this modest civil wedding Sandra had chosen a long ivory flounced lace-edged V-neck wedding gown with large puffed sleeves, a halo of flowers with a short tiered veil, pearl drop earrings, a pearl bracelet and a sapphire engagement ring. She was distinctly surprised to see, emerging behind Ted and Sandra, and all looking like naughty children caught smoking behind the bike shed, her son Elvis, her daughter-in-law Jenny, her protégé Carol and her employers and old friends Rodney and Betty Sillitoe. A passing planner, who was planning to start work that very afternoon on plans to build a separate entrance for the register office, glanced at the scene with his usual faint interest, and was struck by something unusual in the way in which the two groups were facing each other, like opposing buttonholed armies.

If they had been armies, Rita's would have been heavily outnumbered. Sandra's friends and relations were still pouring out of the register office, and they included several burly young men who might prove useful in a scrap.

Ted and Sandra, still arm in arm, approached Rita and Geoffrey slowly.

Elvis scurried past them, said, 'He swore us to secrecy, Mum,' and scampered back to the safety of the larger group.

The two couples, one just married, the other about to be, faced each other warily. Ted was smiling uneasily. Sandra's smile had an understandable touch of smugness. Geoffrey smiled cautiously.

Rita, who didn't smile at all, was the first to speak.

'Well, quite a coincidence, Ted.'

'Oh no. Not a coincidence, Rita.'

'So what's the big idea, then? Sabotage our wedding day?'

'No. No! Absolutely not! Do you think I'd do that? Look at all Sandra's lot. There'll be even more at the reception. How many have I rustled up? Five. I'm a social outcast.'

'Please, Ted,' said Geoffrey. 'I don't want to cry on my wedding day.'

'Could I have formally invited my ex-wife and her fiancé? Could I have formally invited . . . ?'

'Your ex-lover?'

'Rita!' Ted seemed hurt. 'Not today! I want today to be a day of reconciliation, all round.'

'Do you?'

'Yes! So I thought . . . when I bumped into you here, I could informally say, "Please pop into our reception."'

'Strangely enough, Ted,' said Geoffrey in his gentle, dry way, 'Rita and I have both decided to go to our reception.'

'But this is the whole point,' said Ted. 'They're in the same hotel.'

'You what, Ted?' said Rita.

'You're in the Sir Leonard Hutton Room. We're in the Geoffrey Boycott Room. Much smaller, and the service is very slow; we aren't trying to upstage you. I've asked the others to try and pop in for half an hour and have a drink with us. Rodney and Betty seemed quite keen. So please, come and have a glass of champagne.'

'Asti spumante,' said Sandra. 'We prefer it.'

'Thank you,' said Rita. 'Well . . . it's a bit . . . we'll see, shall we?' Ted had the advantage of surprise. She couldn't help resenting being thrown on the defensive on her wedding day.

'Please do,' said Sandra. 'Hey, I think you look right belting, Mrs Simcock.'

'Well, thank you, Sandra,' said Rita. 'You don't . . . er . . . you don't look too bad yourself, Mrs . . . Simcock.'

'Hello, Mum,' said Jenny Simcock, *née* Rodenhurst, nervously. She was wearing a long, ethnic skirt in black, pink and red, with a pink-shot silk fitted jacket.

'Hello, stranger,' said Liz, who'd been unable to pretend not to be interested in the confrontation between the two wedding couples, but had just resumed her study of distant space.

'Well, I wasn't sure what sort of reception you'd give me.'

'Jenny! Friendly, of course. After all, you've twice walked out on Simcock boys, and I applaud that.'

'Mum!'

'The only slight cloud being that both times it's been to move in with his brother, but that's a mere detail.'

'Mum!'

Jenny hurried off.

298

Elvis intercepted her.

'Crying?' he asked.

'Yes,' she sobbed.

'Good.'

'Oh!'

Elvis strolled on, trying to look as if it was by chance that he was approaching Carol, who was talking with the Sillitoes near the door of the register office.

'Hello, Carol,' he said.

She turned to look at him gravely.

'Jenny's gone back to Paul,' said the cynical Elvis Simcock.

'Good,' said the long-haired Carol Fordingbridge, who had once loved him.

'Hello, Liz,' said Ted, with what it would be an exaggeration to call *sang-froid*. There was no reply, so he continued. 'Liz? Can we let . . . '

'Bygones be bygones? Let me save you from your banality.'

'No, but . . . I mean . . . will you? Pop in to our reception.'

'Hooray! My life's ambition achieved. The pinnacle climbed.'

Ted began to wince, then stopped, as if realising that she had no power to hurt him any more.

'No, but . . . ' he continued resolutely, ' . . . we're moving away for good, and – '

'Oh, well, that is a cause for celebration. In that case I'll be delighted.'

'Liz!'

Ted sounded disappointed that Liz should fall below an acceptable standard of social behaviour on this happy day. And Liz felt all the more angry, because she knew that Ted's implied rebuke was justified, that he was behaving with more social grace than she was, and that she was unable to do anything about that intolerable state of affairs.

'No Lucinda?' said Elvis. He could never resist turning the knife in the wound, when the wound was Simon's.

'Not yet.'

'Ah.'

'Save your "ah"s, Elvis. She hasn't ditched me.'

'No?'

'No. She wouldn't.'

'Ah.'

'Oh belt up.'

Simon moved off, as if he felt that his devastating wit had rendered further conversation unnecessary.

Jenny approached Elvis anxiously, nervously.

'Can we try to at least be civil today, if not for me, for your mum and dad?' she said.

'Oh all right,' said Elvis.

'I mean, we don't have to talk if we can avoid it, but, if we can't avoid it, and I hope we can, but if we can't, let's be at least coolly polite.'

'Well, all right.'

'Thanks.' Jenny didn't leave, and Elvis didn't say any more, and clearly Jenny thought he ought to say something more, for she repeated, 'Thanks.'

'All right!' he said.

The moment he'd got rid of Jenny, Elvis found that he had Rita to deal with.

'You've offended Simon and Jenny already, haven't you?' she said. 'What have you said?'

'Let's think. To Simon I said, "No Lucinda?", then "Ah", then "No?", then "Ah" again. To Jenny I said . . . er . . . "Oh, all right", "Well, all right", and "All right".'

'My word. You're surpassing even your normal level of inarticulacy.'

'Mum!'

'You should try total silence. Britain's first Trappist philosopher.'

'Mum!'

The moment Rita had moved off, Ted steamed in.

'Have you upset your mother?' he said. 'What have you said?'

'Oh heck. I said "Mum!" and "Mum!"'

'You shouldn't speak to your mother like that.'

'Dad!'

It was becoming a nightmare. The moment Ted had gone, here was Rita again.

'Have you upset your father now?' she said. She saw that he was reeling, and relented. 'Sorry. But . . . I mean . . . on my wedding day . . . not coming to fetch me, as arranged, not telling me why.'

'I couldn't. Look, Mum, I'm here now, at your service, and I want to make this a happy day for you.' He became confidential, as if announcing momentous news. 'I've switched me bleeper off.'

'My God! Greater love hath no man.' Rita saw the hurt on his face. 'Oh, Elvis.' She kissed him. 'Thanks, Elvis.' She slapped his face in maternal exasperation. 'Oh, Elvis.'

At last it was the turn of the somewhat bewildered Elvis to move off. There weren't many people he could approach in safety. He decided to try the Sillitoes. Too late. They were already on their way across the dark foyer to explain themselves to Rita.

'Rita!' said Betty, who was bedecked in a purple and coral tiered dress, with short black shiny gloves, and a pink hat which looked like the intestines of a small, repellent animal. 'We had no alternative. He swore us to secrecy.'

'And for the first time in your life you kept a secret! Congratulations!'

'Don't be like that, Rita,' said the former big wheel behind Cock-A-Doodle Chickens. 'It's not every day we're invited to two receptions in the same hotel.'

'No,' said Rita. 'How will your system work? Will one of you get drunk at each reception?'

'Rita!' Bottomless was Betty's hurt, immense her disappointment at the attitude of her friend and employee.

And Rita felt suitably contrite. 'Oh Lord!' she said. 'I'm sorry. I shouldn't have said that. Not today. I'm just . . . after my previous . . . and seeing Ted and everything . . . I'm . . . '

'We understand,' said Rodney. 'But we believe, don't we, Betty . . . ?'

'Oh, we do. We do. Utterly.'

'That Ted's done it for the very best of motives – a day of reconciliation all round.'

'We wouldn't have accepted if we hadn't believed that, Rita. We are your friends.'

'We want to drink to Ted's health and to Sandra's health.'

'As well as your health and Geoffrey's health.'

'We want to drink to everybody's health.'

Rita looked into the bloodshot eyes of her two old friends, and suddenly felt that she couldn't bear to disappoint them.

'I think I believe you,' she said. 'I really do. Thank you. You're both very dear friends.'

Could she – after all he'd done to her – believe Ted's assurances?

She had to. Otherwise it would be another blighted day. And, if she was just to go from one blighted day to another, why had she fought so hard to change herself and her life? She had once thought that it was a fight that would lead to victory. She knew now that there could be no victory. There could only be the continual avoidance of defeat.

She was ready for it. Ready for the continuation of the endless fight.

Ready for the fray.

She rejoined Geoffrey.

'I'd like to accept Ted's offer,' she said.

'Tremendous. So would I.'

He led Rita straight up to Ted, as if fearing that she might change her mind.

'I'd like to accept your offer and hope you'll come to our reception as well,' she said.

'Thank you, Rita,' said Ted.

'Let's make this a day of reconciliation all round,' said Rita. 'Come on, Geoffrey.'

Rita and Geoffrey walked towards the register office as if proceeding down the aisle of Westminster Abbey.

Their small party of guests followed them in.

Ted took the good news to Sandra.

'Great news,' he said. 'A day of reconciliation all round.'

Simon hurried in from the street, where he had been making a desperate effort to will Lucinda to appear on the horizon.

'Hello, Simon,' said Ted. 'No Lucinda? Ditched you, has she?'

He cackled. Simon entered the register office without deigning to reply. Ted grinned at Sandra, inviting her to bask in his malicious wit. She gave him a look of grave rebuke that made her seem mature beyond her years.

The Angel Hotel had undergone major surgery. The peeling

Georgian façade had been repainted in dark blue and cream. This colour scheme didn't suit its elegant proportions, and its elegant proportions no longer suited the rest of Westgate. On either side of the hotel there were building societies and shoe shops. Opposite it, where there had once been Georgian town houses, was the bleak concrete façade of the Whincliff Centre, known to the locals as Alcatraz, and publicly condemned by Prince Charles.

Inside, the Angel had become a theme hotel. The theme was Yorkshire cricket. The ballroom had become the Sir Leonard Hutton Room. The Ridings Suite had become the Geoffrey Boycott Room. The restaurant was called the Headingley Grill, and served three courses – openers, middle order and tail-enders. The Gaiety Bar had become the Pavilion Bar. The signed photograph of Ian Botham was still there, but those of Terry Wogan, General Dayan and Dame Peggy Ashcroft had moved on for the second time, to lend their handsome tributes to another hotel that they had never visited, in Bowness-on-Windermere.

A not entirely successful picture of Sir Leonard Hutton, painted by Doug Watkin, who was to cricketers what Sir Alfred Munnings was to horses, gazed down upon a cheery, happy scene, in the refurbished green and cream function room. Rita's uncles and aunts and cousins and nephews and nieces hadn't entirely accepted her explanation that there wouldn't have been room for them all at the register office. But she had turned up this time; they could enjoy themselves without feeling guilty, and enjoy themselves they would. Her new councillor friends were more restrained, being conscious that they were public figures, always on display, it was the price they had to pay. There were friends from the almost forgotten past: her old schoolfriend Denise Bowyer, who had once had a crush on her and now had four sons, and Madge Longbottom, from the next desk at the insurance company, whose daughter Glenda had become a Country and Western singer and changed her name to Emmylou Longbottom.

Eric Siddall, barman supreme, replenished the glass of the cynical Elvis Simcock with a smile, and the words, 'There you go, sir. Just the job. Tickety-boo.'

Elvis didn't return the smile.

'Oh dear. We do look glum,' said Eric. 'Cheer up, sir. It may never happen.'

'It has happened, Eric,' said Elvis gloomily.

Eric moved on, to serve Simon Rodenhurst, no longer of Trellis, Trellis, Openshaw and Finch. Simon had a plate piled with food, as was his wont, his years at boarding school having taught him to go for every half chance, whether at rugger or eating. But today he felt sick with anxiety and couldn't eat.

'A touch more of the '82, sir?' said the dapper, ageless Eric Siddall. 'A fine vintage, as you will know, being, I'm sure, something of a connoisseur.'

'Well, yes.' Simon basked briefly in Eric's praise. 'I think I can say I know my way around a wine list.' He watched Eric pouring the golden liquid. 'Thank you, Eric. You're a treasure. But I thought you were working at the Clissold Lodge nowadays.'

'There were problems, sir. Of a personal nature.' Eric changed the subject. 'Is your lovely lady not here? Not indisposed, I trust?'

Eric's change of subject was not an enormous success.

'Why don't you cut the tittle-tattle and concentrate on the job you're paid to do?' said Simon contemptuously, and he stomped off.

Eric raised an ironically self-pitying eyebrow, fought his anger, controlled his breathing, and moved on warily. The wariness fell from his face like fat from a slimmer's cheeks when he saw that he was approaching those two lovely young ladies, Jenny Simcock and Carol Fordingbridge.

'A drop more of the sparkling grape, ladies?' he enquired.

They accepted with thanks.

'There you go,' said Eric as he poured. 'Very special champagne for very special young ladies, who are, if you'll excuse the play on words, as bubbly as the bubbly.'

'Oh Lord,' said Jenny. 'Excuse me.'

Eric looked stunned as Jenny ran off.

'It's just . . . she's all churned up about Elvis,' explained Carol. 'And Paul. And Simon. And her mother and Rita. It was just you being so cheerful upset her, I think.'

For a moment Eric felt sorry for himself. But he soon snapped out of it. He was a fighter. He was a barman supreme. He was even able to acknowledge that he might

304

have been a little at fault. It was possible for a barman to be too cheerful.

'Good afternoon, madam,' he said to Liz with a suitable air of gravity. 'May I replenish your glass at all?'

'It's not a funeral, Eric,' said Liz. 'For goodness sake cheer up or I'll cry.'

Rita circulated busily, smiling at Morris Wigmore, the ever-smiling deputy leader of the Conservatives, whom she had invited because she believed that social life should be non-partisan, smiling at Councillor Mirfield, who smiled at her, lest his resentment of her became public knowledge, smiling at Councillor Wendy Bullock because she liked her, smiling at all her relatives, who were feeling neglected and would feel even more neglected when she went off to Ted and Sandra's reception. Oh why did she still care so much what people thought?

Eventually, inevitably, Rita's smiling tour brought her face to face with an unsmiling Liz.

'Ah!' she said.

'"Ah!"?'

'Yes. Geoffrey tells me you had a chat with him.'

'Ah.'

'Yes. He tells me you regret suggestions at the . . . er . . . '

'Funeral, Rita. My husband's funeral. It's not something I can't face mentioning, although of course I don't want to harp on it and cast a cloud of depression over your joyful day.'

'That you regret saying that we should end our feud.'

'I'll have to be careful what I say to Geoffrey. It'll all come back to you.'

'Well, we are married.'

'Yes. I remember the ceremony. I thought the registry office people did their best to make it seem a happy occasion.'

'Geoffrey also tells me you don't relish the prospect of . . . '

'Intruding on your marital bliss? Amazingly enough, I don't.'

'Well, perhaps one day you'll bring your . . . '

'New man? You seem to assume I want one.'

Behind them, Hutton and Washbrook were walking out to face the Australians until the world ended, or the photograph faded, whichever was the sooner.

'Well . . . ' Rita didn't want to say too much. Not today.
'Er . . . '

'Oh come on, Rita. What?'

'Well, all right. I don't mean it rudely, but . . . I think
you're the sort of woman who finds it difficult to live without
a man.'

'Whereas you don't?'

'No.'

'But you aren't.'

'Well, as it happens, no. But I've married Geoffrey because I
want to, not because I needed to.'

'Are you hinting that I needed Neville?'

'I wouldn't think any the less of you if you did. Look, what
I really want to say . . . '

'You mean all this so far has been small talk?'

'Well – no – but Geoffrey and I are going to pop in soon to
wish Ted and Sandra well. And we wondered if . . . well . . .
you'd find it easier to pop into Ted's reception if you came
with us.'

'Why should I find it difficult?'

'Well, you having . . . er . . . with Ted, and its not being
. . . er . . . '

'My kind of thing? Why are you so frightened of saying it?
No, it isn't. Not my kind of thing. Not my kind of people.
However, I suppose I shall "put in an appearance". But not
tagging along with you, either as a sop to your consciences or a
pathetic lonely figure to remind you of your good fortune. You've
taken my brother, Rita. Cease this pathetic charade that you
want me too.'

'Rita! You came! Geoffrey! You came! Come on in.'

The Geoffrey Boycott Room was about half the size of the Sir
Leonard Hutton Room. Doug Watkin's painting of Sir Leonard
Hutton looked like a Rembrandt by comparison with his portrait
of 'Our Geoff'. It was a grinning grotesque, with a retouched
mouth, who gave his blessing to the boisterous gathering of
the Pickersgill clan, in the spick and span, gold and grey
function room.

Ted's boyish delight at the arrival of Rita and Geoffrey was
irresistible. They found themselves smiling broadly.

306

'Meet everybody,' said Ted. 'Everybody!' he shouted. Gradually, the young men with their pints of beer and the ladies with their asti spumante turned to greet the new arrivals. 'Everybody, this is . . . er . . . my good friend Rita Simc . . . Ellsworth-Sm . . . '

'Spragg,' interrupted Rita. 'Rita Spragg.'

'Spragg. Spragg? Spragg. And her fian . . . husband, Geoffrey Ells . . . er . . . '

'Spragg. Geoffrey Spragg.'

'Spragg. Er . . . Sandra's mum.' A platinum blonde smiled warmly. 'Sandra's dad.' A tall, greying man smiled with shyer warmth. 'Sandra's nan.' A little old lady in frilly black smiled roguishly. 'Sandra's brothers, Darren and Warren and Dean.' Three very large young men, with ruddy faces and big horny hands, squirmed in suits that were too small.

Sandra hurried over to hand the new arrivals glasses of asti spumante.

'Sandra!' said Ted. 'Somebody should be serving *you* today.'

'It doesn't make me inferior, doesn't serving people,' said Sandra. 'And it's my wedding day, and why shouldn't I do what makes me happy, 'cos it's a happy day, i'n't it, Rita?'

'Oh yes, Sandra,' said Rita. 'It certainly is.'

Eric Siddall, barman supreme, realised that he was walking towards the Sillitoes. He pretended not to see them, made a small but vital adjustment to his course, and walked straight past them.

Betty Sillitoe sighed.

'I know,' said Rodney. 'Give a dog a bad name and the mud sticks.'

'You what, Rodney?'

'You sighed because when Eric saw us he turned away because we have a reputation which is no longer justified but which when once won is not easily unwon.'

'No. I sighed because of the young people. Because I noticed, at the registry office. Tensions.'

'Oh . . . well . . . right . . . well . . . you couldn't not notice.'

'And I thought, tensions, sadness, at a wedding – it's a pity. At a double wedding it's a double pity. So, let's go and pour

307

a bit of the calming balm of our experience over the stormy waters of their immature emotions.'

'Well, if you put it like that!'

They looked round for a young person onto whom they could begin to pour their calming balm, and saw Elvis wandering purposelessly across the room, a lover without his woman, a reporter without his bleeper.

'Elvis!' said Betty, intercepting him. 'Rodney and I couldn't help noticing, well, you couldn't . . . '

'Not that we were poking our noses in,' said Rodney. 'Well, we wouldn't.'

'But you couldn't.'

'And we did.'

'Notice that you and Jenny . . . '

Rodney saw a possibility of detaching Jenny from a group of Rita's relatives, and went off to do so.

'That I'm barely speaking to the little cow,' said Elvis to Betty.

'Yes. Well, not the little cow, no, but . . . yes.'

Rodney returned with his prize.

'Children!' said Betty. 'Make your peace, for your mothers.'

'Absolutely,' said Rodney. 'Specially for Rita. On her wedding day.'

'And for your father, Elvis.'

'On his wedding day.'

'Quite unusual, really, both your parents marrying on the same day. When they're not marrying each other, I mean.'

'Betty! So, how about it?'

For a moment, neither Jenny nor Elvis spoke. Then Elvis leapt in.

'Why not? Maybe Jenny meant it when she said she loved me. Maybe our love could have survived anything except martyrdom.'

'Martyrdom?' Jenny was puzzled.

As the argument between the former lovers developed, the Sillitoes found themselves turning their anxious gazes back and forth, like spectators watching Britain's last representative in the second round of the Wimbledon championships.

'You can't resist feeling sorry for people, and with Paul in prison you were bound to feel sorrier for him than for me.'

'That's totally untrue, Elvis.'

'Elvis didn't mean your love for him wasn't genuine,' said Rodney.

His intervention wasn't a great success.

'Yes, he did,' said Jenny.

'Yes, I did,' said Elvis.

'I'm only glad I went back to Paul before you exposed Simon and lost him his job, and it seems his fiancée, because if I'd gone afterwards, everyone would have said I'd gone because you'd exposed him and I went because I love Paul more than ever now after prison, which has matured him.'

'Oh, it's the "suffering matures people" syndrome, is it? Well, I've suffered too, being dragged through the emotional mangle by you, so I'm just as mature as him, so there, fishface. And you needn't think I'm sorry, I'm glad, 'cos it's Carol I love.'

Betty swooped on Carol like a heron and brought her into the group triumphantly. Indeed, Carol looked barely more comfortable than a goldfish that is being swallowed whole.

'Carol!' said Betty. 'Come and get these young people to look on the bright side.'

'I am trying to look on the bright side,' retorted Elvis. 'I'm trying to forget Jenny.'

'I wish you would,' said Jenny.

'Elvis?' said Rodney. 'You and Carol were friendly once. Why don't you ask her out?'

'No chance!' said Carol.

'He's just told us,' said Betty, ' . . . I hope you don't mind, Elvis . . . that he loves you.'

Clearly Elvis minded very much.

'Obviously linguistic analysis wasn't your strong point in philosophy,' Carol told him.

'You what?' said the philosopher.

The Sillitoes were centre court spectators again.

'Words have meanings. Love has a meaning. It means . . . ' the former beauty queen searched for a definition, ' . . . "love". It doesn't mean, "Knock about with till somebody cleverer comes along.'

'Nobody cleverer came along.'

'Are you saying she's cleverer than me?' demanded Jenny.

'No.'

'Are you saying I'm stupider than her?' asserted Carol.

'No. You're of identical intellectual ability.'

'What a cop-out,' said Jenny scornfully.

'Right,' said Carol.

The flickering candle of female solidarity was quickly snuffed out.

'I don't think it was very clever what you did with my husband, Carol,' said Jenny, with unaccustomed aggression.

'Hell's bells, Jenny, nor do I, but that was yonks ago. I was an immature kid, then.'

The removal of youngsters from this social pond continued as Rodney netted Simon, detaching him expertly from Madge Longbottom, who'd just discovered that he'd never heard of Emmylou.

'Simon. Help us sort these young people out,' said Rodney.

'What's wrong?'

'Relationships. Life. Love. Families.'

'Oh, that. Well, they'll all grow up one day.'

'Does that include me?' said Jenny.

'Well, yes, frankly.'

'You pompous idiot.'

'Well said, Jenny,' said Elvis. 'I suppose everybody's right sometimes. Law of averages.'

'Don't start being sarcastic about my sister, you rancid slug.'

Simon smiled at Jenny. She wasn't as grateful as he'd hoped.

'I can defend myself without your support, thank you very much, Simon,' she said.

'I'm glad to hear it. I think I'm well out of it.'

'Well, go then.'

'I will. Don't you worry.'

Simon departed with injured dignity. This was more than Jenny could bear.

'I shouldn't have said that. Not today,' she said, hurrying after her brother.

'Carol, I've been thinking . . . ' began Elvis.

'Wonders will never cease,' retorted Carol. She tossed her long hair like a startled horse, and slid smoothly away.

'Kids!' said Elvis. 'This is the trouble with being mature for your age. All your friends seem so childish.'

Elvis walked listlessly away, a lover without his woman, a reporter without his bleeper.

Rodney and Betty contemplated the wreckage of their hopes.

'Well, we tried,' she said.

'Yes.'

'We were right to try.'

'Yes.'

'The peacemaker was a hard row to hoe.'

'Very true.'

Eric Siddall, barman supreme, realised that he was walking towards the Sillitoes. He pretended not to see them, made a small but vital adjustment to his course, and walked straight past them.

'Let's go and give Ted our blessing,' said Betty.

'Good idea,' said Rodney. 'We may even get a drink there.'

Ted and Rita sat in a corner of the Geoffrey Boycott Room, outside the gaze of its eponymous hero, and talked in undertones which contrasted with the extrovert enjoyment in the room.

'He'll be all right, in time,' said Rita. 'He just couldn't face crowded rooms . . . or Elvis.'

'I'm not surprised,' said Ted. 'How can he go fishing, anyroad? He's a vegetarian.'

'Oh, he doesn't catch things. He just sits by gravel pits and dreams. He'll be all right, in time.'

'They'll be having fishing for vegetarians next.' Ted climbed onto a hobby horse, but it ran without its old spirit. 'Stocking gravel pits with lentil cutlets. Throwing veggieburgers back because they're too small. Ruddy trendy . . . '

'Vegetarianism isn't trendy, Ted. It's popular. If you call things trendy because a lot of people do them you'd say breathing was trendy.'

There was a burst of laughter from Warren and Darren and Sandra's hairdresser, Russell, who, with Darren's friend Wayne, ran 'Peter and Angelo's' in George Street.

'They're a lovely family, Rita,' said Ted. 'I'm a lucky man.'

'Do they . . . are they . . . worried?'

'Because I'm so much older than her?'

'Well, yes. Partly.'

'Well, I suppose they might have preferred somebody younger

at first, but I think as they've come to appreciate my . . . qualities, my . . . maturity, my . . . sincerity . . . what do you mean, "partly"?'

'Well, I mean – are they worried because of your . . . ?'

'Employment prospects? Not at all. We have plans.'

'Because of your reputation.'

'Reputation? What on earth do you mean, Rita . . . reputation?'

'Well, as a bit of a – I mean, take us. Our marriage not working. Doesn't that . . . ? I mean, she's their only daughter.'

'You and I were very young, and still lasted twenty-four years. Par for the course.'

'It was supposed to be love, not golf.' Rita saw Geoffrey, pint glass in hand, chatting surprisingly animatedly with Sandra's parents and her nan, to whom he seemed to be being quite gallant, and she felt so very happy, and she wished she hadn't spoken to tartly. 'Sorry. I don't want to row today, Ted.' Ted looked relieved, almost smug. Rita wished she hadn't spoken so gently. 'But . . . oh Ted! Some of the things you did.'

'Don't you think sometimes we made mountains out of molehills?'

She couldn't let that go. It was outrageous. 'No, Ted, I do not! Doreen from the Frimley Building Society wasn't a molehill. Big Bertha from Nuremberg certainly wasn't a molehill. And as for Liz . . . she was a sexual Alp.'

'All in the past.'

It has to be said, but make it gentle, Rita.

'Leaving Sandra for Corinna? Not that long in the past, Ted.'

'I'm grateful to Corinna, Rita. No, I am. I believe she may have been sent, to show me the error of my ways. Much of my behaviour for much of my life has been that of a berk.' Rita couldn't hide her surprise. 'I've surprised you, haven't I?'

'Well . . . yes.'

'Difficult to see me as a berk.'

'No. I was surprised because *you* saw yourself as a berk.'

'What?'

'Sorry.' He looked so hurt that Rita felt she had to say this.

'Well, all right, but give me a chance. I love Sandra. Maybe I've never before . . . '

'I see.' What a knack the man had for making you sorry you'd said "sorry".

'Well, no, of course I loved you.'

'And it went wrong and now you love Sandra and it won't go wrong.'

'Yes, because . . . Ah! They've come!'

Rodney and Betty Sillitoe were standing by the door, looking for somebody to greet them.

Ted leapt to his feet.

'Danger of meaningful conversation with Ted narrowly averted,' said Rita.

Ted shrugged and approached the Sillitoes.

'Rodney! Betty!' he said. 'You came!'

Sandra hurried up with a tray of glasses.

'Have some champagne,' said Ted.

'Oh!' said Rodney and Betty, as if this was a thought that had never crossed their minds.

Each took two glasses, intending to hand one glass to the other.

'Oh!' they said again.

And they laughed.

But neither of them handed their second glass back.

Elvis approached Carol, who was standing beneath a photograph of Sir Leonard Hutton shaking hands with Sir Donald Bradman after he had beaten the Don's record of the highest score ever made in test cricket.

'You're looking more beautiful than ever,' said Elvis.

'Nice body, pity about the brain.'

'No. You look more intelligent than ever too. I underestimated you.'

'Well, I think so.'

'Is there really no chance at all?'

'None. I'm not sure I don't want to remain without a man forever, but even if I ever decide I don't want to remain without a man I'd be stupid not to look for one who never thought I wasn't good enough for him.'

Carol had sailed through all the double negatives with utter confidence. Elvis plodded behind, trying to work them out.

'All those negatives,' he said at last. 'They seem to add up to one enormous negative.'

'That was the general idea.'

Elvis was beginning to feel that this wasn't his day so far as women were concerned. So he wasn't surprised to see Liz advancing on him almost before Carol had gone. There'd be no comfort here.

'The rat must expect to be deserted by the ships that he's helped to sink,' said Liz, justifying his fears. 'Thank goodness there weren't three of you. Three Simcock sons for my daughter to rebel against me by falling in love with.' Liz, almost as fastidious about her grammar as her appearance, frowned at the inelegance of the sentence.

Her discomfiture gave Elvis room to attack. 'Do you have to be the central figure even in that scenario?' he said.

'Very good. Quite an effective little thrust. In some ways you're improving. What a pity I shall never forgive you for destroying my son's career.'

'He destroyed his own career. I merely did my duty.'

'To what?'

'Justice. Truth.'

'Phooey! Now excuse me. I must go and disconcert Ted.'

Ted was showing the Sillitoes off to Sandra's family as 'my valued old friends'.

Rita set off to rescue Geoffrey. He'd be out of his depth in that heaving throng.

She found her path blocked by Sandra, magnificent in her ivory gown, resolute in her determination to speak to Rita.

'Thanks, Rita,' she began, 'for your concern. It does you credit.'

'You what?'

'I saw you talking to Ted. You're right worried about him. How he'll treat me. Whether he'll look for bits on the side like what he did with you.'

'Well, I wouldn't have put it quite like that, but . . . look, it's none of my business, but . . . no, there's no point. You're married. The damage . . . oh Lord, I don't mean the damage. I hope I don't mean the damage, anyway. Sorry, Sandra. I shouldn't be saying anything.'

314

'You can't understand how I can marry Ted after he ditched me for that con artist.'

'Well . . . no, frankly, I can't.'

Sandra appeared to be staring at the wall behind Rita. Rita knew, from the romantic look in those proud eyes, that she wasn't seeing Geoffrey Boycott acknowledging the applause for his hundredth hundred. What she didn't know was that Sandra was seeing the store cupboard, in the town hall, with its folding chairs, discarded detergents and griffin.

'Ted apologised,' said Sandra, 'and it was right beautiful, it really was. And when I thought about it, I felt he was sincere. With her being so false it opened his eyes to what's real. That's what I reckon, anyroad.'

'Well, I hope so.'

'His having done summat like that before we were married, there's less chance of his doing it afterwards. That's what I reckon, anyroad.'

'Well, I hope you're right.'

There was a roar of beery laughter from the far side of the room. Sandra looked round.

'Your Geoffrey's a right yell, i'n't he?' she said.

'I beg your pardon?' Rita was utterly astounded. 'Are you calling my husband, that dear quiet bearded man over there, a right yell?'

'Yeah. 'Cos he is.'

Liz Badger, *née* Ellsworth-Smythe, stood in the door of the Geoffrey Boycott Room, *née* the Ridings Suite, and gave a cool, brittle smile to anyone who might be privileged enough to be looking in her direction.

Sandra hurried over to her, unself-consciously.

'Mrs . . . Liz! You came!'

Ted wasn't far behind.

'Have some champagne,' he said, handing her a glass.

'Ah, you do have champagne,' she said, with infuriating pretence. 'I heard a dreadful rumour that you only have asti spumante.'

Ted smiled. Rita could have sworn that his eyes twinked. 'We do,' he said, 'as you very well know, but we call it champagne, and we like it.'

Rita also smiled.

'What's so funny, Rita?' asked Liz.

'You're trying to disconcert Ted, and are disconcerted to find that you can't disconcert him, and, since you bring out the worst in me, I find that funny. Sorry.'

Rita surprised Ted and Liz by moving off abruptly. Sandra surprised them even more by saying, 'I'll leave you two together so you can discuss old times.'

Ted Simcock and his ex-lover eyed each other warily.

'Rita's right,' said Ted at last. 'If you have come to laugh at us, don't bother. We're beyond the reach of ridicule.'

'How touching!'

'Yes, Liz. In the peace and tranquillity of my new love . . . ' There was a roar from Sandra and her brothers, ' . . . I feel no old bitterness. I hope – no, I do, I mean it – that you'll find . . . happiness again.'

'A man, you mean.'

'No. Well, yes.'

'Half of me never wants to find another man. Half of me understands too late exactly how Neville felt about Jane's death.'

'And the other half?'

'Screams with loneliness. And I can't tell anybody.'

'You just told me.' Ted sounded slightly indignant, as if Liz might have told him because he wasn't anybody.

'Yes, I did,' Liz sounded surprised, as if she hadn't realised that she'd told him. 'You're cutting a really rather good figure today.' Her body was almost touching his. Ted suddenly felt totally in control. 'It's all absurd, but you're carrying it off. I've always admired that.' She looked into his eyes and spoke very softly. 'Suddenly I remember why I once found you so attractive.'

Ted felt something very like pity for her. He smiled at her, calmly, only a trifle smugly. 'Thanks for coming,' he said as he turned away.

'Geoffrey? Sandra said you're . . . I can hardly say it . . . a right yell.'

'Oh, did she? How nice.' Geoffrey realised that Rita was waiting for an explanation. 'Well, I *am* at ease among her friends and relations.'

'But you've never been even remotely a right yell with me.'

'Of course not. I'm in love with you. But maybe, when passion fades, in the evening of our lives, my right yellishness will take over.'

Rita smiled at Councillors Narbett and Elliot. It was the smile of a hostess. As soon as she'd finished smiling, she realised that she wasn't the hostess here, and she should have given them a different kind of smile, a smile of gratitude for coming to Ted's reception, as she had asked. But she hadn't time now to make fine distinctions between different kinds of smiles.

'What on earth were you talking to them about?' she asked.

Geoffrey spoke so quietly that Rita could only just hear him above the rumbustuous gathering. 'I was talking about the peoples I've studied, their rituals and taboos.' He gave a gentle stroke to his soft, grey beard, the way he did, the way she loved. 'I told them about native women who greet tourists wearing grass skirts and bare breasts, when at the back of their huts there are clothes lines hung with T-shirts and jeans. I told them of Indians who accept American Express cards for shrunken heads. I told them how the advanced world is dragging the primitive world into its clutches. Some see it as a comedy. I see it as a tragedy. The dividing line between the two is wafer-thin.'

'I'm frightened.'

'Why? My love, why?'

'I don't know you.'

'Then what a voyage of discovery awaits you,' said Geoffrey Spragg, *né* Ellsworth-Smythe, softly.

In the Sir Leonard Hutton Room, Jenny approached her husband's brother, her ex-lover, with her jaw set firmly, the way it was when she was doing her duty.

'Elvis,' she said, 'I'm feeling ashamed. I've been talking to some of your mum's councillor friends, and some of them knew your dad and have rather dropped him, and your mum's made them promise to go and give him their blessing. You and I should go in there and be nice to each other, for your parents' sake.'

'You're right,' said Elvis reluctantly, as if circumstances were forcing him to behave well against his will.

'Thanks.'

Next, Jenny tackled Carol, who had surprised Madge Longbottom by admitting that she had never heard of Emmylou.

'And I thought you were young,' Madge Longbottom was saying rather mysteriously. Carol wasn't sorry to have an excuse to leave Madge Longbottom.

'We're burying our differences and going to give Ted and Sandra our blessing,' said Jenny.

'Smashing,' said Carol. 'I'll come too. I'd like to be at peace with every single person in the world.'

'With the possible exception of Simon,' said Elvis. 'Oh, hello, Simon.'

'We're all going to see Ted and Sandra,' said Jenny. 'Coming?'

'I can't really,' said Simon. 'I want to be here when Lucinda arrives.'

The other three exchanged infinitesimal looks. Simon, not usually so sensitive to nuances, spotted them.

'She *will* come,' he said.

'None of us said anything,' said Jenny.

'You didn't need to. Look, sod off if you're going,' said Simon Rodenhurst, no longer of Trellis, Trellis, Openshaw and Finch.

Geoffrey Boycott looked down in frozen amusement upon an animated scene. Although people had come from the other reception with the express purpose of mingling, not much mingling was going on. In one corner, Sandra and her brothers were reminiscing about the farewell party at the Railway Tavern on the night the landlord left to open a bar in Spain. Warren had drunk fifteen Southern Comforts and Darren had been sick over the aspidistra. Sandra's nan was telling a naughty story about a monk, a chef, a black pudding, two rissoles and a contortionist. In another corner several councillors were exchanging councillor jokes. In the centre of the room, there was a small circle formed by Ted and Sandra, Rita and Geoffrey, the Sillitoes, and Liz.

'So what are these plans of yours, Ted?' enquired Rita.

'You what, Rita?'

'You said you had plans. What sort of plans?'

'That must have been half an hour ago.'

'Yes, well, it's only just filtered through.'

There was a noticeable pause, as they waited for Ted to tell them his plans.

'Well, come on,' urged Liz.

'You're not really interested, are you?'

'Not really, but I keep hoping that if I make the right social noises, one day interest may return.'

There was another pause.

'Well, what are these plans?' said Betty.

'Well . . . '

Elvis, Jenny and Carol approached them. They had already got themselves glasses of asti spumante.

Ted seized on the diversion.

'You came!' he said. 'Get yourselves a . . . oh you have.'

'Hello, Our Dad,' said Elvis with rather forced brightness. 'Hello, Our Mum. Hello . . . er . . . ' He looked at Sandra in amazement, as if realising for the first time what their relationship now was. 'Mum?'

He laughed, uneasily. Sandra laughed nervously and tried to look at him maternally. There was some rather forced laughter all round.

The new arrivals raised their glasses and said, 'Cheers.' The others responded. They drank in silence. The silence continued for too long.

'When you came in,' said Geoffrey, 'Ted was *bursting* with eagerness to tell us about his and Sandra's plans. Weren't you, Ted?'

'Well, yes. Yes, I . . . '

'What's all this, then, Dad?'

'Yes, well . . . er . . . we're opening a . . . ' Everyone in the enlarged circle was willing Ted to finish his sentence. 'A . . . er . . . catering outlet.'

'A restaurant, you mean?' said Rita.

'Yes. Yes. Well, in a . . . well, no. Not really.'

'I thought you didn't care what folk thought any more,' said Sandra.

'I won't over there, love, but I know this crabby lot. They'll laugh.'

'"Over there"?' said Betty.

'Over where?' said Rodney.

'The A64,' said Sandra.

'The A64?' said Jenny.

'Go on, Ted,' said Sandra. 'Tell 'em. It's your idea.'

'It's . . . er . . . it's not exactly a restaurant exactly. It's more

319

'. . . a mobile caravanette borrowed off Sandra's brother Dean. We're going to sell snacks from a lay-by on the A64.'

The whole circle stared at the former toasting fork tycoon in amazement.

Sandra began, with uncomplicated enthusiasm, to list the cornucopia of provender that they would offer. 'We'll sell teas, coffees, hot chocolate, Bovril, soup, soft drinks, fizzy *and* still, home-made cakes and scones . . . '

'Sandra's province,' said Ted proudly.

'Crisps, buns, sandwiches. What else?'

'We'll be happy.'

'Oh yeah. That too. It'll be called Ted's Snax.'

'Spelt with an X.'

It seemed that they were having to fight not to reveal that they saw something irresistibly comic in this business venture of Ted's.

'Well . . . tremendous,' said Rita, stifling a laugh. She raised her glass. 'To Ted's Snax, spelt with an X.'

'To Ted's Snax, spelt with an X,' they all said, raising their glasses.

'You think it's so funny, don't you?' said Ted. 'Well, we'll make a success of it, don't you worry. The local farmer's given us permission to put up two gi-normous great signs, fixed to a horse chestnut westwards and a beech tree eastwards, saying "Ted's Snax. 800 yards. Don't miss it!" And folk won't. They'll pour in. It'll be a licence to print money. Rita, I'm surprised at you. Smirking. Liz, yes; she's a snob.'

'Ted! Not today!' pleaded Sandra.

Sandra might as well have asked night not to fall as attempt to stop Ted in mid-grievance. 'Rodney and Betty, yes, they're probably half cut,' he continued.

'Ted!' said Rodney and Betty.

'Elvis, fair enough, cynical little sod. All the youngsters, mock mock, 'cos it's easier than thinking. But you, Rita! I never thought you'd go all high and mighty on me. And Geoffrey! Renouncing your double-barrel. Calling yourself Spragg. You don't fool me.'

'Ted!' said his bride of almost two hours. 'I thought you didn't have a chip any more.'

'More like a jacket potato.'

'Thank you, Elvis. We can do without your helpful comments, thank you very much,' said Rita tartly. She turned to Ted. 'I'm sorry, Ted,' she said. 'It's not funny. It's nice. It's just . . . you . . . Rotarian . . . ex-foundry owner . . . I just . . . sorry.'

'I no longer hanker after worldly honours, Rita,' said Ted with dignity. 'Status. Prestige. Stuff 'em. If they offered me lifelong honorary presidency of the Crown and Walnut Angling Club, I'd tell them where they could stick it. I would. I just want to be happy . . . and have Sandra's kids. Well, she have mine.'

'*Kids?*' Betty realised that her astonishment might be somewhat hurtful. 'Sorry.'

All around the suddenly silent circle there was noise and laughter.

'They're stunned,' said Ted.

'Very touching, Ted,' said Liz.

'No. It is touching,' said Rodney. His ruddy face grew strangely gentle. 'We could never have them, you know. That's why we love other people's so much.'

Betty squeezed his hand consolingly. 'Never mind. We're not going to let an inadequate sperm count spoil a moment of our lives,' said her eloquent squeeze.

'Well if it's what Sandra wants,' said Jenny uncertainly, thinking of Sandra coping with teenagers when Ted was seventy.

'It is,' said Sandra.

'If you're sure . . . ' said Carol.

'I'm not a women's libber, I'm afraid,' said Sandra. 'I want to be dominated by a masterful older man.'

'And I want to dominate a younger woman who wants to be dominated by a masterful older man.'

'Ted!' Rita sounded for a moment as if she was still his wife.

And there, in the Geoffrey Boycott Room of the Angel Hotel, on her wedding day, resplendent in her ivory gown, the cake-loving Sandra Pickersgill made, with grave intensity and admirable brevity, the first political statement of her life.

'What you women want, don't get me wrong, I think it's great,' she said. 'Women should have the right. But it shouldn't be compulsory. There's no cause, no cause in the whole world, more important than the freedom to choose what suits you – if it's legal. That's what I reckon, anyroad.'

Ted put his arm round his young wife, proudly.

'Darling!' said Lucinda Snellmarsh, of Peacock, Tester and Devine. She was simply but elegantly dressed in a blue and cream chiffon top and skirt, with a single row of pearls.

'Darling! You've come!' Simon was too overjoyed to hide his relief.

Eric hovered tactfully, pretending not to listen.

'Well, of course I have, my darling.' She kissed him briskly. 'You didn't doubt me, did you, my darling?'

' 'Course not, my darling.'

'You weren't worried I wouldn't stand by you, were you, my darling?'

' 'Course I wasn't, my darling.'

Eric moved smoothly forward. 'Champagne, my darli . . . madam? Touch of the '82?'

'M'm. Please.'

'There you go, madam. Tickety-boo.' The dapper, ageless Eric Siddall departed, giving Simon a dirty look and no chance to take one of the other glasses on the tray.

'You're awfully late, though,' said Simon.

'I know. Some urgent business cropped up, and it involved you.'

'Me?'

'Yes. It's incredibly exciting, but I can't tell you in front of every . . . where is everybody?'

In his fog of anxiety, Simon hadn't noticed that there were only fifteen guests, mainly somewhat bewildered relatives of Rita, still there.

'Yes, where is everybody?' he said.

It was elbow to elbow in the Geoffrey Boycott Room. Barriers were breaking down. Councillors were rubbing shoulders, sometimes literally, with Sandra's friends and relations. The Sillitoes were joking with Sandra's nan. The beer and the asti spumante were flowing freely, and everybody except Liz was having a wonderful time.

Eric Siddall, eager to find someone to serve, rushed up to Rita and Geoffrey and Liz the moment they returned, even though this meant that he would also have to serve the Sillitoes, who had returned with them.

'Sir, madam, madam, madam, sir? Champagne?' he said.

'Ah. The real stuff,' said Liz. 'Thank you, Eric. Well, if you'll excuse me, I have to . . . '

'Get away from us? Of course you do,' said Rodney.

'Rodney!' said Betty.

Rita also walked away, abruptly. The Sillitoes exchanged raised eyebrows. Geoffrey wasn't sure whether to follow her or leave her alone.

All the function rooms in the town held painful memories for Rita. In choosing the Angel for their reception, they'd been swayed by the fact that the sparkling Sir Leonard Hutton Room looked so different from the old ballroom, whose walls had bubbled with nicotine stains.

Yet now, with no Dale Monsal Quartet, a carpet covering the dance floor, and a shaft of golden October sunshine showing how much dust churns in the air we breathe, Rita was back in the smoky, noisy dentists' dinner dance, where her father had dropped dead during the last waltz.

She didn't believe in a life after death, yet she sometimes imagined her parents looking down, watching her. She looked up at the ceiling now, and imagined her father looking down, and craved his posthumous forgiveness, his approval of what she had become, his approval of Geoffrey, his approval of their decision to adopt that flat cap of a name, Spragg.

She realised that Geoffrey was speaking to her.

'Sorry,' she said. 'What was that?'

'I said, I feel incredibly close to you,' said Geoffrey.

Liz became another in the long line of people who, that afternoon, said, 'You came!' to somebody who couldn't have failed to be aware of the fact.

'Surely you didn't doubt your future daughter-in-law?' said Lucinda, with a faint smugness that grated on Liz's nerves.

'No,' said Liz. 'No! Though why you should think him worth standing by under the circumstances amazes me.'

'Ah, but the circumstances have changed, Mother,' said Simon, oozing brightly onto the scene. His smugness was a Matterhorn compared to Lucinda's Mendip. To Lucinda he said,

'Just phoned him. Seeing him tomorrow, sweetyplum.' He saw Elvis watching him, and called out, with frightful cheeriness, 'Elvis! Pax!'

Elvis joined them reluctantly.

'You what?' he said.

'Thanks, old chum,' said Simon. Seeing Elvis's puzzlement, he added, 'For what you did.'

'"Old chum"?' said Elvis.

Simon turned to Lucinda. 'It's in the bag,' he said.

'Thought it would be!' Lucinda's smugness level rose from Mendip to Brecon Beacon.

'Children, please,' said Liz, almost screaming with irritation. 'What's in what bag?'

'I've been offered a job by a very large, go-ahead firm,' purred Simon.

'*What?*' Elvis couldn't believe his ears. 'Why?'

'They seem impressed by what I did at Trellis, Trellis, Openshaw and Finch.'

'They admire his go-ahead qualities,' said Lucinda.

'You mean his dishonesty,' said Elvis.

'They call it my initiative,' said Simon.

'They would,' said Elvis. 'Who are this firm?'

'I'm not at liberty to say yet.'

'Well what sort of firm are they?' asked Liz. 'What do they make?' She sounded as if she feared that it was something she wouldn't be able to reveal to her friends, like refuse sacks or toilet rolls or condoms.

'They don't make anything,' said Lucinda. 'They own things.'

'That figures,' said Elvis, with the savagery of a young man whose cynicism has lain fallow too long.

'So, Elvis,' said Simon, who seemed to have become a born-again capitalist, unrecognisable as the almost likeable depressive that he had been half an hour ago, 'thank you for making my career, not breaking it.'

'Yes, thank you, Elvis,' said Lucinda. She kissed him softly, demurely, on the cheek, and then peered at him through her thick but not unstylish glasses. 'I've never really seen you properly before. You aren't irredeemably horrendous, are you?' She turned towards her future mother-in-law. 'Isn't it amazing? Simon thought I'd ditched him. And there I was, digging up a new career for him, supporting him morally and practically so that he'll be able to support me in the manner to which I could rapidly become accustomed. Oh ye of little faith.'

Lucinda strode off. Simon hurried after her, then returned.

'I'm only just beginning to realise what a strong personality Lucinda is,' he said. 'Isn't it terrific?'

He beamed.

'Terrific,' said Liz drily.

Alone with Liz, Elvis had no idea what to say. She did.

'Thank you. All obstacles to a beautiful friendship are now removed.'

'But . . . I didn't want to . . . '

'You really don't like him, do you?'

'No, I suppose I don't, but it isn't that. Is he the sort of person that gets on in our society?'

'You'll have to answer that. You're the investigative journalist. Come to dinner on Saturday. I'd like to celebrate Simon's job. I'd like to thank you for making him available to take it.'

Elvis shuddered. 'I don't think I could face them so soon.'

'Oh Simon and Lucinda won't be there,' said Liz airily. 'No one else'll be there.'

Elvis did an impression of a catatonic sardine.

'We'll dine alone. We may find no spark. We may become friends, even perhaps . . . don't look so shocked.'

'But you're . . . '

'So much older than you.' Liz smiled sweetly. 'Congratulations. You've inherited your father's tact. Look at the age difference between Ted and Sandra.'

'That's different. He's a man.'

'Oh, Elvis! How provincial you are.' Liz stood very close to him, gazing into his eyes. 'You and I are unattached. We're nothing to anyone. We're free to . . . explore the possibilities at whatever pace we choose. What do you say?'

'Oh heck.'

'You know I was rather afraid you would.'

She kissed him on the lips. He stood rigid. His belief that it wasn't his day so far as women were concerned was reinforced when, the moment Liz had gone, Carol bore down on him.

'I meant everything I said earlier, Elvis,' she said. 'The answer's still no. But I also meant it when I said I want to be friends with everybody. So I feel no bitterness.' She kissed him on the cheek. 'But there it is.'

Elvis hadn't so much as twitched an eyelid, but Carol had been so intent on what she was saying that she hadn't noticed anything unusual.

Betty noticed immediately.

'What on earth's wrong with you?' she said.

'What? Nothing. Just that . . . women keep kissing me. Lucinda. Liz. Carol. Masses of kisses, and all for the wrong reasons.'

'Poor Elvis. You look as sad and clapped-out as an old teddy bear that doesn't squeak any more. Aaaah!'

She kissed him, and moved on.

Eric approached with champagne, and noticed Elvis's sour look.

'Oh dear!' he said. 'Is there anything I can do for you, sir?'

'If *you* kiss me, I'll clock you one,' said Elvis.

'Well!' said Eric Siddall, barman supreme. 'Young people today! I don't know!'

The Sir Leonard Hutton Room was filling up steadily, as people returned after drinking the health of Ted and Sandra. Now Ted and Sandra themselves arrived, accompanied by several of Sandra's friends and relations, including her three burly brothers and her tiny, exuberant nan.

'Oh Lord,' said Liz, who was watching with Rita and the Sillitoes.

'You were right,' said Rita. 'They're not your sort of people. They're friendly to everyone. You're only friendly to "your sort of people".' She hurried over to them. 'Hello!' she said. 'Welcome! It's really good of you to come.'

'Exaggeratedly effusive to show me up and make me angry,' said Liz. 'Well, I won't rise to it.'

'Very wise,' said Betty. 'Never give people the satisfaction of knowing they've succeeded in annoying you, that's what I always say.'

'Do you really?' said Liz. 'How very boring of you.'

Liz slipped off to a far corner of the room, well out of range of the new arrivals. She was circulating thoroughly, but more because there were so many people to get away from than because there were so many to meet.

'I'd like to hit that woman,' said Betty.

'Don't give her the satisfaction of knowing that she's succeeded in annoying you,' said Rodney, slurring his words somewhat.

'Are you drunk?' said Betty.

'Oh yes.'

'Oh Rodney! But you don't need to get drunk any more because you used to get drunk because you had a guilty conscience about your chickens and you don't have a guilty conscience any more because you don't have any chickens any more.'

'Yes, I do. A guilty conscience, I mean, not chickens. I don't have any chickens. I do have a guilty conscience. But I told you . . . at that thing with those roads. I'm a sham.'

'Your love for me isn't a sham.'

'Oh no, no. That isn't. But how do we know spinach doesn't suffer?'

'You what? Of course it doesn't. It has no nervous central system.'

'Nervous spinach. Neurotic leeks. Paranoid parsnips. Because, if they do, why bother not eating meat?'

'Oh Rodney?'

Betty swayed slightly and clutched him for support.

'Are *you* drunk?' he asked.

'As a rat. But that's all right because I get drunk because I'm happy because of my larger than love of life and today I have been to . . . ' she counted carefully, ' . . . four wedding receptions, but you get drunk because you're sad and that makes me sad because I love you and because I love you I don't want you to be sad . . . ' Betty was getting extremely sad, ' . . . because when you're sad you get all miserable, and that makes me miserable, and being miserable makes me sad.' By this time, she was crying, and her voice was little more than a whisper.

'Oh Betty!' said Rodney.

They embraced, and shook together with gentle sobs.

'Well, it's goodbye, Rita.'

Rita, who was resting her feet beneath a photograph of Sir Leonard Hutton being bowled by Graeme Hole for 79 at Melbourne in 1951, said, 'Yes,' smiled, and indicated that he sit in the empty chair beside her.

He needed no second bidding. 'Rita?' he said. 'I . . . I wish I . . . oh heck . . . I failed you. All those years. Wasted years. Well, not entirely wasted. You gave me two sons. But . . . I let you down.'

'Well . . . ' After saying it for years, Rita found herself wanting to deny it, when Ted admitted it.

'But we had some good times, didn't we?'

'Oh yes, I remember a Thursday.'

'What?' Ted saw that Rita was joking, and relaxed. 'No. We did. Didn't we? We did. Happy memories. Some good laughs.'

'Yes, I suppose we did.'

Ted reflected, and chuckled reflectively, gently, affectionately.

'Remember that time you slipped on that dog shit in Barnard Castle?' he said.

'Ted!' Rita was outraged. 'Is that the humorous highlight of your marital memories?'

'No. 'Course not.' He chuckled again. 'It was funny, though.'

'There's a vicious streak in you.' But Rita was laughing too.

Their other halves stood watching them laughing.

'Ted and Rita are laughing a lot,' said Sandra.

'Yes,' said Geoffrey. 'Expiating the past, so that they can live with us without regret.' He smiled. 'Ted Simcock, the Edith Piaf of the A64.'

Sandra looked at him blankly. 'No, but . . . it's great, i'n't it?' she said.

'Very touching.'

'Remember that very cocky feller with the flash yacht leaning against that big bollard in San Tropez?' said Ted.

'In those very short shorts. That very pretty girl went by. He leant nonchalantly back and missed his bollard.'

'Went base over apex into the harbour.'

'I was nearly ill with laughing.'

'How we laughed!'

How they were laughing now, as they remembered how they'd laughed.

Betty and Rodney were also riveted by their laughter.

'Oh, Rodney!' said Betty, over-specific as usual. 'You don't think . . . they wouldn't, would they? They couldn't.'

'Of course they couldn't. Not on their . . . could they?'

'Well I mean I suppose they could.'

'Well, yes, they could. Of course they could. But they wouldn't. Would they?'

'And that canal holiday, when we took the boys for that bar snack.'

'And that pompous couple came in behind us and she said . . . what did she say?'

Rita made a brave stab at the woman's cut-glass accent. '"Oh my God, Lionel. It's ebsolutely crawling with children."'

'Poor Paul. He nearly died. Are there still people like that around, do you think?'

'Yes, I very much fear there very probably are.'

Ted also made an attempt at the cut-glass accent. 'How ebsolutely appalling.'

'Ebsolutely appalling.'

'They're laughing a hell of a lot.'

'It really is an extremely touching scene.'

'I'd have thought that by now . . . '

'They'd have expiated vast areas of the past. Yes, so should I.' Geoffrey smiled, a trifle wryly. 'I must say I'd have expected a little farewell peck on the cheek to be coming up by now.'

'What a life we could have led, Rita. If . . . I'd had more sense.'

'Oh me too, Ted. Needing to be liked. Worrying what folk thought morning, noon and night. Me too, Ted.'

'What a couple we'd have made, if we'd known what we know now.'

'What a couple we'd have made.'

They gazed solemnly into each other's eyes. They began to kiss.

'There it is.'
   'I wouldn't exactly describe it as a little peck on the cheek, though.'
   'Ruddy hell, no!'

'Oh, I say, Rodney.'
   'Better not, Betty.'
   'Oh, I wouldn't, Betty.'

It was a long kiss. It was an affectionate kiss. At last, it was over.
   'No regrets, though,' said Rita.
   'You what?'
   'About today. We aren't going for second best.'
   'Oh no. No, no, no. Oh no, no. In no way. No. I mean . . . we aren't.'
   'Good luck, Ted.'
   'Good luck, Rita.'
   They kissed again, a brief farewell touching of the lips.
   Ted stood up, slowly. The watchers weren't sure whether the slowness was due to reluctance or to the effects of his recent injury.
   On his way towards Sandra, Ted passed Geoffrey, who was trying to look cool as he approached Rita. The two men's eyes met. Neither was sure what the other was thinking.

'Were you worried?' asked Ted.
   'Daft chuff!' said his bride.

'Were you worried?' asked Rita.
   'No. No!' said her groom. 'I said "no", Rita.'

Jenny willed Rita and Geoffrey to leave, so that she could go back to Paul and the children without seeming rude. She could hardly bring herself to listen to Madge Longbottom, who was saying, 'I'm amazed you've never heard of her. I mean, you're obviously into ethnic, and Emmylou is very ethnic indeed.' She

330

found it difficult to make the right noises as Eric told her why he'd left the Clissold Lodge. 'He said to me, "Why not? I know you're . . . " I had to be frank. I said, "Just because I'm . . . and so are you . . . doesn't mean I have to find you attractive." Well, rub the manager up the wrong way . . . as it were . . . life isn't worth living. The manager here's married. But enough of my . . . how about Paul? He must be thrilled to be with the children again.'

'Oh, he is.' Jenny sprang to life. 'When I visited him, the last time, before he got out, he said, "I'm missing them." I knew, then.'

'He must have. Their little minds, grasping new words. Their little bodies, learning new achievements. Never ever to be repeated moments. I sometimes think I'd have made a wonderful father, if I . . . oh well. Stick to it, Jenny. There aren't many of us left.'

Jenny gave Eric a great big kiss, because he'd talked about Paul.

Rita and Geoffrey began to prepare for the departure that Jenny craved. They advanced upon Liz.

'We'll be off in a minute,' said Rita.

'Ah,' said Liz neutrally.

'One good thing about getting married in middle age,' said Rita, 'you don't have to have a disco in the evening.'

'No,' said Liz.

'Liz . . . ?' said Geoffrey.

'If this is going to be yet another appeal for me to treat your home as my own, forget it,' said Liz. 'Go on. Get off. I'll be all right. I'll stick my claws into some poor, unsuspecting . . . '

She saw Elvis and hesitated.

Elvis saw her and veered away.

'Some poor unsuspecting . . . ?' prompted Rita.

'Some poor unsuspecting unmarried man.'

'Unmarried?'

'I broke up your marriage. I don't want a repeat of that disaster.'

'Disaster?' said Geoffrey. 'You put in chain a series of events which ended in Rita's marrying me.'

'Precisely,' said his sister.

Ted and Sandra were also preparing for departure. Liz found no escape from them.

'So this is goodbye,' she said.

'Not goodbye,' said Sandra. 'We'd be dead chuffed if you ever dropped in for a cuppa.'

Liz gave a thin smile. 'Sadly, I fear you're going to have to remain dead unchuffed,' she said.

'It'll be right hygienic,' said Sandra. 'Not like posh restaurants where you get all the chef's spittle in the soup. Our soup'll be tinned.'

'Sandra!' Ted tried to smile at Liz.

But Sandra wasn't to be diverted from her course that easily. 'If you're embarrassed 'cos you once had a bit of a ding-dong with Ted, there's no need,' she told Liz.

'Thank you, Sandra,' replied Liz. 'You're making this a perfect farewell.'

'You what, Liz?' said Ted.

'Reminding one why one is so pleased that one will never again see the people one will never again see.'

Ted scurried after her.

'But, Liz, one will see one,' he said. 'One has forgotten, hasn't one, that one will be coming to see one's son'.

'No, Ted.'

'You what?'

'You can't offer him a parent's love. It's already too late. You'll drift apart. Long, awkward silences in zoos and burger bars. You'll be an embarrassment to him.'

'You what, Liz? Me, an embarrassment to my son?'

'When he's at boarding school, Ted, a dead lawyer to whom I was married will be less embarrassing than the live owner of a snack bar in a lay-by with whom I once had what your wife so charmingly described as "a bit of a ding-dong".'

'You mean . . . I never see him again?'

'I honestly do think it would be best, Ted.' The finality of it chilled him all the more because she spoke so gently, almost affectionately. He stood rooted to the spot after she'd gone. All right, he hardly deserved . . . he hadn't exactly . . . he could fight for his . . . but.

Sandra was at his side, squeezing his arm.

'Tiny social point, Sandra,' he said. 'Hardly worth mentioning . . . but one doesn't refer to people like Liz having "a bit of a ding-dong".'

'Sorry.'

'No. It was great! Sandra, you're . . . no, you are. I mean it. You really are.'

Simon Rodenhurst, of Projects International plc, and Lucinda Snellmarsh, of Peacock, Tester and Devine, approached the cynical Elvis Simcock, of Radio Gadd.

'We're leaving in a jiffy,' said Simon.

'Good move. Sounds much more up-market than a car.'

'We just wanted to say that we have no hard feelings,' said Lucinda, with a smile that was only fractionally patronising.

'I have no hard feelings at all,' said Simon.

'Several replies spring to mind,' said Elvis. 'I'll settle for "why should you?"'

'Precisely.' Lucinda gave a smile that was only fractionally self-satisfied. 'It all looks like working out really well for us. If only we could get Simon's mother fixed up with some suitable man, life would be perfect.'

'Yes, I suppose if she's lonely she might intrude rather embarrassingly on your yuppie bliss,' said Elvis.

'You're determined to be unpleasant, aren't you?' said Simon.

'He doesn't need determination,' said his fiancée. 'It comes easily to him.'

'Some suitable man?' Elvis looked as if a thought had struck him. 'What sort of suitable man?'

'I don't know,' said Simon. 'Just somebody I'd be happy seeing Mother with, I suppose.'

'It's almost worth it,' mused Elvis, 'to see your face.'

'You've someone in mind?' Simon was intrigued. Elvis didn't muse very often.

'No,' said Elvis, as if he really meant "yes". 'No!' he added, as if he definitely meant "no". 'Not even . . . no.'

'Come on, Simon.' Lucinda was growing impatient. There was no longer time, in her eager young life, for musing. 'There are some people I want you to meet. They could be useful to you.'

She strode off. Simon scurried after her, then returned.

'She's so dynamic and strong and organised,' he said. 'It's wonderful.'

'Hello, Mum,' said Jenny cautiously.

'Don't say anything.'

'What about?'

'Anything. Today. The past. The future. Me. You. Paul. Elvis. Neville. The shanty towns of El Salvador. Anything. I couldn't stand it. Just . . . don't go away.'

'Mum!'

They put their arms round each other and held each other tight. All around them, on that October afternoon, people circulated, groups formed and broke up, plans were made, jokes were told, champagne was poured, butt ends were stuck in the remains of trifle. Mother and daughter stood still and silent, as if they were the eye of a social hurricane.

Councillor Mirfield tried to look thrilled as he listened to encomia on Rita's political abilities. Councillor Morris Wigmore smiled and smiled and smiled, as if, the moment he stopped smiling, he would start to think about his son's sticky end in Brisbane. Rita's Auntie Edie from Normanton smiled fixedly at Madge Longbottom and felt pity for any girl who was so constantly praised by her mother. And Ted Simcock, in his smart grey suit and yellow buttonhole, stopped dead in his tracks. A thought had struck him.

He'd become so involved in his contrasting farewells to Rita and Liz that he had entirely forgotten that he was at Rita's reception, not his!

'We must get back,' he told Sandra.

'Hell's bells, yes.'

They went to say goodbye to Rita and Geoffrey.

'We'd better be getting back to our do,' said Ted. 'Folk'll wonder where we've got to.'

'Oh Lord, yes. I'd forgotten,' said Rita.

'Well . . . er . . . ' said Ted, 'if you . . . er . . . should ever find yourselves in the vicinity of the A64 . . . you can't miss us, you'll see the sign, "Ted's Snax", on the beech tree or the horse chestnut, according to which . . . '

'Well, yes, if we ever do,' said Geoffrey, 'we'll stop by for a

334

cuppa and a slice of Sandra's homemade cake.' Sandra smiled modestly, disclaiming special merit for her baking. 'Won't we, darling?'

'No.'

'Rita!' said Ted.

'I'm not sure I could bear to.'

'Rita!' said Geoffrey.

'In case we found they weren't happy.'

'Rita! We will be!' said Ted. 'I mean . . . we will. Won't we love?'

' 'Course we will!' said Sandra, with the utter certainty that a young woman should feel at her wedding reception.

'There!' said Ted. 'Straight from the horse's . . . well, perhaps that isn't the . . . ' He gave a slightly embarrassed little laugh. They all gave slightly embarrassed little laughs. 'Well, Rita, this is it.'

'Yes.'

Rita kissed Ted and Sandra. Sandra kissed Geoffrey. Ted and Geoffrey shook hands. Rodney and Betty lurched towards the platform.

'It has to be said, Rodney,' said Betty, as she clambered breathlessly onto the platform.

'Oh, I quite agree,' said Rodney. 'I quite agree.'

The joint big wheels behind Sillitoe's turned to face the gathering.

'Ladies and gentlemen,' shouted Rodney. People began to turn towards him. 'Ladies and gentlemen!' he shouted.

'Oh Lord,' said Rita.

'We have an announcement to announce,' announced Betty.

'Oh heck,' said Ted.

The Sillitoes looked down on rows of alarmed, yet slightly excited faces.

'Don't look so alarmed,' slurred Rodney. 'All right, in the past we've let the cat out of the bag, and the cat's killed a few pigeons coming home to roost, when we've had a many too few. No, that's wrong. A few too many.'

'That's wrong too,' said Betty. 'A many too many.' She laughed strangely.

'Oh Lord,' said the dapper, ageless Eric Siddall. 'Just when for once everything seemed . . . how can I put it . . . ?'

335

'Tickety-boo,' said Rita.

'Yes. Incredible. You're both psychic!'

'Have you two finished?' said Rodney. Eric nodded frantically, anxious not to inflame. 'Good. Ladies and gentlemen, we have a message for you all!'

Tension held everybody. A few people shut their eyes, like fans unable to watch their team taking a penalty.

The Sillitoes spoke slowly, carefully, in perfect unison.

'We hope you'll all live happily ever after.'

There was a hiss of escaping tension. Applause broke out throughout the room. Rodney and Betty swayed and smiled.

'Aaaah!' said Ted and Sandra, and they kissed each other.

'Aaaah!' said Rita and Geoffrey, and they kissed each other.

As the applause died down, Betty leant towards Rodney and hissed loudly into his right ear, 'But we're not taking bets on it.'

'Betty!' said Rodney.

A scruffy racing pigeon, a hopeless straggler in a race from Gateshead to Leek, shuffled across the streaked mauve and orange of a late autumn evening, looked down on a huddled jumble of roofs and yards and unkempt gardens, and saw two vehicles depart from the front of what it did not recognise as a hotel. One of the vehicles was a hired Rolls-Royce. It slid smoothly towards the West. The other vehicle was a mobile caravanette. It chugged noisily towards the East.